# SKULL GAMES

# THE FIRST OF A TRILOGY

GUMBO

The Cataloging-in-Publication Data is on file at Library of Congress

**ISBN-13: 978-0692672457**
Reign Publications LLC | Houston, TX

# DEDICATION

On behalf of my Queen and me; this literary piece is dedicated to all the young brothers and sisters that are trapped in the midst of situations and circumstances that contradict what truly lies in their hearts. We are the voice that will tell the "truth" and write the "real" in regards to the misconception that describes who ***"we"*** truly are. We are warriors! We are all able to thrive and endure the hurdles and pitfalls that have been pre-designed for us. The publication of this work is a sign ushering in a "New Era". It's time we rise from the graves of ignorance and awaken the true essence of our natural selves. Take a look around; the world seeks to mimic ***"you"*** my young Kings and Queens. Even in the midst of our misled paths; our influence is felt and often imitated. We are undoubtedly descendants of Pharaohs, Prophets, Kings, Queens, Gods, Goddesses, and the original civilizers. Let's get back to being the light that leads this world back to its true essence of peace. We sincerely dedicate this novel to **you**; my beautiful brothers and sisters.

I hope I've made you proud pops...

## ACKNOWLEDGEMENTS

Without a minute wasted; all honor and praise is due to the creator of love divine and eternal life. I would be nothing without the graceful hand of the Great God of the universe. Second; I have to acknowledge my calm through the storm, my beautiful wife. I know it sounds cliché but there's no me without you. You're the most amazing woman I know. You've been my biggest cheerleader, and my inspiration behind all of this. You're my rock, my love, my superstar, and my peace. I love you divine baby.

## WARNING

This book contains explicit content and is not recommended for children under the age of 18. By no means do I seek to glorify what's vividly painted throughout the pages of this book. I seek to take you down a journey of the unique style and life of the beautiful people of my city. So without further or due; I present to you, ***Skull Games the First of a Trilogy....***

# INTRODUCTION

New Orleans, the city that's known for its famous food and great jazz music consist of a mixture of much more than those known facts. The culture is very intriguing. The birth place of Jazz is famous for its Mardi Gras celebrations, Indian Masking, and Second-Lines; which could be best described as a parade and celebration of death when a loved one passes away. It's really something to experience but, there's a flip side of the game to this picture. The city in itself breeds an evil presence that has caused a lot of young brothers to lose their lives in gruesome murders. It's not a nice subject to talk about but, its reality. It's a killed or be killed mentality that roams through the minds of young African-American men that are bred in the "Crescent City." I want to take you on a journey that is filled with murder, loyalty, sex and everything that goes down in the heart of the city. I call it a taste of Gumbo. For the people out there who don't know what the definition of Gumbo is. It's a mixture of all kinds of tasty concoctions. In the Gumbo you eat it's mixed with all types of meat and seafood in a rue base. The Gumbo I'm about to present is a mixture of the elements of life in the depths of New Orleans. My job as an author and a born and raised citizen of New Orleans, is to give you the raw uncut feel of the party life, the violence and cut throat shit that goes down in my neck of the woods. I felt a strong motivation to share with the world how young brothers have to struggle, kill, and hustle to survive in the concrete jungle of "The Boot." So if you're looking for the usual predictable urban novel, this is the total opposite. Through this book you will be introduced to the day to day life of the goons that lurk in the trenches of New Orleans, and also their unusual dialect and swagger. So sit back and get ready to experience the most electrifying tale of the urban world.

# JAMAL TSION LEE

# "TEELEE"

Teelee sat in deep thought as the afternoon sun beat down on him and his lil rounds. "Rounds" was a phrase they used in the N.O., to refer to their friends. He scanned the block from Big Head Unc porch and noticed the potential for their block to be very lucrative. The fiends were constantly running up and down Rocheblave St.; the "Blade." Teelee and his Rounds fought and struggled to keep a dollar in their pockets, but the cost of living wasn't matching what they were pulling in. He looked at the two closest people to him in the world and made up in his mind that he would get them rolling in the major leagues. Thugga, Lil Man and Teelee came up from diapers on the block. Even through all the separation from getting caught up in Juvenile and other dangerous situations, they still managed to stick by each other's side. Teelee lit up a Camel non-filter cigarette. As he inhaled the deadly smoke into his lungs, his son entered his mind instantly. He wanted to give his son the best life had to offer. He didn't want him to go through all he had endured, as far as all the thugging and hustling was concerned. Sometimes he wished he hadn't got involved with his baby mamma Janae K/A Nunew, but he always pushed that shit out of his mind because he wouldn't have his son. He tried his best to be the best daddy he could; seeing as though he was only 17, and Janae was 15 when his son was born. Teelee also thought about his Pops, who tried his best to keep him from going down the same path he did, which was the same thing he wanted for Lil Jamal. The cycle of life was a motherfucker! He was just too caught up in the streets to look towards anything else at the moment. Teelee had been fending for his self for so long, that the evil presence that roamed through the murderous city of New Orleans had set in his heart. He knew only the power of God could save him from the destruction he was faced with. The 7th Ward of New Orleans, backatown to be exact was all he knew. The motto of his hood was *"Get it out the mud"* and that's exactly what he planned to do. Teelee noticed the hunger and lack of patience in his Lil Rounds. Plies said it best *"When a nigga broke, he ain't supposed to have patience."* Teelee had the same feeling but he knew he had to be the thinker of the clique; if it was up to Thugga and Lil Man they would say "fuck it" and wild out any way they had too. Teelee wasn't taking that route. If they were going to ball, he felt they should ball the correct way. Teelee threw his "Joe", Camel to the ground as a smile came across his face. He had a sure feeling something was about to shake for him and his team real soon.

## JUSTIN WILSON

## "G. LIL MAN"

Lil Man sat twisting one of his dreads, as his black huaraches swung back and forth off Big Head Unc porch. He contemplated on what he and his homey's had been through; from hunger pains, wearing each other's clothes, to even eating off the same plate. Even though he loved his three other brothers, he showed Teelee and Thugga the same amount of love and loyalty. His older brothers Corey and Paul "Corey" and "Pistol" had already been in the game for some time now. He knew if they came up on a nice lick, they could collaborate with Pistol and Corey and have the "Blade" rocking. As freestyle lyrics came to his mind, he bobbed his head to an unheard beat and let his words flow at a low tone. -*Came up from small on the block-me and my niggas don't stop-steady clutching the Glock-hard head niggas run in your spot-come out packing big knots-*. He looked up to the sun, then at his rounds; his brother's for life. He vowed at that moment he would get his family out of the hood and on to bigger and better things off his lyrical talents. As Mario and Tori "Money" and "T-Mac" rolled passed on their bikes, Lil Man felt a stronger desire to make it in the music industry. He wanted his baby brother Money to have more than he had. He knew if he didn't get T-Mac and Money both out of the hood quick they were going to evolve into products of their environment. "Cold Blooded Killers"! T-Mac was like a little brother to all of them, because he was growing up on the "Blade" with Money just like they had. He wanted them to have a better shot at life than the elders on the block. "No matter what I'mma rock till the death of me for my people", he thought to himself with clenched fist.

## RONNIE BENNET

## "THUGGA"

"I wonder what that boy over there smiling about", Thugga thought as he looked toward Teelee. "Ain't shit to smile bout outchere, we broke than a muthafucka. True enough we make $100.00, a day but that's pocket change compared to the money that some of these hoe ass dudes be making. They don't even deserve to have the street money and the street fame. I ain't hating or nuthin like that it's just that; bitch made pussies don't have no business in the same game with some full blooded goons like me and my team. Man I gotta go cop me some new "Geedy Weedys" meaning his Air Force Ones", Thugga thought as he glanced at a single mark on his brand new Nikes. Thugga was real big on his appearance. He was known as the pretty gangster of the trio. As he looked over at his rounds his anger settled and he thought of how close they were. He always said if anybody got out of line with any one of them he would "Smash em" onsite. It didn't matter to Thugga; they were all he had. True enough he had family but, he felt closer to Teelee and Lil Man. That's why it was no limit to what he would do for them two!

Thugga glanced over at his Uncle; "Big Head Unc", and knew they had to pull something off quick. Teelee, Lil Man and Thugga were the only ones that really looked out for him. They bought him beer and other shit he needed. Thugga wanted to get Unc a nurse to help him out. He was getting old and had some mild mental problems. He felt obligated to Unc because he let them hustle out of his house and he never tripped. "I wonder where my Lil bitch Tyler at. I'mma go get my hair braided and afterwards and she can pop me off some of that fire head game she got", Thugga thought while playing with his latest toy. He was fascinated with guns.

# CHAPTER 1

# FIRST JUMPED OFF THE PORCH

Teelee knew he had to get his goal accomplished real soon. As he sat thinking of his master plan, it was like faith came riding down the block. Brian Bailey "Tossy", was the man to see on the cocaine level. The dude was flipping bricks like he was a brick mason. The only problem was he wore his weakness on his sleeve. Hoe's was one and most of all he wasn't cut out to be a certified street soulja. In the N.O. it was a must that you be certified in all areas of the game. You had to have hustle skills, street smarts, and most of all know how to sling that iron. If not, it placed you in a position where someone could take your throne. Besides the boy Tossy was a bitch by blood. He rolled through the hood with his nose stuck up his ass, because he thought he was better off than most people. Having that attitude was about to get him jammed up in the wrong position. "Say Lil Man I gotta get us in the game like yesterday, ya heard me" Teelee said as he jumped off the porch hawking Tossy Ford lighting truck. "I think our meal ticket just rolled down the block." Teelee, Lil Man, and Thugga were doing their thing on a minor level, but nothing too big. Teelee wanted to bring them to bigger, and better things. Like Manny Fresh song said *"House real big, cars real big, money real big, everything real big."* Lil Man jumped off the porch to see what Teelee was getting at. "We could get the Blade rockin once and for all if we lay that clown down, ya heard me." Thugga jumped off the porch to join his lil rounds. "What it do, I ain't never like that bitch anyway after the stunt he pulled. That bitch served Pistol and Corey a package of bad coke. Then on top of that, he didn't want take it back after we found out the shit wasn't right. He could have showed love on the next go round, ya heard me." Teelee scratched his head as he plotted on his next move. Teelee was the brains of his clique. He knew a lot of people that could make things happen. "Well it's on then! We lay on this duck for about a week, then checkmate we get what we need. One thing before we go any further, we got to smash this nigga. If we don't its gon bring a lot of heat to the block. We can't slow the block down if we plan on getting this bitch popping. I know for a fact if we don't smoke him we gon have to bang it out wit him; he's known for puttin change ova ya brain." Lil Man and Thugga agreed and the hunt was on from there.

Early, Friday morning Teelee woke up to see if his timing was right on Tossy. As he walked through the alley of the vacant house right across from Tossy spot, his timing couldn't be any better. Tossy was pulling up in his driveway. Teelee received the low on Tossy from Keedy; one of Tossy's ex-girlfriends. She laced Teelee up on what time Tossy came in every day. Keedy didn't give a fuck about Tossy, because he filled her head up with promises of her being the only one in his life. He ended up leaving her stuck out for his baby mama and all the other low down shit that would make a bitch want to fuck over you. As long as she was getting a cut out of the deal she could give a lovely fuck what happened to Tossy's bitch ass. When Keedy laced Teelee up with the info a thought immediately entered his mind. "This the main reason I don't trust these dumb ass hoes' now." Still in all he played along, because she was given him exactly what he needed. Teelee knew Keedy was a scandalous low down bitch so he always kept his shit tight when dealing with her. She always sent signals that she wanted to fuck Teelee, but he always denied her knowing the type of broad she was. Don't get it twisted Keedy was a bad bitch. Her titties sat up like they were silicone implants, but you could easily tell they were all natural. She was a solid "D" cup so she had enough to satisfy any man desires. "I might have to give that bitch the dick one day, but on my terms" Teelee thought. "Before any of that I gotta get this money. *'Money over Bitches"* is the motto I follow." There was bushes and tall weeds camouflaging the alley where Teelee sat giving him a clear view and perfect spy position. As Tossy fumbled with his keys preparing to go in his house he showed Teelee just what he wanted to see. No sign of a gun or alertness of his surroundings. "This shit go be like taking candy from a baby" Teelee thought. After taking account of Tossy's every move. He headed back to the block to tell Lil Man and Thugga it was on. As soon as Teelee hit the block he ran into Thugga fussing with Tyler, one of his old girlfriends from back in the game. "What it do Thugga" Teelee said as he walked up on the two. "Where Lil Man at? We got business to talk about." Thugga ignored Tyler, and concentrated on what Teelee was saying. Tyler was talking a bunch of bullshit anyway. He was about to leave her standing there looking stupid before Teelee showed up. That was one of the things he hated most; her mouth. She didn't give a damn what she said or who she said it in front of. That was them Creole women for you. They will love you to death and drive you to death all at the same time. "I think that boy still inside sleep, let's go wake his ass up." As they walked off headed in the direction of Lil Man's house Tyler screamed, "Don't come knocking on my fucking window tonight."

Approaching Lil Man's house they ran into Pistol. "What's good wit y'all?" Pistol asked. "Bout to get this money flowing through, ya heard me" Teelee replied. "Well y'all know it's enough money for all of us, fuck wit me and Corey later." Pistol jumped in his whip and headed for the Blade. Soon as they walked in the house they smelled the dro aroma and heard Lil Man stereo blasting Soulja Slim, *"You not invited to my smoke out"* coming from his room. Their nostrils were attacked by a rush of weed smoke upon entering Lil Man's room. "Past the blunt homey" Teelee said as he sat on the bed next to Lil Man. From the looks of it him and Pistol had been cheifing for a minute, their eyes were as low as a Chinese. Teelee took the blunt from Lil Man and began to run down the scheme. "Man I just left Tossy spot, everything official. Tomorrow morning for 7:00 sharp we all meet up ova here. I want us to be posted and ready at least thirty minutes before that bitch get home." "How you got the low on that boy" Thugga asked, taking the blunt from Teelee. "That bitch Keedy put me down" Teelee replied. "You know that boy Tossy fucked over her for his baby momma and besides that, the bitch been wantin to fuck me anyway." "Son you better watch that scandalous bitch" Lil Man said slipping on his high top black Polo boots. "I already know homey, that bitch just a duck in the pond for us." "So it's on" Thugga said cocking the brand new Fortie caliber with the extended 32 round clip. Most people who were street smart in New Orleans knew they called that type of iron work "Fortie with the dick" because the clip hung out from the bottom. Thugga had just copped the impressive piece of steal from a smoker named Blood on the Blade.

Bright and early the next morning while the birds chirped away they all met up at Lil Mans house. They were all dressed in black Dickey uniforms with black long johns to cover any revealing tattoos. Their foot wear was black Polo boots. If anybody besides them would have seen how they were dressed, they would have thought the three were going to combat. Teelee threw Lil Man and Thugga some gloves and two Jason masks to cover their face. Teelee also had a black duffel bag containing some duct tape to contain Tossy while they retrieved what they were looking for. Teelee grabbed the Choppa that was leaning in the corner of the room. Lil Man borrowed his brother's Mac10 for the special occasion. Teelee cocked the chamber on the Choppa, *click clack*. 'Son we ain't letting nuthin come between us. We bout to hit this lick and live hood rich." They all put their guns together placing barrel to barrel while saying in unison, *"Hard Heads 4 Lyfe!!!!"* Hard Heads was symbolic in the 7th Ward of New Orleans. It represented the street niggas on the block getting it how they live, and that was straight out the mud. "Rough, Rugged and Raw!!"

Shit was going down as Teelee planned. They made it to their designated area in enough time to get in position. They parked the stolen car on the back street of Tossy's house. Upon exiting the car, they scanned the block making sure no one was outside, or peeking through their window. "Aight homey shit clear let's rock" Teelee said grabbing the duffel bag and choppa. They all hit the back fence of Tossy backyard and crawled under Tossy's 3ft high elevated home. In New Orleans a lot of the homes were elevated due to the city being under sea level. They positioned themselves under the front porch so when he pulled up they could have the drop on him. Just as Teelee turned his head to see if their target was coming, Tossy was pulling in the driveway. They all got ready to hit the lick. Tossy mind was on one thing, the broad he just picked up from the Daiquiri shop name Kekee. He met her about two weeks ago. The Daiquiri Shop, was a popular spot that jumped on the weekends. A Daiquiri is a solid icy styled liquor concoction that is very popular in New Orleans. Tossy wanted to fuck Kekee the moment he laid eyes on her. The broad was bad, she reminded him of a thicker version of Gabrielle Union. She had enough breast that would fill two mouths. Her ass was so well shaped and plumped that you could sit your drink on it and it wouldn't spill. With his attention focused on Kekee he wasn't aware his life was about to take a turn for the worst. "Boy

I'm bout to show you what this pussy made for" Kekee said stroking Tossy dick through his *LRG* jeans. While Tossy exited his truck; Teelee hands perspired from the anticipation of what was about to go down. He finally was about to get his clique in the game. In his heart he promised his self that they would never fall off or die trying not to. He knew he had to remain the level headed one because Lil Man and Thugga were live wires, ready to buck on site. Tossy grabbed Kekee toned ass as they made their way up the steps of his porch. "Bitch it's about to go down, I want that ass up and face down." Teelee had planned the lick to the tee. He knew Saturday morning's most of the residents in Tossy neighborhood were off work, and in bed sound asleep. Teelee watched in anticipation as Tossy turned the key to his shotgun styled home. Most of the homes in New Orleans were built close together that way. If it wasn't a new home, nine times of out of ten it was shot gun styled. Meaning it was a straight shot through with one long hall way leading to the back. Just as Tossy and Kekee were about to step into the house Lil Man grabbed Kekee and put the Mac in her back. While Thugga keyed in on Tossy with the barrel of the Fortie against the temple of his head. Tossy knew he made a grave mistake by not being on his game and thinking with his little head. "You know what it is" Teelee said violently pushing Tossy in the house making him almost fall over the coffee table. "Pat that bitch down Thugga, see if he got his burner on him." As Thugga patted Tossy down he came across an "FN". An "FN" was the hottest handgun on the street, known as an AR15 handgun. "Bingo" Thugga said disarming Tossy of the rare handgun.

"Lil Man tape that bitch up while me and Thugga deal wit him." "Fasho, I got this hoe. She bet not make a move or I'mma knock this bitch head off." While Lil Man prepared to contain Kekee with the duct tape. Kekee pushed any type of thought of making any sudden moves out of her mind. Kekee's mother always preached to her to do a thorough background check on the men she dated; due to the extreme violence in New Orleans. Not taking her mother's advice got her in a really bad predicament. What Kekee didn't know was, this would be her last moment on this earth. Tossy's arms and legs shook in fear of what was taking place. Three masked gunmen stood in front of him with hunger and death in their eyes. Tossy wasn't built for this part of the game. True enough he was a hustler to the fullest, but the grimy gangsta side he wasn't cut out for. As he sat in anticipation of the ordeal a thought that might save him from this situation came to mind. "Maybe if I give em everything that may spare my life." Through shaking lips, Tossy spoke up. "Man I ain't tryna be stubborn I'mma tell y'all where all the work and money at, just let me keep my life." Teelee stepped up behind Thugga as Thugga held the barrel of his Fortie in between Tossy's eyes. "Aight then bitch, where the shit at?" Teelee proceeded to grab the duffel so they could wrap the lick up. "The work is in the deep freezer in the kitchen under the frozen meat. I gotta open the safe to get ya the money." "Thugga hold this clown down while I go see what we workin wit."

While walking through Tossy's crib Teelee realized just how established Tossy was. Flat screens were in every room, and Louis

XIII style furniture adorned the house. The boy was living hood rich!! Teelee knew shit was about to start rolling for his clique. "If he holdin like this, we bout to come off wit a nice pay off." Upon entering the kitchen Teelee spotted the deep freezer in the corner. He immediately opened it as he threw all the meat to the floor. "Jackpot!!" There were 2 ½ keys of Ya Yo shrink wrapped at the bottom of the freezer. Teelee threw the keys in the bag and headed back to go finish the job. "It's going down Thuggezy, we sittin on 2 ½ keys. Now bitch nigga where the paperwork at?" Teelee yanked Tossy up by the back of his shirt, as he gripped the choppa in his free hand. Tossy led them to his plush bedroom. Above his headboard was a picture of himself, behind it was a small microwave sized safe. As Tossy opened the safe Thugga got excited and taunted Tossy with a quote from *Menace to Society. "Better us than the muthafuckin cops' nigga."* Tossy threw the contents of the safe onto the bed. Tossy had just sold three keys that week. The street value of a key was 21.7, at the time so he was sitting on $65,000. Teelee threw the money in the bag and told Lil Man to bring Kekee, the lick was complete. Entering the bathroom Thugga pushed Tossy in the bathtub making the shower curtain fall to the floor. "Man what's good" Tossy said feeling like the jackboyz wasn't about to come through on their side of the deal. When Lil Man, came with Kekee, they made her get on her knees on the floor. "Please don't hurt us, oh Lord help me!" "Even God can't save you nah, shut up wit all that cryin bitch" Lil Man barked. Teelee halted the execution for a second to go get something that would muffle the noise when they sent Tossy and Kekee to take that long dirt nap. Teelee walked in Tossy's bedroom and retrieved one of his thick pillows off of his bed. "This gon have to do." As Teelee made it back to the bathroom; pillow in hand, Tossy was damn near bout to piss on himself. Thugga immediately grabbed the pillow from Teelee. "Man I thought we had a deal" Tossy said pleading desperately. "Nigga you know how shit go in the N.O." Thugga barked as he put the pillow to Tossy face. "It's cut throat to the bone grizzle ova here, ya heard me!" Following Thugga's words was the bullet exiting his Fortie *"Boom, Boom."* The sound muffled a slight bit, but it didn't muffle Tossy's brains from splattering on the inside of the bathtub. Kekee screamed hysterically, as Tossy body went limp. "Shut up bitch" Lil Man yelled as he hit Kekee in the back of her head with the Mac knocking her unconscious. "Help me put this bitch in the tub" Teelee said grabbing her arms. Soon as they laid her down Lil Man picked up the pillow, and closed the book on Kekee's life as well. They closed the door to the bathroom leaving Tossy and Kekee bodies to drain out in the tub. It was on now, they hit big! It was time to hook up with Pistol and Corey so they could get the Blade rocking. They came off with 65,000, in cash and 2 ½ kilos of that white girl. That was enough to get their show on the road. As they pulled off from Tossy's spot, Teelee lit up a cigarette and told Lil Man to call Pistol and Corey so they could meet them at the house A.S.A.P. Lil Man ended the call with his brothers with a smile across his face.

Soon as Pistol and Corey walked through the door of their lil brothers room they saw the coke and all the stacks of money laid out on the bed. "Son what you lil niggas done pulled off" Corey asked picking up one of the keys off the bed. "I told Pistol we was bout to get this money rolling" Teelee replied as he split the money they had come off with. "It's a long story, we'll run everything down to y'all later. Just know we gotta get a new connect, if ya know what I mean." A devilish grin spread across Teelee face showing his deceitful humor. They ended up having $21,000, a piece. The remaining $2,000, they agreed to give Corey and Pistol a stack a piece since the take was so high. "I'mma give my momma some money to pay the bills, and take Money to get some school clothes" Lil Man said counting his share of the money. "We bout to get the Blade pumping" Teelee said picking up one of the keys. "This how we gon do it. We all get a half a brick a piece. After we finish movin it, we all come together wit the flip money and cop a big package. We gotta score from Nunew brother to keep the coke movin until we can find a good connect with some nice prices." Teelee stood up in the middle of the room and asked everyone to stand with him. "We gon make a vow today to never let no one or nothing corrupt this circle. We brothers and that's how we rockin until death, ya heard me!" Pistol stopped Teelee in mid-sentence. We need to call this circle, *THE SKULL GANG*! Our hood been known for representing and rockin the skull apparel way before anybody else." "Me, myself from the heart I'mma forever rock hard for y'all." Teelee put his hand up. "That's what it is, *Skull Gang 4 Lyfe*!!!!" "It's on then" Thugga said rubbing his hands together. "Say Teelee you gon pop that bitch Keedy off so we won't have to worry bout her runnin her mouth" Lil

Man asked, trying to keep all bullshit out of their circle. "I'mma hook up wit her later on. I might put that dick in her life to celebrate. Tomorrow we gon hit the Blade hard as a rock" Teelee said heading out the door. First stop was to drop off his change, then stop by to see his son. He was planning on giving Nunew some money to take his son shopping. Teelee was anxious for the next day so they could start the beginning of their empire.

## CHAPTER 2

## ROCK HARD ON THE BLOCK

It was a hot sunny day on the block, and the money was coming from every corner on the Blade. Teelee was posted up on the alley on side of Big Head Unc house in full hustle gear. Grey Dickeys, with some grey and white Air Force 1's on. In major hustle mode serving a smoker named Blood. "Break bread Teelee, I got the whole twenty this time. I'm expecting the shit to be right" Blood said eyeballing the bag of boulders that lay in Teelee's hand. Thoughts ran through his mind to grab the bag and run, but he pushed them out quick in fear of what Teelee would do to him. "Say Blood, you ain't paid me for the last twenty I fronted you last week. Don't come at me talkin this better be right shit. As a matter of fact, I should just take this for what you owe me." Teelee peeped Blood eyeballing the bag of crack. He knew Blood wasn't stupid enough to play with him. He gripped the bag tighter, it was no limits on what a smoker would do. "Come on man, you know how many cars I had to wash to get that twenty." Blood was the neighborhood all-purpose smoker. He washed and fixed cars, cut grass and all the other stuff he could get into in the hood. "Say Blood, you betta be planning on being my runner all day." Being a runner meant he was going to run all the sales in Teelee's direction. "I got you Teelee, you know I'm out here all day." As Blood made his way out of the alley, Lil Man was jumping out of the 99 Cutlass Supreme he had just copped. "What it do Blood?" "Chillin, chillin got to go handle my business" Blood said anxious to go hit the twenty that was numbing his tongue. "Say Lil Man when I get back you'll let me wash yo car?" "Yeah you know whuzam, I gotta have this bitch right for the *ROC* tonight." The ROC was a popular night club that popped off every Saturday night in Uptown New Orleans. Your shit had to be on point if you planned on showing your face in that spot. Lil Man walked in the alley where Teelee was posted at. "You outchere early, gettin that paper huh" Lil Man stated giving Teelee some dap. "I told y'all yesterday when we was at the house, I was bout to rock hard on the block" Teelee said counting the money he made that morning. "This our opportunity to do what we been dreamin bout. Plus, when we get enough money, we could put money behind you and say fuck a record deal and do our own thang wit the music." That's whatz up" Lil Man replied leaning against the fence. "Where Pistol and Corey at?" Teelee asked. "They went to go holla at somebody bout some more hardware. They said we gon need em cause soon as the Blade start jumping too hard, niggas gon start hatin." "That's what it is then, there's never enough guns" Teelee said. "Say Teelee, you took care that business wit Keedy?" "No, but I'mma hook up wit her later on. I told her we gettin a room tonight. Man, I been thinkin bout puttin this dick on that bitch all mornin." "I already know" Lil Man replied, fantasizing about how Keedy be moving that ass in the club. "Son see if she bout lettin a nigga flip somethin." "I'mma see what it do, you know I don't handcuff these freaks outchere." "Yo" Lil Man yelled flagging down Papa Bear. Whenever Papa Bear came through he spent big money. "You straight" Papa Bear asked feening for a hit of that straight drop. "You know I stay wit it I'm a block bleeder. How much you tryna get" Lil Man replied jumping in the truck with Papa Bear. "Spin round the block, them people been smokin ever since nigga smashed Tossy and that bitch in his house." "Man that's fucked up with they did that man, it's getting worse and worse down here." A thought entered Lil Man's mind "I wonder what he would do if he knew one of the killers was in the truck with him." "You got slabs?" "Man I got whateva ya money match." "Give me a hundred-dollar slab for now. I'mma be back later to get something else." Lil Man took an eight ball of crack out of his package and handed it to Papa Bear. "You straight wit that" Lil Man asked collecting his money. "Fucking right, this that work. Don't go nowhere I'mma be back fasho." By the time they made their transaction Papa Bear was hitting the corner of the Blade. "Fuck with me, I'mma be outchere" Lil Man said jumping out the truck. As Lil Man exited the truck with Papa Bear, Thugga was coming up the street in his brand new SS Camaro doing donuts in the middle of the block. Being the more flamboyant person in the circle, he always did it big every time he came with it. The little kids on the block was amazed at how the monster machine roared like a lion. In the N.O. most street dudes drove cars like Camaro's, Trans Am, Ram Air, Monte Carlo's, or Cutlass Supremes'. If you had a car in that category, you were labeled to be on your shit. Teelee came out of the alley to see what was going on. As he made it out the alley, he saw Thugga getting out of the candy apple red muscle monster. It had deep dish rims on it. The rims were painted the same color as the inside of the car. "What it do round" Thugga said hitting the remote keypad for his alarm. "You ain't waste no time huh" Teelee said checking out the impressive automobile. "You know how I do, I'm Thugga, Calcutta, number one 7th Ward stunna! Lil Man I see you went cop sumthin ya self huh?" Lil Man had copped a Cutlass Supreme all white with the 5% tint all the way around. It stretched from the windshield to the back glass. "I gotta go get the rims put on it later today." "When you goin whip shoppin Teelee" Thugga asked pulling up his oversized Roc-A-Wear jeans. "I'm going cop, just not right nah. When I do come through y'all boy'." "You always gotta be G14 classified" Lil Man joked. As the three conversed, Pistol and Corey yelled as they passed by. They all jumped in the Cutlass headed to Lil Man's house. When they pulled to the house Corey and Pistol were getting out their whip. "Son we got some shit that could chop down a tree ya heard me" Pistol said referring to the guns they just copped. "Pistol hit the trunk" Corey said heading for the back of the car. Corey grabbed the black duffel bag, and they all went in the house. "Say son, close the door and make sure it's locked" Corey said as he unzipped the big black bag. He removed the first piece of iron work.

It was an AR 15 assault rifle with the muffler on the barrel. "Son that bitch off the chain" Lil Man stated as he stared at the killing machine. "We got three Choppas, the AR 15, and a Tommy Gun wit the hundred round drum" Pistol said exposing the other four deadly machines. "That's not it." Corey pulled out four boxes that contained a forty caliber handgun in each one. "Can't forget these" he pulled out four extended clips that held 32 rounds. Corey handed Teelee, Lil Man and Pistol their Forties. Thugga had already cop one from Blood on the Blade. "I feel if we rockin as, The Skull Gang, we should have some shit that could stop a muthafuckin army" Pistol stated alerting them of the beef that was going to come behind their shine. With him being the oldest, he felt he had to stay on top of the shit the younger ones would over look. Besides, he was a Vet in the game. He already knew the ends and outs of the streets. He knew he had a team of money hungry, blood thirsty goons, that didn't give a fuck. He kept his thinking cap on for all of them. "Son, how y'all come up on this exclusive shit?" Thugga asked. "My white boy that work at Elliot's Gun Store, you know he smoke that work. I just did a lil exchange" Corey replied with a smirk on his face. "Son y'all know that boy Tossy and some bitch was found in his house dead in his bathtub huh?" Pistol asked. "My people say they was shot all in the face." Lil Man, Teelee, and Thugga all looked at each other with smiles on their faces. "That's our work", Teelee replied with an evil grin. "So that's how y'all came up on the coke and the stacks? Well life goes on" Corey stated. Street Soulja's in New Orleans had a very low respect for life, that's why killing was nothing to them. "Son we gotta get back to this money" Teelee emphasized. Teelee wanted the smokers to know that any hour, any day they could come and cop off the Blade. "Oh yeah, I almost forgot bout the FN we got off the nigga Tossy. It's under my momma house on Frenchmen St.," Thugga said. Frenchmen was a street back-a-town right behind the Blade. "Son that nigga had a FN" Pistol asked astonished, finding out about the rare handgun, they retrieved from Tossy.

As all of them headed back to the Blade it was one thing on all of their minds; GETTIN MONEY! Soon as Teelee, Lil Man and Thugga got out of the Cutlass the fiends came running. Pistol and Corey posted up on one end of the block and Teelee, Lil Man and Thugga posted up on the other end. Money, and T-Mac rode up and down the Blade on their new found dirt bike. "Son, let me drive this bitch" T-Mac complained, tired of riding on the back of the bike. "Aight let me make the block one more time, ya heard me." As they made it back around the block Lil Man called for Money. "Say Money, go to the store for me." "What you want?" "Get me a hot sausage Po-boy." Po-boys were highly sold in New Orleans. People came from different cities just to get one of the famous sandwiches. "Say Money grab me a Hawaiian Punch too, I'm hungrier than "Baby Dee" on Friday" Lil Man stressed while rubbing his stomach. "Get me a pack of Camels" Teelee requested, as he pulled a twenty-dollar bill out of the crumpled up ball of money in his pocket. When you was in full hustle mode, there was no time to situate your money. It was just jammed in your pocket as the sales came in. Money was able to get the cigarettes because the owner of the store knew it was for one of his older brothers, or one of the older dudes on the block. "I'm straight, my lil broad made breakfast this morning", Thugga declined leaning back enjoying the breeze that was coming through. The humidity was very high in New Orleans, during the summer months most people stayed indoors. They gave Money more than enough money to get their stuff. They always made sure Money, and T-Mac had money in their pockets. The money was rolling in, and the Blade was still pumping from early that morning. Young Jeezy's, *"I Trap or Die"* came on as Teelee cell phone rang. "What it do" Teelee said answering his phone. "Where the fuck you at?" Nunew screamed. "Bitch why you callin my phone screaming at me?" "Because you said you was gon watch your son today; remember." "Girl you know I'm on the block, bring him round here." "I ain't bringin my son round there!" "Well Nunew you gon have to wait till later." "I gotta get my hair done for the Roc tonight, I don't wanna bring him in the hair salon." "Call my momma, see if she'll watch him till you finish gettin ya hair done" Teelee suggested. "You going to the Roc tonight," Nunew asked. She wanted to know because if she stepped foot in that club showing to much flesh, Teelee was going to A-Town stomp her ass. It wasn't like Teelee was trying to be one of those crazy type dudes. He felt the mother of his child should represent him to the fullest, even if they weren't together. "I might be in there, why?" "No reason I was just askin." "Bitch stop lying, you up to sumthin." "No I'm not boy, you tripping. I'm bout to call yo momma so I could drop Jamal off." "Holla at me when you leave out of there, and don't be runnin yo mouth bout me to none of them hoe's." "Bye boy, ain't nobody worried bout yo ass." "Son Nunew be driving yo stupid ass" Lil Man said laughing at how Nunew got under his skin. "Man fuck that broad," Teelee shot back as he stepped off the porch to serve Lisa. "How much you tryna get?" "Give me something for $15." Teelee broke bread with Lisa because she always came with $15, or more. "Thugga what's up with them hoe's you met at the club last week" Lil Man asked. "See what it do, tell them hoes to come on the block." "You talkin bout Leah, and them Cat Pound hoe's. I'm bout to hit em up and see what's good." As the phone rang, Thugga was entertained with Destiny's Child hit single *"Soulja."* Whatz up boyfriend, where you at?" "I'm cooling outchere gettin this money. Where ya friends from the other night?" "They right chere, we bout to go to the mall and get sumthin to wear to the Roc tonight. Why, what's up?" "My lil rounds tryna to see what it do wit ya friends." "They not ugly huh," Leah asked." "Girl stop playin don't nuthin ugly come off this block." "Boy I'm just playing, we gon pass through when I finish in the mall." "Aight hit the phone when you on yo way, ya heard me." Soon as Thugga hung up the phone, they spotted the police coming up the block. Teelee yelled "Them Hitters!!" The whole block cleared out. Every one either ran in the alleys or hid underneath the houses. You had to constantly stay on your "A Game" because N.O.P.D. always tried to catch the hustlers slipping on the block. They would come up a one way street in the wrong direction trying to jam you up. After the police passed every one came out of their hiding spots. "They gon be back" Thugga said while walking out of the alley. The houses in

New Orleans were built so close together, that it was just enough room for an alley in between. The neighborhood hustlers used the alley way to their advantage. "Them hoes said they be round here after they leave the mall." "Son, I want the lil bitch that had the cat suit on last week. When she was shakin that ass you could see that pussy pokin out from the back" Teelee stated. He replayed the scene in his mind when they had all the niggas in the club drooling on themselves. "I wonder what's taking Money so long. They been gone ova an hour" Lil Man said getting agitated. What they didn't know was Money, and T-Mac got jammed up for that hot dirt bike. "Lil Man you know Money, and T-Mac bad ass just went to jail huh" Ms. Rose said walking back from the store. "Fuck man, those lil niggas stay in some shit! Ms. Rose I know they probably brought em down to juvenile, could you go sign em out for me please." Lil Man's mother was locked up for theft, so he needed someone to sign Money out. "I got you baaby, let me put some clothes on." "Aight Ms. Rose good lookin out. I'mma look out for ya when you get back." Ms. Rose was a long time resident of the 7th Ward. She had practically raised each and every one of the lil kids on the block. "I gotta go get my hair braided for the club tonight" Thugga said hitting the automatic start on his Camaro. "I gotta appointment to get my dreads re-twisted. I guess I'mma just ride wit you" Lil Man said heading for the passenger side of the Camaro. "Where y'all going get y'all shit done at?" Teelee asked. "By Tasha shop in the 9$^{th}$ Ward" Thugga replied hitting the gas on his Camaro. The pipes on the car sounded like thunder. "Well I'mma meet y'all at the mall bout 4:00, its 2:00 nah. I'm bout to go get my hair cut." Teelee opened his phone so he could tell his barber he was on his way. "Aight round them hoes should be finished in the mall by then. You know how long it take females to shop." Thugga grabbed the half smoked blunt from the ash tray, and sparked it up. "Say Teelee, you could push the Cutlass while me and Thugga at the shop" Lil Man offered as he threw Teelee the keys. "Aight homey hit the phone before you on ya way to the mall." Before Thugga pulled off he turned the volume up on his Pioneer touch screen T.V./Radio. The speakers pumped out Soulja Slim's *"I Keep That Muthafuckin Heater on Me."* As they pulled off Lil Man called Pistol. "Say round, we all going to the mall to get sumthin to wear to the club tonight." "That's what it is, we go meet y'all there, which mall y'all going to? Lakeside or Esplanade" Pistol asked. "You know Lakeside don't be really havin shit like Esplanade do." "O yeah, Pistol tell Money bad ass go straight inside when Ms. Rose come back from picking em up. Him and T-Mac went to jail for that hot ass dirt bike." "I'mma holla at his bad ass. I can't wait till momma get outta Conchetta! Look I'mma hit the phone when we in route" Pistol said ending the call with Lil Man.

Teelee pulled up in front of "Good Fellas Barber Shop" ready to get right for the club tonight. He usually went every Friday to get a cut, and during the week to get a lineup so he could stay sharp. Teelee didn't let nobody in his head except Rason. Rason had been cutting his hair for almost seven years now. Teelee got out of the car and spotted Ra smoking a cigarette on the side of the shop. "You waitin for me" Teelee asked giving Ra some dap. "It's crowded like a muthafucka in there, you better be lucky you one of my best customers. Somebody offered me fifty dollars for ya spot." Good Fellas was one of the hottest barber shops in the city. Most of the street niggas that resided in the 7th Ward got their haircut there. "You ready?" Ra asked plucking the cigarette to the ground. "You know it, I gotta get ready for the club tonight. They gon have them hoe's off in there. You going Ra?" "I don't know; it all depends what time I leave outchere. I'mma be here till shop close, cause I ain't bout to pass up no money for a club that'll be there next week. M.O.B. remember!" "Say Teelee, I know you got some of them Wiggers." Wiggers were another name people in the N.O. used for Ecstasy. "Even if I don't get out of here in time. I could still have me sumthin to start the party off right. I got one of my lil females on line, ya heard me." "You just in luck playboy. I just copped a twenty pack before I came ova here. Guess what kind I got?" "I got them throwback Blue Dolphins. These boys gon have whoever comin home with me tryna eat a nigga alive." "Son just gimme two pills for the cut." "Fasho, I got you." Teelee always showed Ra love. He paid him thirty dollars for his haircuts and fifteen for his lineups. Teelee believed firmly in taking care of the people who took care of him. "What's good Teelee boy" Byrd said as he put a precise lineup on his customer's head. "Shid you know me, I'm coolin outchere ya heard me." Ra threw the cape around Teelee preparing to cut his hair. "You going to the Roc tonight Byrd?" Teelee asked. "Nah, I'm going fuck with the House of Blues. My lil people got sumthin in there." "That's what it is" Teelee replied as he closed his eyes while

Ra ran the clippers through his hair. Getting his haircut was a moment of relaxation for him. So he laid back and enjoyed every minute of it. "Man what you think them bum ass Saints bout dis year" Rob asked as he designed the Saints team symbol in his customer's head. Rob owned Good Fellas Barber Shop and a couple of other establishments in the N.O. He had his share of the street life, now he was using his hustle skills on a legal tip. "Hold up Rob, don't be talkin bout my team. I'm not paying you for my cut keep talkin shit." The young dude burst into laughter at his own comment. "I ain't trippin I'mma just fuck yo cut up" Rob replied jerking the clippers in the back of the kids head like he was about to take a patch out of his fresh taper fade. "Say Rob, man I was just playin bruh." He quickly put his hand to the back of his head checking for any gobs. The whole barber shop burst into laughter at the kid as he panicked. "I'm just fuckin with ya, but you betta stop talkin shit while you in my chair." "Man Mayweather gon beat Sugar Shane ass." Two old heads were having a heated debate about the pay-per view fight that was scheduled to come on that night. "Man are you crazy, Shane gon put something on Mayweather pretty ass!" "Hold up nah old school you talkin bout my nigga" Teelee interjected. "Ain't no way Shane garbage can ass beatin Mayweather." Damn near the whole barber shop agreed with Teelee's opinion. "I want the razor shave Ra." "You tell me that shit every time you come in here, I already know." "Just makin sho round, I gotta be on point for tonight ya heard me." Ra had Teelee with the Steve Harvey lineup. He was definitely killing em tonight.

Getting up out the chair, Teelee had to cover up the 32 round clip that was hanging out of his back pocket. "Damn round, you got that heavy equipment huh." "Son you know I stay with that heater on me!" Soulja couldn't have said it better. "Nigga playin for keeps outchere and I ain't never planned on playin no games anyway. It's Zero Tolerance over here ya heard me!" "Come to the car with me Ra." When they got in the car Teelee gave Ra three pills, and twenty dollars. "Son, I said just the pills." "I know you got them lil ones at home, I ain't trippin" Teelee said while lighting up a Camel. "Good lookin my nigga." "I'mma hit you up if I make it out of here in time, but if not be careful my nigga." "Fasho I'mma fuck with ya homey." Teelee shot straight for the mall as he left the barbershop. Soon as he jumped on I-10 his phone rang, *"I Trap or Die Niggaaa Yeeaahh."* "What it do homey, what's yo location," Lil Man asked seeing where Teelee was. "I'm on my way to the mall ya heard me." "Aight round we gon meet up there. As Teelee was about to hang up with Lil Man, Keedy was coming through on the other line. "What it do Keedy?" "I'm trynin to see nah baby boy" Keedy replied seductively. "We still on for tonight huh"? "Fasho" Teelee replied. "You going to the Roc tonight" Teelee asked. "Yeah I'mma be in there looking for you" Keedy said with her sexy voice. "Aight, I'm bout to meet up with my homeys in the mall." "Okay baby boy, me and this pussy can't wait for tonight to come." Teelee's dick got hard just listening to the smooth seductive words coming out of Keedy' s mouth. "Aight Keedy be cool." Moments later Teelee was pulling up to Esplanade Mall. Teelee planned on getting his splurge on tonight. As he made his way through the doors of the mall, he noticed Lil Man and the crew waiting for him in the food court. "What it do, y'all ready to get right" Teelee asked giving all his potnas dap. "Let's hit up the shoe store first, nigga got to get the kicks first" Thugga stated. They headed to Nu Veau, the hip hop store that held all the latest Cole Haans, and anything else a street nigga would have in his wardrobe. Most street cats in the N.O. that was on their shit wore Cole Haans. They were very popular in the city. While walking into the store they all got a glimpse of the new gator skinned Cole Haans. "Son these bitches official" Lil Man said picking up the shoe from the rack. "I'm bout to cop the red ones to match the Camaro." All of them ended up getting the same style Cole Haans, but in different colors. They also got some of that *True Religion* shit that just hit stores. When they stepped off in the club, all eyes would be on them with those type of clothes and footwear. "Hold up, that's them hoe's calling. What's good Leah baby this ya Thugga lover." "Boy you so crazy, where y'all at? We bout to swing through and come see y'all." "We bout to leave the mall and head for the Blade, Thugga replied patting his pockets for his keys. "Alright Thug Love I'mma see y'all when we get there Leah said. "Girl that Lil Man fine than a muthafucka! I wanna put this pussy on his, gangsta looking ass," Yarni declared. Women loved Lil Man's smooth brown baby skin, to top it off he was killing them with his six gold teeth across the top of his grill. His dreadlocks hung shoulder length. He loved to shake his dreads wildly when some gangster music came on in the club. "Bitch long as you ain't got yo eyes on Teelee. That nigga make my pussy wet every time I see him" Carmen said trying to make it known what dick she wanted to jump on out of the Skull Gang. Y'all bitches crazy, but all jokes aside we gotta have a gangsta party with them niggas! They the hottest things on the market right now" Leah said.

They all made it on the Blade damn near at the same time. "There them hoe's go right there" Thugga said to Lil Man. "Watch this shit here!" As Thugga came to the middle of the block, he hit the brakes and the gas of the Camaro at the same time. Making the car spin around in circles several times. After the muscle machine straightened up, he hit the gas once more making the car fish tail leaving a trail of smoke for about half a block. "Man this nigga always gotta show off" Teelee chuckled to his self as he got out of the Cutlass. Soon as Thugga and Lil Man made it back around the block Leah and her girls was getting out of their car. "Bitch Thugga make me want to suck his dick right in the middle of this street" Leah said fantasizing Thugga's dick going deep down her throat. "Girl you see how he was handling that car. His car is almost as pretty as him." Thugga was definitely the pretty gangster out of the clique. He kept his hair freshly braided in eight braids that hung down his back. Like most people from the 7th Ward of New Orleans, Thugga had a soft grain of cold black hair. That attracted a lot of his female crowd. His skin tone was a smooth caramel color. He also had six golds across the top of his teeth. When they first copped their gold teeth, they called themselves the "*dirty half a dozen cousins.*" "Whatz good Leah baaby" Thugga said giving her a big hug while gripping her soft plump ass. Leah was your average hood dime. Big ass, thick baby making hips with a cute face to match. What made her really hot was her skin tone, there wasn't too many men that could turn down a yellow bone. "It's all you hot boy!" "When you got that sexy ass car?" "I copped it this mornin!" Thugga felt good saying that, because it showed they were elevating in the game. "Boy you make a bitch like me bend over on top of that car, and let you put that dick in my life." Leah had to contain herself cause her kitty cat was soaking wet. "Lil Man, Teelee this my girls Carmen and Yarni. They been tweaking to see y'all ever since I talked to Thugga earlier." Yarni and Carmen was holding in the thick department as well. To sum it up they were sevens on the one to ten scale. This my trade right chere Carmen said, grabbing Teelee's arm. Trade was a name the women in the N.O. used to describe a hot nigga. "Come here baby face gangsta, I been wantin you since I saw you at the club last week" Yarni said pulling Lil Man by his Roc jeans. It was a damn shame how broads played themselves cheap behind some dude with a little street fame and a couple of dollars in their pockets. They made small talk, and exchanged numbers with promises to hook up and chill. "Aight I'mma holla later" Leah said pulling off heading to her house so they could get ready for the club. "Son, we gotta flip them hoe's" Thugga stated while rolling up a Keep Moving cigar. "Man we gon hook up with them hoe's another night. I got plans tonight, Keedy said she making that ass clap from the back and I'm the star director." "Son make sho you see if she bout what we talked about." "I got you round, don't trip." They stayed on the Blade and made a couple more dollars before leaving to get ready for the club.

"Say Lil Man I'm ready, come swing through and scoop me" Teelee said as he finished putting on his Cole Haans. Teelee got the burnt orange ones. He loved rocking unusual colors. Teelee's father taught him well in the dress department. Lil Man honked the horn as he pulled up to Teelee's sister house. Soon as Lil Man was about to honk again, Teelee stepped out the door. "What it do, Playboy" Teelee said hopping in the car with Lil Man. Teelee lived with his sister Kyla. They got along most of the time, but Teelee knew he had to get his own spot. You can only live with a person for so long until the discomfort came. Teelee was living with Nunew but that ended quickly due to Nunew's mother always interfering with their personal affairs. "I'm coolin, ready to hit this club scene Lil Man replied, pulling off headed for the Blade. As they approached Touro St. and the "Blade" they saw Thugga, Pistol and Corey posted up on the corner dressed to impress. "What it do Skull Gang, "Teelee yelled, as they pulled up to the curb. "Son, we gon shut the club down"! Thugga said lighting up the blunt he just rolled. "I got them wiggers y'all want one"? Teelee asked pulling the pills from his pocket. They popped and headed to the club.

When they pulled up in front of the *Roc*, it was like "*Freaknick.*" Women were walking around in clothing that resembled bathing suits. The *Roc* was definitely the spot to be on a Saturday night. "Woe Wzup Tiger" Teelee said as they pulled up to the side of the club. Tiger was the head of security of the *Roc*, and a lot of other popular clubs in the N.O. Teelee and Tiger became cool ever since Teelee put him in the game with this lil freak bitch he used to fuck with. "Wzup Teelee, what can I do for you tonight?" Tiger had to keep the line moving because it was starting to get thick. "I need V.I.P. status on the parking tip." "You know I got you bruh, park right there under that tree. I'mma keep my eye on y'all shit." "Fasho, you know I'mma break bread with ya." Tiger got all of em in V.I.P. for half price. The V.I.P. door was $60.00 for the night but they only paid $30.00. Soon as they stepped in the doors of the club, they walked up on two broads swinging their ass like it was made of jelly. *Big Freda "The Dick Eater"*, had the females in the club shaking like there was no tomorrow. Big Freda was a homosexual bounce rapper, he had the club scene on lock with his famous ass shaking music. Females loved to dance to bounce music; which originated in New Orleans. The trigger man beat was laced to damn near every song that came out, and the beat fit right into it like it was made for the song. Bounce music ruled the N.O. It's a mixture of face pace beats that make females go crazy and make they ass shake uncontrollably. Their first stop was at the bar. It was a must you get the alcohol in your system to feel the vibe of the club. "Say homey, give me five Vodka and pineapples", Teelee requested as he pulled the money from his pockets to pay for the drinks. All eyes were on the Skull Gang, in their impressive outfits. In the N.O. it was certain groups out of each Ward that were doing something, meaning they were up on their shit. From the 7th Ward it was the Skull Gang, in the 9th Ward it was the Cut Throat City Niggas, and from Uptown it was the K-Unit from the 3rd Ward. That's just naming a few, there was plenty more. "Son this bitch jumping", Pistol said peeping the vibrant club scene. "That'll be $35.00", the bartender said putting straws in each of the drinks. Teelee handed the bartender two twenties, and told him to keep the change. The club went crazy as Juvenile and Soulja Slim hit single *"Slow Motion,"* came blurring through the speakers. All single or single for the moment women were grabbing dudes and pushing their asses up against them, all while moving in slow motion to the beat. The club was in full stride. All the hustlers, jack boys, and all the freaks of the city was in the club putting on for their city. There were a few respectable women in the club, but few and far between. All the hoes were hunting for the dudes with the big names in the city or hustlers who were on their shit money wise. They were plotting on which dicks they would be sucking for the night. It sounds trifling but that's how these scandalous hoe's rocking in the "Crescent City." If you were on your shit you were guaranteed to leave the club with a hoe, if not two of them. The K-Unit was posted in the V.I.P. The K-Unit was a group of hungry motherfucker's that got money, but most of all slung that iron. Gunplay was their Forte. If you got into it with any of them, you better be up on your shit. The Skull Gang, was posted up by the pool tables. Backs against the wall watching everything move. Teelee got his 32 KelTec mini handgun in the club through Tiger. Just in case anything popped off. All the groupies were running up on the Skull Gang. The lights flickered on them making them look like superstars. "Say Pistol when you gon give ya girl that dick" Kya asked walking up on him. Kya was one of them well known freaks out of the 6th Ward. "We gon see what it do" Pistol replied keeping his schedule open. "Well if you decide to pop a bitch off, I got a friend for ya brother, Corey. We could have ourselves a real gangsta freak party" Kya said before she walked off. Kya was a real certified freak. Word on the street she had real skills. "Son we gon have to flip them hoe's" Corey said letting Pistol know he was all in. "Fasho we gon see what it do." Two females had Thugga jammed up in the corner of the club. From the looks of it they looked like they were having a threesome. "Wzup Thuggezy, you ain't sharing with ya nigga" Lil Man asked playing with Thugga. "Lil Man you know what's mine is yours." "Teelee look at ya baby mamma over there standing by the bar" Lil Man said pointing her out. "Man don't look, she headed over here." "I see you made it in here huh Teelee" Nunew said as she admired her baby daddy's million dollar swag. "I know you bet not be in here hollin at none of these hoe's in here, or I'mma cut ya ass." "Bitch stop playing with me!" "Go buy me a drink baby daddy." "Girl go get ya own drink, who the fuck you take me for? Man here"! Teelee gave her twenty dollars to get her a drink. "I'll be back." Keedy and her friend Tasha walked up as Nunew and her friends went to the bar. "Wzup baby boy, me and this pussy been lookin for you all night, you ready to go?" "Yeah, let's bounce. Lil Man tell the homies I'm out." "Aight round be careful, here take the Cutlass." As soon as Teelee, Keedy, and Tasha headed for the door, Nunew spotted them. That wasn't good, Nunew didn't give Teelee a chance to say shit. "Who the fuck is this bitch," Nunew asked eyes beamed in on Keedy. "Nunew you tripping, don't make a scene in this club." Teelee noticed all the attention starting to direct towards them. "So what you bout to fuck this bitch?" "Bitch I ain't gon be too many more bitches," Keedy fired back. "Bitch I'll stomp yo ass in this club," Nunew yelled taking off her high heeled shoes. "Ain't nobody scared over here bitch, back that shit up." Just as they were about to clash Teelee pulled Keedy, and the security guard grabbed Nunew. "Bitch you trippin I'm bout to get the fuck," Teelee said walking off with Keedy. "So that's how you playing it huh," Nunew said feeling a lump coming up in her throat. She held back the tears, because she didn't want to look weak behind Teelee. Deep down even though Nunew was wild in her past, she had much love for her baby daddy. "It's all good. "I'm bout to find me another nigga to give this pussy too," Nunew said putting her shoes back on. "Do ya thang, you been doing it anyway," Teelee replied as him and Keedy exited the club. Teelee, Keedy and Tasha jumped in the Cutlass and headed to IHOP. IHOP was the spot to go to after the club. So you could call it the official after hour. Upon entering the restaurant, the waitress directed them to their table. "Boy yo baby mamma was bout to get her ass whipped"! "Hold up Keedy, we kicking it and all but you wasn't bout to harm my son momma. You trippin with that shit." Even though Teelee walked out on Nunew looking stupid, he still wasn't gon let nobody hurt the mother of his child. "Y'all got problems," Tasha stated putting her purse on the booth seat of their table. IHOP was packed like the club. Teelee knew he wouldn't be there long though. Besides he couldn't eat anyway, he was in his roll. Ecstasy cut your appetite for food and increased your appetite for sex. Teelee was looking at Keedy like she was a pork chop. "Boy I'mma beat that pussy out the frame" Teelee thought as he watched Keedy lean over the table talking to Tasha. Keedy's back had an arch in it right above her ass, which made it sit out like a trophy. "Man I'm ready to rock out this bitch" Teelee said trying to contain his hormones. "I'm ready, when you ready" Keedy replied thinking bout the same thing Teelee was thinking. As they headed out of IHOP, they ran into Thugga pulling up with one of his females. "What it do round" Teelee said greeting Thugga as he walked up on the Camaro. "I'm cooling. Bout to feed this bitch, so I can go to the room and feed her sumthin else" Thugga replied grabbing his Fortie off the floor of the car. "Where Lil Man at" Teelee asked, wondering where Lil Man could be. Most of the time Thugga and Lil Man was always together. Usually one of Thugga broads would put Lil Man in the game with one of her friends. "That bitch let Gia kidnap him." Gia was Lil Man's old girlfriend from back in high school. "Well I'mma holla at you homey, I'm bout to go get my swerve on wit this bitch. You straight huh." "You know I stay straight, If I can't back em off with this 32 round, I ain't suppose to" Thugga said patting his back pocket where the Fortie was stored. Getting in the car Tasha asked Teelee to put her down with Thugga. "Don't you got somebody at home already, fuck" Teelee asked cranking the car to life. "Yeah but it ain't never enough dick in a bitch collection" Tasha replied sounding like the hoe she was. As they pulled up to Tasha's house, Tasha boyfriend was pulling up right behind them. "You betta get yo crazy ass in that house before he stomp yo ass." "That boy ain't gon do me shit, bye girl don't do nothing I wouldn't do." "That means it's open season if we go by yo code book" Teelee shot back. "Boy fuck you" Tasha said waving by to Keedy as she went in her house. Leaving Tasha's house Teelee and Keedy shot straight to Motel 6. Motel 6 was a very well-known spot for the club people. If you didn't get there early enough all the rooms would be rented out. The advantage was the prices was cheap and the rooms were nice. Keedy proceeded to start the party off early, as she unloosened Teelee's True Religion jeans. "I'm bout to show you what this mouth game like." "Hold up Keedy, I got sumthin for you" Teelee said pulling the *'Dolphins"* from his pocket. "You been holdin out on me huh." Teelee gave her one of the pills with a sly smirk. She took it and put it on the tip of Teelee's dick. Without using water, the pill went down as well as his dick. Teelee almost ran off the road as Keedy took every inch of his meat in her mouth. "Grip my ass while I'm sucking this dick" Keedy demanded. Teelee was turned on from the sound of Keedy slurping on his dick like a freeze pop. As they pulled into the parking lot of the Motel 6, Keedy was still going at it. Teelee pulled up to the front door so Keedy could get the room. "Hold up, Keedy." "What's wrong baby boy you don't like how I'm sucking this dick"? "Uhmm huuum" was the sound she made as she increased the suction in her jaws. "Girl we at the 6, go get the room" Teelee handed Keedy a big face to get the room. Keedy came back as quick as she left. "We in room 308, here's one of the keys. Go park the car and meet me up there." "Why" Teelee asked wondering why the bitch wanted to go to the room before him. "I got a surprise for you" Keedy said slapping her ass as she went through the doors of the Motel. Teelee parked the car and grabbed his Fortie. Whatever it was if it wasn't right that fortie was definitely gon get it right.

Teelee placed the key in the lock, as the light on the lock turned green Keedy pulled Teelee in the room. Keedy began to rip his clothes off, the pill had to just have bust because her hands were freezing cold. When Ecstasy went into effect it gave you all kinds of different feelings. "Damn Keedy yo hands cold than a muthafucka." Keedy was ass naked waiting for Teelee. After she finished stripping him out of all his clothing, she made him lie down on the bed. Keedy took Teelee's dick in her hand and proceeded to try and swallow him whole. "You like how I suck this dick" Keedy asked as the spit from her mouth rolled down the shaft of Teelee's dick. Keedy had a way with words, while she was seducing her men. Keedy' s skills never failed her, she always pleased whoever she had a sexual encounter with. "I want the lights on so you could see me eatin this dick up." Quick as she was up, she was back down continuing on with her dick sucking marathon. Teelee was gone from the feeling of Keedy's expertise. Keedy paused on her dick assault. "I want to feel some of this dick." Teelee stopped her for a second to strap it up. "You can't slip up with these dog ass hoe's" he thought to himself. Keedy proceeded to straddle Teelee, as she began to ride him like he was a Suzuki motorcycle. "Damn this pussy good" Teelee exclaimed as his eyes rolled in the back of his head. "You like that baby boy," Keedy replied in a low tone enjoying the feeling. "I got a trick for you, watch this." Keedy turned backwards, and started riding from the back. Now she was in a reverse cowgirl. Keedy' s cinnamon brown plumped ass clapped as she slammed her self-down on Teelee. Keedy felt a strong orgasm building up. She went even harder as the thick white cum rolled down Teelee's dick. She continued on through the orgasm. She couldn't stop it felt too damn good. Teelee was amazed at how Keedy's ass rolled like waves in a raging river. Teelee and Keedy was making so much noise that the people in the room next to them had to stop their little sexcapade. They put their ears to the wall and heard the sound of Keedy's ass clapping. It actually turned them on and made their sex a little better. Keedy was in full stride, riding Teelee like he was a black stallion. "Ooohhh, tell me when you bout to nut" Keedy said in between breaths. Teelee signaled that he was about to bust. "Uhm hmmm boy you taste like candy, what you been eating?" "Damn Keedy you really put that pussy on a nigga; for real." "All for you baby boy." They took a break and went at it again.

Early the next morning Teelee got up while Keedy was still knocked out from there wild rodeo last night. Teelee left her a few big faces on the nightstand and jetted out the door. As he got in the car Lil Man was calling to check on him. "What it do son"? "Say round that bitch Keedy put that pussy on ya boy last night, I'mma tell you bout it when I get there. I'm in route now."

# CHAPTER 3

## G-CODES

As Teelee pulled in front of Lil Man's house scenes of his little sexcapade with Keedy kept popping in his mind. He couldn't deny it, the hoe had skills. Soon as Teelee got out of the Cutlass, Lil Man was coming out the door in some basketball shorts and a "wife beater." Cheifing on his morning dose of "Purpa." "What's good son? Look like you had a wild night" Lil Man said passing Teelee the blunt. "Shid bitch I did. That hoe Keedy freaked a nigga out the game. She sucked and fucked all the soulja out a nigga." "Son what's the deal, you asked her bout that yet"? "I'm plottin how I'mma put you in the game right nah." The weed smoke had to have went down the wrong pipe, because Teelee went into a coughing frenzy. "Slow down homey you know that ain't that "Reggie Bush" nigga." "I know fuck it just went down the wrong pipe" Teelee said gaining composure of himself. "Finish tellin me bout the freak session you had with Keedy." "It started in the car." "Hold up, wait you ain't skeet on my seats huh"? "Get the fuck out of here, you think I'mma play on you like that"? "No son, I'm just fuckin with you nah finish." "I will if you stop cuttin me off bitch, now where was I. O yeah, I gave her one of them wiggers and the bitch turned into a mad woman. My favorite position was when she rode that dick from the back. That ass was clapping more than a church congregation. No offense to God's house." "Son what it do, I'm tryna see what that's like!" There were certain codes they lived by on the Blade, and not handcuffing a freak was one of them. Now having an ole lady was different. Juvenile said it best, *you can have an ole lady, but them hoe's they for everybody."* "Don't trip round you gon get a chance to see what she working with. Just give me a couple of days and you gon be online. Man fuck that shit, what's this I hear bout you lettin Gia kidnap you last night"? "Son you know that's gon always be my bitch" Lil Man replied swinging his dreads from out the front of his face. "Say round we gotta have a meeting A.S.A.P. All five of us have to sit down and get some things laid out on the table. I want to make sure everybody on the same page, ya heard me. Where Pistol and Corey at anyway" Teelee asked. They ducked off with them sluts from last night. I bet they still at the room. They should be here later on." "You heard from that boy Thugga today" Teelee asked wondering about his where about. "I talked to em this morning. He ain't been to sleep yet. He said sumthin bout hittin the Blade, to catch some early mornin sales." "Son gettin that money early huh." Teelee was glad Thugga was on the same page as him. The harder they grinded, the harder they shined. "Say Teelee, you gon ride with me to get my rims put on the Cuttdog? I was supposed to go yesterday, but I ain't get a chance to." "Where you gettin ya wheels from?" "Rim World Uptown. You know I fuck with the owner. He gave me a fire lil deal on the rims and tires." "Well after we done there, you can bring me to pick up a rental." "Son, go cop you a whip, you know Thugga fuck with that boy Harold that own that shop on St. Claude St. He be havin all types of shit on the lot." "I'mma cop me sumthin homey, I'm just not in a rush right now, ya heard me. When I do pull out, I'mma pull out right." "So what you sayin our shit ain't right." "Nigga get the fuck, you ain't here me say that. You know I like to take my time wit shit. You know you and that boy Thugga shit on point." "Well let me throw on some clothes and we can shoot to the rim shop." "What happen with Money bad ass?" "Ms. Rose got em out, his bad ass went on the Blade early this mornin." Lil Man scanned his closet debating on what he was going to wear for the day. "I'm bout to shoot to Richard's and get some fresh underwear. I'mma jump in the shower over here." You know I couldn't let me guard down wit that hoe Keedy. Especially after she gave us the low on ole boy. "Aight homey, I should be ready when you get back."

As Teelee pulled up to Richard's the fiends rushed the Cutlass tryna get some of that hard white. He made a quick $200, in five minutes. "Damn, Teelee this shit butter, where you gon be at later" Slim asked as he put the rock he just copped under his tongue. "Holla at me on the Blade. I'mma be out there all day, ya heard me." Teelee walked in the store, took off his old white tee and threw it in the trash. "Wzup Mikeezy" Teelee said walking up to the front counter. Mike was busy unpacking a box of fresh "white Tee's".

White Tee's was very hot in the hood. The corner stores sold hundreds of them to the street hustlers during the week. They were something quick, cheap, and fresh to throw on. Also, they went with everything you chose to wear. Mike the owner of Richard's sold socks and boxers as well. He made a lot of money off the block bleeders in the 7th Ward. "Wzup Teelee my boy" Mike said in his strong Iranian accent. "You already know what I'm comin for." Teelee headed straight for the coolers to get an orange juice, as Mike prepared his things. He could still feel some of the effects from the Ecstasy. His plan was to get on some Tropicana to boost his roll. Usually the down part of your roll was horrible, but he didn't feel that way this time. Them *Dolphin's* was some bad motherfucker's. When Teelee made it back to the counter Mike had all his stuff waiting for him. Teelee went to Richard's so much that he didn't even have to tell Mike what he needed. He had been going to Richard's ever since he was small, actually they all did. Mike had Teelee's 2X T-shirt, boxers, socks, and a pack of Winter Fresh gum. Mike also grabbed some Camel non filters, and a box of Keep Moving cigars. "Who did you get lucky with last night" Mike asked while ringing all of Teelee's stuff up. "Mike I had a gansta freak in the bed last night! This thang put that pussy down so good. I gotta let Lil Man get a taste." "Don't forget to put in a word for me with one of them lovely ladies" Mike said as he handed Teelee his change. "I gotcha Mike don't trip." Teelee headed out the store and jumped in the Cutlass. Mike was a big trick; he was going to pop it off to any broad Teelee put him in the game with. Teelee kept a mental note to put that in motion, he was always thinking of a way to make a dollar.

As Teelee rode up Tonti St., he saw Roylee posted up by the store on Annette getting his hustle on. "What it do Roy" Teelee hollered as he honked the horn. "Chillin gettin this money ya know" Roylee replied serving a fiend. Roylee was from the front of back-a-town. They had their block pumping as well. They were cool in spite of the fiend's running back and forth from one side to the other. When Teelee made it to the corner of Tonti and Touro St, he spotted Thugga parked on the Blade. He made the block to go holler at him. As Teelee pulled up to Thugga's Camaro he saw a female's head moving up and down through the window. "This dude just don't stop" Teelee thought as he honked the horn. The unknown female in the car didn't care that someone was on the other side of them. She just kept doing her thang. "What's good homey" Teelee said as he rolled down the window of the Cutlass. "I'm coolin son" Thugga said in a voice that sounded like the girl in the car was doing a good job. "You want some of this?" Thugga asked. "No I'mma have to pass. Look we all hookin up later at Ray's pool hall. We got some things to talk about." "Fasho, after I make a couple more sales. I'mma drop her off, Ahh bitch watch ya teeth!" "I'm sorry baby, let me make that baby feel better" the unknown female said as she continued. "Me and Lil Man going handle some business, he going get his rims put on the Cutlass and I'm going pick up a rental." "Son why you don't?" "Don't even say it, I got sumthin planned for my whip situation." "Aight homey, I'mma holla at y'all when y'all make it back. You show you don't want none of this? She official wit it."

"I'm good homey, I'mma hit ya phone when we make it back," Teelee said pulling off headed to Lil Man's house. Teelee pulled up just as Pistol and Corey was getting out of Pistol's Pontiac Trans Am. "Wzup Teelee," Pistol said hitting the alarm on his car. "Nuthin much," Teelee replied, as he grabbed his stuff from the front seat. "What you boys got into last night?" "Son we flip them hoe's like we was doing gymnastics in that bitch," Corey stated. "I can tell it went down, Corey boy you got passion marks all over your neck. Tiff gon get on that ass!" The expression on Corey's face showed that he had just snapped back into reality. "She ain't gon do shit, cause she ain't gon see em, ya heard me." "If you say so," Teelee replied walking up the steps to the house. "Son them broads was some real freaks," Pistol said unlocking the door walking into the house. New Orleans is a big party city. Most hustler's that ran the streets of the N.O. hit the block, and made money. Hit the mall, and spent money. Went to the club, threw money and fucked with the females. That was a regular day for a street dude in the Crescent city. "Son what took you so long?" Lil Man asked, as he tied his dreads up to the back. "I ran into Thugga getting some brain from this chick on the Blade, so you know how that went." "Oh yeah, they still round there" Lil Man asked. He was always bout getting his rocks off. He wasn't going to pass up the chance to get popped off. "I don't know nigga, even if they was we got business to take care of, remember. Say Pistol we all gon hook up later and sit and discuss some things. I feel we need to get some codes established" Teelee said preparing to hop in the shower. The street life in the N.O. was very fast. If you were involved in the game, you were always on the move. Everything was done in a hurry. Take a quick shower, eat a quick meal and most of all make quick money. Street money came to easy, that's why so many brothers are addicted to the street life. "That's what it is," Pistol said as he kicked off his shoes preparing to take a nap. "We gon fuck with y'all when y'all get back. You going with Lil Man to get his rims put on huh?" "Yeah and I'm bout to go pick up a rental." Teelee hopped in the shower, threw on his fresh underwear and him and Lil Man were off to the rim shop. Teelee was getting his ole school broad to rent the car for him.

As they pulled up to Rim World they saw a nigga pulling off in a Black S550 sitting on some 20inch Ashanti's. Damn that bitch clean Teelee said aloud as he admired the beautiful automobile. "That's the type of shit I'm talkin bout copping." "You gon get yo chance to shine round. Don't even trip" Lil Man said as he pulled up to the garage. "I see you made it" Terrell said giving Lil Man some dap. "Yeah you know I had to come get the shoes put on this bitch. This my lil round Teelee. He gon be doing some business with you in the future." "Well you know I'mma give him a deal he can't refuse" Terrell stated trying to seal a deal with Teelee. "No offense homey, but I don't rock the rims. I leave that stuntin shit up to my lil homies. I'm kinda on a low key tip ya heard me." Teelee closed the deal as quick as Terrell tried to open it up. "It's alright but if you ever change your mind, you know where to find me" Terrell said trying to keep the deal alive. "Step into my office fellas." Terrell's had your usual type of body shop in the hood. Second hand desk and chairs with pictures of all types of cars and rims. The little office reeked with the smell of cigarette smoke. Terrell plopped down in his spring exposed chair and lit up a Kool Filter King. "You can have a seat fellas Terrell offered." "Nah, we good I'm kinda in a hurry. I gotta bring my people somewhere. So how much I owe you?" Lil Man asked pulling a knot of money from his pocket. "$2,200. You got a two-year warranty on the rims and tires. So if you have any trouble bring em back and I'll get everything straight." Lil Man gave him the $2,200, and in return Terrell gave him his receipt and the warranty papers. Lil Man had gotten a great deal. The throw back Lorenzo's were still hot. Not to mention the $5,000, price tag stayed the same from way back when they came out. When they walked out of the office, the garage workers were just finishing up on the Cutlass. "Son you on line," Teelee said checking how the rims brought the car to life. "Them hoe's gon be jumping on the dick like it's a pogo stick when I hit the scene with this thang." True enough when you put the shoes on your whip, it brought its look to a higher level. If you were riding on them your pussy rate was about to shoot through the roof. "Call ya ole school and tell her we on our way," Lil Man told Teelee as he hopped in his new play toy. "I'm bout to hit her up right nah." As Teelee waited for Deborah to pick up her phone, he listened to the Isley Brothers sing, *"I wanna groove with you,"* on her ring tone. Teelee loved the Isley's, they were his favorite male singing group. "Wzup Juvey" Deborah said answering her phone. "You baby girl, I'm on my way to Enterprise you gon meet us there?" "Yeah baby, I'm bout to head that way now."

"Aight I'mma see you there" Teelee said ending the call with Deb.

"Son Deb a bad lil settler" Lil Man commented as he pulled off from the rim shop headed to the rental car place. "What she do for a living?" "She a nurse at Methodist Hospital." "You need to keep her on the team round." "I already know, that's why I always keep it one hunid when she hit me up. Most of the time she just want some of this young meat." Teelee loved how Deb put it down in the bedroom. Just the thought of her backing that round plump ass in the air made him want to knock her socks off.

When they made it to Enterprise they parked and waited for her to pull up. Soon as Lil Man was about to spark up a keep moving cigar she was pulling in the parking lot. "There she go right there," Teelee said signaling for Deb to pull on the side of them. Teelee hopped out of the Cutlass and got in the car with Deb. She had a Benz wagon, one of the perks of being a well-established RN. She worked at the hospital for almost 15 years. Deb was 45 years young giving Lisa Raye a run for her money. Deb was a high yellow, thick old school dime piece. She definitely favored the actress Lisa Raye. They could have passed for sisters if ever compared. Deb liked Teelee because of the way he carried himself. He didn't act like men his age. When she found out he was only 21 years old she couldn't believe it. "Wzup Juvey?" "All you baby girl, what you gettin into today," Teelee asked leaning back in the plush leather of the Benz. "Oh nothing much, just getting ideas in the mall for Essence Fest. You still coming with me huh?" "Yea, you know I'm all in."

"Alright I have our tickets booked online already. What kind of car you trying to get" Deb asked as she gathered all the paperwork she was going to need? "See if they got Impala's, if they don't just get a Grand Prix or sumthin. Just make show it's a full size car." "Alright Juvey stay right here, I'll be right back. You know they can't know you going to be driving this car right." "I know baby girl." Teelee jumped back in the car with Lil Man as Deb headed in the rental car place. Lil Man handed Teelee the blunt soon as he sat down. "Son Deb fine than a muthafucka," Lil Man said damn near breaking his neck trying to see Deb walk in Enterprise. "I already know, that's my fine wine ya heard me," Teelee replied as he inhaled weed smoke into his lungs. "We going to the Essence Fest next month, she got the tickets reserved already." "She a keeper homey!" "I already know playboy, that's why I keep her at the top of the list." As Teelee and Lil Man finished up the blunt, Deb was walking out the rental car place. The rental car agent was showing her the car, and giving her the keys. Within a minute, Teelee's cell phone began to ring. "What's good baby girl." "Meet me around the corner in Target parking lot." "Aight, I'm on my way." "Deb was standing on side of the car when they pulled up. "All they had was Monte Carlo's, here's the keys." "Aight baby girl good looking out, you always come through when I need you." "Well you always come through too, so it's vice versa. By the way stop by the house tonight, I need some of that sex therapy." "I got that covered," Teelee replied as he checked the sound system in the car. "Lil Man gon bring you back to the truck. What time you talkin bout hookin up?" "I'mma be finish around 6:00. Just come to the house for 10:00." "Tell Lil Man meet me in the hood after he drop you off." "Alright Juvey, I'mma see you tonight." As Teelee pulled off out of Target parking lot he contemplated on the thought of settling down with Deb. "It'll never work he thought, she way to old, she got me by 24 years. I can't fuck wit that shit." Deb had everything a man could want. Good job, good looks, and most of all good pussy. Teelee was tempted but the age difference was too far off for him.

Blood ran up to the Monte Carlo soon as Teelee pulled up on the Blade. "Teelee where you been at? The Blade been pumping." "I had to pick this rental up," Teelee said getting out of the Monte Carlo. Lil Man pulled up seconds later. "Son Deb a cool ole school broad. You may need to wife that." "I don't know homey, she kind of too old for ya boy. I'mma always keep her in the side pocket just in case though." "Say Lil Man when you got the rims put on the Cutlass," Blood asked noticing the upgrade of the car. "Me and Teelee just came from gettin em put on. You gon wash it for me?" "You know me, I'm always down for a hustle. Let me get my bucket and shit." "Say Lil Man how you looking on your package," Teelee asked as he lit up a cigarette. "I got bout seven ounces left, ya heard me." "Aight I'mma holla at D-Man so we can cop. We gotta keep the work moving. We gon find out how everybody else looking on their coke tonight. Call Pistol and Corey and I'mma call Thugga. Tell them boyz meet us at Ray's Pool Hall for 7:00." As Teelee and Lil Man related the message to the others, there was a line of smokers waiting to cop some of that hard white. "Them boyz said they gon be there." "Fasho, Thugga said he on his way around here, he had to run to Metairie to make a sale." Teelee's phone rang, it was Keedy. "Wzup baby boy, you just leave a bitch in the room huh." "No it ain't like that, I had some business to handle early this mornin." "What you ain't like how I put this snapper on you?" Keedy asked trying to see if her Kitty Kat passed the test. "That definitely wasn't the case, you broke bread all the way round the board." "So when you gon gimme that dick again?" "Soon, I gotta see what my schedule lookin like ya heard me." "Excuse me Mr. Businessman, I ain't know you was that busy." "Girl be cool. I'm not, but I do have some shit I gotta take care of." "Teelee you know I'm really feelin you and I'm ready to do anything to be down with ya. Just say the word." That's all Teelee needed to hear. He was trying to figure out a way to put Lil Man in the game. She had just given the green light on it. "Aight we gon hook up tomorrow and see what's good, ya heard me." "Aight baby boy, I'mma be waiting." "That's wzup," Teelee said ending the call. "Son, I got her just where I want her." "Who you talkin bout?" Lil Man asked. "Keedy bitch!" "Yeah, you got it like that." "We gon be able to use her in the long run trust me," Teelee said plotting on some upcoming shit. "Say y'all know somebody just got banged up round Richard's huh," Money asked as he pulled up on his bike. "For real, who?" "It was that boy D.J. they fucked over him too. They stood over that boy with the Choppa and let every bullet out the clip loose." Come on Lil Man lets ride round there," Teelee said hitting the locks on the Monte Carlo.

Yellow tape prohibited Teelee and Lil Man from riding any

further down the Blade. They had to park and walk to see what's was good. When they walked up they saw D.J. sprawled out on the concrete. Blood and brain matter was everywhere. He didn't even look like D.J. He was twisted up in an awkward position. Whatever way he fell when he took the first shot was the way he was left when they finished the job. D.J. was a young gunner. He was known for slinging that tool. There's a famous saying that still reigns today, "*You live by the gun, you die by the gun.*" That wisdom was confirmed in D.J.'s situation. D.J.'s mother was going crazy. She ran back and forth up the block hollering and screaming. "They killed my baby, why they do him like that." She very well knew why her son was lying on the ground dead in cold blood. When reality kicks in people are not ready to accept the consequences. The police had to take her away from the crime scene. D.J. face was mangled by the AK47 bullets. In the N.O. a Choppa was very common to the streets. You could get your hands on a Choppa quicker than a handgun. Most of the murders in New Orleans were committed with the deadly assault rifles. If anybody got to chopping at you with that Choppa; God be with you! "I never wanna see none of us like that Teelee told Lil Man," feeling D.J. mother's pain. "You won't son trust me, we gon rock steady. Nigga ain't gon have the chance to cancel any of us out." As they made it back to the Monte Carlo they ran into Roylee and Kinky D sitting on Roylee's grandmother's porch. "What it do, Roy," Lil Man hollered. "Coolin, ya heard me. Y'all seen how they did that boy D.J. huh," Roylee asked as he lit up a cigarette. "Yeah, that's fucked up. I know his people bout to ride behind that shit,"

Teelee replied as he opened the door to the car. "Y'all went to the Roc last night?" Kinky D asked. "Yeah we was off in that bitch. They had all the hoe's in there too," Lil Man replied remembering the awesome night he had. "We stayed on the block bleeding all night. We gon be in Caesars Tuesday. You know that boy Juvey got that "Juvey Tuesday" shit in there nah. He be in that thang buying the bar out. Nigga be gettin there drank on for free, ya heard me." "That's wzup, we gon fuck with y'all if we decide to go," Teelee said starting the Monte Carlo. They headed straight for the pool hall to start their meeting. Seeing D.J. lying on the concrete all twisted up like that gave Teelee a deeper motivation to keep the Skull Gang, on their shit. That was the main reason he wanted to have the meeting with everybody. They needed to discuss the G-Codes, they were going to live and die by. Especially the code of Zero Tolerance.

As Teelee and Lil Man pulled up to Ray's Pool Hall, Ray the owner and longtime friend of Teelee was standing in the front parking lot. He was preparing to spark up the grill. Ray's pool hall was a very popular hangout spot. It was a place where people went and got their drink on, and listened to some of the hottest D.J.'s in town. For the most part, most people came to shoot pool. Ray opened his establishment in the perfect spot. There was an ole school club in the same strip as him called "7140." After 7140, closed all the club goers would go to Ray's to finish off their night. Ray would throw steaks on the grill, boil crawfish, and all types of other things for his customers. It was sort of a thank you gesture for the business they would bring to his establishment. Ray was an ole school cat that wasn't to be played with on a pool table. He taught Teelee all the things he knew. "Wzup Ray," Teelee said getting out of the Monte Carlo. "You know I'm out here trying to please my customers. I think I'mma throw some T-Bones on the grill tonight," Ray said putting the coals at the bottom of the grill. "Wzup Lil Man I haven't seen you in a minute. How's everything been going with you?" "I been coolin tryna keep my head above water you know." "I fell ya, same here. How your brothers been making out?" "They been aight, you gon see em tonight. As a matter of fact, they should be pulling up any minute now." "How bout Lil Money?" Ray asked lighting the grill. A big flame emerged from the grill making Ray back up. "Damn Ray you better be careful," Teelee said about to burst out laughing. "I got this youngin, I been doing this shit before you were even born." "Man you know Money bad ass just got out of Juvenile for a hot dirt bike. I try to keep him away from the lifestyle we living outchere, but you know how it is. He see's fucked up shit every day. It's like he's adapting to it." "We'll just keep trying son. How bout you Teelee, what's been going on with you?" Ray asked throwing the first batch of steaks on the grill. "You know me Ray baaby. I'm tryna get this Mullah, ya heard me." "All I can tell you is be careful in whatever you do." "I'mma keep that in mind, but you know how these streets can get. If these niggas actin crazy, nigga gotta be on some insane shit ya feel me." "Yeah I see where you coming from," Ray replied popping the top on a Heineken. "Y'all want one?" "Yeah give me a Hennessy and Heineken." "Lil Man what you want?" "Woe, woe, woe that's what I got employees for.

Go in there and tell Katy what y'all want. Tell her it's on Ray." Ray always looked out when Teelee came through. Ray sometimes looked at Teelee like a son he never had. Ray had two daughters Tiffany and Chrissy. Tiffany had a hair salon right next door to the pool hall. Ray taught them well in the field of entrepreneurship. Approaching the bar, they were greeted by the cute little bar maid. "What can I get for you guys tonight?" "Give me and my lil homey a Hennessy and Heineken, and an Absolute and pineapple. It's on Ray," Teelee said as he took a seat on the bar stool. Ray's pool hall was small but nice. A full bar with every liquor you had a taste for and six full size pool tables. A small dance floor for people to get their groove on, and last but not least the secluded area in the back. This is where Ray's special table was. If you weren't gambling, you weren't shooting on it. "When you start working here? I never saw you here before," Lil Man said trying to start a conversation with the cute little bartender. Katy was the slim sexy type. Cinnamon skin tone, with a pretty smile. She was definitely a delight to one's eyes. "I just started last week," Katy replied preparing their drinks. "I might have to start comin in here like I used to," Lil Man stated while getting his flirt on. Katy blushed at Lil Man's comment as she put straws in their drinks. "Katy do I have some barbeque sauce back their behind the bar," Ray asked walking in the pool hall. "Yeah Ray here's some right here," Katy replied handing Ray the sauce. "Ray I need to holla at you in private," Teelee requested as he stood up from the bar stool. "Sure son come to the back. Katy keep an eye on that grill for me." "Okay Ray."

Ray I need to use your table for a couple of hours. Me and my people gotta have a lil business meetin. I'll break you off for the time we use." "Everything alright huh?" Ray asked concerned. "Yeah everything cool. I just feel we gotta get some things established as an organization, ya heard me." "What organization is that?" *"The Skull Gang,"* Teelee replied. "We not on no shit like you thinkin. It's just we need to talk about us watching out for each other, while we gettin this money that's flowin through the streets." "Well son, looks like your mind is pretty made up. You can use the table, just make sure y'all don't scratch my baby." "Good looking out Ray. How much I owe you." "Nothing, just be safe youngin," Ray replied as he headed back to tend to his grill. Teelee came from the back and walked up on Katy and Lil Man having a flirtatious conversation. "Wzup homey, I see you made a new friend huh." "I guess I did," Lil Man replied looking at Katy. As Teelee and Lil Man finished up their first round of drinks the rest of the Skull Gang was emerging through the door. Teelee signaled for everyone to go to the back. This wasn't the time to socialize. Teelee wanted to get straight down to the reason why they were having the meeting. Ray sent Katy to take their orders, as they got settled in the back. "What will y'all be having to drink tonight," Katy asked pulling out her note pad to take their orders. "Gimme the same thing from earlier," Teelee requested as he picked up one of the pool sticks from the rack. "You know what I want," Lil Man said giving Katy a sly wink. "Gimme a Belvedere and Cranberry," Thugga said. Pistol and Corey ordered two "Hulks". As Katy went to prepare their drinks they began the meeting. "I wanted us to get together for a few reasons," Teelee said standing at the end of the pool table. I feel we need to get some things established between all of us. We live in one of the most violent cities in America, ya feel me. I feel our top priority should be Zero Tolerance with any beef that's brought to this circle. Lately, a couple of points been running through my mind and I know some things have come up in y'all mind as well. Zero Tolerance is the most important subject I wanted to bring to the table." Pistol was the first to break the silence. "I think we should have a code of notification. I feel we should relate to someone in the circle on our location, before going indoors and shutting off all communication. I think we all have a bad habit of turning off our phones, or just not answering em. That could be bad business if anybody got jammed up in a bad position and nobody knew where that person was." When Katy came back with the drinks, they paused the meeting. After she delivered all the drinks, Lil Man thanked her and gave her a twenty-dollar tip. In return Katy slipped Lil Man her number without anyone noticing. As Katy exited the back area, they continued the meeting. These codes ain't supposed to be known by anyone outside of the Skull Gang, for safety purposes. If anyone of the Skull Gang codes were leaked, they would expose the secrets that kept the clique so tight. That's one thing Teelee never wanted to happen. "We should all know the code to the females Corey iterated. Groupie bitches can be passed along, but ole ladies, wifey, or baby mamas are strictly off limits. If anyone of the women on the "off limit" list should approach any one of us, nigga gotta straight up tell who ever have ties to her. I feel she should be cut off immediately, because that type of broad can cause conflict in the circle. Remember it's always M.O.B., money over bitches." "I got sumthin I been thinkin bout," Lil Man said sinking the nine ball in the left corner pocket. "I think we should put money to the side every month and do sumthin for the kids in the hood. Buy they school clothes and shit, have a D.J., you know anything just to give back. It would keep us with a good name in the community." "What about you Thugga," Teelee asked. "I'm bout whatever y'all bout," Thugga replied, as he removed his Fortie from his waistband and placed it on the pool table. They all followed suit. On this day these codes. "Guns out everything on the line, we will live and die by these codes we have established." As those words came out of Teelee's mouth, he picked up his Fortie and put it in the air. All the rest did the same and in unison they all said, *"SKULL GANG 4 LYFE!"* Before we conclude the meeting, how everybody lookin on their packages?" "We all ready to re-up," Lil Man said pulling out his score money. "That's wzup," Teelee replied. They all gave Teelee their re-up money to get a package from D-man. Teelee knew he had to find another connect soon, because D-man prices were extremely high. "Aight tomorrow we gon meet up by my sister's house so y'all can pick up y'all work.

Ray's was in full stride as all of them headed out the back. The D.J. had R. Kelly's *"Step in The Name of Love,"* blasting from the speakers. There was a nice crowd present. A few couples got their groove on, on the dance floor. Ray's was a real nice place to chill. "I'mma cool out here for a minute," Lil Man said looking towards the bar where Katy stood. "I know what's on yo mind," Teelee replied. "Go do yo thang Playboy. How you gon get back to the Blade?" "I'mma get Thugga to bring me to the Cutlass." "Fasho, you know where I'm bout to go. So if y'all need me just hit me up by Deb. Pistol where you and Corey headed at?" "We bout to hit the Blade, so we can get off the rest of this coke. You comin on the Blade, Thugga," Pistol asked as he finished up the rest of his drink. "Nah I'm bout to go pick up one of my hoes, after I drop Lil Man off. I'mma hustle off my phone tonight." Thugga had a million-dollar phone. He had clientele out the ass calling his phone. The customers ranged from doctors, lawyers, and even car salesmen. They were the type that never showed their faces in the hood. They preferred to have their crack delivered. "Aight y'all I'mma fuck wit y'all later," Teelee said leaving out the doors to the pool hall. As Teelee approached the Monte Carlo, he noticed Ray flipping burgers like he was Chef Boyardee. "Y'all had a good meeting son." "Yeah shit cool, good lookin out Ray." "No problem son, just remember what I said." "I know I'mma be careful, I got you. I'mma holla at you Wednesday night." From there Teelee jumped in the Monte Carlo and headed to get his swerve on with Deb.

Teelee got on I-10, headed in the direction of Deb's house. Just as he was about to slide in his *Reasonable Doubt* CD, his phone rang. "Hey Juvey, where you at?" "I'm headed yo way now," Teelee said lighting up a cigarette. "Well I just got out the shower shaving this kitty kat, she waiting for you to come get her right." "Don't trip, I'mma be there in a hot second baby girl." "Aight Juvey, I'mma see you when you get here."

When Teelee pulled into Deb's subdivision he lowered his music. Deb stayed in Metairie. Metairie was on the outskirts of New Orleans. Most of the people that stayed in Metairie were doctors, lawyers, and judges. You had to watch how you conducted yourself because the area was highly patrolled. Teelee parked the Monte Carlo in Deb's driveway. She always parked her Benz in the garage. Before he got out of the car, he grabbed the box of Keep Moving and half ounce of Purple Haze he stashed in the middle console. Teelee knew Deb got freaky when she got high. She didn't smoke often; she's was what you can call an occasional smoker. Unlike Teelee, he was a real weed head. When Teelee rang the doorbell, the porch lights flicked on. Seconds later Deb came to the door in a sexy robe that showed of her yellow plumped breasts. Teelee often thought of them as juicy cantaloupes. "Come on in." As Teelee followed Deb in the house he watched her ass jiggle in her sheer robe. Deb was well built for her age. She made women that were younger than her look like trash. She always ate healthy and faithfully went to the gym. Her self-discipline definitely had its rewards. "Look what I got baby girl," Teelee said pulling out the purp and cigars. "Boy you read my mind, I needed something to relax myself. I had a real tough week at the hospital." "Well let me go jump in the shower and when I get out we can lay back, smoke and chill." "That sounds good," Deb said as she began to lay back on her queen size pillow top mattress. Deb's house was lavish. There was three bedrooms, two baths, and a swimming pool in the backyard. The feel of the house made you just want to lay down and fall asleep. Teelee hopped in the shower and got the smell of the streets off of him. When he got out, he rolled him and Deb a blunt. Teelee sparked the purpa and began Deb's Sex Therapy. "Here baby girl, don't hit this too hard. That's purple haze." "What's that?" "It's stronger than what I brought you last time." As Deb took a puff off the haze, she coughed lightly and let the weed smoke seep out her nose and mouth. The weed took effect immediately. Deb began to rub and roll her ass all up on Teelee. "Hold on baby girl. I'mma try sumthin different tonight." Teelee proceeded to lay Deb on her stomach. He began to give her a full body massage. He gently rubbed her from her neck to her feet. "Oh baby that feels wonderful," Deb said enjoying the pampering. After he finished massaging her back he licked and kissed from her neck to the lower part of her back. He then turned her over and shot straight for her breasts. The way her nipples stood up in the air, made them look like darts about to shoot off the wall. "Oooh baby, you giving me the works tonight," Deb said in between breaths. Teelee sucked Deb's nipples slightly nibbling on them making her jump from the amazing sensation going through her body. Teelee moved down lower getting closer to her freshly shaven hot box. Deb grabbed Teelee's head using it like it was a steering wheel, while he flickered his tongue on her clit. "Oooh baby, I like how you licking this pussy," Deb said as her eyes rolled in the back of her head. Teelee used his fingers to play with Deb's clit, while his tongue went in and out Deb's juice box like a groundhog ducking the sunlight. "Aaahhh baby, I'm bout to cum," Deb cried as she tightened her grip on Teelee's head. Teelee put his tongue on Deb's clit and pressed against it moving his tongue in circular motions. Deb's body felt like it was on vibrate, as a powerful orgasm ripped through her entire being. "Oh my God" Deb screamed out as she locked her legs around Teelee's head. Deb gained her composure then sat up in the bed and just looked at Teelee. "Damn baby girl, what's wrong?" "Boy you young with an old soul. The way you be working that tongue be fucking my head up. Shit, you had me in another world." Deb tried to give Teelee some of the same treatment but Teelee stopped her. Nah, baby girl tonight is your night." "Aight Juvey, I got something for you, stand up." As Teelee stood to his feet, Deb crawled to the middle of the bed like a cat. She bent over tooting her ass in the air, as she leaned on her arms. She knew that drove Teelee crazy. Her freshly shaved pussy stuck out like a juicy Georgia peach. Deb looked back at Teelee and said, "Come get it baby." The way Deb crawled onto the bed, and instructed Teelee to come get it made his heart skip a beat. Teelee climbed up behind Deb and slid in. "Damn baby girl yo shit good." "You like that baby," Deb moaned. Deb looked back and stared deep into Teelee's eyes. The faces she made were driving him crazy. She didn't know it but what she was doing was about to make him explode. Deb threw her ass back into Teelee making the sounds from their bodies slap together in unison. They went at it non-stop for a while. Teelee held one side of Deb's ass as he felt his big volcano about to explode. He pulled out and shot all over Deb's round plump ass.

"Juvey you really put the dick down tonight," Deb said as she collapsed onto the bed out of breath. "You wasn't too bad ya self." "You hungry Juvey." "No not right nah, probably a lil later." "Teelee had put it down so good, Deb was ready to cook, clean, or even sing him a song. "Well I'mma have a surprise for you when you wake up." "Aight baby girl, right nah I just need some sleep." Teelee's phone rang just as him and Deb were about to slip off into dreamland. "Hello, who this," Teelee barked into the phone. "What's good Teelee boy, this D-Man you still tryna get right huh?" "Yeah, I'mma fuck wit ya tomorrow bout 12:00." "Aight round, hit me on the hip." "That's what it is," Teelee replied before he ended the call. All the rest of the Skull Gang relayed to each other on their locations before they went in for the night. Keeping their G-Codes all in line.

# CHAPTER 4

# WHEN THE GUMBO GOES TO COOKIN

The next morning Deb woke Teelee up to breakfast in bed. The sex was so good, Deb cleaned the house, and cooked breakfast with a smile all over her face. Teelee felt comfortable around Deb, so whenever he slept over he received his proper rest. He didn't have to constantly get up to check his surroundings. In the *"murda cappe"* he had to watch every move he made; especially when dealing with women in the N.O. It's like 2Pac poetically said, *"Every move is a calculated step."* You had to watch who you got involved with cause them grimy hoes were eager to set you up! Deb had Jill Scott's, *"The way"* playing at a low tone. It was loud enough to feel the vibe of her neyo soul melody. The house was filled with the smell of eggs, bacon, and buttermilk biscuits. Deb sang along with the music as she prepared to bring Teelee his breakfast. *"Is it the wayyyy, you lovveeee me babbyyyyy."* Deb's sex therapy really helped her to relieve a lot of stress she accumulated from work. She felt she had to show her appreciation for the treatment she received last night, and this was the perfect way of doing it. Deb had Teelee's breakfast tray looking like it was prepared at a five-star restaurant. She heard Teelee snoring lightly as she walked up on the side of the bed. "Good morning my juvey," Deb said placing the tray in front of Teelee. "Wzup baby girl," Teelee said groggily as he set up in bed. "Here you go sweetie I made you breakfast." "Thank you. Let me get up and brush my teeth first, I ain't tryna to hit you with the dragon breath." "Boy you crazy." Deb always had a spare toothbrush available for Teelee whenever he slept over. While Teelee brushed his teeth he contemplated on the cool relationship him and Deb shared. "I wouldn't mind taking this thang with Deb to another level, but I ain't trying to involve her in my lifestyle. Then her age keeps fuckin wit me. She was well past the age I wanted to settle down with. Fuck it only time will tell." Teelee thought to himself as he spits out the mouthwash. Deb was sitting combing her hair when Teelee made it back to the room. "Damn baby girl, you put it down with this breakfast, it smells good than a muthafucka." "Well you put it on me so good, I had to show my appreciation somehow. I told you I would have a surprise for you." Teelee gobbled down his breakfast like he had never eaten a day in his life. "Damn Juvey, slow down, you're going to choke!" Teelee ran the streets so much that he rarely got the chance to eat a home cooked meal, especially when he was in his roll on one of them Ecstasy pills. He might even go a day or two without eating anything at all. Teelee was a very handsome young man. He was your typical hot boy type nigga. He was slugged up with two golds at the top and two on the bottom of his teeth. He didn't want to get as many as all the rest of his niggas had.

Everybody in the Skull Gang clique had six or better. Teelee rocked his baby soft, hair in a taper fade. He had the smoothest cocoa brown skin that was tatted up to the fullest. He was what the girls in N. O. would refer to as "Trade." The boy stayed on top of his gear. You never caught him slipping in the dress department. Even when he was slipping, he wasn't slipping. He could easily put you in the mind frame of the rapper Nas, but nothing about him was Sincere at all. He had the soul of Tommy off the movie *Belly,* with the appearance of Nas. "You did ya thang baby girl," Teelee said as he finished the rest of his breakfast. "You know you my Juvey, I gotta take care of you. What you got on your schedule for today," Deb asked. "I gotta handle some business. Why, Wzup?" "Nothing, just asking. I gotta go get my nails done, my appointment for 2:00. So that's where I'll be for the day." Deb didn't ask Teelee what business he had to handle, or where at, because she felt if he wanted her to know he would have told her. Teelee stepped outside for a minute to smoke a cigarette. As soon as he took his first puff his cell phone rang. "Wzup Teelee where you at?" "What it do playboy, I'm still at my settlers house." "Damn nigga it's almost 12:00! That ole school broad put that pussy on you last night huh." D-Man never interfered in Teelee and Nunew's business. Even when they were together. So he didn't care what broad Teelee was fucking with. As long as his nephew was taken care of, he could care less. "What's your location," Teelee asked as he threw the cigarette to the ground. "I'm on my way back from across that water. I had to drop my baby mamma off at the hair salon. I'll be downtown in bout 10 minutes."

"Aight round meet me by my sister in the 7th Ward. I'm bout to head that way now." "Fasho, I'm in route." Teelee ended the call and headed back inside to tell Deb he was about to leave. He really appreciated the special things Deb did for him. He really didn't want to leave, but his street instincts took over like always. Deb was preparing to leave herself, when Teelee made it in the bedroom. "I'm bout to rock baby girl," Teelee said giving Deb a kiss goodbye. "Aight be careful. Call me when you finish handling your business."

Teelee hit I-10 headed straight for the 7th Ward by his sister's house. Kyla was at work so it was the best time to do his transactions with D-Man. Even though Teelee took care of himself, he still had to keep everything on a respectable level. He always kept that kind of activity away from Kyla's presence. Kyla knew Teelee was a street nigga, who was involved in all types of shit. She wanted more for her little brother, but it was only so much she could say or do. He was a grown man now making his own decisions. The only thing she could do was keep him lifted up in prayer like his mother and father always did. Teelee had three older brothers and sisters, which was his father's children but he didn't fuck with them. He was on some fuck them type shit, because when he was younger he reached out to them; but they didn't reach back. He was a man now; he didn't need them for shit.

Teelee spotted D-Man parked in front of Kyla's house as he pulled up to the corner of Frenchman and Tonti St. D-Man was doing well with his hustle. He was pushing a black Tahoe sitting on some 24 inch black Davens. In spite of all his other clientele, Teelee couldn't find himself fucking with D-Man on a constant basis with his outrageous prices. D-Man hopped out of the truck when Teelee pulled into the driveway. They didn't waste any time. They went straight into the house. "Y'all boys doing y'all thang huh," D-man asked as he removed 3 kilos of cocaine from his duffel bag. "Yeah you could say that. Nigga gotta get this money to feed ya nephew, ya heard me." D-Man let his keys go for 23,000, so Teelee had to come off 69,000. That's the reason he was so eager to find a new connect. "Nigga you must have had a good time last night, you ain't even know what time it was this mornin." "You could say that," Teelee said handing D-Man three healthy stacks of money. "Aight then hit me up when you ready to get right again." "Fasho, I'mma fuck with ya." I won't when I find a better connect, Teelee thought as D-Man left out the door. From there Teelee prepared to call everyone so they could come pick up their work. "We online homey, where you at?" Teelee asked Lil Man as he separated the coke. "I'm on the block just got off the rest of this package." "Call Corey and Pistol and tell em come by my sister house ya heard me." "Aight round we gon see you in a minute." Fasho, I'mma be here waiting on y'all, I'mma call Thugga and tell him be in route." When Teelee called Thugga a female answered the phone on the first ring. "Who this is!" "Bitch stop playin gimme my phone! Whatz good nigga." Thugga said on the verge of strangling the girl. "Man who that be?" "That's Tyler stupid ass, she better get her mind right or I'mma beat that ass!" "Boy you ain't go do shit!" Tyler screamed. "Girl back up, before I bat the fuck out you!" "Say son don't fuck with that broad like that. You know some of em be waiting to call the police on a nigga." "I ain't gon fuck with her, whatz good on yo end? You got right yet?" "Yeah that's what I'm callin bout now, everybody on the way to pick up." "Aight round I'mma be there. I'm bout to go drop this crazy bitch off."

They all pulled up to Kyla's house one after the other. The Blade had been on fire all week. So they were all in need of that *"White Girl."* The block was coming along well. Every hour of the day someone was present on the block grinding. They made sure someone was available to serve the fiends. "What it do Thugga," Lil Man said hitting the alarm on the Cutlass. "Shit nigga stashed lovely last night. The Blade was flowing like the pumping station." "Say Lil Man, Gia came by the house looking for you," Corey said walking up Kyla's front steps. "Yeah what you told her?" "I told her hit ya phone, I ain't know where you was at." "She think we gon get back together, that girl trippin I don't back pedal." Lil Man hit Teelee on the phone to let him know they were outside. "Say son we outside, ya heard me." "Aight." Soon as Lil Man hung up Teelee was coming to the door. "What'z good wit you boys," Teelee asked while opening the door to let everyone in. Teelee had already divided up all the keys so everything was set and ready to go. As they all walked in Teelee's room he gave everyone their package. "Say homey next time, I'm tryna cop a whole key," Teelee said taking a seat on the bed. "What about y'all, how y'all lookin?" "I'm straight, I'll be ready," Lil Man stated tucking the half of brick in his waistband. "Me and Corey been ready." "What about you Thugga," Teelee asked. "You know I'm a grinder. Its big money heavy weight ova here, ya heard me!" "Fasho that's whatz up. Where y'all bout to go now?" Simultaneously they all said the "Blade." "Aight, then I might be out there later on, I don't know yet. I gotta go pick up my lil homey. I been told Nunew, I was comin get em. So if I don't make it out there y'all know where I'm at." "Aight, tell my godson, I luv him," Lil Man said leaving out the front door. Lil Man had the honor of christening Lil Jamal. He always picked him up and took him shopping.

Ever since they bust the Blade open, Teelee had been neglecting his son. He always made sure he was well taken care of, but the only thing missing was his time. The only reason Nunew pressured him to pick Lil Jamal up was to go run the streets with them scandalous hoe's she called her friends. Nunew was always the follower type. One time Teelee and Nunew's mother had to go bond her out of jail. She let her girl Tanya talk her into stealing out one of the most secured stores in New Orleans. Lord's and Taylor's, in the New Orleans Center Mall. That was one of the reasons Teelee knew it would never work. Ms. Sonya, Nunew's mother was outside playing with Lil Jamal when Teelee pulled up. Nunew was born and raised in the 7th Ward. That's a big reason Teelee got caught up. Most hood niggas fall for hood broads. To sum it up, it's "HOOD LIFE." When Lil Jamal spotted Teelee, he started smiling showing his two teeth at the bottom. "Wzup daddy baby," Teelee said holding his arms out for Lil Jamal to come to him. Lil Jamal had just started walking about three months ago, but when he saw his daddy you would have thought he had been walking for years how he broke out in stride. "Da" Da" Da" Lil Jamal sounded out as he hugged Teelee's neck. "Wzup Ms. Sonya. How you doing today?" "I'm fine, where you been at? You need to start comin get your son more often." "I am Ms. Sonya. I been workin, ya heard me. Gotta have money to take care of my lil homey," Teelee said giving Lil Jamal a kiss on the cheek. Lil Jamal smiled showing off his teeth and gums. Teelee always tried to show respect to Ms. Sonya. Even though she made him want to tell her what was on his mind. That was one of the main reasons he moved out. "Where Nunew at?" Teelee asked. "She went somewhere with that lil girl Tanya. She told me to tell you to bring Lil Jamal home with you tonight. She has a job interview in the morning. I have his bag packed and ready to go." "I had some things to take care of, but I guess I can handle that another day. Where his stuff at?" "Here's his things," Ms. Sonya said handing Teelee Lil Jamal's bag. "Gimme my grandbaby so I can give him a big kiss. Grandma gon see you tomorrow here," Ms. Sonya said planting a kiss on Lil Jamal's chubby cheek. "Aight Ms. Sonya I'll be back tomorrow to drop him off. What time Nunew gon be finish at her interview?" "I don't know, you have to call and ask her that." When they got in the car Teelee looked at Lil Jamal. He knew he had to do better with making time for his son. Lil Jamal got so excited when he came around. It made Teelee feel bad not being there like he was supposed to. Teelee planned on taking Lil Jamal shopping and to Celebration Station. Even though he wasn't big enough for the rides, he still wanted him to have fun. He wanted to take this day and give his son his undivided attention.

When they made it to Lakeside Mall, they headed straight to the Disney store. Lil Jamal loved the Disney store. His favorite stuffed animal was the Tasmanian devil. "May I help you sir," the saleswoman asked. The Disney store was a kid's paradise. There was every stuffed animal you could imagine available. Disney movies and cartoons were playing on the T.V.'s that hung on the walls. There were even people dressed like the Disney characters present at certain times of the day. "Nah, I'm good. Just coming through to get my son a couple of things." "Oh how cute. He looks just like you, hey cutie." Lil Jamal loved women. Every time a woman held him, he would try and grab their breast. Nunew had to stop bathing him with her because he always tried to grab hers. It was in his blood. Teelee was a tittie baby himself. If a woman didn't have nice size breast, he really wasn't interested. Lil Jamal always drew women unto Teelee everywhere they went. "Okay sir, if you need any help just ask. Bye cutie." "Fasho," Teelee said running behind Lil Jamal who was headed towards the stuff animal rack. Lil Jamal ran straight for the Taz. It was almost big as him. "You want this one homey?" "Da "da "da, Lil Jamal mumbled pointing to the stuffed animal. "Aight lil homey, if you want it daddy gon get it for you." They headed for the counter to pay for the Taz. The price of the stuffed animal came out to be $99.99 plus tax. Very expensive for something that was going to sit up and collect dust. That didn't matter though because whatever he wanted he was going to get. After they left the Disney store, they went to Kids Foot Locker to get Lil Jamal some tennis shoes. Teelee got him three pairs of G-Nikes "Air Force Ones." Whenever Teelee bought Lil Jamal shoes he always made sure to get him at least three or four pair. On holidays Teelee and Nunew would go out their way to find him some exclusive shit. Teelee felt if he stepped out nice his son should to. After they finished in Kids Foot Locker, Teelee took Lil Jamal to the food court to get something to eat. Soon as they hit the food court Lil Jamal started pointing at the golden arch. Lil Jamal loved McDonald's French fries. The food court was full of life. Adults and their children flooded the lines of the restaurants that sat in the food court. As they made it to the front of the line Lil Jamal squealed, "Nuggies" "Nuggies." "I hear you homey," Teelee said scanning the menu. Who knows why Teelee felt the need to scan the menu, he went to Mickey D's damn near every day. "Welcome to McDonalds may I take your order," the chipper little cashier asked. "Yeah gimme me a number 3 and a Nugget kid's meal. "Nuggies, Nuggies." "I got you homey she bout to get em now." "He's so cute." "I know and so active too," Teelee replied pulling out his money so he could pay for the food. "That'll be $8.25. Teelee paid for their food and they sat down and ate. After they ate they headed to Celebration Station to finish off their day. Lil Wayne's *"The Block Is Hot"* was on the radio when they got in the car. Lil Jamal bobbed his little head to the beat. "You like that homey? Lemme turn it up for you." Teelee cell phone rung soon as he turned the music up, it was Keedy. "Wzup baby boy?" "I'm coolin, spending the day wit my son, ya heard me." "That's good, where y'all gon be at later?" "Looks like I'mma be inside. I gotta baby sit tonight. His momma got a job interview in the mornin." "Well you think all three of us can spend the night together?" "Nah Keedy, I gotta spend this time wit my son by myself. I been neglecting my lil homey for too long. I just want it to be the two of us." "I understand that, just hit me up tomorrow whenever you get free." "I'mma make sho and get at you, cause I got some shit I wanna run by you. I wanna see if you ready to be down like you say you are." "Believe me baby boy, I am just call me." "Fasho, I'mma fuck wit ya," Teelee said as he ended the call. They ended their day off at Celebration Station. Lil Jamal played all the games he could play and ate all the candy he could eat. Before they made it home, he was passed out in the passenger seat. He was really worn out from the day he spent with his daddy.

Teelee honked the horn, as he pulled up in front the house. He needed Kyla to come and help him with all of Lil Jamal's stuff. Teelee unstrapped Lil Jamal from his car seat and picked him up in his arms. When his little head hit his shoulders, he could hear Lil Jamal snoring in his ear. Kyla turned on the porch lights and stuck her head out the door to see who it was. "You got my nephew, bout time you went picked up your son." "Girl don't start." "Gimme my baby. Hey bogger boo, that baby sleepy," Kyla said in her baby language. Kyla took Lil Jamal inside while Teelee gathered his things from the car. When Teelee came in from getting Lil Jamal's bags from the car, he sat down so he could watch the news Kyla had on T.V. It was very important that you watched the news, because it kept you updated on who got murdered and all the crazy shit that went on in the chaotic streets of New Orleans. Teelee placed Lil Jamal things to the side and proceeded to watch Channel 4's News.

> *Today an unidentified, black man was gunned down in the 1700 block of Magnolia St. in the Uptown area. The police have no witnesses or leads on the murder. Also, in another incident across town, two men were murdered by a mass of bullets in the 800 block of Dumaine St. In the Treme area. Witnesses say the men jumped out of an unmarked black van, wearing black clothing with ski masks over their faces. They carried AK47's assault rifles. Witnesses say it looked like something off of the big screen. Police are looking for suspects in the case, but currently have no leads. If you have any information on any of these cases, please call Crime Stoppers at 1-877-555-0000. In other news today Mayor Marc Morial is meeting with the Superintendent of the School Board......*

Teelee shut off the T.V. All you ever heard on the news was mostly about someone getting killed. It was really sad. He headed to the back to see what Kyla was doing. "Wzup Kay, what you do today?" "After I got off work, I went to the store and got some groceries. By the way nigga you owe me some money for going pick up your clothes from the cleaners." "I got cha, how much I owe you?" "$30.00, plus interest." "Girl you always tryna tax a nigga, here!" Teelee gave Kyla $200.00, for his clothes and a lil something for his room and board. "Big baller, you got it like that huh?" "You could say that. You want me to leave Lil Jamal in here with you?" "Yeah, my baby gon sleep with his Teedy tonight." "Randi still offshore?" "Yea, he had to stay out there, some work came in." Randi was Kyla's husband. He and Teelee were real cool. He tried to help Teelee out by getting him a job offshore, but that didn't last too long. Teelee was too caught up in the street life to change his ways. Every time work would be slow, he would run back to the city. "Aight, I'mma be in my room if he wake up. Oh yeah, where my baby Kayla at?" "She by her friend at a sleep over." Kayla was Kyla's only child. She loved her uncle Teelee very much. The only problem was she barely saw him like the rest of his loved ones. Teelee had a problem with that with everybody. While headed to his room he contemplated on hitting the Blade. He brushed the thought off as quickly as it came. He wanted to be there if Lil Jamal woke up. Instead he prepared to hop in the shower and lay it down for the night. "Damn lemme call this girl and see what time she want me to bring Lil Jamal home." The phone rang three times before this strange dude answered. "Who this!" "This Teelee, Jamal daddy man where Nunew at?" "Say homey why is you callin this phone, Lil Jamal ain't with us." "Look Woe, I don't know who you is, but you can chill out wit all that shit! I'mma call this muthafuckin phone as long as me and ole girl got a baby together, ya heard me!" "Look here play boy you gotta find another way to communicate, cause you can't call this here phone no more." You know what, I'm not bout to be fussin ova no fuckin phone like a bitch! Back a town 7$^{th}$ Ward is where I be, ya heard me!" "That's what it is, we gon see what's really good." Teelee hung up the phone in a rage. He felt Nunew should have had better control over her phone. Something made him feel like she wanted that shit to happen, because of the shit that went down at the club the other night. His first priority was to check that shit bright and early the next morning. Teelee's anger made him want to go see what it do right at that second, but he calmed himself. He knew acting out of impulse would get him jammed up in a bad position.

The next morning Teelee woke up extra early to try and get some info on the unknown nigga who called himself checking him over the phone. Teelee had to be very cautious about shit like that because it could cost him his life. Any potential beef had to be investigated A.S.A.P. Teelee hit Lil Man on the phone to let the rest of the Skull Gang know about the incident. "Wzup homey." "I'm coolin bout to get up. Nigga stayed on the Blade, damn near all night. How you made out with lil homey?" "I took him to the Disney Store, Kids Footlocker, and Celebration Station. That boy fell asleep before we even made it home." "Where he at right nah?" "He right here, I kept him last night. Nunew had a job interview this morning. Say round guess what happen last night." "What?" "I called Nunew phone to see what time she wanted me to bring Lil Jamal home and some nigga answered talkin bout don't call that phone no more. Nigga told me to find another way to communicate. So you know I gotta see what's happening wit that shit!" "What it do, you ready to go see whatz up right nah?" Lil man asked ready to go knock the dude top off! Lil Man was a *"Live Wire"*. "Be cool round, we gon see wzup first. I wanna see what Nunew ass got to say bout it. I feel she let that shit happen on purpose, so I wanna pull her coat tail first, ya heard me!" "I'm bout to swing round there!" "Aight homey, where...... Before Teelee could finish his sentence, Lil Man had hung up on him. Lil Man didn't waste no time. He was pulling in front Kyla's house before Teelee could try and call him back. "Arghhhh". The tires on Lil Man's Cutlass came to a screeching halt as Lil Man hopped out of the car with his Fortie in his hand. "What it do homey? We need to go see wzup wit this shit A.S.A.P.! Remember you said it yourself *"Zero Tolerance'*!" "You right homey, but I don't want the whole fuckin neighborhood in a nigga business either." Lil Man calmed his self and tucked his Fortie in his waistband. Rage was still roaming through his mind, but he suppressed if for a moment. Just as Lil Man put his gun up Kyla was coming out the door. "Hey Lil Man what's up, where you been at stranger?" "Coolin tryna stay out the way, ya heard me." In Lil Man's mind he thought, "I'm lying my ass off." "Hey Teedy baby," Kyla said picking Lil Jamal up from Teelee's lap. "You bout to bring my nephew home?" "Yeah, in a minute, I gotta see wzup with Nunew first." "Aight, you better start going get him more often boy. I'm bout to go get ready for work. Gimme kiss Teedy baby." Kyla gave Lil Jamal a kiss before sitting him back in Teelee's lap. Lil Jamal smiled as Kyla kissed him goodbye. "Lemme call Nunew, to see if she made it back home yet," Teelee said pulling out his phone. The phone rang two times before Nunew picked up. "Hello, where you at", Teelee barked. "I'm at home, I just got back from my interview." Don't go nowhere, I'm on my way ova there." Teelee and Lil Man jumped in the Monte Carlo and headed to see what it do with the situation. Teelee honked the horn, as he pulled up in front on Nunew's house. He didn't want to go inside and talk because he didn't want Ms. Sonya in his business. Nunew stepped out the door waving for him to come in. "No, you come here," Teelee hollered as he got out of the car. Lil Man maintained his position in the passenger seat. "Where my baby at? I know he miss his mommy, Nunew said while approaching the car. "He in the backseat. I need to holla at you bout sumthin." "Wzup." "I'mma ask you a question and don't fuckin lie to me! Who the fuck that nigga was that answered your phone last night tellin me don't call ya phone no more!" "Ain't nobody answered my phone boy, what you talkin bout?" "I'mma ask you one more time," Teelee said trying to keep his composure. "If you lie to me, when I find out who this nigga is you ain't gon be havin no more boyfriend! I hope you don't think I'm trippin bout you havin a nigga! That's the last thing I'm worried about! What I'm trippin off is this nigga call his self checkin sumthin ova the phone!" "Oh yeah, when I went to the restroom at Applebee's Jashawn must have answered my phone." "Who this nigga is? Where the fuck he from?" Teelee was in a rage just thinking about the incident from last night. "He from the East." The East was known as the Suburbs of New Orleans. "How long you been dealing with this cat?" Teelee had to pick Nunew for this information, because there were haters everywhere. This could possibly be one trying to get at him through his baby mama. You had to be on top of every situation dealing in the streets of the N.O., or it could cost you severely. "Not long, I met him at the club last week, when you call ya self tryna shine on me." "I wasn't tryna shine on you. You already know what it is between me and you. We been got that understood, you shined on ya self." "Boy whatever, let me get my baby so you can go by one of ya lil hoe's." "Girl get the fuck, I ain't going by no hoe! You already know what I live by "M.O.B" money ova bitches, including you!" Teelee handled Nunew that way, because a while back she started stripping without him knowing about it. That situation mad him lose all respect for her. Even though she quit, in his mind she had violated beyond reasoning. He felt she didn't respect herself, so why should he. "Don't think that shit ova wit ole dude! As a matter of fact, you betta start watching who you be fuckin wit! Niggas could be tryna get at me through you! I'mma get some more info on this nigga! So if you like ya lil boyfriend, you betta hip him to who the fuck I am", Teelee barked as he looked deep into Nunew eyes. The cold look Teelee gave Nunew made a chill go up her spine. She knew Teelee wasn't to be played with. In this instance though, she saw a whole new dark side of him. "Oh yeah here go his stuff," Teelee said grabbing all Lil Jamal's bags off the back seat. "I'mma give you some more money next week to get him some more shit."

Teelee relayed the info he had just received to Lil Man as they pulled off from Nunew's house. "She said the nigga name, Jashawn. He from the East." "Jashawn huh. Don't trip I'mma find out wzup with him A.S.A.P." New Orleans was a very small city. To find out information on somebody was very easy. Everybody knew everybody. Teelee and Lil Man headed straight for the Blade so they could get their grind on. Thugga was sitting on the porch with Unc when they pulled up. When Teelee and Lil Man hopped out of the Monte, they looked down the block to see if the police were coming up the street. "Whaaan," Thugga hollered greeting Teelee and Lil Man with some dap as they walked up. "What's good Thugga baabyyy, you makin that paper huh" Teelee said taking a seat on one of the milk crates that sat on the porch. "Yeah, you know somebody gotta be out here to feed the block." "You saw Money hard headed ass today?" Lil Man asked. "Him and T-Mac just went to the store for me. Why wzup?" "Nah, I'm just askin, you know how them lil niggas is. I gotta keep my eyes on them, ya heard me." "Say Thugga don't jump to conclusions, but we might have a lil problem." "What problem" Thugga asked standing to his feet. "Nigga I just told you don't jump to conclusions. Be cool lemme tell you what I'm talkin bout. I called Nunew phone last night and this nigga answered makin demands that I don't call Nunew phone no more! I don't know what's behind that there but we definitely gon get to the bottom of it!" "What's the nigga name, where he from?" "We just left Nunew house. She said the nigga name Jashawn. He out the East." "I'mma get the low on the nigga. Don't worry bout that." Lil Man said rolling a Keep Moving cigar into a blunt. "Damn I'm gettin low, I only have like two grams left." Between the three of them they ran through like 2 ounces of Purple Haze a week. "Say round I gotta cop some more purp," Lil Man said pulling out his cell phone so he could call Egghead, the weed man. Egghead was not only the weed man; he was also a long time hood friend to them all. Egghead moved out of the hood for the sake of his baby girl that was recently born. Him and his baby mamma found a nice peaceful spot in Michaud. Michaud was on the borderline between New Orleans and Slidell. The move was beneficial, because not only did Egghead get his fam out the hood, his clientele increased. "Wzup Egg, ya boy need another seven. I'm on the Blade." Seven meaning 7 grams. "Fasho, I'm in route ya heard me." "Egghead dropped off the package and from there Teelee, Thugga and Lil Man jumped in the Monte and hit I-10. They always hit I-10 and got their smoke on. It was a form of relaxation for them. It was their only chance to let their minds reprogram. While the coolness of the A.C. blew the purpa smoke circulated through the air. "Son put that *"Carter 1"* in that bitch, Thugga said laying back in the backseat of the Monte enjoying the cool A.C. "Say y'all know that boy Soulja got a concert in the Roc Saturday huh?" Lil Man asked breaking down a bud of purpa into a Keep Moving. "I got tickets from my lil potna Lil Realone. We official, ya heard me." Lil Realone was an artist on Soulja Slim's label *"Cutthroat Committee."* "That's wzup," Teelee replied, putting the Monte on cruise control. They smoked 3 grams and headed back to the Blade. They hit the block hard the rest of the week, so they could be ready when they elevated their hustle.

It was Saturday afternoon and Teelee had slept in late. The Skull Gang pulled an all-nighter on the Blade. The block was on fire. Fiends were coming around the clock to come and cop. Ever since

Teelee and the gang bust the Blade open their names were heavily flowing through the streets. If it wasn't a smoker talking about them, it was one of them hoe's. If it wasn't the hoe's, it was one of them bitch ass niggas that hated seeing a nigga get his shine on. Every member of the Skull Gang felt in their heart that some friction was about to kick off. It was normal protocol in the streets of New Orleans. If a nigga was getting his shine on, or his name was ringing a lil bit too hard the sharks were about to come to shore. One thing about the Skull Gang, they had some shit to stop a shark and whatever else tried to stop their shine. It's a package deal with the money and fame. The haters and beef definitely fit its way into the equation. So you had better been ready to pick up that Iron and slang that bitch whenever necessary. You couldn't be playing in the dirty streets of the N.O. and just be bout getting money. You had to be bout all of the above. Teelee was awakened by his new ring tone. *"Them boyz in da hood sell any thang for profit/Five in da mornin on da corner clockin."* "What it do Woe," Thugga said as Teelee answered the phone. "What's good wit ya," Teelee replied groggily. "Nigga you still sleep?" "Fuckin right, you should be still sleep after last night." "All I need is a couple of hours and I'm reenergized! When you plan on gettin yo ass up? We gotta feed the block its lunch." "I'm bout to get up, gimme an hour. Where that boy Lil Man at?" "I just talked to him. He bout to meet me on the Blade. You ain't forget bout the cert tonight huh?" "How the hell I'mma forget and that's all Lil Man been talkin bout." "You right that nigga been talkin bout that shit all week. Oh I almost forgot! Lil Man said he found out some info on that nigga Jashawn." "Aight homey I'mma see y'all niggas in a minute." Teelee ended the call with Thugga and hoped in the shower. He shot straight for the Blade, eager to find out what Lil Man had found out about the nigga Jashawn. If it was some flaky shit, he was going to cancel dude contract A.S.A.P.

Teelee pulled up on the Blade an hour later. Everything and everyone was moving like the block had never shut down. The Blade was a 24hr all-purpose strip. You could come and cop you some hard white, get your car washed, score some weed and whatever else the block had to offer. Lil Man was posted in the alley on side of Ciara's house. Ciara was the neighborhood tomboy. She smoked weed and got her gansta on to a certain extent. She kept some fast ass lil girls by her house. Most of the time that's where Money and T-Mac hung out at. They were always trying to get some pussy from the lil girls over there. Thugga was standing on the corner of the Blade and Touro St. so wherever the fiends came from one of them could intercept them. As Teelee got out of the Monte his phone began to ring, *"Them boyz in the hood sell any thang for profit."* "Whatz good Deb baby?" "Nothing much my Juvey, where you at?" "Posted on the block like a light pole, why wzup?" "You're keeping the rental for another week?" "Yeah, I'mma hold it down for like two more weeks. I'mma bring you some money tomorrow so you can pay them people, ya heard me." "Aight Juvey, call me around 12:00, I'll be at lunch. You can bring me the money then. Oh yeah, I'm going out of town to look at this land my grandmother left me. I'll be gone for a couple of days." "Aight baby girl I'mma hit you up tomorrow." "Alright bye Juvey." Teelee ended the call and walked in the alley where Lil Man was. Thugga came right behind him. "What it do son, Teelee said giving them both some dap. "Y'all beat me to the block huh?" Lil Man shared some of his lyrical skills.

*"Yeah you know I gotta get this cake dawg/ Won't stop til the sun drop or the moon fall/ I'm on the block all night/ serving this white y'all."*

"Damn round, you stepping ya free style skills up huh?" Thugga stated, impressed by Lil Man off the dome lyrics. "Say round what's good with this nigga Jashawn?" Teelee asked tweaking to get the low on this clown. "Oh yeah, guess who the nigga people is?" "Who?" "That nigga Tossy! I don't know if he know we smash the nigga, but you know we gotta get at him A.S.A.P. The nigga be hangin in the Goose." The Goose was the slums of the East. "I know the exact spot the nigga be at. "We can handle that whenever y'all get ready!" "Look this how we gon do it" Teelee said coming up with a plan. "We gon swing through the nigga block a couple of times to see what kind of hours the nigga be puttin in. Then when we get an opening, CHECKMATE!" "That's wzup, say Teelee you know that broad Keedy came through lookin for you earlier huh?" Lil Man asked. "Damn I forgot to call her today. I'mma get at her in a minute. Let's go get this money." They all proceeded to go put their hustle down. The block pumped for about a good 2 to 3 hours before they got a break. Pistol and Corey finally made it to the block, so they got a little relief. That gave Teelee a chance to see what was up with Keedy. As Teelee waited for Keedy to answer her phone he was entertained with *Mac the Camouflage Assassins 'My Boss Bitch."* "Hey baby boy, where you been at?" "I been coolin, gettin this money ya know. I heard you came through lookin for ya boy. What it do?" "Oh nuthin just wanted to see ya face. Remember we suppose to hook up today." "Yeah I know my bad, I had some shit to do earlier. Where you at nah? "Just leaving Tasha's house, she cooked breakfast this morning." "Well swing through, we gon duck off and discuss some things." "You go gimme some of that good dick?" "No girl, I'm talkin some real business type shit. That shit you talkin ain't even relevant to the shit I'm tryna run down to you!" "Aight, baby boy I'm on my way. Don't go nowhere." Keedy pulled up to the Blade about 15 minutes later. Teelee ran to the car, from out of the alley on side of Unc house. Before Teelee got in the car, Lil Man hollered "Remember Son don't' forget." "Nigga I told you I got you," Teelee replied before getting in the car and closing the door. "Wzup baby boy where we going?" Keedy asked starting the car. "Just drive around." Teelee had to make sure this broad was down for whatever he told her to do, before he could put her down with the Skull Gang. He had a couple of choice ideas that would determine if she was bout what she said she was. As they cruised the city streets, Teelee observed Keedy closely. "Aight Keedy you say you bout whatever to be down wit me right?" "Of course Keedy replied," glancing at Teelee as she navigated the car. "Why you wanna be down wit me so bad?" "Cause its sumthin bout you that makes me wanna be under you. Even be loyal to you and basically that bitch that would do anything for you." "How I know you wouldn't do me like you did ole boy?" "What ole boy?" "Come on nah Keedy. That bitch ass nigga Tossy." "Oh that's easy, you not a bitch ass nigga like he was. It was a lot of other shit that made me do what I did. That dude use to beat my ass for no damn reason, and a lot other shit I can't even talk about." "Aight Keedy your first test gon be tomorrow night. So you gon have to be ready whenever I call you. If you past these lil tests I got for you, I'mma put you down wit my team. You ain't gon never have to worry bout money, protection or nuthin, ya heard me." "Aight baby boy, we gon see." "No, I'mma see," Teelee replied, as they headed back to the Blade. Within these tests Teelee would definitely find out if Keedy was down like she says she was. Would she past the tests, or wouldn't she was the ultimate question? Teelee relayed what he had in store for Keedy when he made it back to the Blade. They all agreed on his plan. If everything panned out, Keedy would become the newest member of the Notorious Skull Gang. Only time would reveal the outcome.

# CHAPTER 5

# THE CONNECTION

"Say Teelee hit that boy Myron up, so we can get some of them wiggers. Nigga gon need em for tonight," Lil Man said shaking his dreads as he took his rubber band from around them. "I'm tryna feed them duck hoe's them pills like they skittle's." Teelee, Lil Man, and Thugga stood posted up on Ciara's porch feeling their selves. By the way they were rolling, it made them look like they had more money than they actually had. That was basically a young street niggas lifestyle. Always living above his means. Teelee hit Myron on the phone. "Say round I need a twenty pack of them exclusives." "Where you at?" "I'm on the Blade," Teelee replied." "What you want me to swing around there?" "Nah, we gon head yo way on the way to the concert. Y'all niggas not going? That boy Soulja got a concert in the Roc." "You know me and Cash, we might pop up in that bitch." Myron and Cash were blood cousins with a major hustle scheme. Myron pumped the pills, while Cash moved the heroin. Heroin was a big money making drug in the N.O. Myron and Cash had the 6$^{th}$Ward on lock with the pills and *dog food. Dog Food*, was another name used in New Orleans for heroin because it made fiends bite your head off, if you didn't feed them on time. "Where y'all posted up at," Teelee asked. "We on Orleans by the store." "Aight I'mma hit the phone when we on our way," Teelee said disconnecting the call. "Damn Teelee, where y'all boyz going all swagged up," Ciara asked. "Soulja got a cert tonight. You know we had to be right, ya heard me." "Say Lil Man, Keisha said when you gon stop playin and give her that good dick?" "Tell her when she make 18, to fuck wit me. I ain't bout to get jammed up fuckin with her young ass." "Aight Ce Ce, we gon holla at you tomorrow. We bout to push out," Teelee said walking off the porch headed to the Monte. "Aight son, y'all got them burners on deck huh?" "Yeah we bout to go get strapped up like some seat belts right nah."

They pulled from the Blade and shot to Lil Man's house so they could go pick up the AR15. They already had their forties on deck. It was mandatory that they have enough fire power. All due to the tension in the air with the prime suspect Jashawn. They also had enough for all the other haters that were lurking and waiting for them to slip up. "Say Lil Man where Corey and Pistol at?" Thugga asked. "They went to the movies with they baby mamas. "Y'all know how that is." Thugga jumped in his Camaro and from there they headed to the 6$^{th}$ Ward to pick up the pills from Myron. When they made it to the store on Orleans and Galvez St., they saw Myron spraying silly string all over Cash Armada truck. Myron and Cash always played with each other like that. Teelee hopped out of the Monte, while Lil Man waited in the car. They didn't want to be in that spot too long, because the police stayed pushing around that area. The only reason Myron and Cash were able to be posted out there like that is because they knew damn near all the police that patrolled the area. "What it do round, y'all bout to hit the club scene huh?" Cash asked taking off the silly string Myron had sprayed all over his truck. "Yeah we bout to go do the damn thang, ya heard me! Y'all need to come through. You know that boy Soulja gon have them hoe's off in that bitch." "We gon swing through late. You know nigga gotta make that grand entrance, ya heard me." "That's wzup. I would go later too, but nigga gotta get there early so I could get the burner in the club. I ain't gon feel comfortable wit out my girlfriend on my side, ya heard me." "I already know where you comin from," Cash replied checking his miss calls on his cell phone. "I'll be right back," Myron said before walking off headed for his stash on side of the store. Even though they knew damn near all the police in that area, they still took the right precautions that had to be taken. Never knew when a rookie cop could be on duty. As Myron came back from his stash on side of the store, Teelee met him halfway. They didn't want to be on the Ave making an illegal transaction. "Say Teelee, I went in my stash for y'all boyz. I wasn't gon even bring these out until I got off the rest of my other package." "Them bitches must be official, if you doing it like that. What you holdin?" "You said you wanted them exclusive, these them *White Naked Ladies* fresh off the press. Say round don't take two of these pills at one time, ya heard me. These bitches powerful like a muthafucka! I gave this nigga one to see what they do. Homey this nigga roll ain't slow down until yesterday. I gave the nigga the pill day before yesterday!" "Damn round, them bitches that strong?" "I ain't gon lie to you homey. These bitches so good, I gotta charge you extra cause you gon be the only nigga wit these bad muthafuckas! My connect gave me a hunid of em so I could see what he was bout to hit the streets wit." "How much you talkin?" Teelee asked. "Gimme $350.00." Ecstasy was very expensive, but if the pill was right it was well worth it. "Fuck it, gimme them thangs. If they not how you say they is, you know I'm comin back to get my change huh?" "Wit these pills here, I don't have a problem puttin a refund on em, ya heard me. That's just how confident I am son." "Fasho, that's wzup. We gon see y'all at the cert." They hit I-10 from Orleans Ave. headed to the Roc.

As soon as they pulled in front of the club, Tiger spotted Thugga's Camaro. He signaled for them to park in there V.I.P. parking spaces. In the positions they were parked in everyone leaving and coming to the club could see the hot boy play toys. Blood had the cars shining like diamonds. If the rental didn't have the commercial plate on it, people would have thought it was someone's personal whip. "What's good Tiger baabyyy, how it's lookin in that bitch?" Teelee asked hopping out of the Monte. "You can't tell? Soulja got them hoes in there like we given away free hair or sumthin." The club was jumping. The streets were flooded with cars. The line in front of the club, as well as V.I.P. was wrapped around the building. Females flocked to the bouncers in their skimpy clothing, tryna get into see the one and only *Soulja Slim*. "Bitch it's going down tonight! I'mma leave here wit me a trade that's banked up," one girl stressed while looking at herself in her compact mirror. "Them hoes on a prowl tonight huh," Lil Man said leaning on the door of the Monte. "You fuckin right," Thugga replied as he hit the alarm to the Camaro. "Jump in the car Tiger so I could give you this burner, ya heard me." "Aight." As they got into the Monte, Teelee gave Tiger the fortie. Teelee felt if he couldn't get in a spot with the banger, he shouldn't be in that club. Not to just shoot someone for nothing. It was for the protection of him and his people. Tiger got the gun in the club for Teelee, because he knew Teelee wasn't a hot head. Unless he was provoked, then all hell would break loose. Just like Tiger got Teelee's gun in for him, one of the other Security guards was getting their people shit in as well.

Soulja was hitting the stage soon as they stepped into the doors of the Roc. The club went wild as Soulja performed his hit single *"You Gotta Feel Me."* Teelee, Thugga and Lil Man went straight to the bar. As they approached Teelee recognized his pops old friend Joc, standing behind the bar. Joc had become the General Manager of the Roc, ever since he stop working with Teelee's father. "What's good Joc baby," Teelee said leaning over the bar to give Joc some love. "You lookin good boy, the Roc treatin you right huh?" "Yeah, you can say that. You ain't lookin bad yaself, I see you shinning." "I'm doin what I could ya know." "How's pops been doing?" Joc was like a son to Teelee's father so he always called him pops too. Teelee's father took Joc under his wing and taught him well in the area of business. When Tyra came with the bottle, Joc handed it to Teelee. Joc always broke bread whenever Teelee came through.

"Good lookin big homey. I'mma tell pops, I seen you ya heard me." "Aight, tell him I'll be by next week to see him." "Fasho, I got you covered. I'm bout to go fuck wit these females ya heard me." They didn't want to be in the mix. The Roc was jammed packed. Hoes was shaking their ass, and niggas was bucking to Soulja Slim's gangsta vibe. They caught a spot on the leather sectional sofa that sat off to the back of the V.I.P. "Here homey." Teelee handed Thugga and Lil Man the two glasses and proposed a toast. "This for all the hard work we been puttin in on the block. On three Skull Gang 4 Life. One, two, three." *"SKULL GANG 4 LIFE!"* They all took the champagne to the head. "Hey Man Man," Gia said walking up behind Lil Man. Gia had her own personal nickname for Lil Man. That's why he already knew who it was before he even turned around. "Wzup G." "Nuthin baby, where you was at Thursday? I came by the house lookin for you." "I was on the Blade. Say G, you gon have to start callin before you pop up like that. I don't wanna hurt yo feelings, if you run into a broad comin out the house." Man Man when you gon stop playin with me, we need to get back together. I miss you!" "Say G, I'mma fuck wit ya tomorrow. We gon see what's up then," Lil Man said trying to get rid of her. Who could blame her for tryna get back on the team. Teelee and the gang was killing the scene. They all had on that Cooji shit with the Mauris to match. The ice that adorned their necks lit up the club like they were walking Christmas trees. Any groupie in their right mind, would try and get in where they fit in. "Aight Man Man make sure you call me tomorrow. Bye y'all," Gia said before walking off. "Nigga you still love that broad. I could see it in your eyes," Teelee said as he handed Lil Man the bottle of Moet. "Son you fuckin trippin! I told y'all I don't back pedal." Teelee and Thugga both looked at Lil Man like nigga you stunting like a muthafucka. Slim had the Roc jumping. The whole vibe of the club was on some straight gangsta shit. The tension in the club was so thick, you could cut it with a steak knife. Slim always brought that type of vibe to the club scene. He was just that type of nigga. Rough, Raw, and Rugged. The nigga never had security with him. The whole Magnolia project was his security. "Damn son this bottle almost gone," Teelee said holding the bottle up in the air. "I'm bout to go to the bar and get a drink. Y'all straight?" "We good homey. We bout to spark that purpa up ya heard me," Lil Man said taking the Keep Moving from behind his ear. "Aight, I'mma be right back." Walking to the bar Teelee ran into a bad little Latino broad. Teelee was attracted to her and wanted to see what was up, but he resisted. A long time ago, he changed his method of approaching females. He had a really bad experience with a lil broad he used to deal with, but that was a whole different story. He felt if he played the back field and let the woman come to him, we would have the advantage. For one, it gave him a chance to peep the swag of the broad before moving forward with anything. Two, if the broad had the urge to speak first more than likely she was attracted a little bit more than he was. "Gimme a Hennessey and a Heineken," Teelee requested leaning against the bar. Teelee positioned himself so he could be noticed by the Latin beauty as the bartender prepared his drinks. "Here you go sir, that'll be $10.00," the bartender said as she placed a napkin under Teelee's drinks. Teelee gave the bartender $15.00 and went back to admiring the look alike Vida Guerra. As Teelee checked the time on his phone, the Latin Mami approached him. "Wzup Papi, I never seen you in here before." "This my spot, I'm in here almost every weekend. I ain't never seen you before either. Whatz ya name Mami?" Teelee asked, scanning her from her head to her feet. "My name is Selina." "Well they call me Teelee, nice to meet you beautiful." Teelee was turned on by the Latin doll. Selina was exactly five feet tall, with a butter pecan complexion. She had some titties that would make your mouth water, not too big and definitely not too small. They looked fake, but Teelee would find that out when he had the chance to have them in his hands. Another attribute that attracted Teelee was the eight porcelain veneers in her mouth. Teelee knew she had to pay at least two stacks for them. They ran $500.00, a tooth. "Gimme ya phone Papi." Teelee handed her the phone and she proceeded to put her number in his call log. "Here you go cutie, call me tomorrow. We can hook up and do something if you're not busy." "Aight beautiful. What's the best time to call?" "Call me tomorrow evening." "That's wzup, Teelee said putting his phone back in its clip. "Bye Papi," Selina said walking off into the crowd. Teelee loved how she called him Papi. He was intrigued by Latino women. He always wanted to fuck one of them. I guess now this was his chance. Teelee headed back to where Lil Man and Thugga was. As he walked up two twins had them jammed up throwing their asses back on them. "I see y'all," Teelee said before taking a seat on the sofa. As the song mixed into another Lil Man and Thugga went and joined Teelee on the sofa. "I know y'all put them freaks in the call log," Teelee said taking a sip of his drink. "You know it Thugga replied," leaning his head back on the sofa. "Them hoes from the St. Bernard huh," Teelee asked. "Yeah they name Dana and Danny. They some real jump offs." "I already know; they use to be by my lil broad Tasha. That's where I know them from. Nigga I just met Vida Guerra lil sister by the bar." "Nigga stop lying," Lil Man said. "Aight I'm lying about her being Vida Guerra's sister but I'm not lyin bout her lookin like her. This lil thang bad, she gave me her number. She told me call her tomorrow. Say round I think the lil bitch got that money too. She top notch from head to toe, ya heard me." "You know how it go. See if she got a cousin or a sister for a nigga," Lil Man said trying to get in the game. "Let's walk down stairs, and see what's poppin," Teelee said getting up off the sofa. They ran into Roylee and his gang coming down the steps of the V.I.P. What it do Roy," Thugga said. "We chillin, peeping these hoe's, ya heard me." "Well I got them wiggers to make it official with one of these hoe's," Teelee said pulling the pills from his pocket. "What kind you got?" "I got them *White Naked Ladies.* These bitches ain't even hit the streets yet. My lil homey pop me off." "Gimme five of em," Roy said pulling his money from his pockets. "Gimme $150.00." "Damn round, $150.00, you taxing a nigga huh." "I got taxed to my nigga. I paid $350.00 for em. I know one thang, these bitches worth it. I'm rollin on the river right nah. Nigga told me he gave one to this nigga and his roll ain't stop till two days later." "Aight, but if they ain't like you say they is…" "I already know you want ya money back. Nigga that's the same thang I told my lil homey." Teelee paid a pretty penny for the pills, and he felt he should make a least half of his money back. He wasn't hooked on Ecstasy; they were used for fun. Most people would have popped the entire twenty pack; not Teelee though, he was a hustler to the fullest. He was always trying to make a dollar out of fifty cents. Roylee copped the pills, and they all posted up together enjoying the view of all the females circulating around the club. After Soulja Slim finished performing, he chilled in the club as well. He posted up in the V.I.P. area with his entourage. The night was going smooth until the D.J. played C-Murder's song, *"Fuck Them Other Niggas."* A big fight immediately broke out by the pool tables. There were chairs being thrown, and niggas getting hit in the head with pool sticks. It was all kinds of wild shit going on. "Say son come over here" Teelee said pulling Lil Man and Thugga to the wall with him. It was very important that you put your back against the wall, and get away from the crowd whenever a big brawl broke out. You never knew when a nigga was gon start bustin that Iron. If Teelee got his burner in the club, you know somebody else was strapped up also. "Whack" was the sound of a dude getting smashed in the head with a pool stick. It was from one of the comrades of the nigga he was fighting with. That's another thing about a club brawl, you never knew where the blows were coming from. "Let's get the fuck out this bitch", Thugga said heading for the doors of the club. "This ain't ova between these niggas. Its gon be part two of this shit outside." They headed to their cars. It was good they were parked in front of the club, because the bullets could start flying at any given moment. "Say Lil Man get the AR out the trunk and put it in the front wit you," Teelee said as he hit the trunk button on the keypad. "Fasho, I got this covered just drive." These precautions had to be taken. You never knew what was in front of you in the crazy city they called "Murda Cappy" Teelee hit Thugga on the phone and told him to meet them at the Exxon down the street from the club. As they pulled into the gas station, they heard gun shots from the distance. Boom, Boom, Boom, was the sound of the automated rifles. "Nigga bangin that Choppa! I know that sound from anywhere" Thugga said hopping out the Camaro. "I gotta gas this thirsty bitch up. That V8 be drinkin gas like an alcoholic in a liquor warehouse. Say son what y'all bout to get into," Thugga asked handing the cashier his money for the gas. "Remember I told you bout Keedy," Teelee replied as he leaned back and enjoyed the A.C. in the Monte. "Oh yeah, I almost forgot about that. Well I'm bout to meet my lil bitch at the Trolley Stop." The Trolley Stop was another nice place to go and eat after you left the club. Of course Thugga wasn't going for the food though. He was going strictly for the ass. Sometimes you gotta wine and dine before you bump and grind. "Well most likely we gon be at the "6". So if you need us that's where we gon be," Teelee said as he lit up a Camel. "Say son that wigger got me feelin good then a muthafucka," Lil Man said leaning back in the passenger seat. "Aight homey, I'mma fuck wit y'all. That's my lil bitch callin right now"

Teelee hit Keedy on the phone as they hit I-10. He didn't see her in the club, which was strange. She faithfully attended the Roc. Soon as the phone began to ring Keedy picked up. "Wzup baby boy?" "Damn Keedy, what you was waitin by the phone or sumthin?" "You could say that. You told me to be available tonight, that's why I didn't go to the concert." "That's wzup, where you at?" "I'm by my sister in the East." Keedy proceeded to give Teelee directions to her sister's house. Teelee hit Keedy on the phone as they pulled up in front the house. He didn't want to honk the horn because of how late it was. By the looks of the neighborhood it was very peaceful. Knowing an area like that, there was nosy neighbors ready to peep out of their windows. Keedy stayed with her oldest sister Karen. Ever since their mother and father was murdered, Karen had been taking care of Keedy. Keedy was a young woman experiencing life on her own terms. Her mother and father both died while she was still very young. Due to her father being in the drug game, they were kidnapped and killed. Keedy's father was a well-known hustler in the city. The fucked up thing was her father gave the jackboyz everything he had, and they were still killed. It was very unusual that anyone survived a situation like that in the N.O. Through all of that it gave Keedy an urge to be in the streets, and just wild out any way possible. Deep inside she wanted to avenge her parent's death, but they never found out who was responsible. That's one of the reasons she wanted to be under Teelee. She wanted to be a part of something by any means necessary. "Wzup Keedy, I'm outside." "Aight, I'll be out in a minute." Lil Man hopped in the back seat as Keedy stepped out the door. After all, Teelee was running the show, so he had to let him do his thang. "Wzup y'all," Keedy said getting in the car. "We coolin, just left the concert. That bitch was jumping until niggas went to fightin and shit." "Who got killed," Keedy asked. Keedy asked that question to skip all the preliminary things in between. Doesn't matter how it started. It always ended up with someone losing their life. "Shid, we ain't stay around to find out, if somebody did get smashed you gon see it on the news," Teelee replied. "Aight Keedy enough of that, it's time for your first test. Before we get into that, you tryna get your roll on?" "Fuckin right, you know I'm always bout that!" "Now look Keedy these things strong, so don't trip when it takes effect. It did the same thang to me." "Damn baby boy, what you got like that?" "That shit that's gon make you wanna be a naked lady." "You know I'm bout that, give it here." After Teelee gave Keedy the pill they went to the gas station to pick up a few needed items. Teelee got everything they might need, like cigars, rubbers, gum and anything else they might have needed. As Teelee got back in the car, he could tell the pill was taking effect on Keedy. Her head was leaned back and her bottom lip was shaking. These some bad muthafuckin pills, Teelee thought as he turned the key to start the car. "Wzup baby boy, you know I got love for y'all right?" It was official, the wigger was kicking like Bruce Lee. It was something about Ecstasy, that had you feeling all emotional and shit. "Aight Keedy this the deal, I want you to pop my lil potna off like you did wit me. If you do this you'll have one more shot to prove ya loyalty to me, ya heard me. You know what I told you if you follow through. Ain't no respect gon be lost after this, I just gotta see if you down like you say you is." Keedy looked directly at Teelee and said, "I told you Teelee, whateva you got for me to do I'll do it. I just want Lil Man to know this ain't pleasure, this business. It's all for you baby boy," Keedy said never breaking the hard stare she was giving Teelee. In a way Teelee was starting to feel that Keedy was going to be very loyal to his circle. If she was bout doing this with no complaint or problem, she was definitely going to be a key player within the Skull Gang. "It's all good Keedy. I ain't trippin I'm just tryna see what my round been talkin bout.

They pulled out of the gas station parking lot heading for the Motel 6 to start the rest of Keedy's initiation into the Skull Gang. Keedy jumped out of the car eager to get the room keys, while Teelee and Lil Man drove around to park the car. "Say Teelee, this wigger got me feelin like I'm on top of the world." "You ain't by ya self homey. I'm feelin the same way, ya heard me." "Say round, I think Keedy gon be right for the circle. Not cause she bout to break that pussy off either. I feel she loyal ya know." "I already know round, that's why I wanted to test the water wit her first. See what it do ya feel me. Hold up Lil Man, that's her callin right now. Yeah wzup Keedy?" "Guess what room we in?" "I don't know, what?" "Rm. 308." "Damn that's the same room we was in last week. Aight, we gon be up there in a minute." When they walked up to the door of the room, the door was open with the lights off. Soon as they stepped in the room they saw Keedy's naked silhouette standing by the curtains. "Close the door," Keedy demanded as she sat on the bed legs bust wide open. When Teelee closed the door Keedy told both of them to sit on the bed. The Ecstasy was really on over drive, cause she was taking control of the whole situation. Teelee didn't plan on staying in the room while her and Lil Man did what they did but the way Keedy was looking made him change his mind. Keedy's toned body was hard to walk away from. The roll of the Ecstasy didn't make it any better. "Get out them clothes," Keedy demanded once again. While they complied with her request, she played with her pussy making all kinds of freaky fuck faces. In any other situation this type of shit would have felt uncomfortable, but in this situation the pill was disregarding all of that. As they finished stripping out their clothes, Keedy grabbed both their dicks and went to work. She had her cinnamon brown ass pointed in the air, as she tried to suck the life out them both. Teelee was turned on by the way her ass looked. He slapped her on the ass making her let out a moan of pleasure. "Aaahhh." Teelee couldn't take to much more of the four play. He grabbed a magnum off the night stand, slid it on and started jabbing Keedy up from the back. "Oooh baby boy gimme that good dick! Don't stop, I'm bout to nut!" Teelee was long stroking the fuck out of Keedy, but she continued to throw her ass back like a true champ. Keedy threw it back harder as a powerful orgasm ripped through her body. She wasn't finished handling her business. She instructed Lil Man to lay back on the bed. She grabbed a rubber from the night stand, slid it on Lil Man's dick and straddled him backwards. "Come here baby boy, I can't leave you out." Keedy rode Lil Man and sucked Teelee's dick at the same time never missing a beat. "Tell me you love how I suck your dick,"

Keedy said looking into Teelee's eyes. She made his entire dick disappear. Teelee couldn't even get any words out. His facial expression said it all. Even though they were having a threesome Keedy's attention never left Teelee. Lil Man just got his rocks off in the process. Got damn Keedy I'm bout to nut," Teelee said grabbing the back of her head. "Oh good, nut in my mouth baby boy. Teelee had to back up. He just couldn't take it anymore. Keedy proceeded to finish Lil Man off, as she increased the motion in her hips. "Damn Keedy, "Lil Man moaned. He gripped her ass, exploding in the magnum at the same time. "Keedy you official," Lil Man said as he headed to the bathroom to clean himself up. "All for ya boy," Keedy said giving Teelee that look again. "I don't even have to tell you how much loyalty you just showed to me. You should already know it," Teelee said slapping Keedy's naked plumped ass cheeks. "Aight Keedy, this what I need you to do next. You gotta set this clown up for us." "That's it," Keedy said in excitement. That definitely wasn't a problem for her. She did it many of times before. "It requires more than you think, this just the first step. I'mma pick you up tomorrow so I can show you who the nigga is. I want you to fuck wit him. Get him comfortable around you, so we can get him in a position to get him out the way. After you finish this, I'mma put you on the block. You ready to get this money huh?" "Definitely, baby boy." "Say Lil Man we gon swing around the nigga spot tomorrow." "Fasho," Lil Man said coming out the bathroom. "I'm ready when you ready." They smoked a couple of Keep Moving's and crashed out in the room. It didn't make any sense to leave. The room was paid for until 12:00, the next day.

The next morning, they all got up and had breakfast at IHOP. After they ate Teelee dropped Keedy and Lil Man off. He headed to the house so he could prepare for his day. Selina was on his mind ever since last night. He was going to make sure and see what the business was with her.

# CHAPTER 6

# BLAME IT ON THE ALCOHOL

"Boy where your ass was all night?" Kyla asked, as Teelee came through the front door. "That boy Soulja Slim had a concert last night. You know how the rest went." "Boy you ain't nothing but a street runner." "I know you ain't talkin how you be havin yo ass in Joe's Cozy Corner every Saturday night." "I'm grown, I could do that," Kyla said twirling her neck. "Hey Uncle Teelee," Kayla said as she ran and jumped into Teelee arms. "Hey my baby, gimme kiss." "I miss you Uncle Teelee, where's Lil Jamal at?" Kayla loved her little cousin. Every time he came over she would take care of him like she was grown. "He by his momma. I'mma pick him up next weekend so he can sleep ova aight." "Okay Uncle Teelee." "Come on Kayla so I can finish combing ya hair," Kyla screamed from the back room. Kayla ran to the back so she could get her hair finished, while Teelee went to his room so he could get situated for the day. He was anticipating seeing Selina again. She had really caught his attention, he wanted to see why the attraction was so strong between them. He had to also put Keedy on her assignment. That was his first priority. The quicker he got this clown Jashawn out the way, the less worried he would be about bullets flying at his dome. As he took his clothes out for the day, his phone rang. *"Them boyz in da hood sell anything for profit."* "What it do Teelee boy," Thugga said. "I'm coolin, getting ready to step out for the day. Where you be at?" "I'm just leavin ole girl from last night. Ya girl went off the chain last night. I gave her one of them naked ladies, and before we made it to her spot she was damn near a naked lady." "They treated you good to huh," Teelee asked as he shaved the overnight growth off his beard. That was one thing about Teelee, he kept his self together. His hair and facial upkeep stayed on point. "Son them pills had Keedy like a nymphomaniac. She broke it off like a gangsta last night. Lil Man gon tell you when you talk to him." "Well I guess she one step closer to being down with the team huh?" "If she handle this next assignment for me, she all in. This how we gon do it. We gon get Keedy to fuck wit the nigga Jashawn. When she get him in the right position CHECKMATE!" "That's wzup, that's a damn good idea. We won't have to worry bout no in between shit, as far as swinging through the nigga block. We can off dude nice and smooth," Thugga commented. "Now you feelin me," Teelee replied as he prepared to take a bath. He wanted to relax, and let his mind mellow out. It wasn't too often he had a chance to soak, so when he had a window to do it he took it. "Aight homey, I'mma fuck wit you when I hit the streets." "Fasho, fuck wit me" Thugga said before they ended their call. "Oh yeah let me call Deb so I can drop this change off for the rental." Deb's phone began to ring. *"Ooooh, Iiiivvee beeeenn thinking of youuu/ like you've beeeen thinking of meee."* It was something about the Isley's that made Teelee's day every time he heard them. "Hey Jamal, I'm with a patient right now. Just meet me here for twelve, I'll be available then." Deb only called Teelee by his government name when she was in her work place. She knew when to turn the street mentality off. Deb wasn't average, by far she was FDA certified. That's why Teelee fucked with her.

In a way it made Teelee feel good to know he had someone on his team that was a part of regular society. "Aight Deborah, I'll see you then." "Bye boy" Deb said, letting out a little smirk. Teelee always knew how to break the ice in an awkward situation. Teelee jumped in the bathtub for a few seconds because his schedule didn't permit him to chill for too long. He pulled out some of his player gear, instead of his usual hustle gear. He wanted to be presentable when he hooked up with Selina. He chose his linen apparel for the occasion. Women always told him he looked sexy in his linen, so he chose the style most desired by the ladies. Before he hit the door he sprayed on a hint or two of Issey Miyake cologne. That was another area his father taught him a lot about. He constantly preached to Teelee, if your hygiene was not up to par, you weren't up to par as a man. The morals Teelee's father instilled in him were grade A. Teelee noticed how women always tried to sniff all over him when he cologne on. Teelee's first destination was to go to the hospital so he could bring Deb the money for the rental. He wanted to make sure he handled that. The rental was his only means of transportation at the moment. Teelee wanted to go cop a whip, but he resisted because he wanted to make sure when he did cop, it didn't put a dent in his stash. "Wzup Deb baby, I'm pulling in the parking lot." "Aight Juvey, I'm coming out right now." Deb was standing by the emergency room doors, as Teelee pulled to the back of the hospital. Teelee left the Monte running while he went to give Deb the money. "Hey Juvey, you looking mighty clean today. What's the occasion?" "Just felt like being in another mode, ya heard me." Teelee was lying his ass off. He was dressed like that for one reason only; Selina. He damn sure wasn't going to tell Deb that. Even though he and Deb had an understanding about dealing with other people, he still wasn't going to put it in her face that he was going to fuck with another female. Teelee had that much respect for Deb, and she had the same respect for him. They were on common ground, which kept all bullshit out of their relationship. "Here baby girl." Teelee handed Deb $500.00. "Juvey the rental fee is not this much for two weeks." "I know, I just wanted to give you a lil extra so you could go buy ya self sumthin." "Juvey you need your money; I can't accept this." "Baby girl believe me I can afford it. You could use that lil extra money for your trip you bout to go on. I don't care, just take the money trust me." "Aight Juvey, but whatever you doing to get this money be careful." "I am baby girl, don't trip. Ain't nuthin gon happen to ya boy." "I pray not, but anyway I'll be gone for two days. When I get back we can start getting ready for Essence Fest." "Aight, baby girl be careful on the road and hit me when you get back." "Alright I gotta go Juvey, gimme kiss. My co-worker left early. She had an emergency to tend to so I gotta work through lunch". They shared a sensual five second kiss, and Teelee was off to start his day. As Teelee pulled away from the hospital he called Lil Man. They needed to put Keedy on their target. "Wzup Lil Man, you ready?" "Yeah come through. I'm sittin on the porch waitin for you." "Fasho, I'm in route."

When Teelee pulled in front of Lil Man's house, he put the hazard lights on to go holler at Ms. Mary. Lil Man's mom had just gotten out of jail. Teelee had to go see her, she was like a second mother to him. "Wzup moms, when you got out?" "Last night baby. It feels good to be out that cage." "I already know" Teelee replied. "Here ya go moms." Teelee pulled out $200.00, and gave it to Ms. Mary. Teelee was never a stingy person. If he had it to give, he was going to break bread. "Thank you baby." All my sons looked out for mama, I'm going have me a drink tonight. Well let me let y'all talk, I'm bout to go in here and see what Mario bad ass doing." "You ready homey?" Teelee asked. "Yeah let's do this. Say hold up round. You GQ today huh, what's the occasion?" "Ain't no occasion, nigga just can't get his swerve on sometimes." "Hell no nigga, you up to sumthin! Oh yeah I almost forgot, you hookin up wit ole girl from the club last night." "If you already knew, why you drillin a nigga then?" Teelee asked, aggravated at the numerous questions Lil Man was asking him. "Cause nigga, I'm still shook up from last night. I told Thugga how it went down." "He said the lil bitch he was with freaked him out the game too. Them naked ladies some bad muthafuckas, we gotta keep a few of them." "I'm already on top of that homey." "You called Keedy and told her to be ready?" Lil Man asked. "Believe me round, she already ready. All I have to do is call her and tell her to come outside. Watch this shit." Teelee proceeded to call Keedy on the phone. Teelee pressed the speaker phone button and the phone began to ring. After the second ring Keedy picked up. "Wzup, you outside?" "I told ya." "What you said baby boy?" "I wasn't talkin to you Keedy, I was hollin at somebody. You ready, I'm bout to come through and pick you up." "You know I'm ready, I'm not playin no games. I'm down wit ya." "Buleeve Dat." "Aight Keedy, I'mma be there in a minute."

Teelee and Lil Man put the weed in the air, as they headed to pick up Keedy. It didn't matter where they were going, or when they were going they was going to get their smoke on. In their eyes it was good for the soul. Teelee called Keedy and told her to come outside, as they turned on the block to her house. Keedy stepped out the door with some gear on that would make a blind man see. Keedy had some tights on that showed all her curves from the waist down. You could see that camel toe poking through her tights, which made Teelee's nature rise a bit. He shook the feeling, because his mind had to be focused. She also had a Cooji top on that hung slightly off her shoulder, which made her cinnamon skin tone glimmer in the sun. "What's good fellas?" Keedy asked getting into the car. "All you Keedy. Damn you lookin good" Teelee replied. "You ain't lookin bad ya self baby boy. What's the occasion?" "Damn why everybody keep askin me that shit." "You usually in ya gangsta gear" Keedy replied as she checked her makeup in the sun visor mirror. "I guess I gotta come like this more often, so I won't have to worry about being stereo typed. I should be asking you, why you dressed like that." "Well how I'mma get dude attention if I'm dressed like a grandma." "I feel where you coming from" Lil Man commented. "Aight this how we gon do this" Teelee said, pulling off from Keedy's house. "We bout to swing around the nigga spot so we can show you who the nigga is. It's all on you from there, make show you keep us updated on ya progression. Remember we need to get this nigga outta the way A.S.A.P." "Believe me it won't take long at all. Trust me on that." "Here" Teelee went in his pocket and gave Keedy $300 dollars. "This for gas, or anything else you go need. You got a way to get around huh?" "Yeah I'mma use my sister car." Teelee headed to the Goose to put Keedy on their prime suspect. If Keedy handled her business, Teelee had some shit planned for her. Above all a woman could get in and around things that a man couldn't. "Get off on Chef" Lil Man said sparking the Purp back up. They exited Chef Highway and rode until they made it to America St. Lil Man specifically instructed that they turn left on America St. Jashawn spot would be exactly seven houses off to the right. As they rode past Jashawn spot a group of niggas that were standing on the corner glanced in the car. Lil Man instructed Teelee and Keedy that Jashawn was the one standing off to the back by the fence. They had to keep it moving because they didn't want to run the risk of being spotted. "You got the nigga locked and loaded" Teelee asked headed back to the main highway. "Yeah baby boy, he good as done. Don't worry

I'll have him for you in no time." "Aight Keedy nigga countin on you, ya heard me." Teelee dropped Keedy off so she could get started on her assignment. "Aight y'all I'mma hit y'all up when sumthin shakes" Keedy said getting out of the car. "Fasho, hit us up" Teelee replied as he put the Monte in reverse. As Teelee pulled off from Keedy's house his phone began to ring. "What's good Teelee, where you at?" Freddie was one of Teelee weight customers. Him and his cronies had Galier St. in the lower 9th Ward, booming. "I'm leaving the East, why you tryna get right?" "Yeah, I need a set of them twenty eights A.S.A.P." Twenty eights was another name for an "ounce." "What's your location" Teelee asked getting on I-10. "I'm in the nine on G-Strip." "Aight, I'll be round there in five minutes. Where you at, by them boyz Nell and nem?" "Yeah we ova here." "Who that is" Nell asked. "This that boy Teelee, he bout to swing through." "Man tell him I need two sets of them twenty eights." "Say son, Nell said bring him two of them thangs." "I got y'all covered" Teelee replied as he ended the call. "Lil Man you got coke on you" Teelee asked taking an ounce and a half from his package that sat on his lap. "Come on round, you know I keep that "Hard Rock and Roll" on me." "Aight, we can split this sale." "Gimme forty-two grams." Lil Man grabbed the portable scale that sat on the back seat. He weighed out forty-two grams and gave it to Teelee. "Fasho" Teelee said adding what Lil Man gave him to the pack. Minutes later they pulled up on G-Strip. Freddie and Nell were standing on the porch waiting. Teelee jumped out to serve them. He didn't plan on posting up to long, never knew when the jump out boys planned on hitting the block. "What's good wit you niggas" Lil Man asked as he rolled the window down on the Monte. "We coolin gettin this paperwork, ya heard me." "I see y'all, well do the damn thang then." Teelee made his transaction, and him and Lil Man dipped out. "Wzup Lil Man, you tryna go get sumthin to eat?" "I ain't trippin, where you talkin bout going?" "Let's go fuck with Shoney's today." Even though they were straight hood by nature, they still had to act accordingly. Never knew when the law enforcement would be around. They didn't want that kind of attention at all, so they sprayed on cologne to camouflage the weed smell.

"May I help you sir" the cashier asked as Teelee and Lil Man made it to the front counter. "Yeah give us a table for two" Teelee replied picking up a menu from the counter. "She'll take you gentleman to your table" the cashier said as she proceeded to assist the people who were trying to pay for their meal. "Right this way" the waitress said leading Teelee and Lil Man to the back of the restaurant. "What will y'all be having to drink" the waitress asked taking out her note pad. "Gimme a fruit punch" Teelee requested. "I'll take a coke, ya heard me" Lil Man said while scanning the menu. "Alright I'll be right back with y'all drinks. As the waitress walked off to prepare their drinks, Teelee checked his missed calls from yesterday. Nunew had called him at least twenty times. "She spooked out like a muthafucka", Teelee thought as he closed his phone. "What time you pose to be hookin up with ya Latin Mami?" "I'mma see what's good with her after we finish eatin." When the waitress brought their drinks back she took their orders. Teelee ordered the T-bone and bake potato, which included the salad bar. Lil Man ordered the chicken fried steak, with mash potatoes his meal came with the salad bar as well. Shoney's had one of the best salad bars in New Orleans. When their food came they dug right into their plates. It was the closest thing to a home cooked meal. It was better than the fast food they were accustomed to eating every day. After they finished up their food they sat back and chilled for a bit. They brainstormed over some upcoming things they had planned for the Skull Gang. They always shared their ideas with each other to see if they both were on the same page. The communication level was on point between all the members within the circle, which kept everything in tack. Communication was very important in anything because if it's not lined up something or someone would be out of order. "I'mma go get my grill redone" Lil Man said cleaning in between his teeth with a toothpick. "You down? I already hollered at that boy Thugga. You know he bout it." "We could do that" Teelee replied. "It's time to change up anyway. How you tryna get yo shit this time" Teelee asked taking a sip of his fruit punch. "I'mma get six more, and I'mma put that princess cut shit in em." "I might get a couple mo. I wanna get them VVS thangs. Hold up homey lemme call ole girl so I could see what it do." Teelee proceeded to call Selina, as he waited he took the last bite of his steak. The T-bone was too good to leave anything on the plate. "Hello." "Wzup Mami, this Teelee. What you doing?" Oh hey cutie, I'm chilling just finish cooking for my lil brother. Him and his friends over here playing the PS2 on the big screen." "That's wzup, I just finish eatin myself." "Yeah, what you ate?" "I started off with a salad, and ended off with a steak and baked potato." "Where you at now Papi?" "I'm still at Shoney's wit my lil homey, why wzup?" "I'm bout to bake some cookies, and we bout to chill out. You need to come over here and chill with me." "That sounds like a plan. Where you live at?" I live in Kenner right before you get to the Flamingo Casino. Bring your friend along too. He could keep my sister Rosy company." That's wzup I'mma hit you up when I get in the area so you can tell me exactly where your spot at." "Aight Papi, see you in a minute." "Aight Mami" Teelee replied before hanging up with Selina. "You tryna dip with me by ole girl. She said her sista ova there." "Damn round, I would but I gotta go handle some business in Slidell." "You passing up the chance to get put in the game. I can't believe this shit!" "I know I can't believe it myself, but it's always money ova bitches. I gotta bring a couple Oz's to my clientele out there." "That's what it is, get ya money homey. I'mma call Thugga see if he want to fuck with me." Teelee called Thugga on his phone, he was in luck. Thugga didn't have one of his hoe's with him, and he didn't plan on picking one up. They paid for their food, and headed to the 7$^{th}$ Ward. Teelee was about to drop Lil Man off so he could go handle his business in Slidell.

"What it do Thuggezy, you ready?" Teelee asked pulling in front of Lil Man's house. "Yeah pick me up off the Blade, I'mma ride with you." "Aight, I'm round the corner droppin Lil Man off by his car. I'mma be that way in a minute." "Say Teelee, I almost forgot. Pistol told me to tell you he got a package of some good dro. He said fuck with him." Lil Man said while hopping in his car. "That's what it is. Tell him I'mma get at him. Hit me up when you make it back from Slidell." "Fasho, I'mma fuck with y'all. Tell Selina you got another lil potna. Keep one of her cousins on line for me." "I got ya homey." As Teelee pulled off he headed to pick up Thugga, so they could go get their chill on with the Latin beauty's. "What's up Thugga, I see ya car but I don't see you. Where you be's at?" "I'm on Tonti and Touro by twin house." "Aight, I'm comin up the block. Come outside, ya heard me." "I'm comin out now my nigga." When Teelee pulled up to twin's house, Thugga jumped in and they were in route to Kenner. When Teelee got to the Williams Blvd. exit he called Selina to get the exact location of her spot. "What's good Mami, I'm on Williams now. Where I go from here?" "Come up Williams until you get to the jewelry store on side of the canal. Make a left by the canal, the first corner you get to make a right. We live in the second house on your left. You'll see my black Benz in the driveway." "Aight, I'm in route. I'll be there in a few" Teelee said before hanging up with Selina. "I knew it, ole girl holdin she got a Benz nigga." "O yeah, she might be connected" Thugga replied as he turned his fitted cap to the back. "I don't know, but I'mma find out. She might just have a good paying job."

As Teelee and Thugga pulled in front of the house they saw the black Benz, which let them know they were at the right spot. Soon as Teelee rang the doorbell, Selina came to the door looking even better than she did in the club. The funny thing was she didn't even have on any makeup. She was naturally beautiful. "Hey Papi, you made it." "Yeah beautiful, I had to see your face again. This my brother from another." "What it do, they call me Thugga." "Nice to meet you, y'all come on in." As they stepped into the house, they could tell Selina was living way above average. Marble tile covered the floors, furniture that you would see on MTV cribs, and a flat screen that looked as big as the ones at the movie theater. "Guys this is my lil brother and his friends." "What's good with y'all" Teelee said extending his hand to Selina's lil brother. "We chillin playin Madden. My name is Carlos. This my lil patinas Recio and Adam." "Fasho, I'm Teelee and this my brother Thugga. "Who the best on this here" Thugga asked taking a seat on the couch. All of them replied at the same time. "I AM!" "Well I'm bout to see. I got winners, I'mma see if y'all got sumthin on me." "Thugga this my sister Rosy, Rosy this Thugga" Selina said introducing the two. "Nice to meet you. I guess beauty run thick in y'all family." Rosy and Selina favored a lot. The only thing that separated the two was Rosie's thickness. Girl had hips and ass for days. "You don't look bad ya self Papi" Rosy replied taking a seat next to Thugga. "Y'all want some homemade chocolate chip cookies?" Selina asked heading to the kitchen. "I just took them out the oven, so their warm and fresh." "Yeah you could bring me a couple. You good Thugga?" "Yeah, I'll take a few" Thugga replied never taking his eyes of Rosy. "Wzup Papi, where that good at?" Selina asked as she brought the cookies on a tray. "Y'all smoke? I wish I would have known that. I coulda cop some before I came through. We could take a ride to the city and get some. Thugga hit Pistol up and tell him we need a couple grams of that dro. Y'all wanna take a ride" Teelee asked getting up walking towards the door." "Yeah sure, we can take my truck" Rosy replied picking up her keys from the counter. Thugga ended the call with Pistol. "He said he at the house come through, he waitin on us." They jumped in Rosie's GMC Envoy and headed to Lil Man's house. While Teelee and Selina was getting to know each other a little better in the back seat, Rosy and Thugga looked like they had been knowing each other for quite some time by the way they clicked. Thugga leaned over the middle console talking loud enough just so Rosy could hear, while Rosy smiled and blushed like a little school girl. "Looks like y'all hitting it off well" Selina said leaning in Teelee's arm. "He's so crazy, he keeps making me laugh." "You don't want me to be serious all the time do you? Gangsta's laugh too" Thugga said smiling at Rosy. "Keep doing ya thang boo. I love your sense of humor" Rosy replied. "Do ya thang lil sis" Selina said snapping her fingers. Teelee jumped out of the truck, as they pulled up in front Lil Man's house. "Wzup Teelee, who you lookin for" Money asked coming out the front door. "Where Pistol at?" "He in the back room. Lock the door when you leave, I'm bout to go on the Blade." Teelee was met by the potent smell of Hydro, as he made it to the back of the house. "Damn that shit smell good" Teelee said walking into the room where Pistol was at. Pistol was busy breaking a pound down into ounces and grams. "Here homey, gimme $50 dollars" Pistol said throwing Teelee an ounce. "Good lookin my nigga." "It's all good, you know how we rockin" Pistol replied handing Teelee the Keep Moving cigars. I'm bout to hit the block with this so you know the Blade really bout to be over flooded with the customers." "Get ya money my nigga" Teelee responded. "What you and Thugga bout to get into?" "We bout to go cool out with these lil Latin Mami's." "Oh yeah, Lil Man told me you had met a bad lil mamacita. That's why you gettin ya Denzel on huh.?" I really gotta mix my style up Teelee thought. "Well I'm bout to bounce. I'mma fuck with you later, ya heard me." "Aight round, go do ya thang." From there they headed back to Selina's spot. When they made it in the door Carlos and his friends were still at it on the PS2. "Carlos bring your friends upstairs and play in your room." "Aight Selina, come on y'all." Carlos and his friends went upstairs, while the grownups began their grown up party. Teelee rolled up a couple of Keep Moving's, while Selina broke out the liquor. "What's this" Teelee asked picking up the rain drop shaped bottle. "It's called Rain, it's really good" Selina said pouring each of them a glass. They all got lifted off the dro and alcohol to the point where they were stuck in a zone between themselves. Teelee and Selina were off in their own zone on one side of the sofa, and Thugga and Rosy were doing their thang on the other side. Before Selina and Teelee could notice, Rosy and Thugga had made their way upstairs. "Come on Papi, let me give you a small tour of the house." As they walked up the stairs Teelee beamed in on Selina's small waist line that led down to her nice sized ass. For Latina's Selina and Rosy were working with a lot in the ass department. Selina led Teelee into her room. She gotta be connected Teelee thought looking around the room. Selina's closet door was open revealing her Chinchilla furs. Yes, she had a shit load of furs. You wasn't about to rock Chinchilla's if your paper work wasn't right. Seeing those things sealed the deal. All he had to do was here it from the horse's mouth. If she was connected, that was all Teelee needed to bring the Skull Gang to another level. She then led him to another room. "This my little girls room, she's spending time with her daddy right now. Hopefully you'll get to meet her someday. Well I guess that's all of it. I would show you Rosie's room, but sounds like her and Thugga is kinda busy at the moment." Busy wasn't the word. You could hear Rosy all throughout the house. "Aye Papi, Aaaaahh, Aaaahh." Luckily Carlos and his friends had already left. "Come with me Papi." Selina took Teelee by the hand and led him back into her room. As they made it into the room she pushed him on the bed. Selina turned her back on him removing her shirt. As soon as she turned around her perky size 36D's made Teelee's soulja stand at attention. Selina had some of the most succulent breast you would ever lay your eyes on. "I know I'mma regret this in the morning, but the mixture of weed and alcohol got me wanting you inside of me Papi." The money wasn't the only thing that came quick, the sex came just as fast. Every aspect of a street nigga lifestyle moved at least 100mph nonstop, especially in the never sleep streets of the N.O. Teelee grabbed Selina by the arm pulling her into him making her breast press up against his stomach. He gently kissed her on the forehead, and then proceeded to her lips. As they kissed, they undressed each other. Teelee worked his way to the reason why his engine was on overdrive. When his lips touched Selina's breast something felt odd. Before he could say anything, Selina looked at him and said, "You like em?" "I love em" Teelee replied continuing on with his four play. Deep inside he really didn't. They felt like water balloons, but he wasn't bout to ruin the moment by saying so. Teelee gently pulled Selina's panties off. Selina's neatly shaven kitty cat almost looked good enough to eat, but not good enough for Teelee to break bread like that. Upping the head game was out of the question. Selina opened her legs playing with herself, as she rambled on speaking in Spanish, "Te gusta esto." Whatever it was she was saying made Teelee go crazy. He quickly peeled the wrapper of his "anti-children" device and went to work. "Aye Papi, gimme that dick! No Pares, please don't stop." Hearing Selina scream out Papi made Teelee dig deeper. "Aaaaahh, Aaaaahh! Go deeper Papi, don't stop! Aahh!" Teelee made Selina stand up and touch her toes. As he reentered her she let out a moan of pleasure. Teelee was in full stride. He had Selina's head jammed up by the wall where she could do nothing but take the dick. "Oohhhh, I'm bout to nut! Oooh shit, I'm cumin" Selina screamed out as an orgasm burst through her insides. The way Selina came shocked the fuck out of Teelee. He had never had a woman cum like that before. It came out like running water. It wasn't over, Teelee picked Selina up by her small frame and sat her on his dick as he thrust into her in midair. "Aaaahh, Papi you beatin this pussy up. Give it to me! Aaaahh, Papppiii." Teelee grabbed Selina's ass and thrust one more time, as his seed shot out like a fire hydrant. They both collapsed on the bed feeling satisfied. They caught their breath and went straight to sleep. The sex was definitely good. There wasn't a need for pillow talk, nor getting up to get something to drink. Straight Zzzzz's. I guess you can blame it on the alcohol……...

# CHAPTER 7

# NEVER TRUST A BIG BUTT AND A SMILE

Keedy didn't waste any time, she went right back to the Goose. She wanted to see what strategy she would have to use to get the nigga Jashawn to recognize her. Once he was placed in her presence, it was *Murda She Wrote.* Keedy knew what area to target first when dealing with men. Most men let their little head think for them. Keedy knew that all too well, so she was going to use that to her advantage. She knew it wouldn't be hard. She went with the oldest trick in the book, woman in distress. As Keedy drove by Jashawn spot she faked a break down. She proceeded to pull her Cooji top a little bit further off her shoulder so her voluptuous breast would protrude. As soon as Keedy popped the hood on her sister's Impala and bent over, it was like feeding time in the zoo. All the lil niggas that were standing on the corner dropped what they were doing and tried to render aid to the so called woman in distress. "Wzup baabyyy, you need some help?" said the track star that beat everyone to the punch. "Yeah I don't know what's wrong with it. This damn thing just cut off on me. "Well lemme see what's"….. "Hold up lil homey. I got this here." Just what Keedy wanted to see. The bird had flown into the trap quite easy. "Now what you said happened?" "I don't know; it was driving fine earlier. I was on my way to pick up my sister, and it just cut off on me." "Well lemme see whatz up. Just sit down and relax. I got you." In all actuality Jashawn didn't know what the hell he was doing. As he went under the hood of the car he shook a couple of wires, and told Keedy to try it. Of course it cranked right up, nothing was ever wrong with it in the first place. Now it was time for Keedy to put her skills to work. Just to seal the deal, Keedy pretended as though she lost something on the back floor of the car. When Jashawn came from under the hood, he noticed Keedy bending over with the crack or her cinnamon brown ass showing. He was right where she wanted him. He was immediately caught up by her sex appeal. As Keedy turned around Jashawn was still mesmerized by her "Buffy The Body" booty. "Everything good?" Keedy asked. "Yeah, yeah, yeah you good to go. By the way what's yo name?" "I'm Keisha, and you?" Of course she wasn't giving this clown her real name. She didn't want her name, or any of the members of the Skull Gang implicated when dude came up missing. "My name Jashawn, but they call me Jay. You from outchere in the East?" "No, I'm from the West Bank." "Well what you getting into later?" "I didn't have anything planned. Why you had sumthin special in mind?" "Maybe we can duck off and go get sumthin to eat. You know, get to know each other a lil better." "That sounds like a plan. What time you talkin?" "I'mma be done outchere bout 7:00, so any time after that." "How bout 8:00?" "I'm cool wit that, you want me to pick you up, or what?" No, I'mma come back around here." Keedy didn't want to risk exposing any information on her whereabouts. "Well Ms. Keisha, I'mma see you at 8:00." As Keedy pulled off she called Teelee to inform him on the situation. Keedy planned on having the assignment covered by the end of the week. Once dude felt the "Art of Seduction" from Keedy, it didn't matter where she wanted him to go or what she needed him to do. Jashawn would definitely oblige. The saying is true, "pussy is power". It's crazy but, it's life. A lot of young brothers have lost their lives chasing pussy. This clown definitely wouldn't be the last.

"Damn lil sis, what trick you tryna catch with them clothes on." Keedy had a sheer black Dolce & Gabbana dress on that showed every curve on her body. If the lighting hit her at the right angle, you would be able to see all of her valuables. "I'm just going out with a friend." "I guess you tryna use my car to huh?" "Yeah, but don't worry I got you." Keedy went in her purse and gave her sister a hundred-dollar bill. "I'mma have your tank on full too." "Shid, if you doing it like that, you can take that bitch more often." "Aight I'm bout to be out, don't wait up." As Keedy walked out the door, she contemplated on the fact of her becoming a part of something that had meaning. Well before Teelee formed the Skull Gang he always stood for something, which indeed sparked the flame in Keedy towards Teelee.

When Keedy pulled up Jashawn signaled for her to pull in the driveway. "How we gon do this? You gon ride wit me, or what?" Jashawn asked, opening the door to the car. "Come on, you could ride wit me" Keedy replied. When the dome light of the car came on Jashawn eyes got big as silver dollars. The sight of Keedy's enticing clothing had him all entranced. "Got damn, you lookin good than a mutha. You make a nigga wanna bite you and see what you taste like girl". Those comments alone made Keedy know she had the clown in the palm of her hands. "You like it? I wanted to make a good second impression." "Well you definitely passed that test." "So where we going to eat at Jay?" "Lookin good as you lookin, I could eat you for dinner" Jashawn said drooling over Keedy's beautiful body. "Boy you crazy, but for real though where we going?" "Let's go to Houston's on St. Charles St." "Aight, come on close the door" Keedy said attempting to back out of the driveway. "I don't want this light to go off. I'm enjoying my view." "This shit to easy Keedy" thought. "I ain't even gotta seduce this nigga, shit I could get this shit ova tonight. Well fuck it, I'mma get me a free meal before I feed his duck ass to the wolves."

They hit I-10, and headed for Houston's. When they pulled up Jashawn paid for Keedy's car to be valet. After peeping the scenery, they decided to dine at the bar. Well actually Keedy persuaded Jashawn to eat at the bar, because she knew a touch of alcohol gave some niggas diarrhea of the mouth. "Can I get y'all a drink before I take y'all orders" the bartender asked wiping down the bar. "Yeah gimme a Hennessey on the rocks" Jashawn requested. "For you ma'am" the bartender asked. "Give me a Thug Passion" Keedy said winking at Jashawn. As the bartender went to prepare their drinks, Keedy decoded to break the ice. "Well Mr. Jashawn tell me a lil bit about the person who has all my attention." "It ain't much to me, I'm just a street nigga. I survive off street money, ya heard me. No kids, no baby mama's. Anything else you wanna know?" Keedy proceeded to feed him a bunch of lies about herself. As the night went on, they ate and continued to get their drink on. Keedy wanted to throw some bait in the air to see if the nigga would catch it. She wanted to see Jashawn' s true intentions towards Teelee and his circle. "I been hearing a lot of things about these dudes that call themselves the Skull Gang. The streets talkin bout they got the hustle game on lock." "Man fuck them ole bitch ass niggas!" Now she was finally getting somewhere. Before the night was over Keedy would have all the information she needed for Teelee. "You know em?" Keedy asked moving in closer so she could soak up all this good information. "I don't know fasho, but I think them niggas had sumthin to do wit my cousin gettin smashed. I'm tryna work my way in on one of them nigga's baby mama. See if I could get some info through her." In the game there will always be a nigga that loves to run his mouth, and make his self look like something he wasn't, especially in front of a female. Real gangsters didn't talk, they walked. Most importantly a gangster wouldn't talk his business to a broad he barely even knew. Another true statement, "loose lips, sink ships." Keedy offered her fake condolences to Jashawn. "I'm sorry to hear that, I hope you get some closure on that situation Jay." Keedy could have received an Oscar for the grade A acting she was doing. "Enough of all that. Where you think our night will lead us to?" Jashawn asked inching closer to Keedy's bar stool. "You, to your house, and me to mine. I'm really starting to like you, so let's not rush things. If you really feelin me, you can wait on this pussy can't you?" Keedy asked while opening her legs a little so Jashawn could get a glimpse of her bald kitty cat. Keedy had to throw that out there to keep his mind captivated, and tweaking for more. "I guess we can take the slow route" Jashawn replied. He paid for their food and drinks and headed back to the East. When they pulled into the driveway, Jashawn tried one last time. "Can a nigga at least get a kiss, or sumthin?" This was Keedy's chance to put the strong hold on him, securing the position she needed. Keedy proceeded to kiss Jashawn from his ear to his neck. As she worked her way down, she unbuckled his Girbaud jeans giving the head of his dick a kiss as well. Keedy was a real grimy bitch. She did whatever she had to do to accomplish her goal. "Damn babyyy, you gon just leave a nigga like that" Jashawn asked sitting in the passenger seat with a stiff one. "That'll keep me on your mind until next time. Who knows; maybe next time I'll give you that P.A.M." "You definitely know how to get a nigga hot" Jashawn said putting his dick back in his pants. "So when I'mma see you again Ms. Keisha?" "I don't know Jay; I have some stuff to take care of this week. My schedule is always subject to change. Just stay available for me baby." "Don't worry, I'm on the block all day, so my schedule always open. Just make sure you get at me." "Don't trip, I'mma definitely get at you." The fucked up thing was he didn't even know the true meaning behind those words.

What he thought was meant for his good, was really meant for his death. When Keedy pulled off she called Teelee and told him she needed to meet him first thing in the morning.

Early the next morning Teelee woke up with a slight headache and a beautiful Latin bitch on his side. He knew he had to shake the hangover due to the great news Keedy informed him on. He was tweaking to see what Keedy had acquired while on her mission. Just as Teelee got out of the bed to go use the restroom, Selina woke up. "Hey Papi." Selina said in a voice that sound like she felt the same way as Teelee. "Wzup beautiful, how you feelin this morning?" "I got a headache. Would you get me two of those Aleve's out of the medicine cabinet in the restroom?" "I got you Mami." As Teelee went to relieve his self from the Rain vodka exiting his system, he grabbed the pills from the medicine cabinet. He went downstairs to get Selina something to drink to wash them down. When he made it downstairs he heard Thugga and Rosy in the kitchen. They were preparing to cook breakfast. From the looks of it they didn't feel the way Teelee and Selina did. "What it do Teelee, you finally got ya ass up huh?" "Yeah and I got a bad ass headache. Y'all don't feel fucked up from last night?" Teelee asked going into the refrigerator to get Selina a bottle of water. "Nah we good, but if we did Rosy sure as hell knocked it out this morning." Thugga replied, as he slapped Rosy bare ass. The only thing she had on was Thugga's oversized T-Shirt. It was something about how a chick looked in your T-shirt after some good ass sex. It made you want to go for a couple of more rounds. Teelee grabbed the bottle of water and headed back upstairs. From the looks of it round twelve was about to pop off on the kitchen counter. When Teelee made it back to the bedroom Selina was in the bathroom brushing her teeth. "Here you go Mami, I'mma be right back." Teelee went to grab his travel toothbrush from the car. He always kept one on deck just in case a situation like this happened. His little "sexcapade" with Selina was proof of his theory. As he came back into the bedroom, Selina was laid across the bed. He proceeded to go brush last night's funk out of his mouth. When he made it back into the bedroom, Selina signaled for him to come and lie down. "Well, well, well, Papi you got my goodies quicker than I anticipated." "You know what I figured out Selina? Dealing with the opposite sex you never know what's going to happen. One thing I do know is I enjoyed our night, and I haven't lost any respect for you. We live in a fast city which means fast living, ya heard me." I understand what you saying Papi, but I just think you're not going to be interested in me as you were before," Selina replied with her head down. "Believe me when I tell you, if I say I didn't lose any respect, I didn't. I'm still standing here right now so my interest is still on you Mami." "Aight Papi, I can believe that. If you don't mind me asking, what do you do for a living?" Teelee paused for a second before speaking again. "My first instinct was to tell you a lie, but that would be going against my own principles. I hustle cocaine." "Well I'm glad you didn't lie to me. I respect that, everyone has their own hustle. Whether it's working a nine to five or whatever, I appreciate you being straight up" Selina said as she kissed Teelee on the cheek. "Aight Ms. Selina, what you do for a living with all this luxurious shit around here. You gotta be a doctor or sumthin." "Well let's just say this, if this here last long enough you'll find out." That really left Teelee confused. One part of him wanted to believe she was connected, and the other part of him wanted to believe she was a rich kid of some wealthy parents. He didn't know what to believe, but one thing was certain he was going to definitely stick around and find out. Selina and Teelee went downstairs to join Thugga and Rosy. They ate breakfast, kicked if for a minute, and made plans to hook up later in the week. It was time to shake the spot. Teelee had to meet up with Keedy so she could run down what happened during her date with the dead man walking.

"Wzup Keedy, where you at?" Teelee asked as they headed back to the city. "I'm in the Seven by Manchu's." Manchu was a very popular corner store. They sold fried chicken plates that was so good, people even came in the morning to order them. "I'm on my way" Teelee replied. When Teelee and Thugga pulled up they spotted Keedy standing outside in front of the store. "What it do Keedy baaby, what you got for me?" Teelee asked jumping out of the Monte Carlo. "I got everything you need, and I got the nigga in position to go wherever I want him to go. All you gotta do is say the word." "Come get ya plate gurl" Ms. Chan said swinging the door to the store open. Ms. Chan was a cool, ole school, Chinese woman. Her and her husband had been owning Manchu's for over fifteen years now. She was real familiar with everyone that came through on a regular basis. "Hold up baby boy lemme go get my plate, when I get back I'mma run everything to you" Keedy said walking into the store. When Keedy came out of the store, they jumped in the Monte. From there she ran everything down. Even the part about her kissing the nigga dick. "So he think we killed that bitch ass nigga" Teelee said gripping the steering wheel of the Monte. "Well that just shortened his life term. When the quickest time you can set this up Keedy?" Teelee asked. "Shid, we can get this shit ova wit tonight. I told you I got the duck tweaking for this pussy" Keedy replied proudly. "Aight, this how we gon do this. Get the nigga to bring you to the spillway. I got everything from there." The spillway was an area located by Lake Pontchartrain, where people would go to fish and cast their crab nets. It was also a good swamp area. "Aight Keedy call me after you set the shit up." From there they parted ways. Keedy was off to arrange her side of things, and Teelee went to prepare to finish this shit for good. He was going to make sure that Jashawn wouldn't be heard from, or seen ever again. Teelee, Thugga, and Lil Man spent the whole day preparing for the night. The shit they had up their sleeves was full proof, and really gruesome. Teelee didn't want nothing to be traced back to them, so he planned on experimenting something he had been having in mind. If it worked out the way he planned he was going to use this as his method of disposal. "Say Lil Man, you picked up the raw meat from Wagner's" Teelee asked. "Yeah everything covered. You talked to Keedy yet?" "Yeah, she got everything locked and loaded. Look I'm on my way ova there. Thugga made it ova there yet?" "Yeah, he just came back. He said he got what you wanted him to get, ya heard me." "Aight homey, I'mma be ova there in a few." When Teelee pulled up to Lil Man's house, Thugga and Lil Man jumped in the Monte and they were off to Keedy's spot to make sure everyone was on the same page. "Wzup Keedy, we outside" Teelee said as he pulled in front of Keedy's sister house. "Y'all come in, my sister and them gone." When they went into the house, Keedy led them to the garage. "We gotta smoke out here y'all." "Aight Keedy, we gon already be out there. Just do what you gotta do until we step on the scene." "I got you baby boy, don't worry bout nuthin." They sparked up a couple of Keep Moving's to stimulate their minds, then they headed to their positions.

Keedy was once again dressed to kill. She thought she should at least give the nigga something good to look at before he took his last breath. Keedy had on a dress that resembled a T-Shirt, with nothing on underneath of course. She really threw the nigga off with the "I wanna have a picnic under the stars' line". "Who knows what might happen tonight Jay." That sentence alone sealed the deal. That really had the nigga gone. As long as she was speaking on that level, he didn't give a damn where the picnic was going to be.

"Wzup Jay, where you at? I'm ready" Keedy said making some last minute adjustments on her makeup. "I'm bout to leave the block, how I get to ya spot?" Keedy gave him directions to her and her sister's old house. No one was living there at the moment, so if he did tell anyone where he was going they would find a vacant home. Keedy was really on her shit. She made sure all her tracks were covered. Jashawn pulled up minutes later. "Yeah Keisha, I'm outside." The house still had their old blinds up, and the neighbor kept the grass cut. He didn't want to make his house look tacky; it really looked like someone was still staying there. Keedy came out with a picnic basket filled with fried chicken she had prepared before she left home, and some cheap ass bubbly to make everything look official. "Damn baby, you stay in something to entice a nigga huh" Jashawn said lusting off Keedy's firm juicy breast. "Is it workin?" Keedy asked getting into the car. "Does a fat bitch love cake? Of course it's workin" Jashawn replied pulling off. They shot straight to the Spillway. Keedy had the nigga about to go crazy the entire ride. She licked, kissed and sucked his neck. She even put his fingers in her warm, wet pussy and all type of other shit that would make a nigga hot off the heater. He was just how Teelee wanted him stupid and dumb found.

There wasn't a person in sight. They were ducked off so when Keedy and the nigga pulled up they wouldn't be spotted. This would be the end of Teelee's worries. If everything played out right, there would be a new member inducted into the Skull Gang tonight.

"Park right here, so we can be close to the water. I always wanted to fuck a nigga by the water under the stars" Keedy said getting out of the car. Jashawn grabbed the blanket Keedy packed in the basket and laid it on the grass. From the looks of the whole scene one would have thought that it was a real romantic picnic. They proceeded to eat and drink the cheap ass bubbly Keedy purchased. "This is so romantic. It's making me real freaky" Keedy said straddling Jashawn. She started kissing him from his neck working her way down to his chest. She slid his shirt off, as she made a trail with her tongue all the way down his stomach. Before you knew it Jashawn' s pants were unbuckled and his dick was in her mouth. The way Keedy sucked and stroked made Jashawn' s eyes roll to the back of his head. When he opened his eyes up, he was face to face with the barrel of Teelee's Fortie. "Well, well, well Mr. Jashawn look like you was really enjoying ya self." "Man what the fuck! Bitch you set me up!" "No nigga you set yaself up. Maybe next time you'll use ya big head, instead of that lil muthafucka in ya pants. Oh my bad, it ain't gon be a next time" Keedy said in an evil giggle. "Bitch, I'mma kill you!" Just as Jashawn tried to leap at Keedy, Teelee whacked him in the mouth with the gun, "POP." "Say Lil Man see if our lil potnas ready to come to land." Lil Man grabbed the raw meat from the trunk of the Monte they bought from Wagner's Meat Market. He threw a couple pieces of the bloody meat in the Bayou. For a few seconds the meat floated at the top of the water, but with the blink of an eye the meat was gone, and there appeared three very hungry alligators. "What the fuck y'all did that for?" Jashawn asked still fucked up at what was going on. "You gon see" Teelee said. "Oh my bad, you won't" Teelee smirked. An evil grin spread across Teelee's face as he made Jashawn stand to his feet. "Well I guess you now fasho it was us that smashed yo bitch ass cousin." "Nigga fuck you" Jashawn growled as spit flew from his mouth. "No nigga you fucked yaself behind some pussy". "Lemme shoot that bitch Teelee" Thugga said cocking his Fortie. "CLAK,

CLACK." "Nah homey, I got this." When Teelee lifted the Fortie to Jashawn's head he looked directly at Keedy. "Well Keedy remember I said your test wasn't finish. This ya last one. Here, bust that bitch head open!" Teelee handed Keedy the Fortie. Keedy took the gun from Teelee's hand. She looked nervous, holding the massive gun in her hands. As she lifted the gun to Jashawn's head, she squeezed the trigger with no hesitation, "BOOM!" The hollow point from Teelee's Fortie exploded as it exited the back of Jashawn' s head, leaving a huge hole. Keedy stood over Jashawn body starring with a cold look in her eyes. She had tasted her first blood and she liked it. There was brain fragment everywhere, which drew the gators to land. They all backed up as the water monsters came to land to drag Jashawn' s lifeless body to the water. They wrestled back and forth over who would devour most of his body. "SNAP" was the sound Jashawn' s bones made as they tore his body apart. After they finished with him there was nothing left, not even a finger. Teelee took some lye and threw it over the blood that splattered across the ground when the gators drug Jashawn body to the water. They took Jashawn' s car and burned it on Almonaster Rd. Almonaster was a dark strip leading into the Eastern part of New Orleans. There were many bodies dumped and cars burned on this road. While passing through the area you would always smell the scent of death in the air. They picked up some Grey Goose Vodka, and headed back to the 7$^{th}$ Ward to celebrate Keedy's initiation into the deadly Skull Gang. They posted up on the Blade drinking and giving Keedy all the G-Codes to the circle. It was just one thing left to do. Teelee stepped up to Keedy, as she sat on the hood of the Monte turning the bottle of Goose to the head. Keedy didn't even look like Keedy anymore. She had a whole new demeanor about herself. She had pure evil in her eyes. "Thugga let me get that" Teelee said reaching out for the black box Thugga had in his hands. "Keedy you no longer go by the name Keedy" Teelee said looking directly into her eyes. "Your new name gon be "K-Real". Keedy you apart of us now, and we vow to ride for you till death. As those words came out of Teelee's mouth he opened the box. It contained a baby Glock 40 with a 32 round clip. It was official, she had received the Fortie with the dick. It was no turning back now, Keedy was in until death. "Say y'all come here." K-Real wanted all of them to hear what she had to say. "As long as I got breath in my fuckin body. I'mma rock to the muthafuckin wheels fall off for all you niggas." Teelee took his Fortie from his waistband, and instructed that the rest of the clique do the same. "On three Skull Gang for life, and after that I wanna hear them Forties bark! 1, 2, 3, *SKULL GANG FOR 4-LYFE!*" As they all screamed those words, they squeezed the triggers on their Forties. Making the Blade light up like the 4$^{th}$ of July. "BOOM, BOOM, BOOM, BOOM, BOOM!"

# CHAPTER 8

## LET'S EAT

It had been weeks since K-Real popped her cherry into the game. She was really becoming a real live Gangstress. Teelee and the gang put a lot of work into K-Real. They showed her the most important shit like how to cook coke, sell coke, and all the other street etiquette she was going to need to survive in the Concrete Jungle. Along with shaping and molding K-Real, the money was coming in like clockwork. They were still stuck with D-Man as a connect, but they flipped and scored so fast it didn't even matter. Teelee had been kicking it with Selina heavy for the past few weeks, so much so that he felt her secret lifestyle was about to be revealed. She wanted him to come over that night for dinner. Selina said she had something real important to speak to Teelee about, and she wanted him to meet her oldest brother. That really intrigued Teelee's curiosity. Whether she was connected or a rich kid, Teelee would finally get to the bottom of Ms. Selina's luxurious living. Today was the day they all were going get their grills upgraded. Teelee planned on stepping K-Real's gangsta appearance up a bit by putting a ten piece in her mouth. She wasn't aware of it yet, he wanted to surprise her. K-Real had been putting in so many hours on the block, it made Teelee proud to see the persistence of her hustle. He felt like he had to compensate her for her commitment and loyalty she showed towards the circle.

As Teelee pulled up on the Blade he spotted K-Real posted on the corner like a light pole. She had been bleeding the block hard for the past few weeks. K-Real whole swagger had changed since she became a member of the Skull Gang. She really carried herself like a grimy street nigga, but don't get it twisted she was far from being lesbian. She still loved dick and wouldn't replace it for nothing in the world. Her new found life took away from her sexual pleasures. Her block wear was a black t-shirt and black Dickey pants. She wore her hair in a crinkled style, like she had just took it out of corn rolls. She even got a cross tattooed in the middle of her forehead that symbolized her Soulja sign. The crushed out grill was going to put the finishing touches on the G'd up and Soulja down gangstress.

"What it do Real baaby" Teelee said jumping out of the Yukon Denali, Deb had rented for him. "You know me baby boy outchere tryna get this money, ya heard me. Whatz good wit ya?" "I'm coolin me. You saw Lil Man today?" "No, but I seen Thugga. He just pulled off. He said sumthin bout us going somewhere. You know what he talkin bout?" "Yeah that's what I wanted to talk to you bout. I got a surprise for you. When you first put me down with that bitch ass nigga Tossy; I thought you was low down and conniving. Through this time though, you been down wit the team. You showed persistence and loyalty. I just want to say I appreciate you for that. Too show my appreciation I'm treatin you to a grill makeover. That's what Thugga was talkin bout." "Oh thank you baby boy!" "Just keep on rockin like you rockin. That's all that counts." As Teelee and K-Real conversed on the corner of the Blade, Lil Man pulled up. "What it do y'all" Lil Man said jumping out the Cutlass. "Y'all ready to get right?" "Yeah, but we gotta wait till Thugga get back" Teelee said leaning against the grill of the Denali. "I'mma just hit him up and tell him meet us there" Lil Man replied. As Lil Man hung up with Thugga they all jumped in the Denali and they were off to Saks Fifth Avenue. They had their diamond work done at Jack Sutton's Jewelry store. Jack was the hottest, and most well respected jeweler in the N.O. When you entered the place you were greeted with Champagne. It was a real upscale jewelry store. Lil Man decided to get the princess cuts, with invisible sets. Thugga got the one carat diamond on each of the twelve slugs he was going to put in his mouth. Teelee got the VVS settings in his. He was going to surprise K-Real by just getting hers done up, but he decided against it. He felt she should pick out what she wanted in her own mouth. When they walked in the jewelry store they spotted Jack appraising some diamonds. "What's good Jack baaby" Teelee said extending his hand to the jeweler. "Teelee my boy, I see y'all made it. Karen put this away for me" Jack said. He handed his assistant the tray of beautiful diamonds. "So did you all go to get your mold work done at the dentist?" "No, we going after we leave here. I just wanted to bring my people ova so she could pick out what she wanted." "Well let me get Karen to help her decide. Karen would you show the young lady our variety of diamonds and settings." "Sure Jack, right this way ma'am." As K-Real and Karen went to see what she wanted to get, Jack showed Lil Man, Teelee, and Thugga a replica of what their grill was going to look like. "Son we go light up the room with all this ice" Thugga said, admiring the impressive work Jack did with their mouth pieces. "Jack you really out did yaself this time" Teelee stated examining the precise work of Jack's craftiness. "Make sure you all have the dentist call and let me know when the molds will be ready. I will take care everything from there. I'll have the dentist notify you all so you can go and get them put in." With that being said K-Real had picked out what she wanted to get and they were off to get their mold work done from Mr. Smiles on First and Claiborne St. K-Real went with the pink VVS settings. The Skull Gang came off a pretty penny for their upgrades. Jack Sutton's was not only upscale; it was also very expensive. On his and K-Real's alone Teelee paid $30,000. Thugga's one carat diamonds came up to $15,000, and Lil Man came off paying $10,000 for his. After they left the dentist they went and got their grub on at the Two Sister's Soul Food Restaurant, and then headed back to the Blade.

Corey and Pistol and been babysitting the block until they made it back. "Son y'all just missed it. We had an afternoon rush" Corey stated as he organized the big ball of money in his hands. "It's all good we outchere now" Lil Man said turning his N.O. fitted cap to the back preparing to put his hustle down. Even though the Skull Gang was moving kilos, they still bled the Blade like they were still some petty hustlers. Work moved off the Blade so quick you could get off a whole key just selling quarters, twenties, and dimes. No exaggeration, the Blade was a real gold mine.

As soon as Teelee ducked his stash in the alley under Unc house, there was at least seven cars waiting to cop. He proceeded to grab his issue and get back to it. Once that line of customers was gone it was like seconds later another line of cars was pulling up to come cop some of that "Hard White Girl." The Blade pumped like that throughout the rest of the day.

Teelee had to shake the spot. He had made a substantial amount of money for the day. Besides tonight was the night that he was going have dinner with Selina and her brother. He was really anticipating to hear what Selina wanted to speak with him about. It had been weighing heavy on his mind since she told him. Over the past month Teelee had been contemplating on bringing the Skull Gang to bigger and better things. For one he felt it was time to move out and get his own spot. True enough he was comfortable staying with Kyla, but it's only so much you could do staying under somebody else's roof. He felt since his money was elevating he should elevate to a better living environment. He didn't want to be like the majority of dudes, and leech off someone else. He was more than able to handle the responsibility of putting a roof over his own head. Another big issue was he felt it was time to get out of the rental and cop his own shit. He had been slick slide dipping to numerous car lots window shopping. He wanted to see what would be suitable enough to transport him around. If things went the way he was plotting, he would be in his own spot and driving his own shit by the end of the month.

Teelee really wanted to look presentable not just for Selina, but for her brother as well. He didn't know what type of person to expect. Her brother could have been the white collar boogie type, or he could be a down to earth understanding type of person. He didn't know that's why he chose to wear his Polo button down, with a black Polo undershirt. Some navy blue cargo Polo pants, and his high top Prada tennis shoes. He also sported his two and a half carat diamond earring. Along with his gold chain and crushed out cross. The boy was really sharp. If Selina's brother didn't except him like that, he wasn't going to except him at all. When he was walking out the door, he ran into Kyla pulling in the driveway. "Where you going all dressed up?" Kyla asked getting out of her car. I got a dinner date with my Latin doll. "Yeah, I hear you, go do ya thang playboy. Oh yeah, I'm going get Lil Jamal myself. You promised Kayla you was going get him and she's looking forward to it, liar." "It slipped my mind, I been so busy I forgot. It's all good you got my back though big sis." "Boy get the fuck. I'm only doing it because I miss my baby and Kayla wanna see her lil cousin. Other than that Lil Jamal is your responsibility, remember." Hearing those words really made Teelee feel guilty; he told his self that he was going to make sure he made time for his son. Like always he let the streets consume all of his time. "Good lookin anyway" Teelee said as he jumped in the truck. As Teelee headed to Selina's house he changed the musical atmosphere to his collection of R&B. It gave him a chance to relax his mind, and allow him to think better. The sounds of Musiq Soul Child crooning his hit song *"Love"* gave Teelee an inner peace as he cruised on I-10. *"Looove sooo many people use your name in vainnnnn."* Although the Skull Gang worked together as a team. Teelee always was on some thinking outside of the boundaries type shit. He knew all his thugging and hustling wasn't going to last long. Especially in the grimy streets of New Orleans, it's either death or prison. Teelee's father and mother continuously preached that to him. He wanted to back up, but he was too caught up. The question was would it be too late when he decided to give it up.

As Teelee exited Williams Blvd, he called Selina to let her know he was in the area. "Wzup Mami, I'm around the corner. I'mma be pulling up in a few seconds." "Aight Papi, we're waiting on you." Soon as Teelee turned the corner to Selina's house he could see a GT Bentley parked behind Selina's Benz. "Man whatever they do, these muthafuckas got crazy Louche" Teelee thought as he parked. He called and let her know he was in front the door. "Yeah, I'm outside" Teelee said as he made his last minute adjustments on his attire. Selina came to the door looking beautiful. She looked better and better every time Teelee laid eyes on her. Money really elevated your look and everything about you. That was big reason this world was in the condition it's in now. Everybody desired to have the power, looks, and status. They'd do anything and everything to have it in their possession. "Come on Papi, we been waiting on you." When Teelee walked in the living room, he was greeted by her brother. From the looks of it he was a business man. Standing about 6'2, looking similar to the actor Antonio Bandera's. He was draped in an Armani pin striped suit, with an amphibious foot wear. The estimated cost of his whole attire had to be close to $4,500. That's not including the Frank Muller he sported on his wrist. The watch had so many diamonds in it making it look similar to a baby chandelier. "Teelee this is my big brother Lanzo. Lanzo this is my sweetie Teelee" Selina said preparing to get their dinner date started. "Nice to meet you Teelee. Selina has told me so much about you" Lanzo said in his strong Latino slur. "Same here. Man that's a nice suit your wearing" Teelee said admiring the tailor made Mercedes Benz of suits. "You like it? I have plenty of them. Maybe one day I'll take you to my tailor so you can get yourself one." "I would like that, I need to upgrade my apparel anyway." "Come on fellas. Dinner is ready" Selina said leading the way to the dining room. Selina had the table set up like they were dining at a five-star restaurant, and the food smelled delicious. Even though Selina was Latin, she had been living in New Orleans for so long she picked up the customs of Creole style cooking. Selina prepared Red beans and rice, and corn bread. She also had a wine beverage. As they sat down to eat, Teelee couldn't help but to compliment Selina on how great the food was. "Selina you really put it down. The food taste good." Teelee called Selina by her name out of respect for her brother being present. They ate and made small talk while getting better acquainted with one another. Teelee began to feel more and more comfortable around Lanzo. Teelee shared with him about the struggle of being a young parent and surviving in the rough streets of New Orleans. Lanzo expressed to him that he too struggled through parts of his life so he understood Teelee to the utmost. Lanzo had a real cool demeanor about himself. The way he spoke and explained things made it evident that he was a boss of whatever area of business he was involved in. After they finished their entrees, Selina prepared to bring out dessert. "You really out did ya self Selina" Teelee said wiping his mouth with a napkin. Just as Teelee said that Selina was coming to the dining room with a homemade sweet pie. "This must be some big news you gotta tell me cause you done pulled out all the stops" Teelee said as his mouth watered over the delicious looking pie. "I'm glad you're enjoying yourself." As they ate dessert Selina spoke up. "To get down to it, Teelee I'm pregnant." Teelee almost choked on the pie. "For real!" Selina and Lanzo burst into laughter at how Teelee's face looked when he heard Selina say those words. "I'm just playing" Selina said trying to gain composure of herself from laughing so hard. "For real though, I've been telling my brother about you and he was eager to meet you." Just then Lanzo interceded. "Teelee tonight I've got the feel of what type of person you are, and I'm impressed. I like your, how do you young people say it *Swag.* So what I want you to do is, meet me at this restaurant tomorrow at twelve sharp." Lanzo handed Teelee a card with all the information that he would need. Even his cell phone number. "Bull's Eye Point huh. I know where that's at" Teelee thought as he tucked the card in his shirt pocket. "I'll let you know everything from there." With that being said Lanzo kissed Selina and excused his self from their presence. That really left Teelee confused, but eager to see why Lanzo wanted him to meet at this expensive restaurant. Whatever it was he would get to the bottom of it tomorrow. "You know why he wanna meet with me?" "No Papi, I really don't." Selina knew, but Lanzo made specific instructions not to relay any information to Teelee. She had to play dumb to the whole situation. Selina and Teelee kicked it a little bit longer, then Teelee was on his way back to the Blade. It had been a mystery ever since he laid eyes on Ms. Selina. Tomorrow all the guessing would be over.

As Teelee exited Elysian Fields St., he hit Lil Man on his phone. Webbie's hit single *"Gimme That Pussy"* came on as Teelee waited for him to pick up. *"Gurl Gimme That Pussy, Gurl Gimme, Gurl Gimme Gurl Gimme That Pussssy."* "What it do Round, you back from ya dinner date huh?" "Yeah homey. It was nice, Selina put it down. Ole gurl cooked Red beans and rice, corn bread and homemade pie." "Damn son, I shoulda came through" Lil Man said mad that he missed the soul food dinner. "Nigga fuck the food, I met her brother. Dude on a whole nother level. Picture the nigga pushin a GT Bent." "Yeah, the nigga doing it like that?" "Nigga he gotta be rollin deep. Look where you at?" Teelee asked making a left turn under the Elysian Fields overpass. "I'm on the Blade, come fuck wit me." "I'm round the corner, I'mma see you in a few." When Teelee pulled up on the

Blade it looked like a block party was popping off. Everybody was outside from young to old. That wasn't new to Teelee, their block had people outside 24/7. Ciara had her DJ speakers on the porch bumping that bounce music. The lil chicks who always hung out at her house was pussy popping all on their head trying to see who could shake their ass the best. It didn't matter how fast or slow the beat was their ass was in sequence with it. New Orleans females held the title in the ass shaking department. Teelee jumped out of the truck to go holler at Lil Man. As he walked up Lil Man was sparking up that good. "What it do homey" Lil Man said giving Teelee some dap. "I'm coolin son. How things been lookin outchere?" Teelee said throwing his button down shirt in the truck. "Shid, you know the Blade always gon bleed my nigga." "I'm already knowing, ya heard me. Look back to what we was talkin bout. Homey name Lanzo. He want me to meet him at that expensive restaurant on the lake. He said he gon let me know everything from there." "What restaurant you talkin bout son?" "You know the one by Joe's Crab Shack. The Bull's Eye Point. How the fuck you forgot and you took Gia there for her birthday." "Oh yeah, I know what you talkin bout. You know these drugs have a nigga memory all fucked up," Lil Man replied holding the blunt up in the air. "Well what the nigga said y'all having the meeting for?" "I don't' know. All he said was he like my swag, and to meet him tomorrow for 12:00, sharp." "The nigga might just want to put you down with some legal shit." "I don't know, but whatever it is it's gon benefit all of us cause dude on some other shit. The nigga whole swag scream I'MMA BOSS." "Well I guess you go find out tomorrow then. You need me to go wit you?" "Nah, I'mma go by myself, see what it do first." "Oh yeah I almost forgot. You still going to Essence Fest with Deb?" "Fuckin right, why wzup?" "Gia want a nigga to go wit her. We could all hook up and go" Lil Man said passing Teelee the blunt. "That's wzup. What about Thugga?" "You know him. He ain't gon wanna go inside, but the nigga gon definitely be round there showing his ass." "Where K-Real and nem at?" "Real ran to the East by her sister. She said sumthin bout going put some money up. Pistol and Corey went to Bogalusa. They went to go check on some trap spot out there. You know every drug you could think of be pumping out there, and we can put our tax game down. If everything official out there we can extend our territory ya heard me." "That's wzup" Teelee replied passing the gar back to Lil Man. "Where that bitch Thugga at anyway?" "Last time I talked to him, he was at the gambling shack shootin dice." "My nigga stay on his hustle" Teelee said lighting up a camel to mellow out his high. "Son look at them lil girls. They be wildin" Lil Man said noticing one of them shaking with no underwear on. "If I ever have a lil girl, I'mma beat her ass if I ever catch her doing that shit." "I feel ya homey, same here" Teelee replied. Lil Man and Teelee smoked another blunt, made a few dollars then parted ways. Teelee wanted to make sure he got enough rest, so he could wake up and be on time to meet with Lanzo. Whatever it was he wanted to talk to him about, he didn't want to show up late and make a bad impression. Fucking with the night life of the N.O., you could lose track of time really quick. Before you know it, you'd be waking up late for whatever business you had to take care of.

The next morning Teelee woke up extra early. Even though his meeting wasn't until 12:00, he wanted to make sure he had everything in line. He picked out what clothes he was going to wear the night before. He decided to wear his lime green Polo sweater vest, with a black Polo underneath. Some black Levi jeans, and his lime green Cole Haans with the black soles. Teelee loved Ralph Lauren. To take off the edge he jumped in the shower and smoked a cigar of Purpa. He was anxious to find out why Lanzo wanted to have this meeting with him. While he smoked the haze, he enjoyed he cool breeze of the morning. He loved doing things like that. It gave his soul peace. It was getting close to that time, so he prepared to head to the restaurant. He grabbed the Fortie and a couple of grams of Purpa and hit the streets.

It was about 11:45, when Teelee made it to the restaurant, so he was official on his timing. As he stepped into the restaurant he was greeted by a beautiful hostess. "Do you have reservations sir?" "No I'm meeting someone." "Okay if you need anything just ask." As Teelee was about to pull out his cell phone to call Lanzo the hostess was approaching. "Right this way sir. Mr. Gomez is waiting for you." For a minute Teelee was lost and didn't know who she was talking about, and then it snapped. Selina last name is Gomez. When they walked up Lanzo was seated in a secluded area to the back of the restaurant. Lanzo stood as Teelee approached, greeting him with a firm handshake. "You made it and you're early. I like that" Lanzo said taking a seat. "Yeah when you said you wanted to meet here, it had to be sumthin important. So wzup?" Teelee asked ready to get to the reason they were there. "Let's have a drink. What would you like?" Lanzo asked. "Gimme a Hennessy, no ice." Lanzo signaled for the waitress to come over to their table. How he was acting you would have thought he owned the place. When the waitress came over, he proceeded to give her their order. "Kelli get me a double shot of Louis XIII, and my friend here a Hennessy no ice." "Right away Mr. Gomez." The waitress moved quickly to go prepare their drinks. "Lanzo can I ask you sumthin?" "Sure what is it." "Man you call shots like you own this place. Do you know the owner or sumthin?" "Yeah son I know him. You want to know how I know him?" "Yeah, how?" "I am the owner." Yeah the nigga was a heavy hitter Teelee thought. He owns one of the most expensive restaurants in the N.O. The waitress brought their drinks and Lanzo ordered her not to come back to their table until he called her. "Well Teelee, I know you're wondering why I wanted to have this meeting with you, so I'mma get down to it. As you can see I have power legally by owning a restaurant of this caliber. Well I have more establishments also. I know your familiar with the clear port on the other side of the lake." "Yeah, I know what your talkin bout" Teelee said while taking a sip of his drink. Well just like I have power legally, I have power illegally as well. I know your familiar with the Colombian Cartel." "Of course, who don't know what the Colombian Cartel is" Teelee replied with a sarcastic look on his face. "Good, because I'm one of the head under bosses." "JACKPOT!"

All the curiosity about Selina and her luxurious lifestyle had been revealed. Teelee had hit big once again. Who knew he was going to run into the sister of not only a drug Lord, but a Big Dawg in the legal side of life also. "I hear you and your team have one of the hottest blocks in the city" Lanzo said lighting up a Cuban cigar. "Yeah we doin our thang." "Well how would you like to have not only your block locked down, but numerous of blocks?" Lanzo asked. "I would love it" Teelee replied. "I have a proposition for you" Lanzo said plucking the ashes to the cigar. "What would that be?" Teelee asked ready to get the ball rolling. "How many kilos of cocaine do you think you can handle a week?" "Just to start off bout twenty, and if me and my circle get this territory out here in Bogalusa we can escalate to a bigger amount." "I'm glad you didn't bite off more than you can chew, because what you have with Selina is personal. What you have with me is business. As long as we keep our business together and straight up. You and your friends will be eating off one of the biggest plates in New Orleans." "I feel where you comin from and to let you know a little bit about myself. If it ain't straight up I can't fuck wit it. I'mma keep it one hunid wit ya longest you do the same. I know if shit go to lookin flaky you will apply force. Well just know me and my team rockin on the same level. I ain't got no push over's behind me either. F.Y.I. we rockin on that Guerrilla shit too, but it won't get to that because we on some straight up shit right" Teelee replied as he extended his hand to Lanzo. Teelee had to let Lanzo know that he and his team wasn't scared by the least, even though they wouldn't stand a chance against the Colombian Cartel. He still had to get it clear that they was rocking until death for theirs. Lanzo respected Teelee for his boldness. "You got balls kid" Lanzo said shaking Teelee's hand. "Well as long as we on the same page, we can get this show on the road. Oh yeah, also Teelee I do business with you and you only. You understand?" "I got you Lanzo." "Alright this what I want you to do. I'mma have my guy meet you at the clear port when you leave here. He will give you twenty kilos and I will see you next week same time, same place." "Hold up Lanzo, what the prices gon be like?" Teelee asked tryna see the range he was playing with. "How much you paying for them now?" "$23,000." "Well cut that in half." As Lanzo said those words he got up and left Teelee sitting there dumbfounded. Teelee couldn't believe it. He had gotten plugged into the best plug you could get. Teelee shook the shock of Lanzo' s last words and headed to the clear port. When he pulled up it was like he had a radar attached to the Denali. A tall Spanish guy that resembled Andre the Giant, signaled for him to hit the locks. The big guy opened the back door of the truck and threw in a black duffel bag. He walked off without saying anything. He jumped in a black Hummer and pulled off. Teelee quickly unzipped the bag and sure enough twenty kilos lay in the bag lined up like piano keys. Teelee immediately hit Lil Man on his cell phone. "What's good homey, how everything go at the meeting?" Lil Man asked. "Say round, you ready to eat?" "Fuckin right" Lil Man replied excitedly. "Well get ya bib, fork, and knife cause it's on nah my nigga."

# CHAPTER 9

# CAUGHT SLIPPING

Teelee sat in the Marriott Hotel in Slidell gazing over the twenty kilos that laid in front of him. He felt in his heart this was his chance to take the team to the top. It was definitely time for new protocol, dealing on this type of level. He called an immediate meeting with all the members of the Skull Gang. As he sat and waited, he couldn't help but to contemplate on the joy and pain that was about to come about. Joy; because of the levels he could take him and his people to. He could provide whatever his loved ones would need and want. Even though Teelee was married to the streets, deep down family was a big part of his life. Now he had the chance to shower his family with whatever their hearts desired. That was his biggest joy, to see his family happy. Pain; because it's more than likely someone might get hurt or die; especially when haters and hungry sharks peeping your progression. Not saying he was looking for one of them to be in that position, but he wasn't going to be naïve about the situation either. One thing he did stand on was, to rock until death for his street family. Teelee's cell phone rang breaking his deep thought, it was Lil Man. "I'm downstairs, I'mma be up in a few." "Fasho" Teelee replied ending the call. Teelee got up to take a piss. As he washed his hands, Lil Man was knocking at the door. Teelee dried his hands and let him in. "What it do" Lil Man said dapping Teelee off. "Shid, I'm coolin round. I'm tryna see what we gon do wit all of these." Lil Man's eyes lit up like Christmas lights as he got a glimpse of the bricks lined up on the bed. "Son, dude put you in the game wit all this?" Lil Man asked still shocked from seeing all the kilos of cocaine. "Yeah homey, we online like Yahoo. Where Thugga and the rest of the team at?" Teelee asked. "They all in route. Pistol and Corey coming straight ova here. They on their way back from Bogalusa. They said it's ours for the takin. Pistol gon set up shop by his lil bitch in the projects down there. So this here couldn't have come at a better time. We official like a referee whistle." "Nigga who you tellin. Lanzo got whatever we need. Dude got ties with the Colombian Cartel and he got big dawg status with the big wigs of the city." "Hold up homey" Lil Man said answering his phone. "Yeah, we in room 3705. Aight son, I'mma see you in a minute. Yeah that was Pistol and Corey. They said they gon be here in like 10 minutes." "That's wzup" Teelee replied as he pulled a box of Keep Moving cigars and a half ounce of granddaddy purpa from his back pocket. He threw Lil Man half the box so they could roll up for the meeting. All the rest of the members of the Skull Gang arrived and were shocked just like Lil Man. Seeing all the bricks in front of them, they knew shit was about to start popping like champagne bottles. Teelee grabbed one of the thick hotel towels that was in the bathroom, and put it under the door so they could get started. Teelee sparked the first blunt and proceeded. "As y'all all can see we been given the privilege to bring our hustle to a higher level. We plugged into the best shit we could get. All we have to do is move em quick. Our time line is a one-week span. From right now, to this time next week. We need to put the word out that the bricks going for seventeen and pump em. I ain't tryna be greedy. We gon break bread and try and keep everybody satisfied. Corey, and Pistol y'all control the spot in Bogalusa. Take what y'all need, set up and take ova. I also want everybody to get a burner phone. We go do all business ova these lines. Don't give clientele none of your personal lines. Put them in bogus names so if the heat turns up, we can ditch em and not be traced. Inform all clientele not to use any government names across these lines. Also due to the increase in weight, our money is about to extremely elevate. The haters and jack boyz bout to be lurkin. We gotta step our game up as far as being alert, and knowing who we dealin wit. Most of all staying cocked and ready for that dumb shit. Whenever anyone of us has a sale, I don't give a fuck if it's one brick; make sure somebody round in case of any jack play. We get em for 11.5, so quick as we move em the bigger our pockets get." "Me and Corey gon take five of them thangs out there to start off wit" Pistol said taking the blunt from Lil Man. "Fasho, whatever y'all think y'all could handle. I ain't doing no trippin. We all in this together. There's just one thing I want us to do. Keep our eyes and ears open to the streets, cause shit bout to start popping money wise and beef wise. We gotta be on our "A" game. With that being said, I ain't got nothing else to say. If anybody else got sumthin to bring to the table, you got the floor." Everyone said no and from there Teelee distributed the coke to each one of them. K-Real advised Teelee that she wanted to roll with him, so she could get the feel of how he wanted things done. That was one of the biggest things Teelee liked about K-Real; he promised himself that she would be official on all the ends and outs of the game.

A week had passed and the work was moving faster than a smoker trying to get to the crack house. Pistol and Corey had set up shop in Bogalusa, while Thugga, K-Real, Teelee, and Lil Man locked the city down. The money was coming in quicker than they could blink their eyes. Teelee met up with Lanzo like they had agreed. Lanzo was shocked to hear that they would be increasing in the amount of keys by the following week. So instead of twenty bricks, they would be pushing forty. As Lanzo and Teelee's relationship increased, Teelee and Selina's decreased. Selina's baby daddy started coming back around, so Teelee backed up and let Selina do her. Besides he wasn't looking for a relationship with her anyway. He considered the two of them to just be sex partners anyway. He also looked at Selina as a real good friend, because if it wasn't for her he wouldn't have been in business with Lanzo. Teelee had been car shopping, and finally decided what he was about to pull out with. He loved to be different, so he didn't go with the typical hot boyz play toys his lil rounds was pushing. He decided to go with the Audi A8. Today was the day his father and him was going to do the rest of the paperwork. Teelee talked his pops into co-signing for him. It wasn't easy at first, but eventually the old man gave in. When Teelee was younger him and his father had a really strong bond. They used to do all kinds of things together. As Teelee got older and got his first piece of pussy, and tasted the streets; he hadn't been the same since. Teelee reminded his pops so much of himself. That was the reason Mr. Daniel tried so hard to pull Teelee away from the street life. He had been down that route, and didn't want to see his so go down the same destructive path he did.

Just as Teelee finished putting on his low top shell toe Adidas, his cell phone rang. It was his father. "Wzup Pops" Teelee said putting his money and cigarettes in his pocket. "Nuthin much my nigga. You ready? I'm outside." Teelee looked just like his father. Everywhere they went together people would always say, "Daniel that's your twin." "Yeah Pops, I'mma be out in a minute." As Teelee was about to head for the door Kyla came from her room looking like she had just woke up. "Where you going boy?" Kyla asked, tying her robe being nosey. "You know I told you, me and pops going pick my whip up today." "Daddy outside? Hold up, I gotta tell him sumthin." Soon as Kyla ran in her room, Randi came out with a Keep Moving hanging out the side of his mouth. "What's good homey" Teelee said dapping his brother-in-law off. Teelee was always happy to see Randi, because above all he knew he took good care of Kyla and Kayla to the fullest. He respected him in a way, because he held a job down and didn't fuck with the streets. "I'm chillin bout to spark this blunt up ya heard me. Where you bout to head to?" "I'm bout to go pick my whip up." "You talked him into it huh?" "You know he can't tell me no. I'm the baby boy." "I already know. If it's within his means. He gon make it happen for your crazy ass. You wanna hit this? Randi asked holding out the cigar. "What you smoking on?" Teelee asked knowing it was probably some regular. If it was green and labeled as Marijuana, Randi was go chief it. "Shid, you know me. If it's good I'mma smoke it. Regular, or Dro it don't matter." "I'mma have to pass my nigga. If it ain't Purpa, it ain't me ya heard me." "Boy get out the way" Kyla said pushing Teelee to the side headed out the front door. "Girl stop pushin me" Teelee said catching his balance so he wouldn't fall. "Well holla at a nigga when you get back. Let a nigga check out ya whip game. I'mma be here" Randi said heading for the back door so he could blaze his blunt. "That's wzup." Teelee walked up to his father's car to hear Kyla hating as usual. "Daddy why you co-signing that kind of car for that boy? He don't need that." "Girl get out the way" Teelee said moving Kyla to the side so he could get in the car. "Why you hatin, you got a new car. Let me do me." Teelee couldn't stand when Kyla hated on him. She had been doing so ever since they were kids. He eventually got used to it, but it still struck a nerve in him. "Baby he using his own money, and he promised to pay his own notes. Besides he needs a car of his own, so he could stop giving that damn rental car place all of his money." "Well that's on you daddy" Kyla said turning her lip up at Teelee.

"Look I'm gonna take you out to lunch when I get back. You gonna be here?" Mr. Daniel always tried to keep his kids satisfied. He knew Kyla just wanted some attention. "Yeah, I'm off today. Just call me when you on your way" Kyla said blocking the sun out of her eyes. The sun was on extra beam this afternoon. "Aight Daddy gon see you when I get back. Come gimme some sugar." Kyla went around to the other side of the car. Gave her daddy a kiss and him and Teelee was off to the Audi dealership on Tulane Ave.

When they walked into the dealership, the salesman that had been assisting them greeted Mr. Daniel and Teelee with a smile. They headed to his office to finalize the paperwork. Not long after Teelee was pulling off the lot with his midnight blue Audi A8. It had peanut butter interior, a sunroof, navigation, plush seats that heated up at the touch of a button, and it was sitting on 20inch alloy rims. Teelee cruised down Tulane Ave. with his sunroof back, feeling good about himself in his foreign beauty. He hit the volume on the steering wheel as his phone began to ring. It was his father. "Hey son, make sure you meet me in the morning so we can go get your insurance ya hear." "I got you pops. Where you bout to go?" "I'm bout to go get Kyla and take her to lunch. Why, you wanna come with us?" Mr. Daniel asked hopping Teelee would say yes. "Nah, y'all go do y'all. I'm bout to go get the windows tinted. I want to be low key, you know. We could go eat lunch tomorrow after we leave the insurance place, my treat." Teelee knew his father wanted him to say yes. He also missed the closeness between them. He was just in too deep in the streets. He couldn't get the grip it had on his heart to let up. "Alright son, I'm lookin forward to it." Truly he was. He missed his son. "Aight pops. I'mma see you tomorrow" Teelee replied ending the call. Teelee cruised down Broad St. feeling like he was on top of the world. Who could blame him. He had come from being broke sitting on Unc porch, to now driving an expensive car. Now he was moving forty keys a week, and labeled as the nigga to see in the N.O. His next stop was Platinum Performance to get the 5% tint all the way around the Audi, even the windshield would be blacked out. He was going to be able to move like that because of what kind of car it was. The police always suspected a white business man to be driving that type of automobile. That was the main reason he decided to cop that type of car. As long as he didn't put flashy ass rims on it, he was good to go. He planned on keeping the vehicle just like it was. It already had a good sound system. He didn't want to bring the value of the car down by putting all that extra bullshit on it. He was going to eventually trade it.

Ciara woke up today in the mood to have a splash. It was extremely hot so it definitely called for a cool down. They pulled out the DJ speakers and the water guns and prepared to get it popping. It was no need to call people to advise them of the splash. Once it kicked off, word was going to spread quick that it was going down. Lil Man started it off as he crept up behind K-Real with a double barrel super soaker. K-Real didn't see it coming. She turned and met the huge water gun face to face. "Don't shoot me wit that fuckin water gun" K-Real said putting her hands in front of her face. Lil Man flashed a shining smile. The princess cuts that flooded his mouth twinkled in the sun as he advised her that he wasn't going to shoot her. Soon as K-Real turned around, she felt a rush of cold water hit the back of her hair. "It's on!" K-Real screamed shaking the water out of her hair. It was all out war. The whole block ran around like crazy, shooting each other with water guns, throwing water balloons, and drenching each other with ten gallon buckets filled with water. There was water everywhere on the block. It was always a group of people that came to a splash not appropriately dressed, and expecting not to get wet. A group of females stood on the corner of Tonti and Touro dressed to impress. Swaying their hips to the beat of the bounce music coming from Ciara's porch. They never noticed Thugga, Pistol, and Corey sneak up behind them. As soon as they turned to see someone approaching them, it was too late. They drenched them with gallons of cold water. They ran off cursing and yelling. Their freshly done weaves and clothing was soaked by the water. They couldn't do nothing but laugh it off and join in the madness. The Skull Gang got all the kids on the block water guns and sent someone to go get food for the neighborhood. The event wasn't planned. That's just how it went down. Whatever came to mind that day, that's what it was going to be. They lived by the spur of the moment motto. As the Skull Gang stood posted up on the corner of the Blade an unrecognized car pulled up. They all reached for their Forties. They couldn't see who was behind the wheel. Thugga exposed the Fortie, letting the person behind the wheel of the car know to reveal their self. The driver side door opened up and everybody eased up. It was Teelee in his foreign flossed out boss of the road. “Son this bitch smoking” Lil Man said opening the passenger side door. “What you just come from picking it up?” “I picked it up earlier. I just came from Platinum gettin the tint did up, ya heard me.” “I guess you wasn’t gon cop till you had the chance to out shine a nigga huh?” Thugga asked dapping Teelee off. “Get off the gas. You know I like to take my time wit shit. I know you heard bout ya boy from the females” Teelee said arrogantly. “Nigga get the fuck” Thugga replied laughing at Teelee’s comment. “Say son, all bullshit to the side. That bitch nasty” Pistol said taking a toke off the blunt. So this what you been duckin off doing huh?” K-Real asked enjoying the feel of the plush leather. “What it hit you for?” Thugga asked contemplating on upgrading his whip game. I put nine stacks down, but the window sticker hittin for $75,000.” “So we eatin off paper plates now huh?” Corey asked referring to the temp tags on the back license plate area. “Fuckin well right. The more money we make, the better we live ya heard me” Lil Man said. The splash continued on until the moon was on full beam in the sky. It was a semi cool night. The wind blew briskly, making all the people on the block clear out. Wet clothes and cool air didn’t mix. Definitely not with the young kids on the block. Mothers were pulling their children inside to keep from having to sit in the hospital all night with a sick child. As the splash reached its end everyone complimented Teelee on his beautiful car. Everybody liked it, even the elders. “Say Lil Man where Corey at?” Pistol asked scanning the block trying to locate him. “I don’t know. Last time I saw him; he was posted on Ciara porch.” “BOOM, BOOM, BOOM,

BOOM, BOOM, BOOM" was all everyone heard, as a black Lumina sped up the block. First instinct of all the members of the Skull Gang was to draw their heat and see what it do. Teelee ran to the alley, retrieving the Choppa that was leaning against Big Head Unc house. He headed towards the crowd that was formed on the corner by twin's spot. As all of them approached, they were all shocked to see that it was Corey laying on the ground with blood everywhere. Ms. Mary was screaming and crying to keep his head elevated. "Call the fuckin ambulance" Ms. Mary screamed as she swung at people trying to come close. Lil Man, Thugga and Teelee jumped in the Cutlass to see if they could catch the black Lumina. It they caught up with that car God bless their soul, because every bullet that was in the Cutlass was ripping into the body of everybody in the car. Pistol and K-Real stayed behind tending to Corey. He was still holding on. From the looks of it, he was hit in the stomach, the legs, and in one of his arms. "The ambulance is on the way" Lil Man's grandmother screamed. "Get some towels. I gotta try to slow the bleeding" Ms. Mary yelled. Pistol and K-Real grabbed the towels from grandma hands, and gave them to Ms. Mary. "Help me apply pressure to where he's bleeding." While they tried to slow the bleeding, you could hear the ambulance from the distance. "Hold on baby, the ambulance on its way." The paramedics arrived ordering everyone to clear out. They checked Corey vital signs, immediately put him on the stretcher and they were off to Charity Hospital. Ms. Mary rode with the ambulance, while Pistol and K-Real proceeded to follow behind them. Teelee, Lil Man, and Thugga pulled up right before they were about to pull off. "We couldn't catch them bitches" Lil Man growled as he jumped out the Cutlass, with the AR15 tight in his grip. "Oh but when we do catch up with them bitch ass niggas, they gon have to get cremated for their funeral." Lil Man's words were venomous. He definitely meant every word he said. "Wzup wit Corey?" Teelee asked. "They on the way to Charity. Come on let's go" Pistol said running for his car. Pistol and K-Real rode together, while Teelee, Thugga, and Lil Man rode in the Cutlass with the big boy toyz. They were tweaking to kill somebody. Hopefully no one got in their way, because it would be a sad day for them.

Charity hospital specialized in gunshot wounds. As long as they got Corey there in enough time, he was more than likely going to survive. The nurses and doctors dealt with gunshot victims every hour on the hour. It's like the old saying, "There is a baby born every day." Well there's someone getting shot every hour in the bloody streets of New Orleans. When they arrived, they ran into Ms. Mary seated in the chairs of the emergency room. Her eyes were puffy and red; she was still slightly crying. Ms. Mary knew the life her sons lived, but they were all grown. All she could do was keep them in prayer. This was one of her biggest fears. Now she was faced with it. "What's up Ma, what the doctors say?" Lil Man asked as he put his arm around his mother trying to calm her down. "They took him to straight to surgery" Ms. Mary stuttered as the tears welled back up in her eyes. "He gon make it Ma" Pistol said. "My nigga a soulja." All of them waited in the waiting area anticipating the news from the doctors. Corey was in surgery for at least three hours.

Everyone sat still not saying one word to each other. Each person was deep in their own thoughts. "Lord please spare my son. I can't lose him like this." Ms. Mary prayed silently to herself. Everyone else had one thing on their mind, MURDER. Whoever was responsible for this had just signed their death certificates. Maybe the certificates of their loved ones as well. As Ms. Mary attempted to close her eyes and plead with God once more; the doctor approached them. "Well Ma'am he was pretty banged up, but the surgery went well. He will make a full recovery. He's just still a little groggy from the morphine. You will be able to visit with him in about another hour or so. The nurses are getting him situated." "Thank you Lord" Ms. Mary screamed out. "Thank you so much doctor." "No problem ma'am. I'm just happy everything went well. Another thing, are all of you here for Corey?" The doctor asked looking around at everyone. All of them immediately said "Yes." "This is all of his brothers and his cousin Kenisha" Ms. Mary said. "Okay, you will have to inform the police of their relations for them to visit. If there's nothing else, I'll see you in a minute." The doctor headed through the double doors of the Trauma area. Everyone let out a sigh of relief. They conversed amongst each other, as they waited for the nurses to finish. "Shit done got real" Lil Man said with murder in his eyes and his tone. "Y'all need to stop all this shit." Ms. Mary still had jitters in her stomach. She knew this shit wasn't anywhere near over. Whoever shot Corey, she knew her boys were going after them. Once beef kicked off, it never died until no one was left standing. "Ma be cool. Everything gon be aight" Pistol said trying to defuse the situation. Just as Pistol put his arm around Ms. Mary, the nurse came from the back. "Are you the family of Corey Williams?" "Yes, I'm the mother" Ms. Mary said standing to her feet. "Okay you can see him now. You have to sign in with the police officer to verify anyone else that will be visiting. You can come with me and I will bring you so you can get everything straightened out." "Alright, I'll be back y'all" Ms. Mary said as she followed the nurse to the back. N.O.P.D. did that for the victim's safety. If word got out that the victim wasn't dead, if they were some real killers; they were going to make their way to finish the job. Of course N.O.P.D. wanted to try and get some sort of information on whoever may have been involved. They knew they were pissing in the wind, but they were going to definitely try. "Come on, one of y'all come with me" Ms. Mary said walking from the back. "I'mma go first" Pistol said jumping out of his seat. Of course Pistol was going to go first. Even though all of them were brothers in a sense. Pistol and Corey were like Frick and Frack. Pistol wanted to go see what it do with them niggas A.S.A.P., but he knew he had to be there for his mother. He knew Lil Man would just make her nerves bad. He couldn't control his self or his mouth. They didn't call Pistol, "Pistol" for nothing. He just lived and learned. He understood acting off impulse always got you jammed up in a bad position. He knew this would be handled, and handled correctly. Too much shit was at stake. "Lil Man you know what this shit could be bout?" Teelee asked. "Nah son, I don't know but I'mma definitely find out. I gotta ask Corey some shit." "This shit ain't gon be hard to figure out though, ya heard me. It's probably behind one of them dumb ass hoe's" Thugga stated as he paced back and forth across the hospital floor. Thugga wasn't talking too much, but it didn't have to be said. His whole demeanor said it all. It was time to slang that iron point blank. "One thing I do know" Thugga said standing in front all of them. "We gotta make an example outchere in these streets. We gotta let these niggas know them Skull Gang niggas ain't playin no games, ya heard me." "Believe me we bout to turn the heat up under these bitch niggas" Teelee replied letting Thugga know he was on the same shit as him. Teelee felt real fucked up because he told his self he didn't want to see none of his lil potnas in a position like that. The other members of the Skull Gang didn't know it, but that incident had transformed Teelee in rare form. He was about to be on some kill first, ask questions later type shit from there on out. "Well when this ground hog decides to show his head. We gon be there to knock his fuckin head off his shoulders and mail it to his mama" Teelee said rubbing his temple. Teelee had a rage boiling up inside of him. "Two of y'all can go up there now. Just sign in with the officer at the desk on the 8th floor. Y'all names are already listed." Ms. Mary took a seat next to K-Real who was in a daze with death in her eyes. Even though she hadn't been around for that long. She still felt obligated to bury whoever was responsible for this. "What he lookin like Pistol?" Lil Man asked as he ran his hands through his shoulder length dread locks. "You know that nigga a soulja. He was sittin up talkin and shit. You already know what type of shit he on. Oh yeah, he said he know who shot him to ya heard me." "Who that be like?"

Lil Man asked tweaking to hear who had the nuts to shoot his flesh and blood. "You remember the lil nigga Corey had to pistol whip behind comin up short? He said that's the nigga that shot him. He didn't recognize the other niggas. Crazy bitch was tryna get out the bed wit the IV in his arm. I told him to be cool. We gon handle that, he just need to get right first. Oh I almost forgot he said don't fuck wit that. He want to be the grim reaper that takes the nigga soul." Teelee and Lil Man went to the 8th floor. As they approached the officers desk they greeted the cop. He gave them a look that showed he was one of them dick head types. To keep him off their backs they complied with everything he said so they could get in to see Corey. One slip up from them would give the officer a reason to deny their visit. As they walked in the door another officer was trying to get some info out of Corey. Homey wasn't having it. You would have thought Corey was talking to a regular person how he was handling the short stubby detective. "Man get the fuck out my face" Corey said waving the cop off with his good arm. "I'm trying to get this information to help you Sir" the detective said pretending to sound concerned. In all actuality he didn't give a fuck. As long as he got a lead to solve a case, because they rarely did in the N.O. You would sit 60 to 120, days and if the district attorney's office didn't accept the charges, you would be released on a motion called a 701. Which means they would release you but they kept the case on the side. Just in case they gathered more evidence, which rarely happened. Catching another case made them reopen the case as well. "I ain't see shit. How you want me to tell you sumthin if I didn't see nobody. All I saw was the fire come out the barrel. Besides if I did see sumbody, I wouldn't tell you. I ain't rockin like that homey." "Well it's your funeral if they come back and try to finish the job" the detective said in an aggravated tone. He realized he wasn't about to crack this safe, so he put his little notepad up and took a deep breath. "Well I guess that's what its gon be, cause I ain't telling you nuthin." "Use this if you ever get some sense. Here's my card." The detective sat his business card on Corey food tray. "Yeah when hell freezes ova pig" Corey spat. He picked the card up ripped it and threw it in the trash can beside his bed. The detective walked out the room cursing Corey out under his breath.

"What it do Homey" Lil Man said pulling a chair close to the hospital bed. "Shid you know I'm a gangsta. I'mma make it. Y'all heard dude, he thought I was go actually tell him sumthin. He would have done betta tryna get some info from them dead muthafuckas down there in the morgue. What's good Teelee? Why you standin ova there lookin like a lil bitch. Come give a nigga some dap. I ain't gon break if you touch me. I'm not a sensitive thug." "Nigga you still crazy. You know it's all love ova here round. I'm just fucked up to see you like this, ya heard me. I told myself I didn't want to see none of my niggas like this." "Well homey shit happens, but guess what nigga ain't kill me. That's a blessing, but it's gon be a curse when I catch that lil bitch that shot me." "Oh yeah son, why you don't want us to handle that?" Lil Man asked tryna get Corey to change his mind so they could handle it for him. "Because the nigga shot me. I want to be the one to return the favor, but the only thing is he ain't gon live to be talkin to nobody in the hospital ya heard me." The way Corey said those words and the facial expression he had on his face made you feel the intensity behind his revenge. Hell he had the right to want to handle his own shit. A real nigga gon handle his own business, and call for back up only when needed. Pussy niggas ran and let the next man handle their beefs. "However you wanna do this shit. We behind you 100% ya heard me" Teelee said. It didn't matter how Corey wanted to handle the situation. Teelee was bout whatever. Ms. Mary stayed at the hospital with Corey. After Thugga and K-Real went up to visit with him. They all headed back to the Blade to tell everyone that Corey was okay. Tiff; Corey's baby mama had just made it right before everyone was about to leave. She rushed back from Baton Rouge when she received the news. When they made it on the Blade everybody was worried so the news eased a lot of troubled minds. Everyone on the Blade was like family, so the incident with Corey had the whole block on edge awaiting the outcome.

# CHAPTER 10

# FROM NOTHING TO SOMETHING

For the past few weeks the Skull Gang had the Blade on major monitor mode. Every unfamiliar car that pulled on the block received the third degree. They could have been simply asking for directions, they were greeted with big guns. Corey was coming along well. It had been exactly a week since he came home from the hospital. He was already trying to hit the block, with his crutches and all. Ms. Mary and Tiff had to threaten him to get his ass to sit down somewhere. Everybody stopped by the house and shared their part of helping out. That also gave Ms. Mary and Tiff a chance to take a break to handle other affairs. A gunshot victim who had been hit in all the wrong places needed help doing almost everything; from feeding them to washing their ass. Corey was in need of both. If the bullet that hit his stomach had hit a little closer to his intestines, the doctor informed them that he would have needed a colostomy bag.

The weekend of the Essence Festival had finally arrived. Lil Man and Teelee went all out getting right for the event. It was mandatory because the Essence was a major event that took place in New Orleans. People flocked from all across the United States to attend the three day concert. Different artist performed each night of the weekend. Deb made sure she reserved tickets on the night *Maze featuring Frankie Beverly* performed. They were one of her favorite singing groups. *Maze featuring Frankie Beverly* were known as New Orleans adopted sons. They performed every year, but all the other artist varied. The concert was held in the Superdome. The home of the *New Orleans Saints.* Unlike other concerts, this event caused the city to go in party mania. Well anything caused New Orleans to go in party mode, whether it be baby showers, graduations, or birthdays it was bound to be a celebration. During Essence weekend every club in the city was open and packed to capacity, especially Canal St. and the French Quarters. It looked like Mardi Gras every night of the weekend. If you attempted to drive up the strip, you were liable to be stuck in traffic the entire night. Your best bet was to park your whip, and walk the strip. Bourbon St. was so packed; you would think they were giving away free money. The event gave all the D-boyz and street niggas a chance to show off their hard earned work in the game. Teelee and Lil Man did it big for the occasion. They rented a stretch white Cadillac Truck for the weekend. Thugga and K-Real chose to hit Canal St. They made plans to hook up with the rest of the crew after the concert ended for the night. Pistol stayed home with Corey. Actually that's where

Pistol spent most of his time. If he wasn't on the Blade, he was right by his brother's side. Corey didn't miss out on any money. Pistol hustled for the both of them. Loyalty was a big part of the Skull Gang. If one was down, they all picked up the slack.

Teelee got Lanzo's tailor to hook him up something special for the night. Teelee sprayed on his Armani cologne as he looked over himself in his full body length mirror. The black Armani blazer fit to perfection, with a brandy colored crème de le silk button down shirt underneath. Black Armani slacks with brandy colored Mauri gator low quarter boots to complete his attire. He sported his custom made Skull Gang piece. Courtesy of Jack Sutton's jewelry store. The skull head was damn near the size of a cantaloupe, with the letters Skull Gang crushed out in white diamonds. His four inch diamond encrusted bracelet and pinky ring had a shine that would temporarily blind you. To complete his jewelry ensemble. He chose to wear his hog head Jacob watch, with his brown replacement band to keep everything color coordinated. He had gotten a fresh taper from Rason earlier that day. The boy was on his shit from head to toe. As he put a final buff on the VVS diamonds in his mouth, he looked in the mirror once more. He felt good to see where he was now, compared to where he came from just a few months ago. He also thought about how long would his run last. With the street life he knew there were high times, and definitely low times. This was definitely one of his high times, but he kept in mind the possibility of the low times that could transpire. That was one thing about Teelee. He always faced reality. In the event something bad did happen, he wasn't caught off guard. However, the cut fell, he was going to keep grinding and stacking his dollars. He knew deep down it was bound to happen. Kyla's close friend Deon hooked him up on a great deal on a condo that sat on Esplanade. The condos sat off the bayou, right across from city park. Deon's seniority at the real estate company she worked for put Teelee straight in the door. It had 2 bedrooms, 2 ½ baths, a fire place that was controlled by remote, and a balcony giving you a great view of the park. The master bedroom had a huge glass window extending from wall to wall and ceiling to floor. It was very luxurious for someone coming straight out the hood. He gave Kyla $20,000 to furnish the place, plus $1,000 for her services. He didn't mind paying his sister to do it. He was going to have to pay someone to handle it anyway. Why not his family. He planned on moving in the weekend after the Essence Fest. Kyla informed him that everything would be all set by next Friday. That gave him ample enough time to get packed up and situated.

Teelee tucked his two twin Glock 40's in his back strap holster. He increased his fire power due to Corey's little incident. Now instead of toting thirty-two rounds, he was holding sixty-four. He had enough rounds to go to war with fifty niggas if need be. The ground hog hadn't showed his head yet. Oh but when he did, Corey was planning on putting him in the ground for good. That was all Corey conversation consisted of. He could run but Woadie couldn't hide for too long; unless he planned on leaving the city. Corey knew it wasn't going down like that. Lil homey was eating all because of the Skull Gang. Now that his water was cut short, he was going to come out eventually trying to get money. That day was going to be his official death day.

Just as Teelee clamped his Nextel I-30 on its clip, *Soulja Slim's* song *Gangsta Shit* came on his ring tone. *"We want gangsta shit-We need gangsta shit-listening to Soulja Slim-Gangsta Shit is all ya get."* "Yes is this Jamal?" "Yeah this me." "How are you doing Sir? This is Elegant Limo Services. I am in front 1555 Tonti St. Am I at the correct address?" the limo driver asked. "Yeah you in the right spot. I'mma be out in a minute" Teelee replied. He turned off the lights and locked the door to his room. He had to make sure his room was secured, because he didn't want Kayla to go in there and get a hold of any of his guns. When he stepped out of his room, Kyla couldn't help but to compliment him on his attire. "Damn Teelee, you look like you stepped straight out GQ Magazine." "I'm in there?" Teelee asked as he turned from side to side like he was on Top Model for men. "Yeah lil brother, you gon hurt they heads with that gear you got on. Hold up let me snap you up before you go." Kyla came back with her digital camera, took a couple of flicks, and Teelee was out the door. Teelee was greeted by the limo driver as he stepped out the door. "How are you doing tonight Sir?" The driver asked, as he opened the door to the limo. "I'm cool, how you doin?" Teelee replied getting into the limo. "Just fine Sir." The driver closed the door, and they were headed to pick up Lil Man and Gia. Teelee hit Lil Man on his phone to let him know he was pulling up in front his door. "Homey I'm outside" Teelee said as he laid back in the luxurious Escalade super stretch. He felt like the King of New

Orleans. Lil Man and Gia came out looking real snazzy. Lil Man treated Gia to a mini shopping spree for the occasion. Gia stepped out in a black Chanel spaghetti strapped dress, with some 6-inch Stiletto black heels. Her long black natural hair was parted down the middle, and hung down pass her 36c's. Gia was a real cute broad. Her beautiful caramel skin tone, and slanted eyes gave the impression that she was mixed with black and Asian. Lil Man had love for Gia, but he couldn't commit again. Gia was a very jealous, over protective type of broad. She would try and fight anyone trying to bring harm to him. Lil Man loved that part of her, but the jealousy he couldn't cope with. He tried, but it was just in her genes to be a jealous person. Lil Man stepped out Gucci down to the socks. Gucci fisher man bucket hat, Gucci button down shirt, Gucci print pants and the Gucci loafers to top everything off. He also wore his Skull Gang piece, four carat pinky ring and his crushed out ocean water blue faced Techno Marina watch. They were in need of some Charmin cause they were shitting on niggas with the gear they had on. Gia and Lil Man stepped in the stretch and was amazed at how nice it was. It came with two bottles of Dom Perignon, and two dozens of red roses. Well Teelee actually made a special request for the roses. It was equipped with a mini bar stocked to the top shelf with all the liquor you could ask for. Grey Goose, Hennessy, Patron, etc. It also had a 42-inch Plasma television and could seat up to twenty people. The truck was a home on wheels. "Y'all this is nice" Gia said looking around in amazement. "Shid it cost enough! This bitch betta be nice" Lil Man replied as he recalled how much it hit them for. If it wasn't something that was putting more money in his pocket, he was going to have a complaint about it. They came off $7,000 for three days. They felt they might as well splurge the whole weekend. "Nigga stop crying. You got it to spend. All that cheese you makin" Teelee replied. He nudged Lil Man's leg letting him know the roses were for Gia. Lil Man winked at Teelee, as he picked up one of the dozens of roses to give to Gia. When Gia turned around from looking throughout the limo, Lil Man greeted her with the beautiful roses. "Thank you Man Man. You so sweet. You just bought yo self an all-expense paid trip to G-World." Lil Man's face lit up at the thought of Gia's definition of G-World. He knew she was going to freak him out the game. "Say we could skip the concert, and get straight to G-World ya heard me" Lil Man offered. He began to caress Gia half exposed thigh. "Boy stop playin. We got all night for that. Wzup Teelee, I see you ova there lookin like you own half of New Orleans" Gia said stroking Teelee's ego. "Don't buck that nigga head up. He already think his shit don't stank" Lil Man said pulling at Teelee's pants leg. "Nigga go head wit that shit. You the same way. Wzup wit Corey, he good huh?" "Yeah that nigga in there running Tiff around like a chicken wit her head cut off." "Shid that's good. You can't find too many loyal broads these days" Teelee said as he thought about the huge amount of bullshit ass females they had walking the face of the earth. "Where Pistol be at?" Teelee asked. "You know that boy huggin the block, like he hug the Glock. He been puttin in overtime. He handling shit in Bogalusa and down here. He got his hands full, ya heard me." "Well I'mma let K-Real help him out. Remind me to run that by her tonight" Teelee replied. He took an ounce of Purple Haze from his jacket pocket. "Guess what I got?" Teelee asked. "Nigga what you workin wit?" Lil Man asked. Teelee pulled out the legendary "Naked Ladies" from the night Keedy had freaked them out the game. That was when she was just plain ole Keedy. Shit had drastically changed for the 7th Ward hard head girl. She wasn't far from becoming a full bloodied Soulja girl. "You tucked some of them boyz huh?" Lil Man was glad Teelee had stashed some. It was really official if he could get Gia to take one of the freak pills. "I told you I was going under wit some of em" Teelee said while pouring his self a shot of Hennessy from the bar. "G, you want one?" Lil Man asked hoping she would accept. Lil Man knew if Gia took one of those pills, it was going down for sure. Gia was going to give him the roller coaster ride of his life, fuckin with those bad muthafuckas. "Sure why not. You only live once" Gia replied. She took the pill from Lil Man. "Yes!" Lil Man thought to himself. It's official like two refs with two whistles. "Gimme a shot of that Goose Teelee" Gia requested. She was on her way to a world she had never experienced before. Teelee handed Gia the shot. As she took the Naked Lady and the shot of Goose to the head, they were pulling up in front of Deb's house. Teelee dialed Deb's number to let her know they were outside. She was unaware of what they were riding in. When she opened the door, and got a glimpse of the stretch Escalade her mouth dropped. She knew Teelee was making a nice bit of money, but the way he was dressed made her panties get soaked. Deb was decked out in a brandy colored Dolce & Gabanna strapless dress. She felt their attire should coordinate for the occasion. "Damn Juvey, we rolling like this tonight huh?" Deb asked walking with a confident strut. "You know ya boy gotta do it big for ya, you know" Teelee replied. Even though he knew what he did in the streets was wrong, he still appreciated what the street life was doing for him and his team. "Hey y'all" Deb said as she took a seat next to Teelee. "What it do Deb baaby" Lil Man said giving Deb a hug. "This my girl Gia. Gia this Deb, Teelee's ole school sweetheart." "Boy I'm not that old" Deb said. She playfully slapped Lil Man on the hand. "Don't call her old, she fine wine" Teelee said kissing Deb on the cheek. Teelee grabbed one of the bottles, pop the cork and began their fun filled night. They smoked two blunts, downed a bottle of champagne and was now ready to get their groove on. When they pulled up in front of the Super Dome they sat and chilled for a second before getting out. There was people everywhere in their best attire heading in the dome. People stopped and stared wondering who was about to jump out the stretch. Before they exited the limo, they adjusted their clothing making sure everything was in line. "Y'all ready, cause the party ain't gon end till the sun come up" Teelee said as he took a few last tokes off the blunt. "It's about to go down" Deb exclaimed. "I could hear Frankie Beverly now, Happy Feelings in the Air" Deb sung out loud. As they were about to step out the limo Deb told Teelee she had something important to speak with him about. "Wzup baby, tell me now. You know I don't like surprises." "No Juvey, I'mma tell you later. Let's go have fun" Deb replied. When they got out of the limo, people gazed over how good they looked. A couple of minds wondered which celebrities this group might be. Not knowing they were regular people grinding for the better things in life. The driver of the limo informed Teelee that he would be out there waiting for them. As soon as they took their seats the concert began. Alicia Keys performed first followed by the soulful Musiq Soulchild. They gave a short intermission to give the crowd a chance to go to the restroom, or the bar before they continued on with the next artist. "Y'all want sumthin to drink?" Teelee asked getting up about to head to the bar. "Yeah Juvey get me some water" Deb replied. She was dabbing the sweat that had formed on her forehead from singing along with Musiq and Alicia. "Man Man get me some too, my mouth is dry" Gia wined. "I love you baby, you know that huh?" The pill had Gia rambling. "Y'all this pill got me feelin so good. I can't take no more of this. I'mma mess around and be addicted. I feel like we the hottest thangs off in here." Lil Man and Teelee walked off. If they would have stayed there and listened to her the next artist would have got on the stage. Teelee knew Deb didn't fuck with Ecstasy so he didn't even bother asking her. Deb stuck with the liquor and weed. She witnessed to many people come in the hospital messed up on those things. When Teelee and Lil Man made it back Maze and Frankie Beverly was hitting the stage. They rocked the Dome with their old school classics. From "*Southern Girl*" to "*Golden Time of Day*" to "*Silky Soul Singer.*" The concert ended for the night, but the party had just begun. They all headed back to the limo. Teelee hit Thugga and K-Real up to find out their whereabouts so they could all hook up. Teelee dialed Thugga's number, as he waited for him to answer. He was entertained with the *Hot Boyz* hit song *"Project Bitch." "I need a project bitch-I need a hood rat bitch-One that don't give a fuck-and said she took that dick."* "What it do Teelee baaby" Thugga said in a slurred tone that said one thing. He was on it. "I'm coolin. We just left the concert. Where y'all at?" "Shid me and Real posted on Canal St. Y'all come through. We in front of Popeye's on Rampart." "Where the whip at?" Teelee asked sparking up another blunt. "It's parked in the Marriot parking garage. We just came back from walkin the strip, and hittin Bourbon St. It's off the chain outchere, ya heard me." "Let me holla at Real." "Say Real, this Teelee. He wanna holla at cha." "What'z good baaby" Real said sounding exactly like Thugga. High as fuck! "Shid we headed y'all way now. You ready to do the damn thang?" "We waitin on y'all." "Aight we go be pullin up in a few minutes" Teelee replied ending the call. Lil Man and Teelee kept the stretch Escalade to themselves, they wanted to surprise everyone. So far everybody was pleased with the gesture.

It was a beautiful night for the concert. Not to cool, and not too hot. The temperature was just right. The traffic was jammed packed bumper to bumper. There were people everywhere walking up and down Canal St. Hoe's was walking around dick chasing in their dick chasing outfits and niggas was trying to get a sex partner for the night. It looked like the Kappa beach party on Galveston beach. When the driver swung the super stretch around the curb, Teelee spotted Thugga and K-Real turning up a bottle of Patron. "That bitch killin shit" K-Real commented as the stretch pulled in front of

Popeye's. Teelee and Lil Man waited for a second before they revealed themselves. As if they were waiting for the red carpet to roll out. K-Real eyes stayed fixed in on the Cadillac "Sexcalade." When the driver opened the door Teelee stepped out only showing his Mauri gator boot. When he exposed his whole body, K-Real and Thugga ran up to the truck giving props on how they represented for the team. "Skull Gang shit" Thugga yelled while holding up his Skull Gang chain. Lil Man, Gia and Deb emerged from the limo joining the others. "Damn y'all look like y'all just came from the awards or sumthin" Real complimented. "You know we had to do the damn thing" Lil Man replied shaking his dreads as he took his Gucci hat off. "When one step out, they speakin for all ya heard me. Wzup Deb, Gia? Y'all lookin top notch" Thugga said hugging both of them. "Oh look, they all color coordinated. This had to be the ladies' idea" K-Real said. "Why you don't think it was our idea. Look, I got taste too" Teelee replied. "You know we had our say so in things" Deb said winking at Real. Everyone that passed had to slow up to admire the group of fine young people posted next to the Escalade. "Girl that's a bad ass limo" replied one girl passing by. "Man Man, that pill got me hotter than Africa in the summer time" Gia said rubbing her ass up against Lil Man. "What'z good, you ready to go?" Lil Man asked pulling her closer to him. Lil Man could care less about the club scene. That pill had him feeling freakier than a porn star with no work. "Nah, we gon enjoy the night. Y'all drop some big dollars. We go have all night. I mean all morning for what I got planned for this." Gia grabbed Lil Man's dick not caring who was watching. "Get a room" Thugga said playfully. "How I'm feelin. We don't need a room. I'll give it to em in this limo." "G, stop playing. You gon start sumthin you can't finish" Lil Man said trying to hide the erection she had caused. "Everything I start; I finish baaby. Trust that. You gon see soon as we make it home." "Y'all ready? Teelee asked while jumping back in the limo. Everyone got in the limo, and they made their way to Club 360. They all had a ball. They popped, smoked, and drank until they could barely stand. Luckily they had a designated driver. Everyone was dropped off to their destinations so they could get their freak on. Teelee and Deb was the last ones left. Teelee rented a room at the Ritz Carlton on Canal St. When they pulled into the carport, Teelee tipped the driver extremely well. He advised him that he would call when they were ready to be picked up. The driver agreed and Teelee and Deb were headed up to their suite.

When they walked through the doors of the room, Deb fell in love with the layout. There was a living room area with a fire place. The bedroom had a Jacuzzi in the middle of the floor. It was really nice. The carpet was so soft and thick when you walked across it your feet sank in. It felt as if you were walking on cotton. "This is beautiful" Deb said taking a tour of the suite. "I know you was excited about the concert, so I wanted to make it a night you could remember." Teelee picked up the bottle of complimentary Cristal, popped the cork and poured them a glass. "Oh no. I had enough, I'm already lit." "Come on baby girl, just one mo." "Oh alright, but this the last one. I'mma pass out on you, and you ain't go be able to get none of this." Deb slapped her soft round ass, as her Dolce dress fell to the floor. The way Deb's ass jiggled when she slapped it made Teelee's dick jump in his pants. "Believe me I'm not bout to let that happen" Teelee replied as he undressed. "This thang to fine for her own damn good" Teelee thought as Deb pranced around in her Victoria Secret boy shorts. Teelee turned the water on in the Jacuzzi so him and Deb could relax and calm their high down a bit. The pill had him on full force. It was no way he was letting Deb wipe out on him. Teelee walked up behind Deb, and kissed her gently on her neck. The warmth from his tongue brought chills up her spine. From the moment Teelee's lips touched Deb's neck it made her boy shorts get soaked. She was already hot from the alcohol and weed, the kiss just intensified her want for him to be inside of her. She was having second thoughts about telling him what she had to tell him. She knew she had to even if it hurt. She wished the circumstances were different, but she just couldn't risk being involved with him. She knew the life he lived. Even though he never brought any of it around her. She was far from being green to the streets. She was well aware of the dangers of being involved with a street nigga in the N.O. When niggas drew those guns, nothing or no one was spared, not even children. Teelee led Deb to the Jacuzzi. As he slid her panties and bra off, he gently ran his hands across her body. It gave her a tingling sensation all over. "Man this boy knows how to handle a woman" Deb thought as she got into the steaming hot, bubbling water. They sat and let the jets of the Jacuzzi massage their bodies. Deb felt the urge to tell Teelee what she had to tell him. She hoped it wouldn't ruin the moment. She had to get it off her chest, it was killing her not to. In the back of her mind she knew Teelee was before his time. He would handle it like a mature adult. Deb took a deep breath before speaking. She wanted to make sure her words came out correct. "Teelee baby I have something I need to tell you." "All lawd it got to be serious. You called me Teelee, not Juvey. What's up, what it do?" "Well through these past months, I really enjoyed the time we spent together. You've been so supportive, caring and kind to me. I appreciate all that you've done for me." Deb took another deep breath. It was hard to say, but she knew she had to. "Juvey, I know the life you live. Even though you try your best not to involve me. I also know you are playing a very dangerous game. Compared to other cities; we just so happen to live in the most violent, heartless one. I know when serious beef kicks off. Lives are meaningless to both parties. I just don't want to get caught up in any of that. So before my feelings grow any deeper and I can't let you go. I have to end this now. As bad as it hurts me too, I have to for the safety of myself. I wanna ask you to stop what you doing, but I know you're too caught up in the game." Teelee didn't have to let Deb know these things. She knew by the way he hugged the streets like they were his child. "I feel what you sayin, I'm not mad at how you feelin. A lil disappointed, but not mad. I just want us to remain friends, ya heard me." Teelee pulled Deb close to him so he could feel her soft skin rub against his. "Juvey you will always be my friend, and I will always have love for you" Deb replied looking deep into Teelee's brown eyes. "I will always pray for your safety. I've been with men in the past way older than you. They could never amount to your level of knowing how to treat a woman. Whoever does get the chance to be that woman, is a very lucky lady. If she don't treat you right, holla at ya girl. I'll beat that ass for you" Deb said smiling as she kissed Teelee on his forehead. "Well since this our last night together. I'mma make it unforgettable." Teelee began to passionately kiss Deb making her lose herself in the moment. Teelee led Deb to the bed without drying him or her off. As he laid her down on the bed, he cupped her wet breast in his hands. He sucked on them like they were mango fruit. He moved his tongue around in circular motions, slightly nibbling on them. The feeling going through Deb's body was breath taking. She closed her eyes and drifted off into a zone of pure pleasure. Teelee let his tongue glide down her erotic water fall. As Teelee's tongue slid down Deb's clit, she arched her back and let out a deep moan. "Aaahh." Teelee worked his tongue up and down making her pull back. She couldn't take it, it felt to damn good. Teelee locked her legs down with his arms. Disabling her from going anywhere. He lifted one of her legs, putting his arm in the arch behind her knee. Her other leg hung to the side, while he played with her clit with his free hand. His tongue continued to move in and out of her hot cozy cut. Deb felt like she was in a whole different realm. "Oooh baby, I'm bout to cum." Deb grabbed Teelee's head with a firm grip, while his tongue continued to work her clit. Her hot, volcanic vagina immediately released its sweet lava. Teelee didn't even give her a chance to catch her breath. He replayed the scene making her cum once more. He planned on keeping the pleasure going nonstop. He wanted her to yearn to feel him inside of her. Deb pulled him into her. Teelee paused to strap up so he could go all in. As he slid in they both let out sounds of pure ecstasy. Teelee's rhythmical strokes took Deb's pleasure peak through the roof. "Got Damn" she thought. "I might take a chance. This feels too good to let go." She knew it was Ms. Kitty talking, so she didn't take hold to that thought. People always say men let their dicks think for them but sometimes their kitty kat try to make decisions too. Teelee's speed increased, as they both were about to explode. They both released their powerful orgasms, holding each other tight throughout it.

Deb settled her body next to Teelee, as they tried to regroup from the amazing sexual experience they had just shared. "You must have been trying to change my mind, cause you went flip mode in this kitty kat" Deb said trying to regain composure of her breathing. "I just wanted to leave you with sumthin to remember ya boy" Teelee replied. Her hair style was out of there, from the intensified sex session. "I will never forget what we shared, and I won't' ever forget" Deb said kissing Teelee gently on his lips. Teelee and Deb went to sleep sexually fulfilled and on common ground. The same way their whole relationship stood throughout the time they shared.

# CHAPTER 11

# KILL EVERYTHING, LEAVE NOTHING BREATHING

As the morning sunshine came through the curtains of the Marriott suite, Gia laid next to Lil Man unable to get a wink of sleep. The Ecstasy still hadn't worn off in her system. Lil Man had been popping for so long that his system was immune to it. He was able to go to sleep when his body gave sign that it was time to get some rest. Gia stared at the ceiling while Lil Man snored like he hadn't slept in years. Gia put it on him so good, before she knew it Lil Man was out like a light. After she regained her composure from the powerful orgasm she experienced she opened her eyes. She placed her hands on Lil Man's chest to give him a kiss, and his ass was sleeping like he had been asleep the entire time. Gia was pissed. She tried waking him up, but it was to no avail. He slept through all the nudges, kisses and nibbles. She even tried to suck his dick, that didn't even work. She thought he might have been dead, but his sudden snoring gave him away. She was still hot off the heater from their wild sex session they had last night. They sexed in damn near every position known to man. Gia gave Lil Man the G-ride of his life. She couldn't take it anymore. She woke Lil Man up with the best thing a man could receive before waking up, some fire head. "I'mma fix his ass. He wanna give me that fuckin pill and go to sleep on me" Gia thought while working her way under the thick covers. Lil Man was still knocked out until Gia put her warm mouth around his dick. He immediately let out a sound of pleasure. Got damn G, you sure know how to wake a nigga up" Lil Man said grabbing Gia's head trying to put his dick through her neck. It looked like a cobra snake was under the covers how Gia was going to town under there. She began licking the head of his dick as she took him slow in her mouth with extra suction in her jaws. She was driving Lil Man crazy. Suddenly Gia stopped and threw the covers back, exposing her naked body. She straddled Lil Man backwards with her nicely shaped ass high in the air. Gia gave Lil Man a Benz ride. Nice and smooth. After they both released, Gia collapsed on Lil Man and they began their pillow talk. "G, you know I got big love for you right?" Lil Man asked as he put his hand under her chin. He looked deep into her eyes to let her know he was serious. "Yeah Man Man, why you ask me that?" Gia sat up because she sensed that something wasn't right in Lil Man's statement. "Gia I enjoyed last night and all the past few days we been kickin it, but I can't play this game no more." "What game Lil Man?" Gia was already standing up with her hands on her hips. Good as she looked, Lil Man wanted to hit that ass one more time before he broke the news to her. "G, I know you want us to get back together. I gotta be real witcha, I ain't feelin it. We tried this before and it always ends up the same way. Shit bout to get real with me and my people in the streets. I can't be going through what you gon bring." "Hold up Man Man, how you know what I'm gon do, or how I'm gon act. So what you a mind reader now?" Gia started putting on her underwear. It angered her to hear Lil Man say those words. She was very confident that she had her man back. "Look G, I ain't tryna end this on a bad note. You always gon hold a spot in my heart. I just can't do this right now. I hope you can understand where I'm comin from, and we can be adults about this shit." Lil Man wanted to try his luck again with Gia, but he knew shit was about to hit the fan in the streets. He had to be on his A game at all times. "I don't wanna let you go baby" Gia wined as she took a seat on the bed next to Lil Man. Her sad puppy face touched Lil Man's heart, but he knew he had to stand firm. The safety of his self and his niggas depended on it. In the streets of the N.O., you had to be alert and on point when beef kicked off. Lil Man knew if he gave into making it work with Gia, it would take him off his basis. She would have been cool for about a month. Then the jealous Gia would have shown up from out of nowhere. "Look if it's meant to be, its go be. Right now I just got too much shit on my plate. My brother tryna shake back from getting banged up and I know when he gets right its go be on. Let's end this on good terms. You gon always be a friend in my book." Lil Man looked in Gia's eyes and she realized that he was sincere. At first she thought he wanted to leave her because he had another hoe waiting on the side line. Now she realized how serious things were. She was very aware of how brutal the streets of New Orleans could get. "Well Man Man, I guess this is it huh?" Tears rolled down her beautiful face from losing her man and the realization of the dangerous life he was living. Lil Man wiped the tears from her eyes and pulled her into his arms. "G, look at me." Gia looked into Lil Man's big brown eyes and felt like a little girl again. Gia felt so protected when she was in his arms, even though she knew he was a live wire. She also knew he would go all out keeping her safe. That's why she felt so attracted to him, and besides that he was the first man to ever still her heart. "No matter what I'mma always be here for you. If you ever need me, or anything you know the number. I just gotta do this", Lil Man said as he gently kissed her neck and lips. Well we know what happen from there. One more ride for the road.

Teelee woke up to an empty spot beside him. As he rubbed his eyes from last night's sleep he recognized a note propped up on the night stand. It was from Deb.

> *"To my Juvey. I thank you from the bottom of my heart for the beautiful time you showed me last night. I woke up this morning having second thoughts. As I came back from the bathroom, I paused and looked at you. It was like my feelings for you were growing deeper by the second. If I wouldn't have left like I did, I wouldn't have been able to. I just can't risk my life. Something was telling me to stay, but I had to use my better judgment. Sometimes the heart leads us in the wrong*

*direction. Always remember that as you continue to experience life. I want to leave something important with you.* ***If you gon play the game; hold it down to the fullest, like the gangsta I know you are.*** *I love you juvey and I will always have love for you. My number will never change. If you ever need me, you know where to find me.*

*Love Always, Deb…*

A smile came across Teelee's face as he thought about all the good times he and Deb shared. He knew all those times were over now, it was time to keep it moving. He let Deb's last words sink into his heart. *"If you gon play the game. Hold it down to the fullest, like the gangsta I know you are."* He put the note back on the nightstand. He got up, took a shower, and threw on his brand new Roca wear fit. He called the driver to let him know that he was ready to be picked up.

Thugga sat in his Crown Victoria, clutching a Chinese choppa with a 75 round clip in it. He was staking out on Pauger St. The block where the nigga that shot Corey use to hustle on. Thugga was camouflaged really good. Seeing that every window on it was blacked out. Thugga copped the car from a police auction. It still had the bright spot light connected to it. No one suspected him out there. Thugga had been lurking for the past few weeks. Confident that the lil nigga Woadie would show his face soon. Even though Corey made specific instructions that he wanted to be the one to handle that situation. Thugga wasn't trying to hear it. If he caught his bitch ass first, he was going to make sure the city talked about that murder for years. It hurt Thugga deep to see his nigga blood all over the pavement that day. He always told his self if anyone brought harm to anyone of his people, he was going to smash them on site. He definitely meant every word. As a car pulled up on Pauger St. Thugga noticed it to be Pie, Woadie's girlfriend. Thugga started the Crown Vic, and took the opportunity to send Woadie bitch ass a message. As Thugga pulled alongside Pie's Grand Prix, he caught everyone on the block off guard. He jumped out in the middle of the street ready for whatever. It was broad daylight, and everybody and their momma was on the block. "Ya bitch ass ole man did this to ya" Thugga growled as he swung the Choppa in Pie's face. When Pie got a glimpse of the massive gun, she screamed. She attempted to pull off, but it was too late. Thugga let loose at least twenty baby missiles in the Grand Prix, before she could do anything. The constant BOOM coming from the Choppa drowned out all the screams coming from everyone scattering. The AK47 bullets rocked the car. The whole block ran and took cover. Some people hit the ground some ran indoors. The car looked like a target at a gun range. Thugga sped off the block feeling slightly satisfied. He had hit the niggas heart in a major way. He knew by killing Woadie's girl it would bring him out of hiding. When one of the hustlers on the block walked up on the car, he gasped when he seen Pie's face torn off. The Choppa bullets ripped through Pie's head and body like it was paper. "Call the coroner, fuck the police! Ole girl ripped up in that bitch."

Teelee rolled down Canal St., just leaving the Ritz. He was on his way to the Blade. Deb's last words kept replaying in his mind. She was right. *"If he was gon play the game. He had to hold it down to the fullest."* It was time to change protocol within himself. He knew the dangers of being involved in the game. He realized even though they had big guns that didn't stop a nigga from touching him or somebody he loved. Goons didn't think, they just went wild. A real gangsta will make sure all his ducks in a row. He definitely would secure all aspects of himself and the people around him. This didn't call for a meeting with everyone in the Skull Gang. This was up to him to tighten up the loose ends in his own affairs. He planned to never expose his blood family to the streets. He was in the game full throttle. He couldn't risk the lives of his family by associating so loosely with them. They would just have to understand, even if they didn't want too. It was for their own safety. As Teelee stared out the window of the stretch, his Nextel walkie talkie chirped through. It was Lil Man. "BEEP, BEEP." "Where you at Teelee?" Lil Man asked hastily. "I'm on my way to the 7th. Why, what it do?" Teelee asked sitting up from his reclined position. He knew something had popped off by the tone of Lil Man's voice. "Come round the house A.S.A.P." "BEEP, BEEP." "Aight, I'm in route" Teelee replied disconnecting the chirp. Some shit just kicked off and it was no time for talk, just action!

When Teelee pulled up in the limo he noticed all the members of the Skull Gang posted up on Lil Man's porch, even Corey. "This shit gotta be serious" Teelee thought as he exited the stretch. "Say Son, homey just smashed Woadie's girl" Lil Man said with an evil grin spread across his face. "Who?" Teelee asked as he pulled his cigarettes from his pocket. "Thugga" Lil Man replied putting his arm around Thugga's neck like he had just graduated from high school or something. Teelee hit the back of the Camel pack with the back of his hand. Making sure the tobacco was tightly stuffed to the back of the cigarettes. He ripped the corner off the back of the pack. Slid one out, lit it and analyzed how they were going to attack the situation. "Where you caught that bitch at?" Teelee asked exhaling smoke from his nose like a dragon. "I caught that bitch on the nigga block. I been lurkin round there for a few weeks, tryna see what it do. I had to send the nigga a message so he can come out and stop hiding like a bitch." "Longest you don't touch him. I want that bitch myself" Corey said with a serious mean mug on his face. "Well this what we bout to do. Say Real." "Wzup?" "I need you to get us a F-350. It don't matter what kind, as long as it's big. Starting today, I want you to link up with Pistol. Help him wit the spot in Bogalusa." "Fasho, I got you covered" Real replied sealing the Keep Moving cigar she had just rolled. "Corey we go save that nigga for you, but we bout to shut down that whole block. We ain't bout to take no chances for them niggas to spend the block on us no more. Pistol after we sweep the block. Form a team to take ova round there. For now, let's go get our chief on." They all jumped in the stretch, rode and got blowed. They were planning on shaking Pauger St. like a monstrous earthquake. They all parted ways except for Lil Man, Teelee, and Thugga. K-Real went to go handle her business. Pistol had to shoot to Bogalusa, and Corey went back inside before Tiff and

Ms. Mary had a fit. Teelee told the driver to take them to Slidell. He wanted to eat dinner and discuss some important things with his lil rounds. They chose to eat at Ryan's. Teelee wanted to eat at their incredible buffet. As they entered the restaurant, they were greeted by the hostess and led to their table. Thugga ordered the steak and shrimp, while Teelee and Lil Man went with the buffet. "Say son, you shoulda seen that bitch face when I swung that yappa in her window. I ain't really wanna kill the bitch, but she was associated wit a marked man. She was guilty by association. I heard that bitch had some good head too. I shoulda got my dick sucked first, then killed her." Thugga burst into laughter at his evil thinking. "I gave Gia her walking papers, ya heard me." Both Teelee and Thugga were shocked. They thought for sure Gia had whopped that pussy on him so good, he was going to be singing love songs today. "Nigga you lying" Teelee said. "I know Gia put that snapper on you last night. How y'all was actin before we dropped y'all off at the hotel. Y'all was damn near fuckin in front a nigga." "Yea, she rocked a nigga socks last night, but I had to cut it short. Shit bout to get real ugly, and I can't have Gia worrisome ass fuckin wit me. You know how she is. Once she gets comfortable, she gon start trippin like always. I gotta be game tight for me and y'all. I just couldn't risk it, ya heard me." "I feel ya homey. Shid don't trip I guess everybody parted ways last night. Deb kited out." "Get the fuck outta here" Thugga said not believing shit Teelee was saying. Thugga knew Teelee was breaking bread with Deb. He couldn't believe she let Teelee's ass go. "I'm serious round. She told me she couldn't risk her life and shit. I understood where she was comin from and we ended it on a good note, ya heard me." "Nigga you think you slick. You ended on good terms so you could always have a key to that pussy" Thugga said peeping Teelee's game. "Gotta always keep that shit kosher. You never know when you gon need that same broad." Teelee explained his actions, and also gave them a piece of advice at the same time. He always dropped jewels on them that way. He didn't want them to feel like he was trying to tell them what to do. "You broke shit off with Gia without a fight? Nigga what you did to avoid that?" Teelee asked. "I just kept it real wit her. She eventually understood, and I waxed that ass one more time for the road." "I'm feelin that. I did the same thang. I had to hit Deb ass one more time before letting that ole jugg go." The waitress dropped the bill and gave Thugga a flirty look. "I got it" Teelee said going into his pocket for his money. "Nah homey, I got this. I'mma meet y'all in the limo" Thugga said heading in the direction of the shapely waitress. "Do ya thang playboy" Teelee replied getting up from the table. Thugga jumped in the limo cheesing like a chess cat. "Damn nigga you smiling like she just sucked ya dick in the bathroom" Teelee said blazing a Joe. "Nah she ain't break it off yet, but it won't be long. I just depends on when I plan on shootin back outchere. I guess I'mma have me another duck off spot, ya heard me." "That's wzup" Teelee replied. "What it do with our hoes?" Lil Man asked laid back across the seat of the stretch. He put in his copy of the gangsta movie "*Shottas*" in the DVD player. "I talked to Carmen one time after they left the block that day. She been callin, but I been sending her ass straight to voicemail. Bitches that eager is a turn off to me" Teelee commented. "Shid, call them hoe's" Lil Man said sparking a blunt. "We ain't gotta get a room, we in our room right now." He wasn't lying. They could have had an orgy with 50 women in that big muthafucka. "Call yo hoe Lil Man, I'm bout to hit Leah up" Thugga said flipping his Nextel open. "Hold up this my part. Them lil niggas pulled off one of our moves, ya heard me. They dropped they nuts, and took what they wanted. What it do Leah baby" Thugga said talking and looking at *Shottas* at the same time. *Shottas* was their favorite movie. They had watched it so much, they had to buy it more than once. "I'm chillin. Where you been at Mr. Man?" "Makin moves, ya heard me. Where ya big fine ass posted up at?" Me, Carmen, and Yarni out here on the lake enjoying the summer breeze. Why wzup?" "Shid you tell me." Thugga replied rubbing his dick, anticipating her lips around it. "Where Teelee and Lil Man at? My girls been tryna get at em." Soon as Leah said those words Yarni and Carmen peeped who she was talking to. They immediately hit Teelee and Lil Man on their walkie talkies. "Hey boyfriend, where you been hiding at?" Carmen asked as she came through on Teelee's chirp. "I been coolin gettin money, ya heard me." "Well, I miss you. I ain't heard or seen you since that night in the 7th Ward." "I been meaning to get at you, but I been having a lot of shit going on." "Well when I'mma see your cute ass again?" Carmen asked hoping he would say today. "Where you at?" "I'm on the lake with my girls." "Well let me holla at my niggas and see what's good, ya heard me." "Alright just hit me on my chirp soon as you see what's up." "I got ya baby" Teelee replied disconnecting the chirp. Yarni hit Lil Man on the walkie talkie soon as Carmen finished talking to Teelee. They didn't want to look to obvious. "Hey baby" Yarni said excited to finally hear from Lil Man. They had been trying their hardest to hook up with the trio, but never succeeded. They knew the Skull Gang were the niggas to see. They wanted a piece of that action. If they had to suck, and fuck they was all for it. "What it do sweetie" Lil Man said with a blunt in between his fingers and a shot of Patron in his hand. "You; is what I wanna do. I been tryna get at you but your voicemail keep picking up. I see I'mma have to start hittin you on the chirp." The only reason she got in touch with him this time was because he wanted some of that mouth and lip service. Juvey said it best, "*Don't get mad/ Don't act bad/ That's all I could do with you/ Cause I don't want yo ass.*" "Well you got me now, so what it do?" Lil Man asked. "That's on you to come find out. We on the lake, so come fuck wit me if you tryna see." "That's what the business is. I'mma hit you up when a nigga in route, ya heard me." "Aight bae, I'mma holla" Yarni replied disconnecting the chirp. "Aight we out here waitin on y'all. Don't have us sittin out here for nuthin. Y'all know how y'all be pullin off acts" Leah said. "I got you, we be out there in about twenty minutes. Just be cool. We on our way back from Slidell, ya heard me." Thugga replied. "Aight Thug Love, I'mma see you in a minute" Leah replied disconnecting the chirp. "Son them hoe's tweakin to see a nigga" Thugga said clapping his Nextel in its case. "I already know, ya heard me" Teelee replied pressing the button on the glass that separated them from the driver.

"Head to the lake on the black side." "Headed that way sir." The lakefront was a well-known hang out spot in the summer time. It was a great place to take your kids to play, or just chill out and eat some crawfish. On Easter Sunday the lake was always jammed packed. If you showed up late, you might have to park three miles away and walk.

When the limo pulled up on the lake, it caught stares from numerous of people. It wasn't packed as it usually would be, and it wasn't empty either. There was a substantial amount of people out enjoying the nice summer day. There were people barbecuing, eating crawfish and most of all laying their stunt down. The lake was another spot you couldn't go half stepping. You couldn't pull up in an old beat up 79 Pinto. You would get your ass clowned. You always had to be ready to make a fashion statement, and your wheels had to be on point. Teelee, Thugga, and Lil Man were definitely fulfilling both categories to the max. They were all rocking that Roca Wear shit. Roca Wear was the hottest clothing on the market in the N.O. Teelee had on a yellow polo styled Roca Wear shirt. Thugga had on the red, and Lil Man had on the green. They all wore dark denim Roc shorts, and Cole Haans to match their fits. Their jewelry was on full beam as usual. They always dressed kind of similar ever since they were young. If one would get a certain style, they would get the same but in different colors. When the driver parked the limo damn near seven parking spaces was taken. Thugga hit Leah on the chirp. He wanted to fuck with her head before they revealed themselves. "Where you at girl?" Thugga asked in a demanding tone.

"I'm waitin on you boy" Leah replied with the same aggression. "I'm lookin at yo ass right now." "Boy no you not, where you at?" Leah asked scanning the area to see is she could spot Thugga. "I don't see you." "I'm not too far from where you standin" Thugga replied. "Boy stop lying! What I got on then?" Leah asked. "Some Apple Bottom shorts, and I gotta say that thang lookin good yeah." "Stop playin, for real where you at." Leah was very anxious to see Thugga. The games he was playing was really starting to aggravate her. "Look to ya left girl." When Leah turned around Thugga opened the door to the stretch. All of their panties got wet instantly as they got a glimpse of how Teelee, Thugga, and Lil Man were rolling. They were shinning like diamonds. Females were hawking, and niggas were hating. Most of all cause the hood rat bitches was in a trance looking at the hot boyz in the super stretch Cadillac truck. It was all good though, they wouldn't dare step to that limo. There was enough arsenal in there to go to war with a few terrorists. A couple of nobody's that claimed they knew the gang tried to come and holla, but they were brushed off quickly. The Skull Gang wasn't trusting no one. If they didn't really know you, you were getting the cold shoulder. As they approached the stretch Lil Man, and Thugga got out and leaned against the truck with the door open. Teelee sat in the limo with the Tommy Gun on his lap. He really wasn't feeling those hoes like that. His lil rounds wanted to play a little so he did it for them. Even though he was a young nigga, deep down he was looking for a woman he could call his own. He was tired of the groupie bitches. He knew they all were looking for the same thing.

Money and the thrill to say they were fucking with some major playas in the game. Teelee yearned for that ride or die chick. A real woman that was willing to love him for him and not for what he had, or what they could benefit from. "Hey baby" Leah said wrapping her arms around Thugga's neck. "Wzup lil girl" Thugga replied gripping her apple in her bottoms. "Ain't nuthin lil ova here." Leah took Thugga's hand and placed it on her hot cat. "Damn you ready for ya boy huh." Thugga cupped his hand so he could get a better feel of Leah's throbbing hot box. "Yeah you definitely not a lil girl, but I'mma see if you know how to use that." "Believe me you gon find out." Leah replied. "Where my baby at?" Carmen asked. "That nigga in there" Lil Man said with a handful of Yarni's ass in his hands. "Why you hidin in here?" Carmen asked. When Carmen climbed in the stretch, she got spooked when she saw the Tommy gun on Teelee's lap. "Girl don't be scared, I ain't gon shoot you." "Why you got that big ass gun on your lap like that?" Carmen asked still frightened by the gun. "You see what you sitting in right now." "Yeah, why?" Carmen replied. "You think a nigga won't run up and try to jack sumthin, seein me and my niggas rollin like this. This here gon keep anybody from tryna run up on me and my team." Teelee replied with the Tommy gun in the air. Teelee's words was stern. He wanted the bitch to know she could get it too. Carmen recognized the two Choppas laid out on the seat across from him, and knew the Skull Gang wasn't to be played with. "I feel where you comin from, but how I'mma show you how much I miss you with that in the way." Teelee sat the Tommy gun to the side of him, but not too far.

Carmen sat next to Teelee feeling better that the gun wasn't pointed at her anymore. "I missed you" Carmen said giving Teelee a hug. She made sure her juicy 34DD's pressed up against him while he was in her grasp. Teelee didn't bother to say he missed her because he barely even knew the broad. "What's been up with you Ms. Carmen?" "I been chilling dealing with my kids." "Kids, how many children do this bitch have" Teelee thought. "Yeah, that's good. How many you got?" "Three boys and a girl." Teelee was really turned off now. "This bitch had a whole Brady bunch, looking for a Mr. Brady" he thought. "They all for the same dude?" Teelee already knew she was about to say no, but he just had to ask. "No, I got three baby daddies. One locked up in Orleans Parish jail, and the other two let's just say they still free." "That's wzup" Teelee replied as he poured himself a shot of Hennessy. "You want a drink?" "Yeah you got some Goose?" as her eyes roamed throughout the stretch. "Y'all watchin Shottas. That's my movie. I got the DVD at home." Carmen said. "That's me and my niggas theme movie" Teelee commented handing Carmen her drink. "Say Teelee, they got this nigga talkin bout he know you" Lil Man said sticking his head in the limo. "What's his name?" "Say what's yo name playa?" Lil Man asked mean muggin the dude. "Tell em this Muddy, ya heard me." "He say his name Muddy, round." Teelee slid over to the seat next to the door with the Tommy gun not too far behind. "What's good wit ya homey" Teelee said maintaining his position and a tight grip on the Tommy gun. He knew the nigga but he ain't know the nigga like that. Muddy had been trying get Teelee to put him on. Teelee knew the nigga had a dope habit. He wasn't about to put nothing in the nigga's hand and he play games and lose his life. "Wzup wit ya Teelee baby. I recognized the stretch, and I came to holla at you, ya heard me. Y'all boyz did y'all thang at the Essence last night" Muddy said lighting up a cigarette. "Well what's good wit ya homey. You was tryna ask me sumthin?" Teelee asked, ready to get this clown away from him. "You still remember what I hollered at you bout huh?" "Look homey that ain't what this is right now. You go have to get at me later on that, ya heard me." "Well when you want me to holla at you?" "Look here Whoa, holla at him later. Now ain't the time" Lil Man said stepping in front Teelee with his Fortie in a tight grip in his pocket. "Aight, I'mma get wit you" Muddy replied getting the picture that he wasn't wanted over there. "What it do round, y'all ready?" Teelee asked sliding back over to Carmen who was watching the movie like she had never seen it before. "Yeah, lets bounce" Lil Man replied getting into the limo. Teelee signaled for the driver. "Swing around West End." West End was on the rich side of the lakefront. Teelee knew it wouldn't be any danger in that area. That side of the lake was heavily patrolled day and night. You couldn't even have your radio bumping to loud. The police would have been harassing you, trying to run your name. When they pulled up to the spot, Teelee changed the movie in the DVD player. He popped in their all-time favorite movie, *Scarface*. He knew them hoes was going to like that. "Ooh this my shit" Yarni said with her legs laid across Lil Man. The stretch was so spacious that they had their own little area to themselves. They smoked a couple of cigars filled with purple haze, and took a couple of shots as they watched Al Pacino get his gangster on throughout the movie. Before everybody knew it the freak show began. Leah started it off. She began to kiss Thugga on the neck, making blood rush to his head. Definitely not the big one. "Say girl lick my chain" Thugga demanded while holding up his crushed out Skull Gang piece. Leah was so turned on by Thugga's aggressiveness. She accommodated Thugga's request, seductively licking the diamonds. From there Leah went for what she knew. She unzipped Thugga's shorts and took him into her mouth as if nobody else was in the limo with them. Leah didn't have any shame in her game. On cue Yarni and Carmen followed the lead of Leah, and began their dick sucking marathon. Lil Man and Thugga chose to bang Yarni and Leah's back out, while Teelee just opted for some head. After Teelee busted in Carmen's mouth, she swallowed like she was drinking a cold glass of milk. She thought she was about to get some of that good jugg. Carmen was sadly mistaken when Teelee buttoned his shorts back up and cocked back in the seat. "Boy what is you doing?" Carmen asked disgusted at Teelee's action. "I don't fuck on the first date, ya heard me." Lil Man and Thugga smirked at they lil round in action. "So you could fuck my mouth though huh?" Carmen asked as she put her big tits back in their holsters. Thugga and Lil Man had Yarni and Leah screaming their names, which made Carmen hotter than a firecracker. She wanted some dick, and she wanted some now. Yarni and Leah was making so much noise that it made the driver sneak a peek through the slightly cracked glass. He thought he was slick; like they didn't know he was watching. They just didn't care; those broads were just jump offs. If he would have asked, they would have let him get him. "Shid, nigga you ain't said nuthin." Carmen said while sliding over joining the foursome. They gladly invited her in, the more the merrier. Teelee hopped out the stretch and blazed up a Camel. He wasn't feeling that bitch enough to stick his dick in her even with a condom. Her big juicy DD's didn't even turn him on. He most definitely didn't give a fuck about her joining in the party Lil Man and Thugga had going on. After the stretch stop rocking, he jumped back in and they dropped them off. They headed back to the hood.

When they pulled up on the Blade, Teelee called K-Real on her phone to see if she made any progress. Lil Man and Thugga jumped out the stretch to go holla at grandma who was sitting in front her door. "What it do Real baaby, where you at?" "I'm bout to be on the Blade in about 10 minutes. I just picked that issue up ya heard me." "Aight, I'm round here waitin on you" Teelee replied. "Alright, I'mma see you in a minute." Teelee clamped his phone in the case and hoped out the limo to go holla at grandma. "Hey grandma, I see you outchere chillin catchin the evening breeze huh." Teelee said as he walked up on the sidewalk. "Yeah baaby, I'm just chillin. Watching these bad ass children run up and down the street, especially Mario and Tori, with they never want to go inside asses. They act like they gon miss sumthin if they go inside." "Gimme my ball" Corey son Budda yelled. "Boy you betta share wit that boy!" Grandma screamed. "I swear these children gon give me a heart attack. How my babies doing?" "We been aight, grandma" Lil Man replied taking a seat on the ground next to her. He always sat on the side of her when she was out in front the door. Lil Man wouldn't move until she went inside. He was very overprotective of her. True enough Ms. Mary did what she could for Lil Man and his brothers, but grandma was always there to pick up the slack when she couldn't. Every time Lil Man asked for something it was no question, he had it. Lil Man was her baby. Lil Man offered to move her out of the hood, but she refused to leave. She had been in the 7th Ward on the Blade all her life. "You need anything Grandma?" Thugga asked with his arm on the back of her chair. "Nah baby, Grandma alright. I just want y'all to be careful out here. I don't want to see no more of y'all laying on the ground like that. Knowing Corey spiteful ass, he gon try and get the person that shot him." "Everything gon be alright grandma" Lil Man said. "You ain't gotta worry." Lil Man always tried to keep grandma nerves calm. He knew her pressure shot through the roof any time something went on with any of them. Just as Lil Man put his hand on grandma lap, K-Real pulled up in a black Ford F-350 with an extended cab. "Aight grandma, we gon holla at you later" Lil Man said getting up from the ground. Lil Man kissed grandma, and they all headed to see what it do with K-Real. Before Teelee walked off he hugged and kissed grandma, leaving $500, in her lap. Teelee didn't care that she said she was alright; he was gon make sure of it. Lil Man made sure everything around her house was tight. She had new furniture, and new flat screen televisions. They made sure she was comfortable. Teelee winked at grandma and walked off. "Thank you, grandson! Grandma love all y'all; remember. Be careful, y'all here me." Grandma said sticking the money in her bra. K-Real jumped out the big truck and tossed the keys to Teelee. "It's official. my people got it out in Slidell. It ain't in N.O.P.D. system yet." "Aight Real, good lookin out. You got wit Pistol yet?" Teelee asked. "Yeah I'm going out there wit him tonight so he could show me what it do out there." "Aight hold it down, cause we bout to shut that whole block down. I'mma call you and let you know when shit good, ya heard me." "Aight baby boy, I'm bout to go get me some head from this duck ass nigga, ya heard me." "You got it like that?" Lil Man asked peeping Real swag. "You know I gotta do me, ya heard me. Y'all ain't the only ones gettin served," Real replied. "That's wzup. Go do you Real baaby," Thugga said dapping K-Real off. As K-Real walked off she hit the locks on a brand new platinum Maxima with the custom rims to match. "You went and copped on a nigga huh?" Teelee asked recognizing Real had a brand new whip. "I pulled off one of yo moves," K-Real replied getting in her car. She sped up the block bumping Remy Ma's "*Conceited.*"

The next day Teelee had someone scope the scene on Pauger St. to make sure everybody that he wanted to eliminate was out there. He wanted to make a clean sweep, not leaving anyone but Woadie. This would leave him naked without anyone, or anything to lean on. Thugga had definitely sent a message that would bring anyone that was bout their business to an extreme rage. Teelee knew what could transpire from Thugga's actions. Which gave him a deeper urge to eliminate everyone on that block. He wanted to get any and everybody out the way that could pose a threat to him or his team.

The muddy water of the game was getting deeper and deeper. They had to take all precautions to stay afloat, and on top of their game. One slip up could cost severely. Teelee was awaiting the call on clearance of the area. He called in some reinforcements for the occasion, just in case things got ugly. Even though they had the man power and artillery to go to war with half the city, not making the right move could cost them their lives. Teelee knew the most important part of war was your strategy. You could have all the man power in the world, but if your plan wasn't devised correctly; it could cause you to lose the war. Just as Teelee was about to light up another cigarette, Roylee came through on his Nextel. "This pussy ready to get fucked, ya heard me." "Aight, we bout to come through. All yo people in position?" Teelee asked cocking the chamber on the AR15. "Yeah we waitin on y'all." "Aight hit the chirp if anything changes before we get round there." "Fasho." Teelee planned to ambush the block. If any stragglers got away Roylee and his team would deal with them.

When the F-350 came up to the corner of Pauger and Villere St. one of the hustlers ran up to the truck expecting a sale. "Gimme sumthin for twenty?" Blood asked as beads of sweat ran down his dark skin. The younger hustler didn't even pay attention to the four gunmen in the bed of the truck. As he went for his stash his instincts told him to look in the back of the truck. Before he could get his hand out of his pocket, Teelee was letting off the first shot to his head. "BOOM!" The shot took him off his feet and his brains in the air. Woadie's right hand man Rico reached for his Glock 9, but it was too late. Pistol, Thugga and Lil Man hopped off the back of the truck spraying a swarm of bullets. Every soul on the block broke for cover. Rico never had a chance, as he gripped his gun Pistol walked him down with the Choppa. "BOOM, BOOM, BOOM, BOOM, BOOM." The other three that was posted on the corner tried to make a run for it. They came to the next block with Lil Man and Thugga hot on their trail. They came to a complete halt as they stared down the barrel of Roylee's desert eagle. "Going somewhere?" Roylee asked with a menacing look on his face. Just as Roylee was about to squeeze the trigger, Teelee came through on his chirp. "They got three ducks flying yo way." "I got em right here." "Smash them bitches" Teelee growled through clenched teeth. Tell Thugga and Lil Man to ride wit you. Y'all meet me in the hood." "Fasho, I got you" Roylee replied disconnecting the chirp. Hearing their death sentences over the walkie talkie had the three in extreme fear, pleading for their lives. As Thugga and Lil Man approached, Roylee relayed the message from Teelee. The three escapees were brutally gunned down leaving a strong message; ***"THEM SKULL GANG NIGGAS AIN'T PLAYING!"***

# CHAPTER 12

# LAY BACK AND CHILL OUT

Back on the Blade Teelee informed everybody to lay low for a couple of weeks. He knew the police was about to be all through the $7^{th}$ Ward asking questions and harassing everything moving. He also knew the money they generated from the $7^{th}$ was about to slow up due to the abundance of police patrolling the blocks. Six people were slaughtered within a week in one area. He knew it was going to be some shit brewing with the police and snitch niggas. Even though the rate on solving a murder case was very low in New Orleans, Teelee always kept in the back of his mind the chance for somebody to run their mouth. True enough they wouldn't make it to court, but it was always that one out of a million. It remained normal protocol as far as their quota that had to be met with Lanzo. Business was business. He had to continue to keep his name good with their bread and butter. He planned on extending territory to a spot Randi had recommended. Randi was familiar with the area because of his offshore job. When work was slow on the rig, he often ventured out to a small country town called Raceland. He went there to re-up on his weed supply. It was outside of New Orleans not more than an hour away. There was money to be made out there, and the Skull Gang was going to be the ones to reap the benefits. They already had Bogalusa on lock, and would soon have the Raceland area too. The loss of the cash flow from the 7th wouldn't hurt their pockets by the least. Besides laying low for safety reasons, he wanted to back away from the scene to rearrange his own affairs. For some reason the statement Deb made in her note sank deep in his heart. He knew there were things he needed to tighten up as far as his personal life. They were knee deep in the game, and he didn't want any of his family members to be harmed because of his affairs in the streets. If anything would happen to anyone of his family members, he wouldn't be able to live with himself. To be safe, he planned on moving Kyla and his son out of the hood. They were the only ones in harm's way. Being that they reside in the heart of the 7th Ward. He encouraged Thugga and Lil Man to do the same. He made them realize that if they left their loved ones vulnerable, it would be nothing for the enemy to do the same thing they did. They both agreed, and began to evacuate their families. It wasn't easy to get Grandma to relocate. Once they made her realize the dangers of her being where she was, she agreed. Teelee also decided to make alliance with Roylee and his team for their assistance. Pistol and K-Real would continue to hold the fort down in Bogalusa, while Corey was still trying to recover. Under the command of Thugga; Roylee and his team would take over the spot in Raceland. Teelee and Lil

Man would continue to deal with clientele in the city. Teelee gave Kyla and Nunew a price range to deal with as they shopped around for houses. He knew he had to give them a price range because he knew how outrageous they both could get. He could afford whatever but he still kept in mind the importance of stacking his paper. He was comfortably sitting on well over a quarter of a million, but he knew how quick it could dwindle due to loose spending.

As Teelee turned over on his Paul Bunyan king size mattress, he opened his eyes to a beautiful sunrise. The view he had from his bedroom was magnificent. Soon as he picked up his remote and turned on his 70inch Plasma screen T.V., Channel 4's rebroadcast was showing the incidents that took place on Pauger St.

> *"I'm Keith Black reporting live from Pauger St. in the 7th Ward of New Orleans. It has been yet another bloody day in the Crescent City. Where I stand is the spot where two young, black males were brutally gunned down. Witnesses say four heavily armed gunmen jumped off the back of a new model Ford F-350 pickup truck, and heartlessly killed anyone they aimed at. There is no positive ID of the suspects. Detectives are investigating the incident as we speak. Right around the corner from here, three men were also gunned down just seconds later. The men were apparently trying to flee from the gunmen. They were caught and killed execution style in the middle of the street. Police believe the gruesome murders are also linked to the death of a 23-year-old woman that was killed in this same*

*area just days ago. If you have any information on any of these incidents you're being asked to call Crime Stoppers at 1-877-555-0000. Back to you Mary Ann.*

Teelee shut off the T.V. and stared at the ceiling. The murders they committed didn't bother him one bit. The only thing he was concerned with was the risk of anyone running their mouth. That was something he would have to deal with if it happened. He glanced around his luxurious condo and was pleased with the layout. Kyla did extremely well furnishing his bachelor pad. Everything coordinated together, from the drapes to the floor rugs. She went with dark chocolate and black for colors. His king size sleigh bed matched all the other furniture to perfection. Kyla went out her way precisely fitting everything together. She had all his furniture specially ordered, and his custom made Scorpion lamps imported from Thailand. She knew he would really like the lamps, because he was a Scorpio by sign. To complete the master bedroom, she had the 70-inch flat screen hung on the long wall directly in front of his bed. She also included an additional 47-inch flat screen built in the ceiling right above the bed. She remembered him speaking aloud about how he wanted his own place decorated. She decked the living room area out with a plush suede sectional sofa, with a matching Lazy boy. She had another 70-inch flat screen on the wall of the living room. She had the previous carpet removed and replaced with 2 ½ inch ultra-soft carpet. Even though the Condo was decked out for a bachelor, Teelee had a different feeling in his heart. He would have liked to establish something with Deb. He knew even if the circumstances were different, her age would still be a big factor. He felt she was just too old to even consider settling down with. Teelee would have been in his mid-thirties while Deb would have been pushing her early sixties. He would have been changing her diapers and tryna hit the club scene at the same time. As the thought ran across his mind and he got over Deb being a candidate A.S.A.P. She did him a favor ending things between them. As he stretched his arms from the wonderful sleep he had gotten, courtesy of his Paul Bunyan, Kyla ran across his mind. He really appreciated how she put so much thought into making his place comfortable as possible. He slid his feet into his Daniel Green men's slippers and headed to the bathroom to tighten up his hygiene. Teelee got up extra early to meet up with Kyla. She had found a place and wanted him to see it. Of course she also needed him to pop off the loot to get the process started. When she told him the number she was working with, he was relieved to hear she had been sensible with the price range. He had given Nunew the privilege to house shop on her own, but quickly withdrew his offer. He knew how materialistic she was. He got Kyla to get Deon to locate a nice safe spot for her and his son. Deon advised Teelee on some secured town homes in Kenner behind Lakeside Mall. Teelee agreed, and had the place furnished and moved Nunew and his son out of harm's way. After he handled things with Kyla, his worries of his family's safety would be over. As he thoroughly flossed in between his VVS diamonds that flooded his mouth, his cell phone rang. It was Kyla. "You up yet?" Kyla asked. "Yeah, I'm brushing my teeth. Where you at?" Teelee replied pouring a cap of

Scope so he could gargle with. "I'm bout to pull up." "Damn you early! Nigga ain't even put his clothes on yet." "Boy, shut up! I was planning on taking yo stupid ass to breakfast, but if you not ready I'll just go by myself." "Girl stop playin, I'm coming." Teelee exited the bathroom and prepared to throw on his clothes. "Aight, if you not out in five minutes I'm leaving" Kyla replied playfully. "Tell that shit to somebody else. You ain't bout to pull off, and leave the money man." "You know what you sho right bout that big bank Hank." Teelee finished getting dressed, and him and Kyla were off to Anita's on Tulane Ave. for breakfast.

As Kyla pulled into the extremely small parking lot the restaurant had to offer, Lil Man came through on Teelee's chirp. "What it do round, where you be's at?" "I'm with Kyla at Anita's, ya heard me. Why, wzup?" "Nuthin major, I was just gettin at ya. Look I want you to go to this party wit me this weekend. They gon have some top notch broads off in that thang, ya heard me." "I'm bout that. Where its gon be at?" Teelee asked. "I'm going get the table. Lock my doors when you get out boy" Kyla said sliding her big Dolce & Gabbana sunglasses from her eyes. "Aight, I'mma be in there" Teelee replied getting back to his conversation. "It's gon be at the Wisdom Hall on St. Bernard Ave. by Circle Food Store. Go do ya thang, holla at a nigga when you finish with Kyla, ya heard me." "That's wzup" Teelee said disconnecting the chirp. Teelee slid his phone in its case, locked the doors to Kyla's car, and headed in the restaurant. When he approached the table, an old sugar daddy was tryna put his Mack down on Kyla. Kyla was grinning from ear to ear listening to pops run that throw back ass game. "She wouldn't be smiling like that if my nigga Randi was here" Teelee thought as he took a seat across from Kyla. Soon as Teelee sat down, pops walked off leaving Kyla looking dumbfounded. "I guess the old nigga thought I was ya man" Teelee said propping his leg up across the seat. "See you, why you ain't walk yo ass to the bathroom or sumthin. I almost had pops trick ass in the bag." "You playin games huh? You betta be cool before Randi catch ya stupid ass." "Boy please, I know Randi be doing him. Why can't I?" Kyla asked giving Teelee a for your information look. "How y'all doing baaby? Glad to see y'all again" Ms. Anita greeted as she leaned over the front counter. Anita's parking lot wasn't the only thing that was small. The restaurant was quite small itself. It kind of reminded you of an old fashion diner from back in the days. A long counter with separate stools ran in front the grill where the cooks prepared the food. There were also booth seats that sat along a long window that gave you a clear view of Tulane Ave. The food was delicious. Everybody and they mama went to Anita's to get their share of her tasty soul food. "Wzup Ms. Anita" Teelee replied with a smirk on his face. Ms. Anita had been in business for a very long time, which linked her to a lot of her usual customers. Teelee's father was also a regular and had known Ms. Anita from back in high school. Every time Teelee or Kyla came through they were treated really well. "How you doing ya self-Ms. Hot girl?" Kyla asked. To say Ms. Anita was in her fifties, she kept her shit tight. Ms. Anita wasn't bad looking either. Her coco brown skin was smooth and flawless. Not a wrinkle in sight. You could clearly tell she was a dime piece in her day. "You know Ms. Anita gotta be presentable, ya feel me." Ms. Anita was a very down to earth type of person. She kept it real, which motivated a lot of people to dine in her establishment. Can't nobody deny realness, unless they fake themselves. "So what y'all having today?" Ms. Anita asked signaling one of the waitress to attend to their table. Kyla scanned through the menu like she hadn't eaten there before. Teelee on the other hand knew off top what he wanted. "Mona gon take care of y'all. Just holla at me before y'all leave okay." "Aight Ms. Anita, good lookin out" Teelee replied. Kyla ended up ordering pancakes, scrambled eggs, and sausage links. Teelee went with his usual. Pork chops, scrambled eggs, and a side order of grits and cheese. As the waitress went to go prepare their orders, Kyla spoke up. "I know why you moving us out the 7th Ward." Teelee almost spit out the water he was drinking. "Girl what you talkin bout. I'm just lookin out for my big sister" Teelee replied with an "I'm lying" look on his face. "Boy miss me wit that shit. What you got yourself into out here that you gotta move us somewhere else?" Kyla asked waiting for an answer. "Look I'mma be real wit ya, but you gotta promise me you ain't go tell mama and daddy. I don't want them worrying and shit." "Aight, so what it is?" Kyla responded. "Look shit done got real as far as beef. So you know how that shit go outchere. Ain't no rules. So before I give the enemy a chance to touch my fam. I'm moving y'all out the way." "So what about you? You ain't moved out the way. What you think gon happen if sumthin happens to you?" "Look Kyla I understand all that. I considered all that shit before I placed my foot in the game. I'm ready to deal wit the consequences that might come about." "You might be, but have you ever considered your family dummy." "Girl get the fuck callin me names and shit. Yea I considered the fact, but guess what. I ain't playin this game to lose. I'm not in it to stay forever. I'mma get me and back up." "What if it's too late." "Well that's the chance I'mma have to take, ya heard me." "Look Teelee you a grown man now, so I can't tell you what to do. All I'm saying is please be careful lil brother. I ain't tryna be wearing ya T-shirt, second lining behind a hearse." "I got this, just be cool. Keep on doing what you been doing. Pray for me." The waitress arrived with their food. They ate, and conversed a little bit more. On their way out the door they said their goodbyes to Ms. Anita and promised they would be back soon.

They headed to meet Deon at the house. It was located in Slidell in a middle class neighborhood. When they turned the corner that the house sat on, they spotted Deon parked in the driveway. "That's it right there?" Teelee asked. "Yeah, it's nice huh. Deon got me a good deal on it. That's why I wanted to bring you to see it. Now we can close the deal before somebody else snatch it." When they drove up, Deon got out of her car greeting them both with a smile. Kyla hopped out and went and gave her longtime friend a hug, while Teelee lagged behind. As long as Kyla liked the spot, Teelee was good. It was no need for him to be there. He had a lot more things to deal with. He planned on giving Kyla the down payment and be out. She could deal with the rest of the paperwork bullshit by herself.

He felt his position was to provide the money, and leave the rest up to the women. Not saying he was unable to handle his business. It was just he felt he could use that time to be on his grind. Besides he wanted to see what it do with this party Lil Man was talking about. He had been so wrapped up in his street empire that his personal life was in shambles. The Essence Fest was the last time he really enjoyed himself. "Come on boy. You moving all slow and shit" Kyla said heading towards the front door of the house. "Girl don't rush me." "Hey Mr. Jamal. How are you doing today?" Deon asked with a flirty look on her face. "I'm coolin. What's up wit ya baby girl?" Teelee replied pulling his Michael Kors jeans up around his waist. Deon was a cool broad, but way out of Teelee's lead. She was what you called a big boned sista. Teelee loved his women thick, but not that thick. Teelee had grown into a fine young man. Deon knew the boy was caked up like Duncan Hines. Those two combinations he had drew many women to him. "Look Kyla lemme holla at you. You see the inside yet?" Teelee asked. "Yeah why?" "If this what you want go head and get it. Ain't no need for me to see it. I'mma see it when you move in. I got a lot of shit I need to do today. You can handle the rest wit Deon, ya heard me." "You that busy, you can't take 15-20 minutes to see the inside?" "Yeah pretty much. How much you said the down payment is?" Teelee asked pulling a knot of hundred dollar bills from his pocket. Deon's eyes lit up at the healthy knot of money in Teelee's hand. "$10,000 plus home owners' insurance" Kyla replied tryna get all she could get. "Girl you always tryna get sumthin extra. Here, that's 11 stacks. So don't look for no more money for another month. Here Deon, this for ya services." Teelee handed Deon $500. He wanted to break bread, seeing that she assisted him with getting his family out of the danger zone. "Thank you Jamal. Anytime you need my assistance just give me a call" Deon stated with that same flirty look on her face. "Bitch stop flirting wit my lil brother. He don't want you." "Oh I smell a hater in the air" Deon replied sticking her nose in the air making a sniffing sound. "Girl go head wit yo crazy ass" Kyla said pushing Deon on her arm. "Why you ain't say this shit before we came all the way out here. I could have dropped you off after we left Anita's." "I ain't wanna hurt ya feelings." "Boy please, the only thing that would have hurt my feelings is you not puttin this money in my hand" Kyla replied flashing the stack of hundreds Teelee had given her. "Aight then. Look Deon I'mma meet you at your office after I bring the cash king home." "Girl come on" Teelee said headed to the car. "Boy don't rush me. All you tryna go do is hook up with Lil Man crazy ass. Aight Dee, I'mma see you in a minute." "Alright bye Teelee, and remember what I told you" Deon said trying to throw her last piece of bait in the air. Teelee quickly deflected by hopping in the car, and closing the door without responding. Kyla dropped Teelee off, and headed to Deon's office so she could get the paperwork process started. Teelee didn't bother going back in his crib. He jumped straight in the Audi, and shot to the 7th Ward.

He cruised down Esplanade Ave. and hit Lil Man on the phone. "What's good homey, where you at?" Teelee asked lowering Benie Siegel from speaking the truth. "I'm just leaving Egg head house, ya heard me." "You got that Purp?" Teelee asked ready to get his morning dose of smoke. "You know it" Lil Man replied. "Aight meet me under the Claiborne Bridge by the Wing Shack, ya heard me." "I'm in route" Lil Man said punching the gas to his brand new 750I BMW.

They both pulled up almost simultaneously. They hopped out greeting each other with daps and hugs. "What it do my nigga" Teelee said leaning against the Audi. "Shid you know me, coolin like a fan ya heard me. How you made out wit Kyla and the house situation?" "I gave her the loot, and let her handle the rest. She don't need me for that other shit. Guess what homey? Deon big ass tried to holla at a nigga." "Shid, who could blame her. You big money. All these gold diggin bitches tryna get a position on a nigga team." "You ain't lying bout that round. One thang fasho can't none of them dog hoe's get a nickel out ya boy. The only way a broad gon get sumthin out of me is if I choose to break bread. Other than that, I lock my fuckin pockets, you can't pick it, or pop it." "Nigga get the fuck that's Juvey shit" Lil Man replied laughing at Teelee's statement. "Come on nigga lets ride. You wanna ride wit me or take yo shit? No, matter fact we bout to christen yo shit. It still smell like it came off the lot." "Yeah I know, but we bout to fix that" Lil Man said holding an ounce of granddaddy Purpa in Teelee's face. "That's what I'm talkin bout. Let's rock nigga. Hold up lemme lock my shit." Teelee spotted one of the drunks sitting on the column of the bridge and summoned him. "Say skool come here lemme holla at you." As he walked up Teelee could smell the

Thunderbird liquor oozing from his pores. "What's up youngin?" the drunk asked. "Look here skool I need you to keep an eye on my shit. Here, this twenty dollars. When I get back I'mma pop you off wit some mo. You gotta make sho nobody don't fuck wit my shit, ya heard me." "I got you youngin. You ain't gotta worry bout shit. I'mma be on this bitch like white on rice." Teelee knew his shit was in good hands fucking with the old head. For one, he was about to use the twenty Teelee gave him to go buy another bottle of Thunderbird. For two, he would be tweaking for the other half of his payment. He was going to be stuck to that Audi like a smoker's lip stuck to that glass dick. "Let's ride whoa" Teelee said hitting the alarm to the Audi. When they pulled off from under the Claiborne Bridge Lil Man hit I-10 from Orleans St., destination Raceland. Since they were just locing getting their smoke on, they thought it would be good to go check on their spot out there. Roylee had been coming along real well. It was bout time that they go make their presence known. As Lil Man hit the cruise control on the 750, he slid Jay-Z's Blueprint in the six-disc changer. Teelee finished rolling up and sparked the blunt. "This shit good", Teelee said inhaling a large amount of purpa smoke into his lungs. "I already know. Egg just copped this shit, so this that first batch of fire." "So tell me bout this party you talkin bout." "Oh yeah my lil college chick told me bout a lil party at the Wisdom Hall. This shit gon be totally different from what we use to fuckin wit. You gotta come wit it, ya heard me." "Nigga I always come wit it, what you talkin bout" Teelee said handing Lil Man the cigar. "I'm just fuckin wit you. I know you stay on ya GQ shit." "Say round I been on some other shit lately. You know nigga got the bachelor pad and shit, but I ain't feelin the bachelor status. I'm lookin for that ride or die type chick ya heard me." *"All I need"* came through the speakers as Lil Man passed the cigar back to Teelee. They loved to listen to Jay-Z while they got their smoke on. Jay-Z's boss type mentality gave them the confidence to push further and accomplish more. "Where Thugga at?" Teelee asked reclined back in the plush leather seat of the 750I. "He told me he had to take his bitch to the abortion clinic." "Son just don't quit huh?" "You know how that nigga get down. Don Juan ain't got shit on homey." "I couldn't do it. I ain't bout to kill my seed. Nunew people tried to get her to get an abortion. I wasn't tryna hear that shit. I look at it this way, what if our people aborted us. We wouldn't be here today, ya heard me." "I feel that" Lil Man replied picking up his ringing Nextel phone. "Oh this ole girl. Hold up homey." While Lil Man talked on the phone, Teelee proceeded to roll up another blunt. He changed the musical atmosphere as well. He hit slot five where Jeezy's *"Trap or Die"* underground disc was at. He sat back listening to Lil Man sweet talk on the phone. "Listen to this nigga here, talkin all low and shit. Sounds like he done found a ride or die" Teelee thought as he flicked his Bic lighting the Purpa stick. Lil Man wrapped his phone conversation up with promises to hook up later. "Why you lookin at a nigga like that" Lil Man asked with a look on his face that said he was really feeling ole girl. "Shid sound like my nigga done found him sumthin special." "I don't know. It might be official. My lil potna Sparky put me down wit this bad lil thang. I'm just feelin her out right now. She seems cool, but you know how that go. She could be cool one minute, and as soon as you rock the boat; she done transformed on a nigga." "I feel where you comin from. Where she from?" Teelee asked. "The East. Her people got that paper, ya heard me. I didn't tell you she got a twin huh?" "Nigga you know you ain't tell me that shit." "Well you go see em eventually. Gotta make sho she official before I start introducing her to the fam you know." "Hold up round, my phone ringin" Teelee said shifting in his seat so he could retrieve his phone off its clip. *"This is the Orleans Parish Prison. You have a collect call from."* "Thugga, Teelee press 1." "To accept this call press 1." Before the operator could say another word Teelee was pushing one. "Wzup homey, what happen" Teelee asked lowering the music so he could hear clearly. "Thugga in jail round." "Damn for what?" Lil Man asked. His high had immediately vacated upon hearing that Thugga was in jail. "Son they got me for that murder on that bitch Pie. They jammed me up comin out Tyler spot. Somebody runnin they mouth." "Hold up son don't say too much. I'mma get the details later. That phone you on ain't right. What's ya bond?" Teelee asked. "I don't know. I ain't been to Magistrate court yet." "Look don't trip. Whatever it is you know we bout to drop them stacks. We was bout to shoot out to Raceland, but we on our way back down there. We bout to go holla at Ralph. He should be able to go holla at one of them judges, and get the process started." "Fasho, I'm waitin on y'all." "Tell that nigga be cool, we on the way" Lil Man said exiting I-10. "Aight homey we on it. Hit the phone when they call you out for court. We gon be down there waitin." "Aight homey" Thugga replied ending the call. "I knew some shit like this was gon happen" Teelee said rubbing his hands through his hair. "Somebody runnin they mouth" Lil Man barked. "I already know. Thugga just said the same thing. Whoever it is they won't have a chance to talk, cause I'mma knock they fuckin mouth off they face" Teelee growled. Teelee knew they had to get the info on this rat and smash em quick. Like the old saying goes, "Dead people can't talk."

Lil Man and Teelee spotted Ralph Benz parked in front his office, as they came off the Broad over pass. That was good because Ralph could get straight on it. They really didn't want to deal with his workers. They couldn't get things done like he could. Ralph was a well-known bails bondsman in the N.O. Most people dealt with him when their people got jammed up. Teelee and the gang had been dealing with Ralph for a long time. On occasions they dropped money on him just for rainy days like this one. Lil Man pulled up behind Ralph Benz. As they got out of the car, Lil Man threw his keys to Sharper. Sharper owned the car wash right next door to the bails bond office. Lil Man felt he might as well get his whip washed, because they were going to be there for a while. Dealing with the judicial system in the N.O. consisted of a lot of time and money spent. No telling how much negotiating Ralph had to do with his people in the courts. One thing was for sure. If your money was right anything was possible in the New Orleans court system. As they entered the office, Ralph deep husky voice could be heard from his personal office. They were greeted by his secretary Linda. Linda had been working for Ralph for quite some time. Rumor had it when Ralph was living his pimp life. Linda was his bottom bitch. Linda was a brick house. Wide ass, slim waist, and a cute face. She definitely caught a lot of attention from the different men that came in and out of the office. "Hi Jamal, Justin. How may I help y'all today?" Linda was very familiar with Teelee and Lil Man by the many times Ralph bailed them out of jail. They had what you call a business type of relationship, which enabled them to be cordial with each other. "Wzup Ms. Linda" Teelee replied taking a seat in a chair in front of her desk. "We got a problem. Ronnie went to jail this morning and we need to get him out A.S.A.P. Can you tell Ralph we here?" Lil Man took a seat on the leather sofa that was located right off to the side of the front door. He greeted Linda with a nod. Linda nodded back acknowledging Lil Man. Linda was very familiar with Lil Man so she understood why his greeting was so nonchalant. Actually everyone that really knew Lil Man, knew when things were serious. He spoke less and listened more. He let Teelee do all the talking, and only interceded when he felt uneasy about something. He was a silent killer. "Hold on let me see if he's finished with his phone meeting. Yes, Ralph, Jamal and Justin are here to see you. Okay, he said come in his office" Linda said standing up leading the way. As the door opened the smell of Cuban cigar smoke lingered in the air. "Wzup Teelee, Lil Man what can I do for y'all today?" Ralph was extremely tall. Standing 6'4 with massive shoulders. You would think he was an ex-football player. Ralph had his fair share of the street life. Before he obtained his pimp crown, he was the muscle in a notorious crew. Lucky for him he ventured off to the pimp game, before the heat of the Feds came. Everybody in the notorious crew all ended up getting life sentences. "We got a big problem" Teelee said as he took a seat in front of Ralph's desk. Lil Man followed suit and occupied the other chair. "Well tell me what it is so we can get started fixing it." "Thugga went to jail this morning, and we need to get him out A.S.A.P." "Hold up for a minute" Ralph said picking up his telephone. "Linda pull up Ronnie Bennett's name and find out what his bond is, and what magistrate court he's in. Call me back when you pull up that information." When Ralph hung up the phone with Linda, he leaned back in his huge leather chair and relit the half smoked cigar that lay in his ashtray. "So what's the background on this situation? I need to know exactly what we're dealing with." Ralph was able to ask those type of questions because of the relationship they shared. When Teelee and the crew were small timing they handled a couple of situations for Ralph. Let's just say some people didn't believe in paying what they owed. Ralph applied a little pressure by sending in the goons. Before you knew it money owed was paid off. "A couple of incidents went down. I know you probably heard about it." "Don't tell me the Pauger St. massacre." Lil Man nodded giving affirmation to Ralph. "Hold up a second. Yeah Linda, what you got for me" Ralph asked blowing smoke O's in the air. "Alright print a copy of his file and bring it to me. Okay. Look he's set for court at 3:00, this evening for a bond setting. The only problem is he's in Judge Hanson's court section." "What, you ain't got no stroke in there?" Teelee asked starting to get aggravated. "Ever since they been having that investigation in the court's he's been cutting ties with people like me. I'll try my best though" Ralph replied putting the cigar out in the ashtray. Before Ralph could look up again Teelee had dropped 10 stacks on his desk. "Do whatever you gotta do. I need my nigga out there A.S.A.P. We ain't going nowhere until we see what's good. Hit the phone when you get some word, ya heard me." "Excuse me" Linda said as she opened the door to the office. "Here you go Ralph." Linda handed Ralph, Thugga's file and exited the office as quick as she came. Even though Linda was never left in the dark about anything. She always stayed out the way giving respect to Ralph. Ralph glanced through the file before speaking. As he closed it, he checked the time on his Rolex and stood to his feet. "Look it's almost 3:00 now. I'm about to head over there and see what's up. Stay in reach because I'mma call your phone soon as I get word." "We ain't going nowhere. We might run to McDonald's to get sumthin to eat, but that's the farthest we going" Teelee replied. By now all of them were standing. Teelee held his hand out to shake hands with Ralph. As their hands locked, Teelee looked into Ralph eyes gripping his hand with a firm grip. "I need my round out of there Ralph." "Don't worry youngin, I got you. Lemme go see what I can do." From there Ralph made his way across the street to the courts, and Teelee and Lil Man opted to smoke another blunt. The situation was fucking with their nerves. When they stepped out of the bail bonds office, Shaper was finishing Lil Man's tires. He made sure they left satisfied. Sharper had workers but he cleaned his VIP clients his self. The 750I was shining like a star on a clear night. Lil Man called it his own personal space ship. It was entitled to be called a space ship because of how big and out of this world it looked. "I see you ain't lost ya touch huh Sharper baaby" Lil Man said giving him dap for the great job he done. "You know I gotta keep my best customers satisfied" Sharper replied tossing Lil Man his keys. "Wzup Teelee, where that big boy Audi you got?" "It's parked, ya heard me. I chose to ride wit my homey today. You know, break his shit in" Teelee said pulling a cigar of purpa from his pocket. "I hear ya loud and clear. Y'all ain't got none of that purp y'all wanna sell?" Sharper was your usual street type of cat. He was raised in the hood, but he chose different methods of getting his paper. The carwash was one of them. "Yeah I got ya" Lil Man replied hitting the locks on the 750. He hopped in grabbed a nice size bud from his middle console and signaled for Sharper to get in the back seat. "Here ya go homey. That's enough to roll you two of them thangs ya heard me." "Fasho, good lookin homey. Where that boy Thugga at?" Sharper asked. "That's why we down this way. My nigga went to jail this morning." "Well y'all go do y'all thang. Tell that boy I said, wzup. I'mma get at y'all, I gotta get back to this money. I got cars waitin." When Sharper said those words, three cars were pulling up to get Sharp's shinning touch. "Go get ya grind on round. We gon fuck wit ya" Teelee said sparking the blunt. "Say Sharp, we gon pull in the back of ya lot ya heard me." Lil Man threw the 750 in reverse. "We ain't tryna get jammed up right by the jail house. That'll be the shortest time it ever took me to go to jail, ya heard me." Lil Man joked. They all had to laugh because it was so true. The police could have walked them right through the doors. No squad car needed. "Do y'all thang. As a matter of fact, pull under that tree by the fence. Don't nobody go back there, but me or my workers." "That's wzup" Lil Man replied. Sharper got back to his business and Teelee and Lil Man enjoyed the comfort of the 750I. They smoked and awaited word from Ralph. "We gotta dissect this situation correctly" Teelee said as he handed Lil Man the blunt. "I already know homey. You wanna fuck wit Mickey D's or wait to go to the Two Sisters?" Teelee asked. "I could wait round. I'm tired of fuckin wit McDonald's." "Hold up homey, that's my phone. Turn the music down" Teelee said flipping his phone open. "Yeah what you got Ralph?" "We got some good news, and we got some bad news. The good news I'mma tell you when I get back to the office." "Well what's the bad news?" Teelee asked. He had a gut feeling he already knew what it was. "Hanson denied his bond. He emphasized him being a threat to society." "Well I was waitin to see what you was gon do, but I'mma go head and call Wayne Williams. He should be able to do sumthin." Wayne Williams was labeled as one of the best criminal lawyers in New Orleans. He got Teelee off of a kidnapping charge a few years ago. "Wayne Williams is most likely going to beat the charge, but I don't know bout getting him out on bond. Hanson specifically stated on record that under no circumstances that he be granted bond by anyone." "Well we'll be waitin at your office so we could hear the good news, cause the bad news got me real fucked up right now." "I'm on my way over there. Gimme like 15 minutes." "Aight" Teelee replied ending the call.

"We got some bad news round." "What happened?" Lil Man asked. "Ralph said that bitch ass Judge Hanson denied his bond." "Fuck" Lil Man screamed as he banged his fist on the steering wheel. "This Thugga right here. I know homey fucked up right now." *"This is the Orleans Parish Prison. You have a collect call from."* "Thugga." Teelee pushed him through before anything else was said. "Them bitches fucked ova me round" Thugga stressed in an exasperated voice. Teelee could hear the frustration in Thugga's voice. It hurt him that he couldn't get his homey out right then and there. One thing he did know was him and Lil Man wouldn't stop until he was out. He wouldn't be back there long. They just had to make a couple of moves. While he was back there Teelee was going to make sure that his stay was comfortable as possible. Teelee had a lot of connects in the Prison. It wasn't going to be nothing to get Thugga some shit to make his time run smooth. "Don't trip round, we on it. Nigga ain't gon rest easy until you up out that bitch, ya heard me." "Do what y'all gotta do homey. I ain't tryna be sittin in this bitch until no trial." "Nigga I told you be cool. We got you" Teelee replied reassuring Thugga of their loyalty to him. "Lemme holla at that boy" Lil Man said reaching for the phone. "Hold on Lil Man wanna holla at you." "What it do round?" Lil Man said taking a long pull on the blunt. "Shid kinda fucked up right now, but I'mma be good. You know I gotta hold it down like a gangsta, ya heard me." "I already know. That's a small thang to a giant. Don't worry bout shit. We gon do everything in our power to get you out that bitch, ya heard me" Lil Man promised. "I already know homey. I ain't trippin." "Look make sho you put us on the visiting list, so we can come up there and see you. As a matter of fact, we gon come down there and do it. Just sign off on it when you get it." "I got y'all homey" Thugga replied. "You had enough money on you when they got you?" Lil Man asked. "Yeah I got a lil sumthin. I gave Tyler most of the money I had on me so she could bond me out." "Don't trip we gon drop a stack on your account when we come down there, ya heard me." "Aight make sho y'all go holla at Roylee. He got 15 G's for me." "We got that covered. You need anything else handled?" Lil Man asked. "Nah that's about it. Oh yeah, go get my Corvette from Tyler spot. I don't want her wreckin my shit." "Aight" Lil Man replied. *"You have one minute remaining."* "Teelee you wanna tell him anything else?" "Yeah tell em I'mma send him a package be lookin out for it." "Teelee said he gon send you a package, be lookin out for it, ya heard me." "Aight I'mma hit y'all up later." "Fasho round. We bout to go holla at Ralph, we gon be down there after that" Lil Man said ending the call. "There Ralph go right there. Let's go see what it do" Teelee said opening the door to the 750. They went straight for Ralph office closing the door behind them. "Aight, what's the good news?" Teelee asked remaining on his feet. All the sitting down shit was over. It was time to get shit shaking, no time for lounging. Thugga's freedom was on the line. "I got info on two people that are cooperating with the state. That's the reason he was held with no bond. The states protecting their witnesses. My girl Rita, the clerk of court hooked me up." "So what's they name?" Lil Man asked. He was eager to find out who they were so he could rock-a-bye baby their ass. "The first name is Stanley Robinson, and the other one is Rahim Wesley." "Get the fuck outta here" Teelee said in shock. "Papa Bear and Woadie bitch ass. I know this bitch ass nigga ain't takin this route, Teelee said. "I'm afraid so" Ralph replied lighting his Cuban cigar. "Well I'mma get Wayne Williams ova there to see Thugga. The rest we gon handle. Just keep me posted on any details between the state and them rat muthafuckas." From there they went to drop Thugga some money in his account, and fill out their visiting forms. It was time to plot, plan, and strategize.

# CHAPTER 13

# TIME TO PLAY CHESS

"Say round, I think them people followin us" Lil Man said as he glanced through his rearview mirror. Teelee made a quick glance to make sure Lil Man wasn't tripping. Sure enough a Black Crown Victoria was trailing them two car lengths behind. "Just keep drivin, see what they gon do. As a matter of fact, just shoot to my whip. I ain't scared of them bitch ass police. They gon do what they do regardless, ya heard me." When they pulled under the Claiborne bridge. The unmarked car pulled right alongside of Teelee's Audi. Teelee hopped out of the 750I with a nonchalant demeanor, paying no attention to the unmarked police car. Teelee signaled for the drunk bum. He gave him the other half of the payment he promised for watching his whip. As Teelee hit the locks on the Audi, two detectives got out of the unmarked car. Teelee sighed when he recognized who they were. Action Jackson and Flat Top. Flat Top was a Caucasian male with similar features to Ivan Drago, the

Russian that played in the movie Rocky. Back in the game Flat Top was a jump out boy. Harassing everything moving. Now he moved up in rank to detective. Why the hell did they do that! Shit was really hectic now that he had a little bit more stroke. Action Jackson was a Creole with silver gray hair that was cut in a fade. He was slim in build, with some speed that would make Usan Bolt look like a turtle in a rabbit race. He was also a jump out boy, just in another precinct. He was more familiar with Teelee and the crew because he worked the 6th, 7th, and 8th Wards. Whereas Flat Top, who worked the Uptown area. Not too many fled from old Action, because the chances of getting away were slim to none. When these two were working the streets, they wasn't showing no love. You could have been caught on the block clean as the board of health; you were still taking a ride to Central Lockup. It was called "Pick Ya Charge." You were given the option to choose what you wanted to go to jail for, or let them pick it for you. Most of the time people went with their own choice. If you left it up to them, you were going and not coming back for at least sixty days. "What's happening Teelee" Jackson said leaning against the hood of the Audi. "I see you done come up in the world huh. "This my people shit. I ain't doin it like this." Teelee wasn't about to agree with his statement and have him looking deeper into his street affairs. So far they managed to avoid that kind of attention. "Come on Lil Man won't you get out and join our little conversation" Flat Top requested pulling at the handle of Lil Man's door. Lil Man cooperated with his request. He felt they didn't have nothing on them. Why not get out and listen to the pigs fish in an empty river. "I see y'all doing big things out here. Must be nice" Jackson stated looking long and hard at the expression Lil Man and Teelee possessed on their faces. It was like looking at stone walls; solid and blank, with nothing leaking through. "I know y'all heard about the Pauger St. killings. As a matter of fact, we got your boy as a main suspect." "Yeah of course we heard what happen on Pauger. We from that area. About my lil homey, he ain't have nuthin to do with that. Y'all just tryna shake some trees. See what y'all can make fall out. I'mma tell you right now. Ain't nuthin happenin ova here, ya heard me. Teelee lit up a cigarette and played the same game Jackson was playing with them. See how statements effect the character of the individual. "Oh so you wanna be the solid type huh. See no evil, speak no evil, hear no evil. Alright let's just take a ride downtown. See what we come up with down there." "What we under arrest?" Lil Man asked. "No y'all not under arrest" Flat Top replied putting his hand on Lil Man shoulder. "It's just questioning, but if y'all refuse we can take that for a sign of guilt." They were really digging, but couldn't come up with no oil. Teelee and Lil Man cooperated with all their request and showed no signs of weakness, which really put a damper on there so called investigation. "Come on lets ride" Teelee said hitting the locks on the Audi. "Lock ya shit homey. Let's see what's good. We ain't got nuthin to hide. They could ask till they tongue fall out they mouth. Its gon be the same response from me. I don't know shit." They hopped in the unmarked car and headed to the Homicide Division on Tulane and Broad, which was located right behind the House of Detention.

Many know it as H.O.D. Ole Parish Prison and H.O.D. mostly housed the like of murders, kidnappers, and armed robbers. All throughout the day inmates were pulled out of their dorms, and brought down to Homicide for questioning. Lil Man and Teelee were put in two different interrogation rooms. They had the impression that if they applied enough pressure, they could try to convince the other that his potna was rating him out. They were sadly mistaken with these two. The Skull Gang had a pledge between each other; "Death before Dishonor." No matter how many years they would be facing in prison, they wouldn't fold under any circumstances. Back in interrogation room #1, Jackson tried every trick in the book to try and pry something out of Teelee. "Look we know you and your little clique are responsible for those murders on Pauger St." Jackson stated with his Glock 9 sitting on the table pointed directly at Teelee. "This nigga done watch too much Menace to Society" Teelee thought as he retrieved his cigarettes from his pocket. "You mind if I smoke?" Teelee asked. "Nah go ahead. You know what, we'll have a smoke together" Jackson replied pulling his cigarettes from his shirt pocket. "Look Teelee, Lil Man already gave up. You betta start talking, or you're going to be left holding all the weight." "Look here Jackson, you could miss me with that bullshit. I ain't tryna hear that shit. You think a nigga not hip to y'all tactics. Even if what your sayin is true. I'm still not tellin you shit, cause I don't know shit. I'm allergic to cheese bruh. You might as well go try and feed that shit to somebody else." "You know the minimum on murder is life right?" Jackson asked in between puffs. He scanned

Teelee's facial expression as if saying those words would shake Teelee. Teelee took a long pull off his cigarette and let out a mild laugh. "I don't give a lovely fuck what the minimum is. The judge gon have to do what he gotta do. I'm fold proof my nigga. You waistin ya time." At that moment Teelee stretched back in his chair. Cool, calm, and collective. While Jackson appeared disgusted at Teelee's arrogance. "Look I'll be back. I see you need a little time to think about this. When I get back you better be ready to tell me something, or it's no more talk. When I get what I need, all deals are off the table. I'mma be shooting to put you and your crew away for life" Jackson said frustrated with Teelee. Teelee smirked and blew smoke in Jackson's direction. "Do what you gotta do. It's gon be the same results when you get back playa." Jackson walked out of the interrogation room slamming the door behind him. "Look you stupid muthafucka. Your potna is in there telling God on Jesus, and you wanna sit here and act stubborn" Flat Top said through clenched teeth. Lil Man had been ignoring him through most of his interrogation. A couple of times he nodded off. Lil Man was doing a great job of pissing Flat Top off. That was his goal. He knew pissed off, desperate for you to talk police didn't have shit. "Man look, you ain't gettin nowhere. You might as well save ya breath, and go eat you a donut or sumthin." "You think you a tough guy huh! Well I'll see how tough you are when the judge bangs that gavel, and say life." "I'm Ford tough nigga. You know how I know fasho you ain't got shit? For one we not under arrest, and for two, cops that have evidence don't beg for information." Lil Man's last statement hit a home run. By the deep breath Flat Top took, he knew he pushed the right button. They didn't have shit, but assumptions. A thought ran across Lil Man's mind. Why they didn't threaten them with the fact that they had cooperation with Woadie and Papa Bear. It quickly dawned on him. They ain't gon reveal that because they trying to protect them rating muthafuckas. "We got a plan for that shit though" Lil Man thought to himself. "The only lead they do have is bout to be "Done Dada." They really ain't gon have shit" Lil Man thought. "You know what Flat Top. You and Jackson both could suck my dick. Y'all ain't got shit. When you gon be finish with this bullshit, so called investigation. I'm ready to go. I got shit to do, like get some pussy. Sumthin you may not be familiar wit." "Fuck You! I guarantee if it's the last thing I do, I'mma take you bitches down" Flat Top yelled while slamming his fist down on the table. "Go for it" Lil man replied quoting a scene from "Rocky" the movie. Flat Top stared Lil Man down as he exited the interrogation room. Lil Man propped his feet up and let out a laugh of victory. He knew he had Flat Top ready to kill him. "What you got?" Jackson asked. "That lil bitch ain't saying shit. This gone be harder than I thought" Flat Top commented. "Well I got the same results. Don't worry though, we got our cats in the bag. They gonna be fucked up when they see our two star witnesses." "I guess we gotta let em go then huh?" Flat Top asked. "Yeah for now, but not for long" Jackson responded. As Teelee and Lil Man walked out of the police station they looked back to see Flat Top and Jackson waving bye. Jackson even hollered, "See you soon! Real soon!" Teelee flipped his middle finger at them as they walked off. "Picture that bitch Flat Top tried to tell me you was runnin ya mouth son." "Jackson tried that same shit on me. They need to get some new tricks, that shit there played out ya heard me." "I already know. They thought they was fuckin wit some amateurs." "I know one thang, we ain't gotta worry about them chumps comin at us like that no more. One thing fasho, they gon be tryin all kinds of other shit. We gotta watch how we movin outchere. Especially when we meet clientele. We don't want them opening up a new can of worms on us, ya heard me" Teelee explained. "You right round. So how we gon play this shit?" Lil Man asked. "First I'mma meet wit Lanzo. I gotta let him know the deal so we could change our way of transacting. I don't wanna bring no heat on him." "Aight do ya thang. After you handle that we need to call a meetin and let everybody know the deal. When you plannin on meetin wit Lanzo?" "Man A.S.A.P." From there they called a cab to bring them back to their cars. It was time to cover their tracks. Definitely not time to be wasted. Jackson and Flat Top were on the prowl. They had to be ready for whatever they had up their sleeves.

Teelee arranged a meeting with Lanzo early the next morning. When Teelee stated that it was urgent, Lanzo cleared his schedule and agreed to attend. Instead of meeting at Lanzo's restaurant Teelee opted to change meeting places. Just in case Jackson and Flat Top decided on doing a little surveillance. He decided to invite Lanzo over to his spot. The more secluded the better. After they left the police station, they went and purchased new cell phone numbers. They used anonymous names, they couldn't risk their phones being tapped. Jackson and Flat Top were real desperate. Teelee sat back on his suede sectional sofa, puffing on his morning dose of purpa. He decided to watch the rebroadcast of Channel 4's news. He tried to catch the news as much as possible to catch the happenings in the streets. The News, CNN, and ESPN was the only stations he watched when he found time. As the meteorologist predicted how hot it would be, Teelee's cell phone rang. Breaking the trance, he sat in. "Teelee I'm on my way up" Lanzo said in his heavy Colombian accent. "Aight I'm waitin on you" Teelee replied ending the call. Teelee gave Kyla the Audi last night. He got her to drop him off at the condo in her car. He made sure to stay on the rearview to peep if someone was trailing them. He planned on posting up at his spot until he got things squared away with Lanzo. Even if Jackson and Flat Top were some where lurking, they wouldn't be able to locate him. Teelee made sure that every move he made was well thought out. One slip up could cost him dearly. Teelee got up and went to pour himself a glass of O.J. Soon as he opened the refrigerator, the doorbell rang. He closed the refrigerator door and went to let Lanzo in. As usual, Lanzo was cleaner than the Board of Health. This time he was on a more casual vibe. Ralph Lauren purple label from head to toe. Selina really kept him in the loop as far as what's hot on the streets. "Come in and make ya self comfortable" Teelee said stepping aside to let Lanzo in. "This a pretty nice spot you got here my friend. I see your spending your money wisely." "Yeah, I feel if I'mma splurge, I should do it where I lay my head at ya heard me." "Yeah I see what you're saying. Smart man, but always remember to invest also. Make your money work for you." Lanzo had been dropping jewels on Teelee every time they met up. Teelee listened attentively as Lanzo shared his sound advice. Seeing that Lanzo was well established, who better to receive advice from. The man was successful in both areas of life; legal and illegal. He had to be doing something right. "You want sumthin to drink Lanzo?" Teelee asked grabbing the bottle of O.J. out of the refrigerator. "Nah I'm cool. Now what's going on that was so urgent I had to clear my golfing date with my colleagues?" Lanzo asked, taking a seat on the sofa. Teelee lowered the T.V. so he could explain the situation. "There was something that had to be taken care of. In the midst of solving my little problem; I accumulated another one. One of my potnas locked up on one of the murder charges on Pauger St. The police suspectin my crew to be responsible for it." "So what you need legal help or something?" Lanzo asked. "Nah I'm pullin in enough to cover all that. I just need to change our method of transaction. I ain't tryna get you pulled into this shit." "Well Teelee I'm glad you brought this to my attention before it was too late." "I told you I'mma deal straight up. I ain't gon never leave you in the blind or draw heat on you. You have my loyalty for life. You've given me a chance to give me and my fam a betta life. It's Death before Dishonor ova here ya heard me." "I know Teelee that's why I gave you the opportunity, because of what I felt about you. I don't just go around giving those opportunities away you know." "I already know Lanzo." "So what do you have in mind as far as transactions?" Lanzo asked. "I'mma use my secret weapon to do the pickups. She all the way off the radar, she won't draw no heat. I keep her off the scene for those type of purposes." "Okay if you can trust her, I trust your judgment. "What about our regular meetings" Lanzo asked. "I'll still handle that, but I wanna change locations every time to keep things tricky. I don't wanna put you in jeopardy." "So what is there someone harassing you all?" "These two bullshit jump out boyz; turned detectives. They familiar with us from patrolling our neighborhood. They feel we were definitely the ones that pulled the shit off." "Are you talking about those murders that happen a couple of weeks ago?" Lanzo asked. "Yeah that's the ones" Teelee replied. "Y'all really caused some havoc. Remind me of me in my younger days." "Nah Lanzo. I think you and yo people a little bit more brutal. Y'all be bout cutting a muthafucka head off and shit." "Sometimes you gotta set those type of examples. How do you say it Teelee, "Ya Heard Me?" Teelee broke out into laughter. Lanzo had to laugh himself. "Say Lanzo you crazy man. You one of the hippest Colombian's I ever met." "Well Selina tries to keep me up to date on the generational change. I don't wanna be behind on time, you know." "I feel that, but back to the business at hand. We call the two detectives "Action Jackson" and "Flat Top." They real names are Charles Henry and Bobby Clark." Lanzo logged the names into the organizer of his blackberry and got up headed towards the door. That's one thing about Lanzo, he didn't stay still for long. After all business was squared away, he vacated the premises immediately. "Look I'mma have my people handle these detectives. You just handle your end." "I got you Lanzo, don't trip. Oh yeah hold up."

Teelee ran to his bedroom retrieving a medium size black bag. As he returned, he tossed the bag to Lanzo. "This for the package last week." "Damn Teelee that was three days ago. Y'all really moving fast huh?" Lanzo asked opening the bag taking a glance at the neatly stacked money. "Ever since we took ova that area in Raceland, business been booming" Teelee replied. "Well keep up the good work and remain alert like you are. When are you going to arrange another pick up?" "Shid today. I just wanted to get this squared away before anything." "Okay I will alert Kia of the change in plans. Just make sure your girl is straight." "Don't worry I got her. She's official. That's my lil protégé." "Alright I'mma see you soon Teelee." From there Lanzo went his way, while Teelee called Kyla to bring him his car.

"Yeah what's good homey?" Teelee asked pulling away from Kyla's house. "Shid I'm posted up waitin on you" Lil Man replied. "Look call everybody and tell em we go meet up at Ray's in an hour." "Aight I got you covered. Oh yeah Corey got cleared from the doctor today. He officially back on the scene ya heard me." "Fasho I'mma see y'all in a minute" Teelee replied disconnecting the call. He planned on shooting to Ray's before everyone made it there. He wanted to make sure Ray didn't have anything going on. With a man of Ray's caliber, he could have had a money scheme brewing at any given moment. As Teelee pulled into the parking lot of the pool hall, he recognized the normal people to be present. Every day around 12:00, a couple of regulars came through and shot a couple of games. Ray opened the pool hall at 12:00 on the weekdays and 7:00 at night on the weekends. When Teelee walked through the doors of the pool hall he saw Ray standing behind the bar as usual. "What it do Ray baaby" Teelee asked as he approached the bar area. "Nuthin much, just finish hittin on the dice" Ray replied shaking the lucky dice he had just hit with. "Damn I missed it. Who was shootin?" Teelee asked taking a seat on the bar stool. "Bald head, Scott, and Wayne. They all left claiming to go get some more money. If they come back, we could pop it off again. I want some of yo money anyway. You hit me last time remember." "Yeah I treated myself to a lil shoppin spree off you." Teelee replied. "How much you hit for again?" Ray asked pulling two Heinekens from the deep freezer. "Bout $2500.0" Teelee replied taking one of the cold Heinekens from Ray. "Yeah I remember that night like yesterday. I lost like $10,000. Sharon had a bitch fit when I went inside. I still hear bullshit behind that. So son, what brings you in this early? You know I don't usually see you till after dark." "Me and my people having a meetin. What betta spot to have it than here." "Well you already know y'all are welcome to the back. How's everything been going anyway?" Ray asked taking a sip off of his Heineken. "Everything been cool up until now. Thugga in jail on a murder charge, and I got these pussy ass cops on my back. I felt it was time to change how we been movin, ya heard me." "That's good, you always gotta be a step ahead of them police. You doing right son. So what time y'all supposed to have y'all meetin?" Ray asked as he wiped the top of the bar down. "Everybody should be here in a minute." "How's Corey coming along?" "Shid he gon be here. The doctor cleared him today."

"That's good. I know next time he gon be on his game after going through that." "Yeah that boy on some other shit." Teelee had one more Heineken. As soon as he swigged down the last of it, every member of the Skull Gang was walking through the doors of the pool hall. Corey was in the lead of the pack. He had slimed up a bit due to the shot he took to the stomach. The Wilson boys looked like identical twins. The only thing that separated them was their different skin tones. They all had baby faces, but souls of stone cold killers. The sternness in Corey eyes showed that he was bout business and nothing else. All of them greeted Ray. Teelee led everyone to the back. Like always when a meeting was called, it was strictly about business. No time for pleasure now with the police trying to bring heat to their mix. They all circled around Ray's customized pool table. For a minute, no one spoke. Everybody had a serious aura about themselves. It was one thing on all their minds; getting their shit tight. Teelee broke the silence in the air with the break of the pool balls. As he chalked his pool stick and prepared to take a shot at the nine ball, he spoke up. "Well fam y'all know why we're here. Shit bout to get real in these streets. I'm not talkin beef either. Jackson and Flat Top are desperate. They gon try any and everything to bring us down." "What's good wit Thugga?" K-Real asked interrupting Teelee's last statement. "He straight ya heard me. Me and Lil Man got an appointment to meet up with Wayne Williams next week. We gon see if we could still get him out on bond. For now, I'mma meet up wit my people down in the Parish and get him some shit. That should make his wait a lil easy, if you know what I mean." "What's the word on the rats?" Corey asked. "I got Ralph on them. Woadie still hidin out, and Papa Bear just don't know we know how he gettin down. We gon off both of em soon as the time presents itself." "Soon as you get word on dude, get at me. I'm tweakin to kill that bitch" Corey stated. "Don't worry my nigga I got you. Pistol how everything doin in Bogalusa"? Teelee asked. "Shid how fast I been puttin them stacks in ya hands" Pistol replied. "Yeah nigga you did come back fast. Lanzo was surprised when I gave him this week's issue. Other than that, no other problems?" "Nah me and Real been gettin it in." "Aight y'all do y'all cause ain't no heat in y'all area. Me and Lil Man the ones gotta watch our ass. We went and cop new burner phones. I want y'all to do the same just in case them bitches try to tap our lines." "Excuse me fellas" Ray said entering the back. "Do y'all want a drink or something?" They all ordered their drinks giving their meeting a short intermission. Even though Ray was a close friend, they kept Skull Gang business between themselves. It was a sworn rule within the crew. No offense to Ray, it was just how their standards were set. You could have been a close relative; you still wouldn't be exposed to the deep secrets within their organization. To many people knowing what's going on leaves you vulnerable. As Ray finished delivering their drinks, they tipped him extremely well. That was the least they could do seeing as though they didn't have to pay to use the back room. "Corey what you gon do, go back to Bogalusa or stay down here wit me and Teelee?" Lil Man sipped his drink awaiting a response from Corey. For a minute Corey stood silent. He spoke up in a demanding tone. "I'm down here. I wanna be on hand when it's time to handle that bitch nigga." Corey soul seemed like it couldn't rest until he got his payback. That was understandable seeing that the little nigga put him out the game for weeks. "Real I got sumthin important I need for you to do" Teelee said. "What it do baby boy?" "You gon be the one doin the pickups from now on. I already arranged it with Lanzo, it's all good on his end. One thang, when you go don't speak at all. Just hit the locks and let Kia do what he gotta do. Ya feel me." "I got you baby boy. When I'mma start?" Real asked. "Today, after we finish up here. I'mma follow you just to make sure shit good." "Aight" Real responded. After they concluded their meeting, Teelee followed K-Real to make the pickup. Teelee sat back in the rented Ford Taurus, observing how Real handled the situation. As she entered the hanger of the clear port, the black H2 trailed behind. Just as quick as they entered, they were coming out in the same instance. Without stopping K-Real pulled out of the lot with Teelee right behind her. They headed to their designated area to distribute the coke. Things went really well, which made Teelee confident in his decision of giving K-Real the assignment.

# CHAPTER 14

# SOMETHING ABOUT THOSE EYEZ

Tonight was the night of the big party Teelee had been anticipating. It had been a while since he had the chance to get away from the business side of life. He planned on being his usual self tonight. Seeing as though he had to be inconspicuous most of the time. Teelee and Lil Man switched rental cars every three days, and only moved when money called. Both of them were in need of some time to just chill. Things were running smooth with their street empire. The only thing that wasn't right was their personal affairs. Tonight was definitely the night to fill the void they had. Teelee and Lil Man pulled up to the Wisdom Hall one behind the other. Lil Man's smoke gray 750I BMW and Teelee's Audi A8 drew a crowd of spectators. As the doors to the foreign beauty's opened it was like watching a Hollywood red carpet event. Teelee stepped out revealing his high top red Prada tennis shoes. He threw the valet attendant his car keys, and tipped him very generously; letting him know to be careful with his whip. Teelee went with for a casual style tonight.

His red, white, and blue Ralph Lauren Polo fit him nicely; not to baggy, not to tight. His denim blue Evsul jeans were slightly tucked in the back of his Prada tennis shoes. Showing a glimpse of the shoe. The boy was so icy he could have chilled every drink in the party. His Skull Gang piece glimmered as it swung back and forth with every move he made. The rubies in the eyes of the skull head twinkled, making them look like flashes of red light. His Cartier watch, pinky ring, and diamond flooded bracelet sealed the deal; giving him the shine of an angel. Lil Man stepped out on his "A" game as well. He sported his black and silver LRG button up, with the jeans to match. He also had on some black high top Prada tennis shoes. He definitely didn't let Teelee out do him. His ice game was sickening. He wore his Skull Gang piece, with his Jacob & Co. hog head watch. He also had his pinky ring and his 2 ½ inch diamond encrusted bracelet.

The night was a beautiful night to step out fly. The stars shined bright in the sky, illuminating the diamonds they adorned. Seeing that it was 1:30 in the morning, the party was still in full swing. St. Bernard Ave. was cluttered with traffic like it usually was. It was known as the strip, because of the four different clubs lined all down the Ave. The younger crowd mostly flocked to a club called the "Duck Off". A club known for its nonstop bounce music. Even though it was considerably small, it stayed jammed pack. It was a real wild atmosphere within the confines of the club. Something the younger crowd seemed to really enjoy. The club stood on its famous motto, "What goes on in the Duck Off, stays in the Duck Off."

"New Edition" and the "Poboyz" were the clubs for the more civilized adults. New Edition and the Poboyz went down as well, they just didn't let the youngsters in. The strip catered to all genres, giving all young and old a chance to get their party on over the weekend. Teelee and Lil Man showed up late giving them a chance to make their grand entrance. They were definitely getting the attention they expected. As they walked through the double doors of the Wisdom Hall, they were greeted with champagne. The Wisdom Hall was a very prestigious establishment. It had to be an exclusive event for the doors of this place to be open. By the look of all the dimes gliding across the hard wood floors of the hall, tonight was going to be yet another exclusive event in the making. "Yeah homey, this wzup right chere" Teelee stated as he scanned through the crowd of fine specimens. The ratio between women and men were 3 to 1, making the scene look even better. "I told ya this thang was gon be on another level. Let's go to the bar" Lil Man said headed in the direction of the bar area. When they made it to the bar they ordered a bottle of Rosé. As the bartender came back with the bottle, two thirsty bitches approached. The hood rat bitches always managed to slip their way into a party. "What's your name cutie?" thirsty bitch #1 asked, grabbing Lil Man's hand. "They call me Lil Man baaby. Look here y'all want a drink. Tell the bartender what y'all want. I got y'all, but y'all can't stand here. My lil broad off in here, ya heard me." "Well he looks available" thirsty bitch #2 replied attempting to put her hand on Teelee's cheek. "Hold up shorty. Don't touch me in my face." "Oh you one of them pretty boyz huh?" "Nah it ain't like that. I just don't like people touching me in my face. Your hands carry the most germs, ya feel me." "Now that you put it that way, I see where you comin from." That was one of Teelee's pet peeves. He knew all the foul things people did with their hands. "Look give them whatever they want, I got it." Lil Man gave the bartender a hundred-dollar bill to cover their expenses, and to rid them of their presence. "Oh I knew I recognized y'all. Gurl this them Skull Gang niggas I was tellin you about" thirsty bitch #1 said in an excited tone. "Well look if the time presents itself again we could talk, but right now y'all enjoy yourselves and have a nice night." Lil Man's tactics had them discombobulated. They didn't know whether to get mad, or thank him for his gesture. "Aight if them women don't treat y'all right we ain't gon be far" thirsty bitch #2 said blowing a kiss in Teelee's direction. They headed to the other side of the bar with their drinks, feeling satisfied for now. "Them broke ass hoes was tryna get in where they fit in" Teelee stated lighting up a cigarette. "Yeah but sometimes you gotta spend a little to get rid of em ya heard me." "I feel ya round" Teelee replied. The party was off the chain. Definitely a change of venue from what Teelee and Lil Man were accustomed to. The women were definitely on a different caliber, well at least most of them were. You had stragglers everywhere you went. The party was more of a grown and sexy feel. Instead of the hot jammed pack clubs they were used to attending. As they downed the first bottle of champagne Teelee signaled for the bartender to bring another one. "Look that's her right there" Lil Man said tapping Teelee on his shoulder. Soon as Teelee turned around from paying for the bottle, Tasha and her friend Kenya was walking up. "Hey Lil Man I see you made it." Tasha resembled a dark china doll. She had some long black silky hair. Her skin tone was a smooth midnight black that looked like Hershey's dark chocolate. Her body was banging like a Sony Explode radio. Coke bottle shaped from head to toe. "Yeah I had to come through and see this face again" Lil Man replied looking Tasha in her eyes as he pulled her in close to him. The smell of Tasha's perfume aroused Lil Man making him give her a small kiss on her neck. "Boy you betta watch it. That's my spot" Tasha said draping her arms around Lil Man's neck. "So this ya ace boom koon huh?" "Yeah this my nigga Teelee. Teelee this Tasha and her friend Kenya." "Wzup wit it" Teelee said in a nonchalant manner. "Lil Man told me so much about you. I feel like I already know you." "Oh yeah, what did he say." Teelee gave Lil Man a questionable look. He knew sometimes Lil Man could be a jokester. "Nigga go head; you act like I told her you wet the bed or sumthin." Lil Man nudged Teelee giving him a sign to lighten up. "Yeah this my nigga if he don't get no bigger" Teelee said referring to Lil Man's baby like features. "Nigga fuck you" Lil Man shot back. "Well Teelee this my girl Kenya." Kenya was average. Carmel brown skin, cute face and petite build. "Wzup up wit ya lil mama." Teelee remained cordial. It wasn't hard to see that he wasn't interested in Kenya. To avoid coming across as rude he still made small talk. As Teelee poured another glass of champagne, his eyes locked on the most beautiful woman in the party. Standing damn near 50ft. away he could clearly see the beautiful eyes of this enchanting beauty. As Teelee stared Lil Man tapped him breaking him out his trance. "Say homey put ya tongue back in ya mouth." "Man who that is ova there?" Teelee asked looking in the direction of "Ms. Pretty Eyez". "That's Tamia Breaux, but people call her Tiger; short for Tiger Eyes." Tasha said interjecting in their conversation. "You know her?" Teelee asked while gulping down the glass of champagne he was holding. He analyzed how he was going to approach the situation. "Yeah we go to the same hairdresser. She real cool people, but its gon be hard to get at her in here. She don't usually mingle wit dudes on the club scene." "I bet I get her pretty ass to mingle. I gotta have that right there." Teelee loved the feeling of being challenged by this beautiful woman. "Alright you could try your luck, but its gon be hard. I'm not saying you not qualified Teelee but I just know how she roll" Tasha stated. "Well you bout to see her get out of her character tonight. I usually don't approach no broad, but I can't let this thang pass me up. Where she from Tasha?" Teelee asked. "She originally from Uptown in the Melph, but she lives in Gentilly now." "Oh she one of them Uptown girls huh. Well she bout to have herself a *"Hard Head"* dude in her life." As Teelee spoke those words his moment of truth had just been born. Tamia was headed in his direction. As she got closer, Teelee got a full view of her. She stood about 4"11, with some hips and ass that fit her body like God sculpted her himself. Her "Seven" jeans fit like a glove, giving a nice view of her frame. As Teelee's eyes made their way up to her chest, he almost got an erection. She had the most plumped nice size breast he had ever laid eyes on. The bling across her shirt spelled out, "My Eyes Say It All." You could tell it was custom to say that. Her eyes were definitely speaking volumes. When he finally got to her face from his full observation of her miraculous body, he paused allowing her to pass him up. Tamia had the face of an angel. Her honey blonde hair flowed just below her shoulders and her flawless honey colored skin intensified the glow of her hazel eyes; which caused Teelee to pause for a minute to get his words together. Teelee noticed her about to walk back to her table. As she approached, he said the first words that came to his mind. "What that "T" stand for, Teelee huh" he asked referring to the diamond encrusted "T" that lay on her voluptuous breast. "No, it stands for Tamia" she replied giving off a small smile as she walked off. "Man, I think I just met wifey." "Damn nigga you sprung already, and you ain't have a full convo wit her yet. I hate to see when you get to know her a lil betta. "Gurl that dude by the bar is so handsome and got a nice swag, but he looks so young" Tamia said taking a sip of her Green Apple Martini. Tamia's sister Denise swayed her hips to the beat of R-Kelly's, "*Move Ya Body like a Snake.*" "Gurl do ya thang. He gotta be old enough if he up in here." Tamia and Denise were like night and day. Tamia was the quiet, shy type. Whereas Denise was the fuck who's listening, do what ya feel, betta not play with me type of person. Don't get it twisted Tamia had a dark side, but most of the time she tried to contain it. Tamia, Denise, and their other sister Cherrelle grew up together in the Melpomene projects, in Uptown New Orleans. Tamia's oldest sister Tangi was raised by her dad and grandma in the Eastern part of New Orleans. Their mother Cheryl who everyone called "Shorty C" raised the three girls quite well, seeing as though their father Eric was hardly around. When he was present Shorty C tried her hardest to get him to share in his parental duties, which usually resulted in an altercation. Eventually Shorty gave up hope, and raised her girls on her own. Denise was the oldest of the three in the house, so she stepped up to the plate to help Shorty C with her little sisters. Even though the girls weren't far apart in age, Denise was always in charge when Shorty C worked. Denise outweighed both of them in size, and was always ready to fight whoever played with any one of them. Cherrelle on the other hand was more of the nurturing motherly type. When Shorty C was slaving at her 9 to 5, Cherrelle made sure there was something on the stove and the house was clean. Tamia was the baby and the spoil one of the three. Shorty C would always receive compliments on her girls, especially the beauty of Tamia. This made Shorty C keep a close guard over her. She was a mini version of Shorty C. Tamia slept with Shorty up until she was fourteen. She never really played outside with the other children. Most of the time she would just watch the kids from the third floor balcony as they ran around downstairs. Cherrelle and Tamia both had a beautiful set of eyes, but it was just something about Tamia that drew many compliments. She looked like a living baby doll. Growing into adults Cherrelle became love struck by her high school sweetheart, which caused her to settle down well before Tamia and Denise. The relationship between Tamia and Denise drew closer because they were relationship free.

They both had their little relationships here and there, but nothing too serious.

As the D.J. switched the mood up, Tamia and Teelee stole glances at each other. It was obvious of the attraction between the two. The question was which one of them was going to break the ice. "Gurl you know you wanna holla at him. What you waitin for?" Denise asked wiping the sweat from her forehead from feeling the beat. "I don't know, what if he one of them dog ass dudes." "You'll never find out if you don't bust a move, wit ya scary ass. He ain't gon bite you, if he do you know I'mma break that nigga jaw." Denise was dead serious. Behind her little sister, she would have beaten up half the party. Teelee sat on the barstool pretending to be occupied by his phone, until Lil Man tapped him on his shoulder. "Say round, looks like somebody tryna get ya attention." "Who?" Teelee asked lifting his head taking a glance around the party. "Ms. Pretty Eyez", he stated as he directed Teelee's attention in Tamia's direction. She signaled for him to come over. Teelee placed his phone in its case and proceeded to meet this challenge head on. As Teelee headed over to Tamia's table it was like the D.J. read his mind. He let the Isley's Brothers "Choosey Lover" spend on the ones and two's. *"Chooseyy Looover-Girl I'm so proud of ya-I'm so glad you chooose mee baaaabyy".* Teelee smelled the scent of Tamia's perfume as he approached. The soft smell of Vanilla gave his nostrils a breath of fresh air. Just the sight and feeling that he got when he looked in her Tigress eyes, made him realize she was definitely different from what he was used of. "Wzup Ms. Teelee" he said as he extended his hand to greet the beauty. "Oh you're quite confident huh. How you know I was calling you over here for that?" Tamia asked as she shook Teelee's hand. "Damn her hands are so small and soft" Teelee thought as he tried not to grip her hand to long. "Because I could tell by the look you gave me from across the room." "How you know I was lookin at you from across the room?" "Because, I was lookin just as much as you was. I ain't tryna come at you wit all that to cool to tell the truth shit. I'm interested just as much as you are. I ain't tryna prolong this here too much longer. I rather keep it 100% real wit ya." "I appreciate your honesty. You don't find too many dudes being straight up like that." "I try to keep my own swag, and not be like a lot of these clown ass niggas." "Well since we keeping it 100, you're right I am interested. How old are you though Teelee?" Tamia asked looking directly into Teelee's eyes. The way those dangerous eyes pierced his soul, it was like she could see if he was lying or telling the truth. Still in all he couldn't blow it by telling her his real age. Looking at the way Tamia handled herself and the wisdom that invigorated from her, gave Teelee the idea that she was in her mid or latter twenties. If he wouldn't have observed her out the gate; just by looking in her face he would have thought, she wasn't a day over twenty-one. "I'm twenty-four and you" Teelee replied with confidence like the shit he was saying was the truth. "I'm twenty-five years young" Tamia stated proudly. "I like how you put that. I gotta used that one sumtimes." Teelee stated. "This my sister Denise." "Wzup Denise? What y'all drinkin on?" Teelee asked taking a seat next to Tamia. "As a matter of fact I got this. I'll be right back." Teelee got up and headed to the bar. When he walked up Lil Man, Tasha, and Kenya was still standing in the same spot. Kenya gazed off in her own world. While Lil Man and Tasha explored each other's body like no one was around. Teelee broke up the passionate moment by pulling one of Lil Man's dreads. "What it do homey?" Teelee asked leaning over the bar. "Shid we coolin" Lil Man replied. "What happen wit lil mama?" "Man it's sumthin about her eyes. It's like she pullin me in. When I locked eyes wit her I felt close to her homey." "Maybe this what you been lookin for round" Lil Man replied as he let his fingers glide through Tasha's silky black hair. "I don't know but I'm definitely bout to find out." The bartender came to take Teelee's order. "Gimme another bottle of Rosé wit three glasses. What you bout to get into Lil Man?" Teelee asked pulling out his money to pay for the bottle. "I'm bout to take Tasha and Kenya to get sumthin to eat. After that it's all up to Tasha" Lil Man stated looking at Tasha with lust filled eyes. "Boy you ain't even gotta ask that question. You know wzup ova here" Tasha replied answering Lil Man's assumptions. "Well I'm bout to get back to shorty. It was nice meeting y'all. Take care my lil homey, ya heard me." "Don't worry bout that, I got him" Tasha said putting her arm around Lil Man's waist. "If she's the one Teelee make sure you treat her right. Good females don't come around too often" Kenya stated. The statement Kenya made caught Teelee by surprise. Usually when you brush a female off for another one, they don't have nothing nice to say. "Thank you shorty, I'mma definitely keep that in mind." From there Teelee paid for the bottle, dapped Lil Man off and headed back to Tamia and Denise's table. "I hope y'all drink champagne." Teelee sat the bottle on the table and passed Tamia and Denise their glass. "Thank you, but you didn't have to go buy a whole bottle of champagne." That was one point for Tamia. If it was an average female, they wouldn't have said shit. They would have just reached for their glasses. Just Tamia's statement alone made Teelee even more intrigued to see what else she had to offer. They sipped the champagne, exchanged numbers, and got better acquainted as the D.J. kept them in the mood. They kept their eyes glued to one another. Denise excused herself as she headed to the bathroom, giving Teelee and Tamia a moment by their self. "So Tiger what's ya plans for tonight?" "How did you find out my nickname so fast?" "Let's just say I have my sources" Teelee replied. "Well since we're on the name subject. What's your real name? I know your momma didn't name you Teelee." "My name Jamal. I got my nickname from my lil potnas." "Oh alright. Teelee there's something different about you. I haven't quite put my hand on it yet. Lately I been meeting dudes that always hiding something. Even their introductions are phony, but you seem so different from all that. I don't know if I'm making the right assumption are not, but that's the vibe I'm getting." "Tamia whether you know it or not, I feel the same way about you. You mind finishing this conversation ova breakfast?" "I'm cool wit that. You have to follow me so I can drop my sister off first." "See if she wanna come wit us" Teelee replied. "Okay, I'll ask her when she gets back ova here" Tamia replied as she crossed her nicely shaped legs. The sight of them caused Teelee to stare. He had to stop the thoughts that were running through his mind. He had no intentions of disrespecting Tamia. Denise made her way back to the table. By the exasperated look on her face, she was ready to shake the spot. "Denise, Teelee wants us to go grab breakfast wit him. You down?" Tamia asked. "I would Tee, but you know I gotta go get Dantel bad ass, before he drive his baby sitter crazy. Thank you Teelee baaby, maybe some other time. I think you and Tamia got a lot to talk about anyway" Denise said with a smile on her face. "Fasho" Teelee replied. From there Teelee followed Tamia so she could drop Denise off at home.

Denise still resided in the Melpomene projects. As they turned off Martin Luther King Blvd. into the project, N.O.P.D. had four young black men pulled over in the front entrance of one of the buildings. They were on their knees with their hands behind their head. Their car was being flipped inside out by the "jump out boys". It seemed like every time Teelee ventured Uptown the police would have somebody pulled over. Coming off of the Claiborne Bridge entering into Uptown, was known as an easy spot to get harassed by the boys in blue. To be truthful the police had to patrol the area in that manner. The Calliope projects sat on the left hand side of Claiborne Ave. and the Melph sat to the right. That caused the area to be high in crime. It got so bad in the Melph that the police had to set up a substation in the heart of the project. That still didn't stop the violence and drugs that flowed through. It only made the hustlers more aware of their surroundings. The entire time Tamia was driving through the project, she sat on the phone talking to

Teelee. Teelee heard Denise in the background ranting. "Dem bitches always fuckin wit somebody." Tamia pulled up to Denise's building as Teelee parked alongside her. To the naked eye, one would have thought the jets was deserted. The hustlers and crack heads stayed within the dark alleys and hallways. Almost every light in the hallways of the project were knocked out to prevent the police from seeing any illegal activity. As Teelee sat in the Audi awaiting Tamia, he admired how beautiful she was. She was definitely above the trash he dealt with in the past. Not saying he fucked with ugly broads, their inner person was just trash to him. As she made her way around to the driver side window of the car Teelee watched her every move. When Teelee rolled his window down, Tamia leaned in. The smell of her Carefree gum made Teelee want to kiss her MAC, glossed lips. He controlled his self nevertheless. He didn't want her to think he was only out for one thing from her. "I'm about to run upstairs and use the restroom, I'll be right back okay" Tamia stated. "Take your time sweetie. I ain't goin nowhere" Teelee replied. While she was upstairs she made sure to give Denise, Teelee's cell phone number and his license plate number. You can never be too careful. Teelee slid in Usher's latest CD *"Confessions"* into his Pioneer touch screen T.V.\Radio. As Usher crooned about confessing his mistakes, Teelee noticed his potna Big Hulk headed in his direction. Teelee got out to greet his old friend. "What's good my nigga" Teelee said giving Hulk some dap. "Shid I'm coolin. What you doing back here?" "I'm waitin on my lil friend. You still at it huh?" Teelee asked. "Yeah man, you know a nigga gotta get it. Dem bitch ass police tried to stop a nigga hustle, but you know that wasn't gon happen." "I feel that. What you fuckin wit nah?" Teelee asked plotting on a money scheme. "Shid whatever gon make a profit." Teelee and Big Hulk went back like an ole skool Cadillac. Teelee and Hulk met back in the game through one of Teelee's lady friends. The old saying "Real Recognize Real" brought the two to have a close friendship. Even though they didn't hang on an everyday basis, when they did hook up it was all love. Big Hulk was highly respected in the Melph as well as the Calliope. His hustle game was official. Anything he got his hands on was good as flipped and profited to the fullest. Big Hulk stood 6'2, solid as an Ox. He was known as the knock out artist of the 3rd Ward. You had to be ignorant to the fact, or just plain dumb to step in front of Big Hulk's massive frame. His hand game wasn't the only thing that was lethal. The boy would slang that iron until the sun shine if need be. Just like his hustle game his dress game was on point too. You never caught him slipping. He stayed in exclusive gear, from Polo Rugby to Prada. "I see you rockin the Fendi loafs. Nigga you stay wit that hot shit huh" Teelee said checking out Hulk's attire. "You know I gotta stay above average ya heard me" Hulk replied as he brushed the invisible lent off his shoulders. "Shid nigga speakin of exclusive shit, I see ya wit the A8. This thing nasty." Big Hulk gave the foreign beauty a look over and nodded in agreement. "Yeah nigga you done stepped ya game up. That 7th must be pumpin money like a dialysis center." "You could say that" Teelee replied grabbing his cigarettes from the middle console of the Audi. Teelee slid one out of the pack, lit it up, and blew smoke rings in the air. Just as the smoke vanished he presented Hulk with a proposition. "What's good homey? You ready to bring ya hustle to another level?" "Do a gold digger love trick niggas? Fuckin right I am." Just as Teelee began to tell Hulk the business, Tiger was making her way down the stairs. "Wzup cuz?" Big Hulk said giving Tamia a hug. "This the friend you was talkin bout?" Hulk asked with a grin on his face. "Yeah that's her" Teelee replied looking deep into Tamia's enchanting eyes. It was something about her eyes. Every time he looked into them it was like he couldn't break the trance they left him in. "Y'all know each other" Tamia asked standing beside Hulk. Tamia standing next to Big Hulk made her look even shorter. "Yeah me and ole Hulk go way back" Teelee replied giving Hulk a wink. Hulk got the drift and winked back. Of course Teelee didn't want Tamia to know how they were really acquainted, at least not yet. Even though it was in the past, certain things, or previous situations could taint the way a person looks at you. Teelee didn't want to risk losing the strong connection they shared. "Well I'mma let y'all go do y'all" Hulk said putting his massive arm around Tamia's shoulder. "Aight cuzin, be careful out here. You know them people be trippin. They got a car pulled over round there as we speak. I don't want to have to come bail ya ass outta jail" Tamia stated with extra emphasis in her words. Tamia had big love for her cousin. Like everyone else Big Hulk was very overprotective of Tamia. If they were in the same club together, he made sure she stayed close by. One time Big Hulk broke a dude jaw on the count of niggas and they bullshit pride. While standing by the bar waiting for her drink, Tamia was approached by a very flamboyant type of cat. He just wouldn't take no for an answer. "Wzuppp Red, you rockin them jeans tonight. Can a nigga get in em wit ya" Too cool for T.V. said while adjusting his fake Gucci frames. "Nigga please, who the hell you think you talkin to like that. I ain't one of these nasty ass freaks in here" Tamia shot back while she received her change from the bartender. "Oh you one of them stuck up bitches huh. I can buy that pussy. Like Soulja said, "I'll pay for it-if I want it" bitch ya heard me" too cool said flashing a wad of cash in Tamia's face. While Tamia continued to argue with the nigga, she neither him noticed Big Hulk creep up behind them. Just as "too cool" let bitch flow from his lips one more time his fake Gucci frames flew off and his jaw popped like a fire cracker. "POP." Big Hulk landed a punch on "too cool" that could be heard all over the club. From that point on, niggas made sure to show respect to Tamia every time they saw her. Word on the street was, "Too Cool" had to get reconstructive surgery to fix his jaw. That still didn't help the fact that his jaw had a permanent dent in it. "Put my number in ya phone my nigga. Hit me up tomorrow round noon. I'mma lace you up on what we was talkin bout" Teelee stated. From there they exchanged numbers and said their good byes. Big Hulk didn't bother telling Teelee to take care of Tamia. He knew she was in good hands. It was understood not by words, but by knowing the caliber of nigga he was fucking with. Big Hulk knew Teelee was a solid nigga and didn't have a slight worry whether or not Tamia would be safe. Big Hulk didn't know it but his life was about to change drastically in the financial department.

Tamia left her car parked and got in the A8. Teelee headed to the Trolley Stop on St. Charles Ave. They were well known for their Belgian waffles. As he navigated the Audi, he couldn't help but to steal glances at Tamia. Everywhere she went she received compliments from complete strangers. She really had that effect on people. It wasn't just men; women couldn't deny how beautiful she was. As Usher's song "*Superstar*" came through Teelee's Bose sound system, Tamia broke the silence. "You don't find too many dudes your age with this kind of music in their car." "Well you just met one out of a million lil mama. I can't ride around all day and night listening to rap music. That shit would have my head all fucked up. This my relief music right here" Teelee said as he turned the volume up with his remote. It sound as if Usher was live in concert in the back seat of the car as the sound system blared. Teelee gave it his best shot as he sang along with Usher; while holding Tamia's hand. *"I'll be your groupie babyyy-if you'll be my Superstar- I'm ya number one fan-gimme ya autograph-sign it right here on my heart.*" "Oh that's so sweet, but Teelee baaby you can't sing." "They both had to laugh at the truth. When Teelee made it to the restaurant, he pulled up under the terrace. It smelled like rain would soon be in the atmosphere. As soon as they entered, the waitress led them to their table right by the front window. They had a nice view of St. Charles Ave. Teelee often ordered his food to go on nights when he didn't have a chance to eat during the day. Belgian waffles, scrambled eggs, and sausage links was his usual choice. Most of the waitresses were familiar with him so they already knew what he would be ordering tonight. "Its sumthin bout these waffles they serve" Teelee said rubbing his stomach. "Every time I come through here that's what I order. It's like they be puttin crack in them thangs." "Yeah, they are good. So I guess you come here often?" Tamia asked sitting her purse in the chair beside her." "Yeah I come on the take out tip, but not so much dining in." "Really, why is that? I know a nice looking man like you have plenty of opportunities to eat out with a woman." "I feel if I'mma sit down wit a woman and share a meal wit her, my interest is to get to know her on a deeper level." "I guess I'm a lucky lady then huh Mr. Teelee?" Tamia asked taking a sip of her water. "Let's just put it this way, we both lucky baaby" Teelee replied with a smile. Tamia's smile lit up on the inside and out. Tamia's speculations were being confirmed by the minute as they conversed over their meals. They continued on discovering a little bit more about each other. The basic things people should know upon meeting; like what high school they both attended, what's each other's favorite pass time, and things of the sort. "I know this may come off bad, but I don't want you to leave my side tonight; beautiful. You wanna come ova to my spot and chill wit me?" "Teelee I don't know bout all that." "Look I promise I ain't gon try nuthin wit ya baaby. Ya people know me anyway. I'm just not ready for this to end just yet. It's been a while since I had the chance to enjoy the company of a lady of your caliber. It's something about you that makes me feel comfortable." "Well I guess it's cool. My people know who I'm with just in case you try and kill me" Tamia said sarcastically. Where your spot at anyway?"

Tamia asked so she could let Denise know her whereabouts. "Believe me baby, I ain't tryna hurt a hair on your beautiful head." They finished their food, and headed to Teelee's condo. They held hands the entire ride to his place. The rain had just begun to come down. As they walked in the door, Tamia was greeted with the pleasant smell of Jupe oil. His mother had bought him a variety of oils and an oil burner for a house warming gift. "Damn it smells good in here" Tamia thought as she viewed the nice layout of the condo. As she looked around, she was getting the impression that Teelee had a lady friend. His place was decorated really nice. "What's wrong baaby?" Teelee asked as he turned on the Plasma T.V. "You have a really nice spot Teelee. It's well put together" Tamia replied still standing at the front entrance with a confused look. "Oh what you think a lil broad stay here or sumthin? Nah lil mama this ain't that type of party. My sister decorated this for me." Teelee took Tamia's hand and led her to the sofa. You want sumthin to drink?" Teelee asked scrolling through his 24-disc DVD changer. "No, I'm good. I'm still kind of full." Teelee clicked select on his *Brown Sugar* DVD, dimmed the lights and sat next to Tamia. "This one of my favorite movies" Tamia said kicking off her Christian Louboutins. "Well look like we have sumthin else in common" Teelee said leaning back cuddling up against Tamia. As she snuggled up under his arm, Teelee planted a soft kiss on her forehead which made Tamia blush. He kept his word, he was the perfect gentleman as they conversed a little more during the movie. They both eventually drifted off to sleep mid-way through as the rain poured down outside.

# CHAPTER 15

# SNITCHES GETS NO LOVE

"Y'all set Whoa" Thugga said slamming the ace of spades on the make shift card table. Thugga and his partner were currently up five dollars' worth of commissary. That set put them up one more dollar, making their winnings come out to six. "Run that shit back" Gutter said while picking up the cards, putting his one, two shuffle down. "That bull shit ass deal ain't gon help you homey. You might wanna try sumthin else." Thugga grabbed his pack of buglers that sat on side of him, and prepared to roll a cigarette. "Yeah we gon see bout that. Cut the cards and let's see what it do." Gutter and Thugga were familiar with each other form maneuvering through the streets. Just as Thugga was known for his flamboyant ways, Gutter was like wise. One time during Super Sunday they had the chance to get their shine on together. Super Sunday was an event that fell on specific Sundays out of the year. This was main event for several different Indian groups to show off their beautifully made suits, as they masked against rival Indians. It was also a time for street niggas to lay their stunt down. Gutter and Thugga really put on a show with their tricked out muscle machines. Thugga pleased the crowd as he 360 his candy apple red SS Camaro several times. He left a perfect circle in the middle of the street. Gutter fished tailed his black on black Trans AM up and down the block, leaving a trail of smoke for the onlookers. They really did it up that day, leaving behind their hot boys marks to prove it. From then on everywhere they bumped into each other, they greeted with a show of respect. Gutter held his fort down. Even though he and his team weren't nearly on the level of the Skull Gang. The 8$^{th}$ Ward pulled in a decent amount of money to supply Gutter's lavish lifestyle. There was always a fiend and a hustler to serve them. His stomping grounds was in the heart of the 8$^{th}$ Ward on St. Roch Park. Thugga very well knew the amount of currency flowing through the area. In his mind, he was going to capitalize off of it, and establish alliance with Gutter. "After me and my potna finish beatin y'all ass, I wanna holla at you on some business shit" Thugga requested, while flipping through his hand. "Fasho, but I don't know bout the losing part. I got five by myself" Gutter replied, arranging his hand to suit his playing style. "Feed up" the tier Rep yelled, as the front gate to the tier slammed shut. "Hold ya hand nigga. We ain't finish yet" Gutter said tucking his cards in his waist band. "Say Thugga, I gotta make a phone call after I eat. I gotta see what it do with my bum ass lawyer. We gon have to pause for a sec" Thugga's partner said as he got up to retrieve his peanut butter jar to put his share of fruit in. "What kind of fruit they got Smoke?" Thugga asked stepping in the hallway of the tier. "Peaches my nigga" Smoke replied preparing to serve everyone their food. Thugga was housed in the House of Detention (H.O.D.). The House of Detention was the second oldest facility Orleans Parish had to offer. There were many other housing units besides H.O.D., they had the Old Parish; which was similar to H.O.D. These two places housed the more harden criminals; from murders, kidnappers, and armed robbers. If you wasn't about your business, all your shit was getting snatched and you may end up being somebody's bitch. There was even a sign before entering the old parish that clearly stated, "You are now entering a real jail." Templement 1 through 6, housed the less severe crimes. From purse snatching to burglary. You could have had an armed robbery charge and be housed in Templement, but the likes of that happening was almost slim to none. If you did land in Templement you were lucky, because of the air conditioning. H.O.D. and the Old Parish was short of that privilege. It was freezing in the winter and sweltering in the summer. The advantage of the old jails was the freedom to get anything you wanted through under paid deputies. If your money was right, you could have it your way like Burger King. The crazy part about both jails was how they were structured. Once a person was thrown into the lion's den, as they called it, you had to fend for yourself. You were lucky if you had some affiliates from the streets in there. Thugga was well known throughout the majority of New Orleans. People were well aware of the strong muscle and hustle of the Skull Gang. You had to be rocking on the same level, or above to even think about challenging the menacing group of young, wealthy, cold bloodied killers. That was proven with the Pauger St. slayings. Even though there was no strong evidence linking them to the incident, the streets still knew who was responsible for the heinous acts. Upon entering the cell block, Thugga was greeted with much respect; mostly out of fear of who he was, and what came behind him. The cell block in H.O.D. was similar to cages in a zoo. On each floor sat four different tiers, two on each side. There were three ten man cells that made up one tier. There was a long hallway that was used for the fans and televisions. Also, at the end of the hallway sat a brick bar in caged shower, which was used by everyone on the tier. If you were a shy type nigga, that wasn't the place for you. The odds of you showering alone was unlikely. Most of the time it was six niggas in the shower all at once, utilizing two shower heads. The guard was stationed outside of the tier, positioned directly in the middle of all four tiers. If someone was beating that ass, or tryna take your ass, your chances of a guard hearing were real slim. That didn't matter if they heard you or not, some guards didn't care. Their famous phrase was, "You better get it how you live." As Thugga placed his share of pepper sausage on the unoccupied bunk directly above his, Smoke called him from the end of the hallway. Thugga was housed in cell #1, with the tier rep, which meant all extras came to them. The tier rep was responsible for the cleaning of the hallway, the showers and distributing the food. If you were a weak dude sometimes you were jacked out your serving for the day. It all depended on the mood of the tier rep that ran the wing. An old school cat named Smoke from the 17th Ward was head tier rep of Thugga's housing. Smoke was known as a real gun slinger back in the day. He was also very surgical with a shank. "What it do round?" Thugga asked opening the gate to the cell. Smoke signaled Thugga to the end of the tier by the entrance. There awaited a cute lil red bone with some army fatigues uniform pants, that hugged her bubble round ass. Her cute pie shaped face was a pleasant sight to see for a dude that had been deprived the presence of a woman. She wore her hair in a ponytail that hung pass her shoulders. "Here boy, this from Teelee." She handed Thugga a brown paper bag through the bars. "Wzup wit my nigga?" Thugga asked as he tucked the bag in his O.P.P. sweat shorts. "Nuthin, he said him and Lil Man going meet wit your lawyer tomorrow." "So what's been up wit ya. You still on the team like Kobe and Fisher huh?" "Boy you know I'mma move when the paper right. Plus, I'm still tryna get in where I fit in wit ya boy." "Keep trying. He gon break one day" Thugga replied as he leaned against the bars of the front gate. "Aight boy let me get back to work. I'mma holla later." Thugga made his way back to his cell to see what Teelee had dropped him. To not expose his hand, he draped his blanket along the four man cut his bunk sat in. As he took a seat, he dumped the contents of the bag onto the bed. There was an ounce of purpa, an ounce of regular, two brand new lighters, two boxes of Keep Moving's, twenty Ecstasy pills, a small compact cell phone with the charger, and a couple of gold cleaning cloths like he requested. No matter what position he was in, he always wanted to get his shine on. "Say Gutter come holla at me for a second homey" Thugga hollered from behind the tent. "Aight round, I'm comin. Here Rell, get me some peach juice ya heard me." Gutter made his way under the tent. As he sat on the bunk Thugga threw him one of the boxes of Keep Moving cigars and the ounce of purpa. Gutter proceeded to roll up a blunt. He quickly rolled it up, sealed it, and put the flame to it to dry the dampness. As he lit the weed, there was an immediate response from the others throughout the tier. Thugga stood up and put his fellow inmates at ease. He grabbed a couple of buds out of the ounce of regular, and handed it to Smoke. "Give everybody a lil bit. I got you later round. I'm tryna get some business straight right now." Smoke walked off to fulfill Thugga's request. Thugga broke bread for two reasons. It was in his best interest to spread the love because you never knew who you were around. Snitch niggas will run off at the mouth if they feel left out. In this case everyone gets a piece, and you don't run a risk of someone telling the police, besides that Thugga wasn't a tight ass dude. He loved the feeling of being top dog. "This that granddaddy" Gutter stated, as he inhaled a large amount of the smoke into his lungs. Just as he blew out the smoke, he went into a coughing frenzy. "Damn nigga" Thugga said patting Gutter on the back. "Nigga this ain't that bullshit you used to smokin. You gotta slow roll this here." Thugga took the blunt and inhaled lightly. He knew due to them being locked up, their lungs were fresh. "Look here homey, we been familiar wit each other for quite some time nah. I know you run yo spot in the $8^{th}$." "Yeah, what good my nigga?" Gutter asked, leaning back on the bunk. The purpa had him feeling so good, he had a tingling feeling running through his feet. "I'mma keep it 100, wit ya. Ya spot got potential to get big money, but you need heavy weight. That's where I come in at." "I'm listening. What you talkin round?" Gutter asked. "When we bounce outta here, I'mma put you in the game wit the cakes for sixteen. If the shit move like I think its gon move, I'mma give you a couple on consignment." "That's whatz up" Gutter replied taking the blunt from Thugga. They took a couple more tokes, and went back to their spade game. The way Thugga was feeling, the business deal with Gutter was going to go just fine.

"Aight what we lookin like?" Teelee asked, as him and Lil Man took a seat in front of one of the best criminal lawyers in New Orleans. Wayne Williams sat back behind his huge desk, smoking a pipe filled with imported Turkish tobacco. His old fashioned modeled office was filled with all kinds of artifacts from all over the world. On his wall hung pictures of legendary people, from Christopher Columbus to Robert Kardashian. Wayne Williams took a puff off of the pipe and let the thick smoke exit his nostrils. The strange odor from the pipe disturbed Teelee's stomach, but he disregarded it to focus on the situation at hand. Wayne Williams was a slender Caucasian. He always wore his hair combed to the back. He had many gray strands from his many years of practice, giving him a crown of wisdom. His long pointed nose always seemed to be red around the edges, due to his nose candy he loved so much. Some people felt his skills were weakening because of his addiction. He proved a lot of people wrong with his 20 and 1, winning streak he had. Wayne Williams picked up Thugga file, glanced through it for a few seconds, and proceeded to tell the details of their situation. "It's simple fellas. No witnesses, no case. As I see here, there are two witnesses that the state has. As your attorney, I can't influence nothing that will break the law. I will tell you what he's up against, and what the loop holes to win the case are." Well don't worry bout nuthin. You just be on your A game this week in court" Lil Man stated firmly. "That I will be my young clients. There is one thing I need from you two. If you could accommodate me." The look in Wayne Williams's eyes gave him away. Teelee knew that look from anywhere. His glassy eyes gave him the attributes of none other than a coke head. "I got you, don't trip. Just be at this address round 3:00. They gon take good care of you. Just don't let this hinder your performance in court." Teelee stated. "Trust me, he won't make it past his motions hearings." From there they headed to H.O.D. to inform Thugga that everything was all good. Visit days were on Saturdays at 12:00, for all the inmates on Thugga's floor. Since they were in the area they decided to drop in and share the good news. The whole time he was gone Teelee, Lil Man and K-Real made sure one of them was up there when Tyler wasn't. The visiting list limited him to four people. So Pistol and Corey just communicated with him via cell phone. His mom stayed in touch as well. Thugga made it clear that he didn't want her to see him in that position. "What it do nigga, I hope I ain't interrupt ya jack session" Lil Man stated. "Nah nigga I'm coolin waitin on Tyler to bring her ass up here." Lil Man called just for that reason. If Tyler would have made it before them, they would have been turned around. "Call Tyler and tell her to hold off today. We got some important shit to tell you." "Where Teelee at?" Thugga asked. "He right here. Talk nigga I got you on ova the radio speakers. You know I'm on that fly shit" Lil Man bragged, as his 760 BMW glided up the street. He traded the 750 for the 760. Even though they looked alike, the 760 was wider and consisted of a lot more accessories in the inside. He added his own touch, giving his space ship looking car a look that was really fascinating. It was sitting on 22inch Giovanni's; they were painted grey with the lip of the rim black. The factory smoke grey paint job blended right with the wheels. He also had a camera/T.V. installed in his steering wheel, so he could be fully aware of whoever was trailing behind him. "What it do homey?" Teelee asked, as he sent Tiger a text on his blackberry. His mind was stuck on her. Every time she ran across his mind a smile came across his face. They had been kicking it real heavy the past couple of months. They planned a picnic this coming Sunday on the lake. He was checking to see if they were still on. "Shid nigga coolin. Oh yeah I got that from ya girl. She said why you ain't call her back last week." "Man I been rockin wit my lil boo. I ain't got time for Penny crazy ass." "Well pass that nigga. She been givin a nigga them looks ever since she dropped that first package." "Do ya thang nigga. You know I ain't bout to hate on my nigga ova no broad ya heard me. I ain't never put her on no exclusive level anyway." "That's wzup" Thugga replied. "Look we gon see you in a minute. We right around the corner" Lil Man said, turning on South White St. He cut the phone call short to put the purpa and the guns in his stash spot in the floor board. Motors did a good job installing the space. With the touch of a button, the whole section on the left back seat floor board, including the carpet slid back. It had enough room to stash up to five kilos of cocaine. When the compartment was closed it didn't even look like it was there. Teelee teased him when he first saw it. "Nigga what you think you James Bond now?" "Nah nigga, I'm being ten steps ahead of these bitch ass cops" Lil Man replied. As they parked in the parking area directly across from H.O.D. Tiger hit back on Teelee's blackberry. "Go head homey, I'mma meet you up there" Teelee said, preparing to read Tiger's message. "Aight don't be long. You know how you get when you talk to pretty eyez." "Nigga go head, I'mma be in there." Teelee pressed the enter button on his keypad of his blackberry. In bold letters Tiger replied, ***"Of course handsome, I can't wait to spend some time with you again."*** The message brought a smile to Teelee's face, and some comfort to his heart. He had finally found someone that appreciated spending time with him, without money being the only reason. That quality made Tiger different from all the other women he had been with. She was a real genuine person, who really wanted the best for him. He just hoped his lifestyle didn't run her off. No matter how much he fell for Tamia, he always kept in mind the commitment he had to the streets and his niggas. Even though he qualified to be a man physically, he still didn't have his priorities together mentally. If Tamia lasted throughout the journey of being committed to a street nigga, she had the qualities to transform Teelee. If only he would let her. Teelee texted back, ***"Me neither my baby. I'm bout to run in and visit Thugga. I'mma***

***hit you when the visit ova."*** Teelee pressed send on the keypad, and sat his blackberry in Lil Man's middle console. After grabbing the keys out of the ignition, he hit the lock button on Lil Man's keyless keypad. *"Bleep, Bleep."* Upon entering the waiting area of the prison, the stale smell of the old jail house hit Teelee nostrils making him sick to his stomach. He hated going down there, but for the sake of his brother, he was gonna go over the limits. He knew if he was in the same position as Thugga they wouldn't hesitate to do it for him. Teelee noticed Lil Man seated on one of the hard benches along the wall. "This nigga here scandalous like a muthafucka" Teelee thought, as he approached Lil Man putting his Mack down on a young cute chick. What made the situation so fucked up, was the fact that she was obviously waiting to visit her significant other. She was giving Lil Man more play than a Tyler Perry show. Luckily the child she had was too small to talk, or he would have busted her low down ass. The visiting area was crowded as always. Young women and their children waited patiently to see their loved ones. There was a couple of mother's present also waiting to see their sons in that awful situation. The depressing colors that covered the walls made the situation even worse. It seemed like ugly green, off white, and pale pink were the colors for all institutions. What most people didn't realize was the system was 90% psychological, and 10% physical. Mind games were used to control and further mental stress on inmates. The system had no hope of people getting better. Their focus was keeping inmates in the same destructible position they were in, if not worse. If the incarceration rate went down, their pockets got lighter. It's a money thing. Modernized slavery in other words. They not only played mind games on the inmates, they also made it difficult on their loved ones. The deputies were trained to have nasty attitudes towards visitors. It's all a big game. Frustrate the family and they would get tired of the situation, and give up on their loved ones. It was all downhill from there. "The names I call are the next to go up" the female deputy yelled from behind the desk. "Listen for your name, if you don't step up you will not be able to visit today." The ape looking deputy confirmed the system's tactics, as she tried to anger the awaiting visitors. The room full of people became silent immediately, because "Planet of The Apes" was purposely calling the names out low. "James, Thompson, Victor, Wilson, Lee." As she called out the names her nose flared giving her distinguished looks of an ape. Teelee and Lil Man heard their names being called. Lil Man was short tempered, and Teelee had zero tolerance for bullshit. To avoid any smart comments from "Boozilla" they immediately made their way to the elevator. A voice came over the speaker in the ceiling of the elevator as the doors closed. "Fifteen to the third floor." The elevator arrived at the 3rd floor, the doors opened and everyone flew out to make their way to the visiting booths. Thugga and the other inmates hadn't made it to the visiting area yet, so everyone settled in and conversed amongst one another. Some spoke in a mature manner, regarding their children and high hopes of their loved ones coming home. Some gossiped and discussed their plans for the weekend. "Bitch I can't wait till tonight. I'm going do me ya heard me" stated one hood rat.

"Man some of these broads ain't shit" Teelee commented sick of hearing the bullshit. "That same bitch be in the "Roc" damn near every weekend. I bet she come down here actin like she holdin it down" Teelee stated frustrated by the conversation coming from the hood rats. "Son them niggas know what kind of broads they be havin before they get jammed up. Ain't no sense in actin like that shit brand new" Lil Man commented. "I'm already knowin son. That's why I treat em like I treat em. If a hoe act like a hoe, I'mma treat her like one. If she acts like a woman, I'mma treat her like one. If she got potential, I'mma teach her how to respect herself ya heard me" Teelee said. From the "Hey baaby" and "Hey daddy" shouting out Lil Man and Teelee knew visitation had begun. Thugga walked up with his grill shinning and braids on point. Basically he was on his penitentiary swag. His OPP sweat suit was brand new and he sported a fresh pair of white shower slippers. "Wzup my niggas" Thugga said picking up the phone. Lil Man proceeded to talk first. "We coolin son. What's good wit you in there?" Lil Man asked. "Shid same ole same ole. You know how it go down in this bitch. What's good, what Wayne Williams was talkin bout?" Thugga asked hoping to hear if he was coming home soon. "Nigga just be ready to come home for ya motions hearing." "That's what I'm talkin bout" Thugga replied excitedly. "Nigga I can't wait to get out this bitch." "I already know my nigga" Lil Man stated. "Here talk to Teelee. You know you ain't got that much time" Lil Man stated. "What it do my nigga" Teelee said taking the phone from Lil Man. "Shid, I'm good now. My niggas came through like they supposed to." "Son you know what it is, Skull Gang 4 Lyfe" Teelee said holding up his Skull Gang piece. "Buleeve That" Thugga replied as he put his fist over his heart to confirm his loyalty as well. "Wzup wit ya boo you keep talkin bout?" "She good, she just texted me before I came up here. We havin a lil picnic tomorrow, ya heard me." "That's wzup. I'm glad to see somebody got my nigga happy." They talked and joked around for a lil while longer before the deputy yelled out "Five more minutes." "Oh yeah" Teelee said his tone turning serious. "Look I want you to lay low when you come home. Them bitches Flat Top and Jackson, gon be on you like bees on honey. I don't want them tryna bring you back in this bitch. You still gon collect from Roylee and his people, but I'mma get somebody else to transport the work." "I ain't doing no trippin boss" Thugga replied sarcastically. "Nigga get the fuck outta here. I ain't no boss, this all our shit. I'm just thinkin bout ya safety homey." "Nigga I know, I'm just fuckin wit ya." "Visit is now over" the deputy yelled as he walked behind Thugga's booth. "Aight round, hit us up later ya heard me" Teelee said as he put his fist to the glass. They all put their fist to the glass and said love as they put their hand over their hearts.

Lil Man and Teelee headed to Pampy's Steak and Seafood on Broad and Bruxsell, in the 7th Ward. They were meeting Roylee there to pick up this week's money drop. When they pulled up on the neutral ground, across from the restaurant, they noticed Roylee was already there. He was talking on his cell phone, leaning against a brand new Royal blue H2, sitting on 28's. When he saw Teelee and

Lil Man pull up, he ended his call. He grabbed a chrome briefcase from the backseat, and greeted his business partners. "I see ya boy. You done upgraded huh?" Teelee asked, giving Roylee props on his whip. Roylee had definitely upgraded overall. Instead of black tall tees, and black Dickey pants, he now wore Cooji and Polo. He even cleaned his appearance up. He traded the rough Freeway beard, he loved so much, for a nicely shaven goatee. Looking at his taper fade and his ocean waves in his head, he had really shaded the grimy nigga look. His dark chocolate skin tone and strong jaw line gave him the appearance of "Stringer Bell" from "The Wire." "You know I'm tryna keep up wit y'all boyz, ya heard me." "It's all love my nigga. Let's go get this here started" Lil Man said headed for the restaurant. Roylee was satisfied with where he was at. He knew everyone had a position to play and he played his role well. When they entered Pampy's, they were greeted and led to their table by the hostess. Pampy's was a nice restaurant to dine in day, or night. It was more on a level of an upscale soul food place. The bar area was to the left of the front door. It was stocked with every liquor you could think of; from Ace of Spade, to Louis XIII. There were round tables spread all around the lantern lit restaurant. Some sat parties of 4 to 10, people. They were also equipped to accommodate large parties; ranging from 25 to 50, people and still have enough room for other customers. While you ate you were entertained with classical jazz music; anywhere from the likes of Fats Domino and the up and coming trumpet player, Kermit Ruffin. During the evening hours a live jazz band, or pianist played throughout the duration of business hours. "So how things lookin out there in "Moneyland" I mean Raceland?" Teelee asked signaling for the waitress. "It's just like you said. It's Moneyland" Roylee replied as he slid the briefcase over to Teelee. "May I help you sir?" the waitress asked approaching the table. "Yeah gimme two shots of Henny, chilled. What y'all drinkin?" Teelee asked placing the briefcase in his lap. "Gimme a double shot of Patron" Lil Man requested. "I'm good, I'm waitin on my girl" Roylee said checking the time on his watch. As the waitress went to prepare their drinks, Teelee peeked in the briefcase to get a glimpse of the neatly stack money. "$100 Grand even" Roylee stated. "Not a penny more, not a penny less." "I know you official wit it. You been on point every drop you made" Teelee replied sitting the briefcase on side of him. "So how ya niggas livin, everything good huh?" Lil Man asked as he wiped a smudge of his 5 carat pinky ring. "Yeah they good, everybody eatin." "That's wzup. I'm just makin sho. I want everybody to get them, ya heard me." They downed their drinks, and got ready to part ways. Roylee's girl had just entered the restaurant prepared to have lunch with her man. "We gon get at cha homey. K-Real gon be out there to drop ya package off tomorrow" Teelee said as he picked up the briefcase and stood to his feet. "Aight, I'mma hit y'all later." Roylee stood up to greet his girl. As Teelee and Lil Man were on their way out, they greeted Tanya with a nod and wzup. She was familiar with them from hearing little things through Roylee, but didn't know them too well. Teelee and Lil Man wanted to keep it that way. Word on the street was Tanya was the voice of the 7$^{th}$, meaning she was a "Motor

Mouth."

Tamia and Teelee sat at one of the many picnic tables that flooded the lakefront. The summer breeze blew lightly, as the sun shinned bright in the sky. It was very few clouds visible, giving the sky's ocean blue color more radiance. They sat feeding each other crawfish tails, while they lost themselves in one another's gaze. "Everything go okay with the lawyer" Tamia asked as she ripped the head off a crawfish, preparing to feed it to Teelee. "Yeah everything good. He coming home for his motions hearing." As Tamia placed the peeled crawfish tail to Teelee's lips he received it and licked the juice left on her finger. "Boy, you too much" Tamia smiled. "Nah, I'm just enough for you, beautiful. Let me ask you a question Tiger" Teelee stated looking into Tamia's hypnotizing eyes. "Wzup boo." "What you doin to me?" "Boy what you talkin about?" Tamia asked with a confused look on her face. Teelee noticed the look of confusion on Tamia's face. He gently took her tiny hand into his, and looked into her dangerous eyes. "What I mean is, I ain't never met a woman that made me feel like you do. What I'm sayin is, you care about me genuinely. You don't wanna be wit me for what I can do for you. You accept me for me. I never had a woman that was interested in just Teelee. All the other ones was always on some bullshit like, *"Oh gurl, he got some good hair. I wanna have a baby wit him"* Teelee said, mocking the ghetto, gold digging hoe's he had encountered in his past. "Most of all, they always tryna see what they can get out a nigga. When I'm wit you, you see me as Jamal and not Teelee." Teelee's statement really touched Tamia, almost to the point that she was on the verge of tears. "Awe baby, I appreciate you for understanding me. From my first glimpse of you in that party, I thought you was the dog type. Through this time we spent together you've proven me wrong. I know you still doing ya thug thang in the streets, but I'm willing to work with you on that. I see so much good in you behind that hard exterior. You're very smart Teelee, and you could be so much more. I'm not saying you're not doing your thang in the position you're in. I'm saying what I see is far beyond what you see. I see you being a great father, great husband, and a strong leader." Suddenly Teelee felt a lump in his throat. He couldn't even get his words out at first. Tamia gave him so much confidence to be more, and to strive for a better position in life. For the second time since they've met, this woman had him lost for words. He finally said what came to his heart. "Look bae, I can't promise that I'mma be inside on time every night cause I'm a street dude and that's where my hustle is at. I can't promise that I'm not gon go to jail. What I can promise is that I'll take good care of you and I'll try to be the best man I could be for you. I'm also open to letting you teach me how to love too. Oh yeah, you gotta stop doing that shit wit ya eyes too." "Why you keep saying that, what am I doing with my eyes?" Tamia asked giving him that same look that drove him crazy. "See you did it again!" "Come here boy." Tamia pulled Teelee into her arms, and passionately kissed him. The intensity from her kiss and her voluptuous breast up against his chest gave Teelee an instant erection. "You betta stop. You gon start sumthin out here" Teelee said meaning every word he said. Tamia peeped the bulge in Teelee's

LRG cargo shorts and her head began to fill with many lustful thoughts. They still hadn't had sex as of yet, but the moment was creeping up on them. All it was going to take was for them to be in a room alone, and it was going down like the Titanic. Just when Teelee felt he was having the perfect day, an unmarked car pulled up behind his Porsche truck. When the two occupants got out of the car it was like his day had took a turn for the worst, instantly. Still in all he maintained his composure. It's like the old sayin, *"Never let em see ya sweat."* Jackson and Flat Top were two people he really didn't feel like being bothered with today. Ever since Lanzo used his legal power, they backed off. Thugga's hearing was approaching real fast. They must have felt like they were on the verge of taking the ruthless Skull Gang out of commission. What they didn't know was Teelee and the gang was ten steps ahead of them. Their so called secret weapons, were about to be worm food. "I'll be right back sweetie. Let me go see what these two clowns want." As Teelee approached Jackson and Flat Top he couldn't do nothing but laugh. "What's so funny Lee?" Flat Top asked feeling like the joke was on them. "Y'all funny, y'all just won't quit huh? I guess I'mma have to call my business associate again." Lanzo had ties so deep, that he even had the mayor of New Orleans on speed dial. One phone call was made and the worry of Jackson and Flat Top harassing them was history. "No you don't. We didn't come to fuck with you about that" Jackson replied. "We just want to wish you and your partners the best of luck." "We don't need no luck. We A1 yola, ya heard me" Teelee replied. "Y'all what" Flat Top asked confused by Teelee's statement. "It means, they're good. You really gotta get wit the street slang" Jackson stressed. Teelee burst into laughter again. "What's so funny this time?" Flat Top questioned. You two muthafuckas remind me of the two police on Sanford and Son." "Ha ha ha, very funny. We gon see how funny shit is when the judge sends your little friend away for life" Flat Top growled. Teelee laughed again because he knew he was pressing the right buttons. "Come on let's go" Jackson said headed to the driver side of the unmarked car. "Oh Teelee, I see you got another new car. Who's this one for, your uncle?" "No it's for your wife. She let me use it after I left your house last night." Jackson's smirk turned into a frown instantly. "Just have your boots laced up slick talkin muthafucka." They sped off in the unmarked and Teelee went back to his picnic with Tamia. "What was that about? I saw you laughing in those police face. They could have taken you to jail." "Bae I'm not worried bout them two clowns. Instead of them havin me by the balls, I got them by theirs. That's why they so heated." "Whatever you do be careful. I ain't tryna lose you baby." "Don't worry bout that. I'm here, I ain't going nowhere. Now where were we?" Teelee kissed Tamia and it was even more electrifying than the last one. "I'm ready to shake this spot" Teelee stated trying to control his raging hormones. By the look on Teelee's face and his body language, Tamia knew he was about to explode. She had already decided that today was going to be the day that she finalized the deal. She had been anticipating making love to Teelee for a while now. "Come on let's get out of this heat. We can go back to my place"

Tamia offered. "Oh yeah, I almost forgot. When Tia comin back in town?" Teelee asked. "I wanna meet my step daughter." Teelee began gathering all of their things. "She'll be back next week. I talk to her last night" Tamia replied helping Teelee with the rest of their stuff. "You told her about me?" "Of course, I don't keep much from my baby." From there they headed to Tamia's spot not too far from the lakefront. She had a nice cozy spot. Tamia really had skills in the decorating department. She could really make something out of nothing. Her whole house was decorated with Asian décor. Pretty simple, but very well put together. The place was spotless, nothing out of order. Tamia had every quality of the virtuous woman the bible spoke of. Teelee had really hit the jackpot. The only thing was, could he maintain it. When they walked in the front door of Tamia's place, Teelee took a seat on the sofa, while Tamia went to the back. "You want something cold to drink baby?" Tamia asked as she came back into the living room and hit play on her CD player. She wanted to set the mood for Teelee. She had a mix R & B disc penetrating the airwaves. Destiny's Child *"Cater to You"* flowed beautifully in the background. "Yeah, I want sumthin sweet, sumthin like you" Teelee replied pulling Tamia into his lap. "We can start wit these" Teelee said while grabbing a handful of Tamia's voluptuous breast. Teelee kissed Tamia so passionately that it made her knees weak. They slowly stripped each other naked and kissed every part of each other's body. Tamia straddled her legs around Teelee as he slowly sucked on her breast. He took his time pleasing every inch of her body. She meant a lot to him and he wanted to make sure she knew it. As he worked his way down to her sweet spot Tamia couldn't do nothing but let out moans of pleasure. "Ahhh Teelee baby." They made love right on the sofa in the living room. They went at it intensely for a couple of rounds and ended up in Tamia's bedroom, out of breath and fulfilled. "Boy what you was tryna dig for gold or something?" Tamia asked still slightly out of breath. "Did I find your treasure" Teelee smiled. "Did you! Feel my legs, there still shaking." They both burst into laughter at the site of Tamia's legs trembling. Suddenly they both became silent and looked into each other's eyes. Tiger decided to break the silence by saying four words that opened Teelee's heart to her forever. "I love you Teelee." He kissed her on the forehead and replied, "I love you too beautiful." They drifted off to sleep under the cool air conditioning, cuddled in each other's embrace.

"Teelee this Ralph, meet me at Roosevelt's on Claiborne. Teelee was just leaving Mr. Bubbles in the 6$^{th}$ Ward. He was having the Audi detailed inside, out. He was already in the area, so he shot straight to Roosevelt's. He knew if Ralph was requesting to meet him, it was some good info regarding the snitches. It was time to clean house, and Ralph knew what was about to transpire. That's the main reason he requested to meet Teelee in person. The phone was way too risky, to relay the kind of info, he was about to give Teelee. Teelee was surprised to see Ralph waiting for him when he pulled up. They both hopped out, and headed inside of the restaurant. They sat at a table close to the front entrance, away from any other customers. Roosevelt's had a substantial amount of regular customers that came in on their lunch break. Their Ox tails, and greens kept em coming. "You beat me here and I was around the corner. This must be what I need. What's good?" Teelee asked leaning in to hear every word Ralph said. "This the deal" Ralph replied in a low whisper. "Rahim will be in court on Ronnie's motions hearing. He will be driving a black Lincoln Town car. Y'all gotta do what y'all do, because if he hit's the stand Ronnie is through. Stanley is also scheduled to testify. I already gave y'all the info on him. It's all on you now, I've done my part. Contact me when everything is all said and done." 'I got you" Teelee replied as they shook hands. "Good lookin OG. I got sumthin for you after this ova wit." "I'm not tripping. Just handle ya business, and handle it like I know you know how." They both locked eyes and once Ralph saw that killer look in Teelee's eyes, there was nothing else to be said. Ralph knew Woadie and Papa Bear ass was grass. There was one thing he knew about Teelee and his team, they were some ruthless, cold blooded killers. Every time he called for their assistance, he was never unsatisfied. The job was always handled with no mistakes.

"All rise the honorable judge Julius Parker presiding. Court is now in session" the deputy called out. "You all may be seated. Counselor call your first case." "Yes your honor. Case #1221613, Johnson vs. The State of Louisiana is ready for trial. First we have a motion's hearing set for Ronnie Bennett. Case #2341516. The states witnesses are available and should be here today." David Silver, was a young up and coming D.A. in Orleans Parish court system. He was determined to establish a name for himself by any means necessary.

A college graduate from Loyola University, Caucasian and in his mid-thirties. To say he was so young, he sank a lot of young brothers down the rotten toilet hole, we call the rehabilitation system. Silver, Jackson, and Flat Top were all in cahoots to bring down the notorious Skull Gang. By the looks of it, they were going to accomplish their goal today. What they didn't know was their witness, base case was about to crumble right before their eyes. "Is the defense team here for the Johnson trial?" The judge asked, as he glanced through a file. Judge Julius Parker, was a hammer in a sense. He wasn't just stern with the criminals that came through his courtroom, he was the same with the district attorneys. He refused to let any D.A. run his courtroom, giving him a non-bias eye 90% of the time. The other 10%, was the little leeway he gave the D.A.'s on frivolous extensions. It was in most people favor to be in his section, if the state didn't have a strong case. If they did and they could prove beyond a reasonable doubt that you were guilty, you had better call on God, because there was no saving your ass. He once sentenced a man to four hundred years for killing a food delivery truck driver. His exact words were, "You deliberately killed a man in cold blood. Now I'm going to take your life." The remark led to the man throwing a chair at him, but if he had you; you were good as done. Julius Parker was a Creole coon ass. That's what some called his blood line. His strong Creole features gave some people the impression that he was a Caucasian man. He was in his early sixties, and been on the bench for twenty-five years. He was born to be what he was, and he vowed to do it to the best of his ability until he took his last breath. He was willing to die on the bench if need be. As the deputy brought the inmates from the back, Thugga glanced through the crowded court room. He noticed Lil Man on the back row. Lil Man gave him a nod letting him know everything was in motion. There was no sign of Teelee and the others, but he very well knew the deal. Shit was in process to make it possible for him to walk away a free man. "Yes your honor. The defense team is ready for the Johnson trial. Just give me a moment to speak with my client." Jonathan Fuller was another top dog in the criminal defense field. He wasn't as good as Wayne Williams, but his track record was growing rapidly. "Get your business straight Mr. Fuller. Counselor lets knock out some of this docket while you're waiting for your witnesses in the Bennett hearing. That should be ample enough time for Mr. Fuller to gather all his information for trial.

Woadie stood on the court room steps on Tulane and Broad St., chain smoking cigarette after cigarette. His nerves were shot to hell. He was really taking a gamble, taking the stand on one of the members of the most notorious organizations in New Orleans. Deep in his heart he wanted to avenge his girlfriend's death, but he knew he wouldn't last a day in war with the Skull Gang. Even if he would have entertained the thought, he still wouldn't stand a chance. After his block was annihilated by Thugga and his crew, he was the only one left standing. Being the bullshit nigga that he was, he took the sucker route. He went to the same people that wouldn't hesitate to lock him up. People like Woadie wasn't built for the game. He was so enticed by the glamour and fame of it all. He was blinded to the fact that the game had consequences, death and the penitentiary. Like everybody that played the game, once upon a time you were faced with the big test of keeping it solid, or folding like a bitch nigga. Woadie was about to become what the game dreaded, "A Snitch." As he proceeded to light up another cigarette, he noticed his snitch rental had a flat tire. He swung his knotted up dread locks out of his face, and contemplated about going check on his dilemma. His instincts told him to leave it until he finished in court. He went against his will and skipped down the many steps of the courthouse. He had a funny feeling in his gut about the situation, but he brushed it off seeing what area he was in. "They ain't gon try nuthin round here. They got to many police ridin up and down the street" he thought as he bent down to inspect the tire. He turned to look behind him, because he could have sworn he felt someone walk up behind him. "Man nuthin but an empty U-Haul parking lot. Damn I'm trippin hard." He ran his hand around the tire to check for any nails. A cold feeling crept up his spine, as he froze from the cold steel aimed at the back of his head. "Yeah bitch nigga turn ya ass around" Corey growled with a tight grip on his Fortie. When Woadie turned around to meet his fate, he saw the look of a stone cold killer in Corey's eyes. "What you thought I wasn't gon catch yo pussy ass!" "Iiii coouuld." Before he could get any more words out, Corey shot him once in the mouth. "BOOM." Another right between his eyes, "BOOM." Brain fragments smeared all over the side of the Lincoln Town car, as Woadie's body slumped under the car. The shots rang out without causing a big scene. It startled a few people on the other side of Tulane Ave., waiting for the RTA bus. "Bitch try and talk now" was Corey's last words before him and Pistol sped off up the back streets of Mid-City New Orleans. The funny thing about the assassination was nobody seen the drama unfold. All was heard was two shots. As a group of children neared the U-Haul parking lot, a young girl spotted Woadie slumped in between the curb and his car. She instantly let out a blood curling scream for "HEEELPP."

Papa Bear and his wife prepared to leave their two bedroom home, headed for the Orleans Parish courthouse. Papa Bear B.K.A. Stanley Robinson, was a hard working citizen that provided for his wife, and his two sons, Ricky and Stanley Jr. He worked for his self as a carpenter for 25 long years. He had a great deal of respect around the city in the construction field. His only downfall was his crack addiction. Stanley had fell victim to the pipe well over five years now. He had done a great job of keeping his addiction from his wife's knowledge. Until a couple of weeks ago when him and his wife were pulled over by two undercover detectives. As the detectives drilled Stanley of his knowledge of the murders that happened on Pauger St., they had his van rummaged. Upon the search the cops found an ounce of crack cocaine. Stanley's wife was shocked by the discovery. She glared at him, as the two detectives drilled even harder about the tragic events on Pauger St. They were pressing the issue because they were informed that Stanley was working on a house a block away at the time of the murders. Stanley stood with beads of sweat rolling down his charcoal black chubby face. He glanced at his wife then at the detectives barking threats at him. "So what you gon do? Go down for this crack or save yourself and go home with your wife; who seems really upset right now." Jackson was really laying it on thick. He knew if he got Papa Bear to take the stand on Thugga, it would put the nail in the coffin. Papa Bear eventually agreed and was scheduled to have a meeting with David Silver, so they could go over the details of the case. He needed to be coached on how trial was going to play out. What Papa Bear didn't know was it didn't matter how you tried to justify snitching. It still meant death on the brutal streets of the N.O. He would definitely suffer the due consequences for taking the forbidden route of the game. "Baby I forgot my purse. Let me go run and get it" Papa Bear's wife said as she ran back into their home. She had been mad with him for the past couple of weeks, but he vowed to never smoke again. He even enrolled in an outpatient rehab program. The tension steadily died down when she saw how serious he was in his efforts to end his horrible addiction. What she wasn't aware of was even though he gave his life of smoking crack up, it still didn't stop the inevitable from happening. The mark was upon her head, for being associated with a marked man. As Papa Bear opened the front gate, he fumbled through his many keys on his key ring. He was stopped dead in his tracks when he heard his wife scream. When he turned around K-Real held his wife in a choke hold, with a massive gun to her head. The huge AR15 handgun made her head look like a peanut. The fear in Papa Bear's heart, as K-Real pressed the cannon to his wife's head, made him want to pass out. He knew what this was all about. As thoughts ran rapidly through his mind,

Teelee called out from behind him. "Papa Bear you bitch ass snitch. You really thought you was gon make it down there to catch the stand on my nigga!" Teelee had a menacing glare in his eyes, as each word flowed from his lips. Papa Bear hands and knees shook uncontrollably, as he dropped to his knees to beg for his life. "Pleaseee Teelee man don't kill me. I won't go. I'll disappear, and you'll never see me in New Orleans again." "Shut up bitch nigga. You might as well save that shit for God cause you bout to see him in a minute. Before I arrange the meetin, I'mma show you what we do to snitches, and anybody that's involved with a bitch ass snitch." Teelee gave K-Real a nod. K-Real then pushed Papa Bear's wife to the ground. She screamed as she looked into K-Real's venomous eyes. K-Real flashed a menacing smile, as her pink VVS diamonds glimmered from the shine of the chrome FN. Papa Bear looked on in horror as K-Real shot his wife in the mouth, "BOOM." Then emptied every last one of the 223, bullets into her lifeless body. "BOOM, BOOM, BOOM BOOM." By now Papa Bear was in tears not caring about life, after seeing his wife gunned down in cold blood. Teelee tapped Papa Bear on the shoulder with the barrel of the baby choppa he held in his grips. Papa Bear looked up, eyes filled with tears, then back down. "Pick ya head up pussy. I wanna look you in ya eyes when you take ya last breath." As quick as Papa Bear looked up, he was taken out. "BOOM, BOOM, BOOM, BOOM, BOOM, BOOM." Teelee unloaded all fifty rounds into Papa Bear's body, leaving his head stuck to the ground, and many of his body parts ripped to shreds. The hits were so gruesome due to the fact of them being snitches. They wanted to set an example for whoever even thought about running their mouths. Snitches get no love in the bloody streets of New Orleans.

Tamia sat in her living room watching T.V. Today was her day off. She just wanted to relax and enjoy the house to herself. She had plans later on to spend the evening with Teelee at his place. Tia wouldn't be home from North Carolina for another two days; so Tiger was taking advantage of the remaining time she had until her baby girl arrived. Her way of relaxing was watching her favorite soap opera. She flipped through the channels until *"The Young and The Restless"* came back on. It was instantly stopped by some breaking news on Fox 8.

> *"We're standing here live in front of the Orleans Parish courthouse where a man was found brutally murdered in front of this U-Haul parking lot. Police say a group of young children found him as they made their way to school. He was shot twice. Coroners say once in the mouth, and then in the head execution style. The victim was a key witness in a murder case that was set for motions this morning. Across town in Metairie, Keith Black is reporting live from a double homicide that is linked to this same case." Yes, Mary Ann I'm standing in front the home of Stanley and Lisa Richardson. The couple was gruesomely murdered in front of their home, as they attempted to make their way to the court house. Stanley Richardson was also a key witness in a murder case that was*

*set for motions today. Police have no leads in the incident. Neighbors say they heard numerous gunshots. When they looked to see what was going on, the suspects had already fled in a late modeled Chevy. The couple was long time citizens of their neighborhood, and were viewed as "good people" by their neighbors. It's really a sad story what happened here today. Back to you Mary Ann." "Yes it is truly sad, especially in this situation. The suspects blatantly disrespected the law enforcements of this city. The heinous act of murdering a man in broad day light, not even 50ft. away from the courthouse, displays the boldness in the murders. We have police spokesman, Martin Doe of the New Orleans Police Department here to give a brief rundown of the situation." "Yes we're doing a thorough investigation of the area, and looking for any leads that would help bring the suspects in that committed these horrible crimes today. The New Orleans Police Department will not rest until the culprits of these crimes are brought into custody." "No one got a glimpse of the incident?" "No ma'am. People are saying they heard shots nearby, but didn't see where they came from. Whoever the suspects are, they were swift in getting away. People in the area also say they didn't see any cars speed off, or any suspicious vehicle in the area." "Thank your Mr. Doe." "No, thank you Mary Ann. We'll be sure to update you of any new information in the upcoming days.*

Tamia cut the television off completely in a state of shock. She knew those same witnesses were the people testifying in Thugga's hearing set for today. The realization of Teelee being what the news described the suspects to be was a rude awakening. The life that Teelee lived was the life of none other than a "True Gangsta." She wasn't green to the streets, and she very well knew that Teelee and his team were the ones responsible for what happened today. Even though her instincts told her to get out and get out now, she just couldn't. The love she had in her heart for Teelee was too deep to back out now. The only thing she could do was try to drown out the evil in his heart, with the unconditional love she had for him. She knew he loved her just as much as she loved him. Could she pull it off was the question and could she do it before the penitentiary took him, or the graveyard swallowed him up?

# CHAPTER 16

# THE AFTER MATH

"Muthafucka! These son of a bitches done slipped through the crack!" Flat Top was furious as he paced up and down the side walk, in front of the court house on Tulane Ave. The feeling of Teelee and his gang getting off on this was eating him alive. Jackson on the other hand felt disappointed, because he couldn't put a cap on the case. In the midst of these tragic events, he was amazed at the boldness of these young cold blooded killers. Today's incidents showed him and many others that the Skull Gang was a forced to be reckoned with. Jackson knew deep in his heart, it was going to take much more than the weak tactics they were using, to take down this brigade. One thing for sure, he wasn't going to stop until every last member of that organization was behind bars. By any means necessary if need be. As the last of the camera crews vacated the area, Jackson and Flat Top headed back into the courthouse to speak with David Silver.

Inside the file room David Silver was in a rage. He couldn't believe the incidents that took place, moments before he was about to seal the deal on one of the most high profiles cases in his career. True enough he could have pushed for an extension, but what good would that have done. None in his favor, because the foundation that the case was built upon had been destroyed in a matter of minutes. Soon as Jackson and Flat Top entered the file room, Silver jumped down their throats. "What the fuck happened? I thought you all had the witnesses secured!" "We did" Jackson replied letting Silver know they handled their part. "We personally followed Rahim up here this morning. Stanley was ambushed before their escort could arrive." "We're dealing with some elites then huh?" Silver asked. "I'm afraid so" Flat Top replied. "Excuse me sir" the deputy said entering the file room. "Yes." Silver stepped forward to see what the deputy wanted. "The judge said he wants you in the courtroom right now." "Okay, I'll be right there." From there the deputy closed the door, leaving Silver, Flat Top and Jackson feeling like they already knew what the judge wanted. "Look I want a full investigation started on these guys." As the three proceeded into the courtroom, they noticed every member of the Skull Gang seated in the back of the courtroom. Ms. Mary was even there to show her support. As Jackson and Flat Top took a seat, Teelee gave both of them a wink of victory. The gesture made Flat Top want to jump across the seats and strangle the shit out of Teelee. They knew Teelee and his crew were responsible for the murders of their witnesses. The only thing was they couldn't prove it. The assassinations were done thoroughly, leaving no trace of evidence linking them to the crimes. The Skull Gang looked like a prestigious organization by the way they were dressed. Everyone from Teelee to Corey to Pistol, was draped in top of the line suits. K-Real even wore a conservative Chanel pants suit. They kept it simple yet classy. They all joined Lil Man, who was already there waiting for them. The judge called a short recess to give the defense teams, and the State time to prepare for the hearing and trial. When the judge got word of the incidents that transpired, he was astonished by the boldness of the criminals that pulled them off. Back when he was first appointed to the bench, it was no such thing as disrespecting the law. As much as he wanted to take these menaces off the street, he couldn't. That was left up to the district attorney's office. Julius Parker knew David Silver based his case upon witness statements. Tangible evidence in so many words. At any given moment that kind of evidence could be touched, and excluded from your arsenal. He knew this all too familiar. Back in his days, while holding down a spot as a District Attorney. He fought to gather evidence that couldn't be weakened by disastrous events like what took place today. He knew this case was closed due to the atrocities that went on. He planned to enforce a thorough investigation of the situation. "All rise, court is now in session" the deputy called out. "You may be seated." The atmosphere of the courtroom was very silent and cold. The sudden murders put fear in a lot of people's heart. Which made them ponder in their thoughts. One thing was certain, the assassinations made people second guess even more about being, or becoming a State's witness. Wayne Williams stepped up sharp as a tack, and ready to attack. "Your Honor, I'm here on behalf of Ronnie Bennett. I'm prepared for motions." As he passed Teelee's seat, he gave his shoulder a squeeze, letting him know everything was okay. "Counselor approach the bench." The look in David Silver eyes gave off the sign of defeat. He approached the bench with his shoulders slumped like his career had been put to an end. Wayne Williams signaled for Teelee to step in the hallway. As they made it through the doors to the lobby, Wayne Williams pulled Teelee to the side. "Yeah what's good?" Teelee asked. "Everything is all set, but we have one problem." "What is it?" Teelee sighed, knowing it wasn't going to be that easy. "The judge is really upset about the murders of the witnesses. I think he might demand an investigation, before he proceeded to accept the State's request to drop the case. I've spoken with the D.A. He's already spoke with the chief D.A.; they are prepared to drop the case. One thing I do need to inform you on." Wayne Williams pulled Teelee in closer. "It's about to be real tight on the streets. If you know what I mean." Teelee knew exactly what he was referring to. He had a plan for that part of the game. "Don't worry bout that. It's time for me to take a lil vacation anyway. We gon be off the scene for a minute. You just handle your part." Wayne Williams's whole demeanor changed. "Before we go back into the courtroom." Teelee cut him off, he already knew what Wayne Williams wanted. "Go to the same place, they gon take care of you." Teelee walked off, leaving him standing there. The thought of the A1 yola made Wayne Williams excited, as he headed back into the courtroom behind Teelee. Teelee took his seat as Wayne

Williams made his way to the defense table. He gave Thugga a nod, letting him know things were in motion. David Silver was shuffling through a file, getting ready to go forward with the court proceedings. Before he got a chance to open his mouth, the judge cut him off. "Before you proceed Counselor. I would like to address the courtroom, and anyone else that's in earshot, of what I'm about to say. Today some heinous acts took place pertaining to a case that was set for motions. I myself, am appalled. There is no more respect for the city's law enforcement, or judicial system. The boldness of the criminals of this city, are outrageous. As an enforcer of the law, it is my duty to thoroughly look into this situation. My guess is by the acts that transpired today, many people are afraid to cooperate with the judicial system. The lack of protection from law enforcement, is absurd." The judge's remark caused murmurs to circulate around the courtroom. "Mr. Silver." The judge looked at David Silver with a look that made him feel even smaller than he already was feeling. "I'm sick and tired of the looseness in the D.A.'s operations. It's your job to secure the witnesses, to a point that they are free from having to worry about situations like these. It's because of the laziness of your department that this happened today. Furthermore, I'm making it an order that anymore cases brought into my courtroom, be based upon solid evidence and not the frivolous garbage that has been brought forth in the past. As for this case Mr. Williams, I'm setting this hearing for a later date. Mrs. Brown, give me a date three weeks from today." The clerk proceeded to find a date suitable to the judge's wishes. "How about June 23 Judge?"

"That's fine. On that date and time, if nothing has arisen about the acts that transpired today, and the state hasn't produced any solid evidence to support this case. I'm dismissing it off of my docket." The fact that he wouldn't be getting out today kind of disappointed Thugga, but honestly he wasn't tripping. He knew his fam had covered all traces. The D.A. wasn't about to come up with any new evidence to keep him any longer. Three weeks wasn't shit, compared to the life sentence he was faced with. As the deputy escorted Thugga out of the courtroom, all of them locked eyes. Nothing was said, the smiles that were spread across their faces was enough.

It hadn't been three days since the murders of Woadie, Papa Bear, and his wife took place and NOPD already had the streets on lock, which was to be expected. Judge Parker made it pretty clear that he wanted some answers. He still couldn't believe the audacity of the criminals. They outright disrespected something he proudly represented; The Judicial system. Flat Top and Jackson were put in control of "Operation Tighten Up." The Chief of Police, labeled this whole operation tighten up for one reason. To tighten up all the loose cracks in his department. They needed to gain back the confidence of all of the citizens of New Orleans. Showing they were still able to protect and serve, the motto they supposedly stood on. Special Task Force teams hit the streets periodically. They were assigned to different wards. Their main objective was to get leads on the murders. All previous and active informants were forced to be on radar for any information on the assassinations. The operation and the investigation was basically a waste of time. Everyone all the way down to the Judge knew it was a useless investigation, but they had to enforce their authority and try to put a top on the pressure cooker; better known to some as the "Murda Cappy." The Skull Gang just sat back and let them do what they do. Of course Jackson and Flat Top put a red light on their turf. It didn't matter much, because all surrounding areas of the Skull Gang's territory; was shut down. The only area that was still pumping was the spots out in Bogalusa and Raceland. Roylee and his team were still in control of the spot in Raceland. The only change was the method of delivery, and payoff. Courtesy of Lanzo and one of his many establishments. The kilos were delivered untraced. Every first Thursday of the month a shipment was delivered to each location. To the naked eye, the spots were supplied with groceries from Conco Food Services. All money was delivered by the head lieutenants in an exclusive place that would never be suspected. Teelee and the gang made sure all their "T's" were crossed and "I's", were dotted. Teelee announced that they would be taking a cruise to get away from the heat of the streets. He got one of his pops friends; that worked at a Traveling Agency, to hook him up with a great group package. He knew Thugga was going to need something like that after getting out of jail. It was sort of a coming home gift. Besides that, he wanted to spend some exclusive time with Tiger. What better way to do so then going on a romantic trip to an exclusive island like, St. Bart's. They were elevating in the game. It was time to see more than just the N.O. If everything went as planned, they all were going to have shares in Lil Man's girlfriend family business. Teelee wasn't the only one that found him a ride or die chick. Sharon and Marion was two wealthy twin sisters from Eastern New Orleans. Their aunt stepped out on faith on an idea that she had been pondering over for years. It blew up overnight. Candy was a middle aged, lifelong resident of New Orleans. Candy had a taste for money and an eye for opportunity. Her never ending ambitions finally paid off. Landing her a string of Pain Management clinics. Business was so good Candy moved her family to an exclusive subdivision in New Orleans East. Lil Wayne was their next door neighbor. Playing around with an idea about investing in Candy's business, became a reality. Teelee ran it by Lil Man, who then presented the proposal to Candy. Candy thought on it and eventually offered Lil Man and the gang a spot in her business. Teelee knew he had to start making some smart business decisions. The first one was to make their dirty money, clean. They were starting to stick out a little too much. All the expensive automobiles, clothing, and other things an ordinary person couldn't afford; they now had it all. It was time for him to start accumulating answers for them people when they started asking questions.

Today was the day Teelee was going to get the chance to meet Tia, and all the rest of Tamia's family. Denise; Tamia's sister, was throwing a crawfish boil and invited Teelee over. When Teelee pulled into the Melpomene project, the scenery was full of life. Kids ran around chasing each other, while most of the residents sat on their porches enjoying the summer breeze. It was a beautiful day for a crawfish boil. The humidity was rather pleasant considering the normal sweltering days that was usually in effect. As Teelee pulled the Audi in front of Denise's building, he laid eyes on Tia for the first time. She was so beautiful. A cute mini version of Tamia. "Damn this girl looks just like Tiger" Teelee thought as he prepared to get out the car. Tamia looked ravishing as usual, in her canary yellow sun dress. Just the sight of her sent Teelee into a complete daze. The feeling he got when he was around her was euphoric. He never felt this type of feeling in the presence of a woman. That made him even more eager to have some intimate time alone with her in St. Bart's. He hadn't informed her as of yet about the trip. He felt today would be a good day to present it to her. Teelee stepped out with his Mauri Gator tennis shoes on his feet and Cooji short set. Of course his bling was on point as usual. The young boy was getting a lot of attention as he got out of the Audi. All the women that were hanging out in the area, gawked at the young hustler's swagger. Knowing the intentions of the horny desperate women, Tamia quickly stated her claim on Teelee. She walked right up on him and planted big kiss on his lips. "Damn someone's happy to see me huh?" Teelee asked, savoring the taste of Tamia's MAC Lip Glass. "Umm, and you're not" Tamia replied cutting her eyes at Teelee. "Shid, I'm probably more excited to see you beautiful." Teelee stole another taste of her sweet lips before she led him to where the rest of the family was. Among the many faces was Tamia's uncles, aunts, cousins, and friends of the family. Tamia formally introduced Teelee to everyone before she led him upstairs to meet Shorty C. Teelee was a little nervous at first, he had never met her, and he didn't know what type of man she wanted for Tamia. True in all Tamia was old enough to make her own decisions, but the acceptance of the mother was always a key point. They ran into Cherrelle, while heading up the stairs to Denise's apartment. "Cherrelle this my baby Teelee. Teelee this my sister, Cherrelle. The way Tamia lit up whenever she introduced Teelee made him feel real special. It was like she was honored to be with him. The feeling was truly mutual. "How you doing Teelee? I heard so much about you. It's nice to finally get a chance to meet the one and only Mr. Teelee" Cherrelle said extending her hand. "Nice to meet you to, sister-in-law" Teelee replied as he shook Cherrelle hand. "What part of the city you from again" Cherrelle asked. "I told you he from the 7th Ward girl" Tamia stated. "Oh yeah, you got one of them "Hard Heads" huh?" "Yeah but I soften up for my baby right chere, ya heard me." Teelee wrapped his arms around Tamia's waist showing his affectionate side. "Ain't nothing wrong with that. Do you brother-in-law." "Where Tia ran off to Tiger, I seen her when I pulled up" Teelee asked anxious to meet her. "Well I'mma let y'all go. I'mma be downstairs if you need me sis. She fixed you something to eat yet Teelee?" Cherrelle asked. "No, I got my baby. I want him to meet momma and Tia first. Tia must be in here with my momma" Tamia said entering Denise's apartment. "Momma where you at?" "I'm back here with Tia cleaning her hands. I'm coming" Shorty yelled from the bathroom. "Have a seat bae. You want something to drink, before I fix your food? They got beer in the coolers." "Yeah baby, gimme a Heineken." As Tamia went to get Teelee's beer, Shorty C and Tia was coming out the bathroom. Tia was even more precious up close. Teelee stood up to introduce himself, since Tamia had walked off for a second. There's nothing like a man with confidence, but still humble in a sense. "How you doing Ms. Cheryl?" "I'm fine. You must be Jamal" Shorty replied taking a seat on the couch. "Yeah that's me. How you doing pretty girl" Teelee asked winking at Tia as she gripped her grandmother's pants leg. "What you actin all shy for? Don't let her fool you Jamal. Once she gets to know you, you won't be able to handle her lil bad self." "I see y'all met already?" Tamia asked, while handing Teelee his beer. She picked up her baby girl and kissed her. She noticed how shy Tia was. "Tia this is Teelee, who I talk to you about. Say Hi." Tia waved and smiled at Teelee, then shyly put her head on her mother's shoulder. You want your food now, or you want to wait?" "I'm cool for now sweetie. I'm just getting acquainted with my mother-in-law and my step daughter." "Oh so you confident you got my baby in a bag huh?" Shorty asked as she pulled her cigarettes from her pocket. "Yeah pretty much. One thing I know fasho; a man can't let a good woman pass him up. They have very few good women left chere ya heard me." Teelee's statement made Tamia's face light up. "Yeah I here ya baby. Gimme a light. Them bad ass kids done picked up my lighter. I don't know where my shit at." "Here you could have this one." Teelee gave Shorty one of the many lighters he had in his pocket. "Damn Jamal, what you got all them lighters for?" "I always have to buy one every time I go to the store. They always fall out my pocket and get lost under the seat of my car. I just had my car detailed today and they pulled about five from under the seat." Teelee and Shorty C got better acquainted, as the crawfish boil progressed. They ended up outside with the rest of the family members. Eventually Tia warmed up to Teelee, or maybe it was the money he was tricking off to her. He couldn't resist, she was so cute. Whatever it was they all seemed to hit if off just fine. The alcohol was flowing, and the crawfish tails was popping. Denise had damn near every type of seafood you could think of. From crabs to oysters, which was Tamia's favorite. "You know this an aphrodisiac huh?" Teelee asked, as he fed Tamia a fried oyster. "Well the more I eat, the betta for you" Tamia replied with a lustful look in her eyes. "Look we gon save that for later. You don't wanna have to leave the party early huh." "Boy you crazy." "Yeah crazy ova you." Just as Teelee tasted those sweet lips once again, Big Hulk walked up. "What it do my nigga" Hulk said interrupting Teelee and Tamia's intimate kiss. "Shid nigga koolading. Just meetin the fam you know. How you livin since you done upgraded?" "Life good round. Thanks to my nigga." Hulk meant every word. Life was truly wonderful for Hulk ever since Teelee plugged him into his connect. Teelee's intentions was to put Hulk down with their operations, but the product Hulk moved was on another level. With a co-sign from Lanzo, Teelee put Hulk in the game with some of the purest Heroin around. Hulk's dope spots pumped 24/7, giving him an extreme boost financially and socially. "Where your daddy at Hulk?" Tamia asked. "Shorty been lookin for him." "He gon be round here in a minute. I just talk to him a few minutes ago." "Well I guess I'll let y'all talk business fellas. I'mma be upstairs with Denise and momma if you need me bae." "Aight, I'mma be up there in a minute. Oh yeah Tiger, I got a surprise for you too." "In that case, don't be long" Tamia said walking off in a sexy glide. "Damn I love that girl" Teelee stated while watching Tamia walk off. "My ole cousin got you sprung huh" Hulk joked. "Call it what you want to playa. I ain't too proud to say it, ya heard me." "Take a walk wit me" Hulk said leading Teelee across the driveway to his brand new, midnight blue Cadillac Escalade XLT. The 28 inch rims made it look like a monster truck. "Share a puff wit ya nigga right quick. Tiger ain't going nowhere." The two proceeded to jump in the truck. Upon entering Teelee was welcomed with the elegance of the Caddy. It was not only tricked out on the outside, it was well put together on the inside also. Ostrich and suede covered the seats. While the numerous amount of TV's lit up the interior. It definitely matched Hulk's persona. Hulk grabbed a zip lock bag from his middle console. It contained some exclusive multi colored marijuana. "This that midnight" Hulk said pulling a nice size bud from the bag. "Well what you waitin for nigga, put it in the air" Teelee replied, while handing Hulk a Keep Moving. Midnight was a well-known weed supplier in Uptown New Orleans. Originally out of the Calliope projects. The weed he supplied was so official, people patented his product by his street name. He was always known for his exotic top of the line Ganja. "Y'all been havin any heat on y'all end lately?" Teelee asked as he glanced at the T.V. monitor installed in the rearview mirror. Nelly's *"Tip Drill"* video was in full stride. "Yeah but it ain't stopping the cash flow. Just gotta keep a tight rein ova my spots you know. Why you ask, them bitches still fuckin wit y'all?"

"Yeah Jackson and Flat Top really got the impression they go catch us slippin." "Well if you need me, you know what it do" Hulk said putting the finishing touches on the blunt. "Fasho, fasho. Look, me and the team going on a lil getaway to duck some of this heat for a minute. If you bout comin, you know you always welcome." "Shid nigga I would, but I just got this new shipment of dope. I gotta oversee the first dose I hit the street wit. You know how that go." "I feel ya, but if you change ya mind, holla at me. We ain't leavin until next week. It's a comin home gift for my nigga Thugga and a treat for my baby." "Say Teelee I ain't never told you, but I'm glad you wit my cousin. I always worried about her gettin hooked up wit one of these fuck boy ass niggas." "Well you know one thing, I'mma take care of her and Tia to the fullest. You ain't gotta worry bout that, I got them." "I already know ya heard me." They smoked and conversed about a few other things before parting ways. Hulk ventured off to check on his spots, while Teelee headed back across the driveway. It was getting late so some of the family had left. The ones that remained made their way up to Denise's apartment. They did like most black folks did and finished the party off with a couple more rounds. Soon as Teelee walked into Denise's apartment, he was pulled by the arm by Shorty, with her Daiquiri cup in the other hand. "Move Jah so my son-in-law can sit down." Jah slick side rolled her eyes, but quickly obliged her grandmother's request. Jah was Denise's eldest daughter. One thing was certain, she wouldn't dare let Shorty catch her rolling her eyes. Shorty and Denise would have jumped on her like she was getting initiated into a gang.

"Excuse me" Shorty said interrupting everyone's conversation. "Have y'all met my new son-in-law?" Of course everyone had met Teelee earlier. "Yeah momma, I already introduced him earlier" Tamia said. "You got you a cutie huh Niecy" Tamia's grandmother commented. The statement made Teelee ease up a bit, because not only did he have the approval of Shorty, but it seemed Tamia's grandmother second the motion. "Yeah grandma, this my other baby" Tamia replied snuggling up next to Teelee while rubbing his soft grain of hair. Iola Breaux had keen eyes for low down men. Especially when it came to her granddaughters. She had her fair share of the street life. She'll be damn if she let her babies go through what she went through. She always spoke her mind, rather you liked it or not. With a beautiful mane of silver gray hair, and a radiant smile, Iola Breaux seemed like she never missed a beat. She refused to be treated as if she was too old. She never missed a chance to share her wonderful wisdom with her loved ones and friends. The sudden gesture gave Tamia confirmation on the love of her life. Usually her first statement towards her male friends would be negative, with Teelee this wasn't the case. Maybe she was headed in the right direction with this thing with Teelee. She didn't know for sure, but one thing was certain; things were looking good. "Jamal where your people from?" Ms. Iola asked crossing one leg over the other. "My daddy people out the 9th Ward and my momma people out the 7th Ward." "I might know some of your people. I used to run in both of those areas." "Well if everything go like I want it to go, you'll be meetin my peeps in due time." "You love my granddaughter, don't you?" Iola asked catching Teelee off guard. "Grandma!" "What gurl. I'm just seeing what the boy intentions are." "It's cool Tiger, I ain't got a problem answering the question. Yeah, I love Tamia. To be real wit you, I ain't never met a woman that made me feel like she do." "That's right son-in-law, tell it like it is" Shorty C said throwing her arm around Teelee's neck. "Momma you ready to go" Tamia replied. "We gon bring you home mother-in-law." "Baby I don't need you to bring me home. I got my own car outside." "Tiger y'all bring her home it's too late for her to be driving by herself. I'mma bring your car in the morning" Cherrelle said grabbing Shorty keys out of her hand. "There y'all go tripping. I can handle myself. I ain't ready to go home." "You may not be ready, but you bout to bring ya ass in ya house. It's too dangerous out there" Ms. Iola said in a demanding tone. Even Shorty couldn't protest to that. Once Iola spoke, that's what it was.

"She straight bae" Teelee asked pushing the passenger side door open so Tamia could get in. "Yeah she on her way to dreamland. She was boarding the plane when I took her shoes off." "That's good. I really enjoyed myself. I got love for the fam already." "I'm glad you did baby. My momma is something else huh?" "She was just feelin good baby that's all. I get like that sometimes. You'll see in the future." "You betta not get like that round me. I'mma take advantage of your ass." "Well shid, you make me wanna get tipsy right nah." "Boy you crazy" Tamia said in a light chuckle. As the Audi glided down I-10 with Tia sleep on the back seat, Tamia gazed out of the moon roof. "It's a beautiful night tonight." "I know a beautiful night to see what you'll say about this." Teelee threw two Carnival Cruise tickets in Tamia's lap. "Bae what's this?" Tamia asked as she picked the tickets up from her lap. "That's my surprise I was talkin bout." As Tamia flipped through the tickets she realized the destination and her whole face lit up. She was even more beautiful in the moonlight. "Damn my baby beautiful" Teelee thought to himself. "We going to St. Bart's baby" Tamia asked excited. "Yeah week after next" Teelee replied feeling good that he could bring happiness into Tamia's life. "Oh, I gotta see who gon watch Tia. I don't know what I'mma wear. I gotta call my job too!" Teelee grabbed Tamia's hand and gently placed his finger on her lips. "Baby girl you just show up. I got the rest."

# CHAPTER 17

# HOME FREE

"Make sure all your property in the bag." The deputy barked at Thugga as she finished processing him out of the system. Thugga was home free. After three more weeks of waiting, Judge Julius Parker, finally accepted the State's request to drop the charges. It took a lot out of the Judge to have to release Thugga back into the streets. Beads of sweat rolled off his balding head, as he banged the gavel dismissing the case. He accepted the lost, but he vowed to put pressure on N.O.P.D. and the D.A.'s office. The two departments would either shape up, or get shipped out. Even though the charges were dismissed and the investigation was terminated, the heat was still on in the streets. Especially any territory ran by the Skull Gang. Teelee felt a relief that he was about to get away from the chaotic streets of the N.O. Spending time away with Tiger made the feeling even more satisfying. "Oohh Thugga baby I miss you, lay down boy, I wanna show you just how much. I can see you miss me too."
"You fuckin right! Now stop talkin and show me what you talkin

bout" Thugga demanded. "Mmmhmm I miss suckin this dick." "Mr. Bennett, I said Mr. Bennett!" "Damn my bad wzup." If you tryna get out of here step by the yellow line. Thugga was so eager to walk through the door of the dreadful place that held him captive. Before he knew it he'd slipped off into a day dream of getting some head from one of his females. Thugga and the rest of the many others that were being released; made their way through the doors of freedom. Everyone dispersed either to greet their awaiting loved ones, or on their way to catch the RTA bus. It was late so Thugga shook the thought of waiting anywhere. It was too dangerous to stand in front of Central Lockup, yet alone walking from the area. In the N.O. you never knew who wanted to push ya top back. It was in your best interest to take all precautions. Several people were gunned down in the past, immediately after being released from Orleans Parish prison. The internet was very useful in many ways nowadays. Anyone could find out your release date just by the press of a button; making the system appear not so helpful in a situation like this. Thugga pulled out his cell phone trying to see if it was still juiced up. To his disadvantage it was deader than a corpse in the morgue. As he looked up a black on black Escalade with dark tinted windows pulled up directly in front of him. Just before he was about to break camp like Carl Lewis, the passenger door to the truck swung open. Lil Man jumped out with a bottle of Cristal in his hand. "Welcome home my nigga!" "Nigga you spooked the fuck outta me." "What it do homey" Teelee asked as he hopped out the driver side of the Lac. "I'm coolin, happy to be out that bitch." "I see you my nigga. What you was getting ya workout on in there." Your lil bird chest kinda stickin out" Lil Man joked. "I see y'all. When y'all cop this thang?" "What this here?" Teelee asked turning towards the beautiful truck. The jet black paint job was so smooth and glossy that the truck appeared to be wet. The 26 inch Giovanni's was painted in black with the lip of the rim in chrome. The whole interior was redone. The seats were wrapped in top of the line alligator skin. The audio and TV systems was hooked up to the fullest. The truck could have been easily put into a car show. "You like this, Round?" Teelee asked, with a big grin on his face. "You fuckin right! Y'all did the damn thang wit this bitch!" "Check out the back, it's even better." Soon as Thugga opened the back door of the Escalade, he was greeted with two Asian beauties. To say they were Asian, their assets were speaking a whole different language. "Damn baby y'all just what a soulja need after getting out that bitch." "We more than you need. We a little extra" the Kimora Lee look alike said as she grabbed a handful of Thugga's private. "Man what it do. Let's get away from this place. I had enough of being round this bitch." "Aight, look bring me and Lil Man to our whips. You go do ya thang wit the Fast and Furious girls. Meet us in the morning for 8:00, at Anita's. We got you a room at the Ritz. All the info in the envelope in the glove box. Oh yeah this here truck for you too." "Good lookin my niggas. Y'all really showed ya brother love in and out this bullshit." "Nigga you know what is. Its Skull Gang for life ova here ya heard me. Before I forget we got you all new clothes. We left two fits you could pick from in the suite. Don't worry ya bling in there too." "That's wzup." From there Thugga dropped Teelee and Lil Man off then headed to the Ritz to get his swerve on with the two Asian dime pieces.

"Wzup homey" you still at the room?" Teelee asked cruising up Tulane on his way to Anita's. He hated to leave Tamia, but he had business to handle. Thugga was laid up in between the two Asian freaks, still on cloud nine from his freak fest. The two really gave Thugga the ride of his life. They popped and plugged each other with numerous Ecstasy pills. He had never experienced that kind of freaky shit in his life. The two fast and furious girls pulled out that Karma Sutra shit. They did positions you would never think possible. It was the least they could do, considering the hefty amount of money Teelee and Lil Man dropped off. "Yeah Whoa, these two thangs wore ya boy out last night, ya heard me." "That's good to hear, cause we popped them hoe's off with a nice lil stack." "I already know. I know they ain't put it on full throttle for nuthin." "So what's good; you gon get ya lazy ass up or what?" "Yeah I'm bout to get up right now, ya heard me." "Aight I'm on my way to Anita's. Lil Man just left Twin house. Hurry up, don't have a nigga waitin." "Nigga go head, I'mma be there." "Fasho" Teelee replied, before disconnecting the call. "I hate to leave these two fine freaks, but I gotta see what it do wit the Fam" Thugga thought as he slapped the bare ass cheek of one of the freaks. All the drugs and wild sex had them both out for the count. Thugga was feeling the effects of their night as well, but he shook the feeling quick. There was nothing that could keep a previously incarcerated person inside, or away from the scene. Especially a young, major playa like Thugga. He loved the limelight, and he was going to definitely shine as much as he could while he was in it. Thugga threw on one of the outfits Teelee and Lil Man had bought for him. He threw six big faces on the night stand, and hit the door. They broke it off so proper that he couldn't help but to leave a lil tip. He also left his cell phone number; couldn't lose contact with two high powered freaks like those two. He never knew when a drought night would occur. When the valet pulled the Escalade to the front of the Ritz, it drew a crowd of admirers. The truck looked even better in the daylight. It looked similar to a Tonka toy. As Thugga jumped in the truck, you would have sworn a celebrity was just spotted; how the traffic on Canal St. slowed up. The all-white Marc Jacob linen short set, with the white high top Cole Haans really made Thugga stand out. His Skull Gang piece really put the icing on the cake. Courtesy of Teelee and Lil Man. They had the whole chain redone. The white diamonds were replaced with black and yellow diamonds; giving it the color of their home team, "The New Orleans Saints." Thugga pulled off from in front of the Ritz headed for Anita's. As he turned to grab his stash of purple haze from his overnight bag, he noticed something he didn't recognize the night before. Teelee and Lil Man had his nickname "Thugezy" stitched in the head rest. He sparked the Keep Moving and contemplated how far they had come in just a matter of months. In his heart, even though he wasn't a religious type of person, he thanked God for blessing him with some genuine solid friends. It was really rare to have some trustworthy riders on your team. It was so cutthroat in the cold streets of New Orleans, even your own blood brother would cross you out. Thugga knew what type of souljas stood behind him, and he would lay his life on the line if need be. Teelee and Lil Man wasn't the only ones that held it down. The whole squad played their part. Each contributed their fair share, especially K-Real She made sure all his clientele was taken care of. She never missed a chance to go and visit him either. Her efforts showed that she was truly loyal to the team; which made everyone in the clique look at her no different than they looked at themselves. "Fam Gang, Skull Gang" to the fullest. Thugga whipped the Escalade into Anita's extremely small parking lot, and parked alongside Teelee and Lil Man. As soon as he entered the restaurant, the smell of eggs and pork chops made him appreciate being home. Being locked up stripped you of having the freedom to eat whatever you wanted; even the little things were appreciated more. Thugga spotted Teelee and Lil Man seated at the back of the restaurant and headed in their direction. "What it do son" Thugga said, sliding in the booth seat next to Teelee. "We coolin, happy to see our nigga home ya heard me" Teelee replied throwing his arm around Thugga's neck. "So what's good. What was so important y'all had to pull me away from them two freaks so quick." "Nigga what you mean. You been gone almost six months, and you don't wanna fuck wit ya niggas." "Damn Lil Man be cool. I'm just fuckin wit y'all. On the real, them two Asian broads some real certified freaks. One of them hoe's tried to lick my ass. I almost broke that bitch jaw." "I'm glad to hear they broke bread like Jesus said. We paid both of them hoe's a stack a piece. Them hoe's better had showed love, like Bub" Teelee said, fiddling with his blackberry. He was sending Tiger a message ***"Wzup beautiful, you up yet".*** "You know money ain't a thang. I'm rockin wit my nigga Slim on that type of shit. I rather pay for it. It keeps the stalker side of a bitch from comin out ya heard me. I even left them hoe's a tip, and the number to the cell." "Man fuck that shit, on to more important things," Lil Man said throwing a manila envelope in Thugga's lap. "What's this homey?" "That's part of your comin home gift" Teelee said as he signaled for the waitress to come to their table. Thugga pulled two carnival cruise tickets and two ten thousand dollar stacks from the envelope. Y'all sending a nigga on a cruise?" Thugga asked with a puzzled look on his face. "No round, we all going on a cruise. I felt it was time to duck the heat in the streets, and besides that it's about time we start seeing different shit anyway." Lil Man got word from his girl auntie, and she said it's a go. We gon be cleaning some of this dope money. Why not parlay on an exotic island for a couple of days." "What's the money for then? Real been handling business wit all my customers." "Nigga stop actin like you green. That's ya splurge money. This trip on me and Lil Man. You just show up when the boat bout to pull off." "That's wzup my niggas. I got mad love for y'all homey. You niggas really held it down like some true gangstas for a nigga." "You know what it is wit us. Nigga we brothers. Anything else would be uncivilized" Lil Man said. "Now stop getting all sentimental on a nigga." "Y'all ready to order baaby?" "Yeah gimme my usual. What y'all eatin?" Teelee asked passing the menu to the waitress. "I'm good, twin cooked breakfast this mornin." "Gimme the same thang my lil homey eatin, but double up on the eggs and grits" Thugga requested. He was anxious to get some good food in his stomach. He was burnt out on the jail house food, especially Orleans Parish favorite dish; "Chicken Alakeen." Soon as the waitress made it back with their orders Thugga dug in. It didn't take long for him to finish off his double serving of cheese grits, eggs, and two fried pork chops. "Damn son you finish already" Teelee asked, barely halfway through with his own food. "Son don't act like you don't know how it is right after you get out that place. "I'm already knowing. I'm just fuckin wit you my nigga." "Say son, y'all know that boy Rafee get out today huh? Damn it feel like son been gone for some months. It don't feel nowhere near five years" Thugga said rubbing his full stomach. "It be like that when you living outchere in the free world" Teelee replied taking the last bite of his pork chop. "So what's good wit the schedule for today?" Thugga asked anxious to let it be known he was back on the scene. "We got some shit planned for you and Rafee. Just be cool, ya heard me." Lil Man threw a hundred-dollar bill on the table and headed for the door. As he made it to the front of the restaurant, he turned and noticed Teelee and Thugga still seated. "What you niggas waitin on?" "Hold up boss playa. Let a nigga finish his OJ" Teelee replied, as he guzzled down the rest of his drink. "Aight Ms. Anita, we gon holla at you next time. We bout to rock." "Alright Teelee, y'all boys be careful.

Follow us" Teelee said hitting the locks on his Audi. The three pulled off from Anita's heading to the 7th Ward. It was a beautiful day for the welcome home events set out for Thugga and Rafee. Rafee had been off the scene way before Teelee and the gang stepped it up, and started rolling with the big dogs. They all grew up together, but due to Rafee's bad luck with the law, he was rarely present on the street. That still didn't hinder Teelee, Lil Man and Thugga from keeping in touch. They made sure his books stayed fat, and his mother's bills were paid in full every month. Rafee was a real menace to society. He had a real itchy trigger finger, and an extremely bad attitude. The combination of the two kept him jammed up in the back of a police car. Teelee was prepared for Rafee and his loose cannon. Instead of giving him his own territory, he decided to let him do the monthly pickups; that way he'd stay away from any hands on operations. That would limit his interaction with too many different people. If he didn't know you, his respect for you was zero. Just by looking at him you would never think he was chaotic as he was. Standing 5'4, 160 lbs., soaking wet, with the face of a kid. You would easily misjudge him for a cool ass dude; just off his looks alone. A lot of people slipped up and made that mistake. After the gun smoke cleared, the ones left standing realized the misjudgment was a grave mistake.

As the three luxury automobiles pulled in front of Rafee's mom's house, Rafee plucked his cigarette to the ground and stood up on the porch. The tinted windows on the three cars prevented him from seeing who was behind the wheel. Soon as Rafee attempted to reach for his 44 bulldog, Teelee hopped out of the Audi greeting his comrade. "What it do son." "Nigga I was bout to make them pretty cars look real ugly." "I already know. That's why I hoped out. Rafee you still crazy than a muthafucka." "Wzup homey" Thugga said, hopping out of the Escalade. "Shid you know me, ain't nuthin change but the season my nigga." The two shared a manly one arm hug. "Damn round you been hittin the weight pile heavy huh?" Thugga asked, recognizing the bulk in Rafee arms. "Nigga I had to focus my time on sumthin. I took my stress out on the weights, ya heard me." Where that boy Lil Man at?" Just as Rafee asked about Lil Man, he jumped out of his 760I talking on his cell phone. "I'mma have to get back at cha, ya heard me" Lil Man said ending his call. "What's good son" Lil Man said with a big smile on his face. "I'm good son. Wzup wit you? I see you jumping out the big 760. All y'all boyz riding fly huh." "Don't trip round, you gon be rockin just like this. We got you son" Lil Man said, happy to see his lil potna. "Mom's said y'all was doing good outchere. I ain't know y'all boyz was rockin like this." "Shid nigga, you ain't seen shit yet" Teelee replied as he retrieved his ringing cell phone off his hip. "Yeah what it do?" "Everybody outchere wit the second line band. We waitin on y'all." "Aight Real, we gon be round there in a minute. Real said she waitin on us. Lil Man, y'all ready?" "Yeah lets rock" Lil Man said, headed for the 760. "Wait a minute. Rafee why you ain't dress my nigga?" Teelee asked, looking at the penitentiary slippers Rafee had on. "Nigga y'all ain't call and tell a nigga y'all was on the way." "You got the clothes we bought for you huh?" "Yeah let me run in and throw sumthin on. I'mma be right back." "Where mom's at?"

Thugga asked. "She at work, ya heard me." "Well here, leave this for her." Thugga pulled out a handful of hundred dollar bills and gave them to Rafee. "Good lookin son. I'mma leave it on her dresser for her." "Hurry up nigga. We got a big day planned for y'all" Teelee said jumping in the Audi. "Fasho, I'mma be right back."

Numerous of people flooded St. Bernard Ave. "Welcome Home" banners covered the front wall of the Autocrat Social Club. The atmosphere was lively, as people mingled and anticipated the second line to crank up. The Money Chasers second line club was set to welcome Rafee and Thugga home in style. They were draped in green and white tailor made suits. With some $1,700, gators on their feet. The head man of the group was Teelee's uncle. They planned to tear up the street with some fancy foot work in honor of Teelee's entourage. New Orleans is well known for its second lines. It starts off with just a few people, but by the middle of the route; hundreds of followers have joined in. The second line crew is led by a live band, which causes the crew to show off their fancy foot work. "Say round, it's crowded like a muthafucka outchere" Lil Man said as he turned onto St. Bernard Ave. Rafee sat in the passenger seat observing the area. It seemed that he wasn't pleased with the crowd. "What's wrong my nigga?" Lil Man asked noticing the uneasiness on Rafee's face. "I'm coolin son. You know a nigga ain't been on the scene for a minute. They got a lot of new faces outchere. You know a nigga like me ain't trusting nuthin." "Don't trip my nigga. We run these streets. Ain't nuthin going down like that." "I'm feelin that, but nigga can't never get to comfortable you feel me. You see what happened to Corey huh?" "Yeah I know where you comin from. Trust me round we ain't slippin by the least" Lil Man said as he flipped a switch on his middle console. Immediately the back seat flipped up exposing an AK47, with a hundred round drum. "Damn whoa, you on some James Bond type shit huh." "Sumthin like that, but on the real be cool my nigga. Everything on point. I want you to enjoy ya self. All this for y'all son. I got you round. Here, roll some of this." Lil Man threw Rafee a half ounce of granddaddy purpa, and a box of Keep Moving. As they pulled up in front of the Autocrat, K-Real approached with two bottles of Dom Perignon. Teelee was the first to hop out. "What it do Real?" "It's all love baby boy. My crew back in full effect. What more could a bitch ask for." Thugga jumped out the Escalade feeling his self. This was definitely Thugga's type of atmosphere. He loved the adrenaline rush that the streets gave him. "What's up Thugga baaby?" Real asked as she threw her arms around Thugga's neck. "Shid you know me Real. I'm back home wit my fam. What more can a nigga want." "Well here baaby, start this shit off right." K-Real handed Thugga one of the bottles of champagne. Thugga turned the bottle up to the sky, as he guzzled down a huge gulp. Lil Man and Rafee exited the 760. Soon as Lil Man feet hit the pavement a flock of females surrounded him. Who could blame em, Lil Man's swag was on full throttle. His neatly twisted dreadlocks hung down his back. The boy was Gucci down to the socks. If you didn't know any better, you would have mistaken him for Lil Weezy Wee. Rafee just stood to the side and watched his lil round in action. They had definitely graduated from the petty hustling, and was now playing in the big leagues. Rafee was proud of his comrades. He always knew they would make a name in the game for themselves. Rafee appreciated all that his lil rounds did for him. Still in all he was always the type that held his own weight. He definitely planned on getting it in now that he was back on the scene. "Say Rafee, come here let me holla at you" Teelee said leaning against the Audi. "What it do son?" "I want you to meet somebody. This K-Real, she down with the clique." "Yeah, that's wzup. What it do Real." "I'm good. Wzup wit you playboy?" "Shid feelin good to be home you know." "Well fam all I can say is, I'm glad your home. Here you go." Real handed Rafee the other bottle of champagne. "Let's start this shit off right." Nothing else had to be said. Rafee took a huge gulp out of the champagne bottle. Soon as he took the bottle from his lips, the Money Chasers burst through the doors of the bar on the side of the Autocrat. The leader of the crew was the first to break out with his fancy foot work. Nuckle, Teelee's uncle went to town as he approached the front of the Autocrat. He did a quick two step all while jerking his shoulders. He dropped down to the ground giving it a slap, to show off for the crowd. That was his favorite move since he first learned how to second line. "It's buck jump time" one of the second line members yelled. The brass band went to town with their rendition of *"Do What You Wanna"* blowing loudly from their instruments. The crowd went crazy. The Money Chasers led the way as the second line proceeded up St. Bernard Ave. Feeling his self Teelee jumped in the middle of the action, and did a couple of choice moves. "Work Teelee" the crowd yelled. He stepped side to side, left to right, and back and forth. All while waving his skull head scarf in the air. Before you knew it everybody was in the middle of the street buck jumping to the beat of the band. The second line was in full swing and had accumulated hundreds of people. They made their way to Harden Park, the heart of backatown. Teelee went ahead of everybody to unveil their surprise for Rafee. As everybody made it into the park, the DJ was already set up blaring his music. In New Orleans damn near every occasion called for a DJ. It didn't matter if it was a baby shower, funeral, or just a plain ole Sunday get together. Teelee leaned against the brand new LS Lexus 430. Everyone chipped in and copped it as one of Rafee's coming home gifts. As the gang approached, Rafee was the first to acknowledge the beautiful car. "Damn son, how many whips y'all holdin?" "We ain't holdin this my nigga. You holdin this one here." The Lex was really beautiful. It was all white with peanut butter interior. The 22 inch shoes was on beam. "Son this wzup right chere. Y'all niggas really showed ya boy love. I promise I'mma hold it down 110%, this time around. "We ain't trippin on that shit homey" Lil Man said putting his hand on Rafee shoulder. "Just stay outchere and enjoy the fruits of our labor." "Don't trip, I'm here. I ain't going back." The party continued on as Pistol, Corey, and the rest of the Fam came through to welcome Rafee and Thugga home. The second half of the welcome home party was a smash. Everyone went to Club 360, and balled like a dog. Rafee ended up leaving the club with three girls. It was definitely a memorable day for them all.

It had been a long time since Teelee and his father shared any quality time together. Ever since Teelee tasted the blood of the game, he and his father's close knit relationship became distant. While growing up Teelee stayed close to his father's side. Everywhere big Dan went, Teelee would be right behind him. Big Dan had given up his life of crime after his beautiful wife Celeste gave birth to their baby boy. Big Dan vowed to his self that he would die before he let his son follow in his footsteps. Unbeknownst to Dan, he hurt Teelee more than he helped him by sheltering him from his past life. Once Teelee got a feel of the enticing life in the streets it was no turning back. All the advice his father tried to give him fell on deaf ears. Celeste kept her baby boy in constant prayer. She knew the danger her son was in with the life he was living. Big Dan was happy to see his son today. Teelee cancelled many commitments to hook up with his pops, due to his street affairs. Big Dan expressed he had something important to share with him. The urgency in his father's voice made Teelee drop everything, and see what was up with his father. Even though their relationship wasn't as close as it was, Teelee still held that special bond in his heart for his pops. "Hey there son. What's your location?" "I'm on my way to come meet you. Where you at pops?" "I'm on I-10 about to exit on Orleans Ave." "Well I'mma be waitin on you. I'm pullin up in front Pampy's now" Teelee said pulling his Porsche Cayenne SUV onto the neutral ground. "Aight son, I'mma be there in a few minutes." As soon as Teelee recognized his father's white cab pulling up, he hopped out to greet him. Big Dan had been a hustler all his life. While growing up, his father taught him the importance of being a thorough hustler. He started out pulling his little red wagon, selling peanuts at Mardi Gras parades and second lines. When big Dan became of age and placed his foot in the game, he was a real ruthless cat. Rumor had it that he burned a man alive for one of his business associates. Those days were long gone now. Big Dan traded in his life of crime for a legal hustle. Before his taxi driving days, he was a chauffeur for a prestigious limousine service. He had the chance to meet all kinds of superstars. From Bill Cosby to Frankie Beverly. Big Dan experienced his share of life's ups and downs. Now his main focus was to save his son from the mistakes he had made. "Wzup pops?" Teelee said opening the door of the cab so Dan could get out. "Happy to see my son that's all. Come here give ya old pops some love." Teelee and his father hugged showing each other they really missed one another. "I see ya pops. You tryin keep ya swag on point huh?" Big Dan always stayed on point with his dress attire. Today was no different. He sported some black Italian tailor made slacks. With a cream colored silk V-neck shirt, and of course some gator skinned loafs. Big Dan was the source behind Teelee's mean swag. That's one thing his father stayed on him about. Never letting his hygiene and outward appearance slip below standard. "I gotta keep up with you youngsters you know." Big Dan and Teelee made their way into Pampy's. They opted to sit at the bar and dine. They both ordered Pampy's famous shrimp Gumbo for appetizers, and the red beans and rice, with grilled chicken breast for entrees. After their meal Teelee probed big Dan about the situation he wanted to share with him. He knew his father didn't like telling him when something was wrong, but used it to confirm a meeting between the two. It wasn't that Teelee didn't want to spend quality time with his pops. The streets absorbed just that much of his time. "So wzup pops, what's going on wit you?" Teelee analyzed his father's face to see if he was trying to hold anything back. "Well son I ain't even going to pull ya chain. I'mma keep it real with ya. Ya pops sick. My ole kidney's giving me trouble. The doctor say I might have to go on dialysis." The sudden news hit Teelee like a ton of bricks. Teelee felt bad, because of all the times he neglected to hook up with his father. Now the time they did get to kick it, it was because of bad news. Teelee looked into the man's face that played a part in bringing him into the world. It was like looking into a mirror. He actually had a live picture of what he would look like when he became up in age. Teelee noticed the happiness it brought his father when they spent time together. He promised his self that he would get better with sharing his time with his loved ones, like he did numerous of other times. His intentions seemed to always go the other way around. The streets had an extreme strong hold over his heart. "Say pops we gon get through this, you'll be aight. Is it official that you have to get on dialysis?" "No son, I suppose to go in for a checkup next week. Then I'll know everything for sure." "Well look here pops, I'mma try my best to make myself available. I been so busy workin." "Go head son. Who you think you talkin to. I know what you doing out here. What you forgot I use to play in these same streets." "I know you still got your ears to the bricks." "I have to, I gotta make sure my baby boy alright." From there Teelee and big Dan kicked it for the rest of the day. To say it had been a long time since they spent time together, it felt like things hadn't changed one bit. They still shared that strong father and son relationship from the past.

"Gurl pull right there" Denise said pointing at the open parking space. Tamia and Denise were about to have themselves a mini shopping spree, of course courtesy of Teelee. It was a beautiful Saturday afternoon. What better way to spend it then shopping and getting pampered at the spa and beauty salon. In a woman's eyes, nothing couldn't be better. Teelee had to damn near force Tamia to take all the money he had given her. In a way Teelee appreciated Tamia's modesty, but he made her realize that she was his woman and he was going to take care of her to the fullest. Deep down Tamia knew Teelee was right. She just didn't want to make it look like she was there only for his money. As Tamia was about to swing the Audi in the open space a soccer mom, in a Toyota SUV, swung in front of the car. Why did she do that? Denise rolled her window down and went off. "You stupid ugly bitch! You saw us about to park right there! I should get out this car and beat the shit outta your ugly ass!" Soon as Denise attempted to grab her door handle, Tamia grabbed her arm. Tamia knew if she would have let Denise get out of the car, their day of enjoyment would have turned into a day at the police station; ruining Tamia's cruise with Teelee. That definitely was not about to happen. "Girl be cool! Fuck that bitch, we can find another spot." Tamia was pissed that she swerved into the spot, but she wasn't about to let that ruin her day. The woman stalled exiting her vehicle until Tamia pulled off. She was obviously scared from the threats Denise through her way. "That's right bitch, you better stay in that car!" "Girl chill out! Don't let that woman fuck our day up." "I just hate when people do that kinda shit! She saw us about to pull in that damn spot! She wanna swing her happy go lucky ass right in front of us!" "Fuck that scary bitch! What you wanna do first?" Tamia asked pulling in a spot closer to the mall than the other one. Esplanade Mall was crowded as usual. They intended on starting there, then heading to the boutiques, outlets and wherever else the money spent. People flooded the mall to get ready for the night life in the N.O. Every club in the city was popping off. By the looks of the crowd in the mall every club was going to get their fair share of business. "Gurl it's all on you. You the Queen bitch. I wish I had a man to treat me to an exotic island, plus a shopping spree to go wit it. I ain't mad at ya chic." "I'm not wit him just for his money girl. That's my baby. I love him regardless of what he can do for me. He treats me and your niece damn good." "Look Tamia that boy know you don't want his money. You gotta realize, he is your man. What real man don't wanna treat his woman to the best of things." "I guess you right bitch." "You know I'm right. Nah let's get our shop on" Denise said getting out of the car. Tamia and Denise hit up damn near every store in the mall. Tamia picked up a few pieces, but intended on doing her major splurging in the boutiques. She even got Teelee a couple of things she thought he might need for the trip. Tamia also grabbed a few special pieces from Victoria Secret. When Teelee got a hold of the pieces Tamia picked out, Victoria would no longer be a secret. Tamia gave Denise

$2000, to do as she pleased. She felt she had more than enough, seeing that Teelee gave her a nice chunk of change to do what she wanted to do. Let's just say she had enough to get her splurge on and pay her bills out for several months. She even went all out for Tia. Tamia and Denise had out done their selves, they ended their day at the spa, treating themselves to a massage, a pedicure and a facial to top it off. The day went really well. Tamia was really anticipating the cruise even more.

Roylee sat in the trap house counting this week's take. The money was definitely rolling in. Raceland was a gold mine. Out of all the territory's the Skull Gang had, Raceland pulled in the most. The Blade couldn't even compare with the network Raceland was working with. Roylee and his crew had definitely made a name for themselves out there in the little country town. On a few incidents they had to flex their muscles, but once that was established, their hustle grew tremendously. Roylee had come a long way in just a matter of months. He still could remember his all night flights, trying to flip a fifty-dollar slab into a quarter. There were murmurs all through his crew. They felt they were not getting the recognition they were supposed to be getting. He killed the tension within his crew quick. He knew very well what kind of problems that type of shit could bring. A beef with Teelee and the gang was not an option in his mind, well not now at least. The money was coming to fast and piling up to high to even think of starting a senseless war, besides that; they practically grew up together in the same hood. They shared a mutual respect for one another. Well at least most of them did.

There was always a hater lurking in the picture. There was a sudden knock at the door. Roylee grabbed the chopper off the sofa and went to see who was knocking. He couldn't get to comfortable. They were the top dogs in the area. Never knew when the hungry dogs was coming looking for food. "Who that be?" "It's me Kinky." Kinky D was one of Roylee's head lieutenants. Kinky D and Roylee came up together; from chasing little girls around the neighborhood, to working the block with that steady rock. They were inseparable growing up. Roylee was the brains and the enforcer behind their hustle, while Kinky D leaned on him and his street creditability. A lot of people knew without Roylee; Kinky D would have been *done dada.* Just off of the respect Roylee had in the streets, no one ever fucked with Kinky D. If you didn't know any better, you would have thought Kinky was about his business by his intimidating bark. If anyone got past that they would have quickly discovered that his bite was nonexistent. On many occasions Roylee had to save Kinky and his loose lips. Roylee frequently stressed to Kinky the importance of backing up the shit he talked. He wanted his boy to hold it down, but if he didn't he was going to definitely take up the slack. The gangsta vibe was just not running through the niggas veins. By looking at him you would have thought he could play his position well. He was tatted up like a subway in Harlem, with a mouth full of gold teeth, and some kinky shoulder length dreadlocks. That's actually where he got his name from. He always had kinky, nappy hair. With a reddish skin complexion, he could have passed for Haitian. "What it do playa" Roylee asked as he opened the door to let Kinky in. "Shid I'm coolin. What's the deal wit you." "Just countin the gwap you know. Lock the door behind you." Roylee sat the chopper back on the sofa and got back to counting the many stacks that laid on the table. "Business lookin good huh?" "You know it" Roylee replied as he pulled a half smoked blunt out of the ash tray. Seeing the many stacks on the kitchen table made Kinky D speak what was on his mind. "Man I'm tired of this hustling for other niggas type shit." "Got damn man, what's the problem now?" Roylee asked as he rubber banned another ten-thousand-dollar stack. "Say son, we pull in all this money. Then we gotta turn around and give damn near half of it to Thugga and them boyz. I'm tired of that shit. It's bout time we upgrade our status, ya heard me." "Sit down round, let me holla at you." Roylee put a pause on counting his cheese. He knew he had to get on top of this negative vibe quick before it grew uncontrollable. "Here light this up." Roylee handed Kinky D a freshly rolled blunt. "You want a shot of this goose?" "No I'm cool." Roylee poured him a shot and took a seat next to Kinky on the sofa. "Look here round, that shit you talkin ain't even an option right now. The money to good and we ain't got no supplier to operate on the level we rockin on now." "Anything's possible when you networking right." "Say Kinky you ever noticed that's how everything go sour. When you beefin, your money slows up. Going to war with them Skull Gang niggas will dry our river up quick." Roylee peeped the anxiousness in his boy. As a matter of fact, he was a little anxious his self. He wanted a higher position as well, but he wasn't going to let his greed fuck up what they had going on. "Shit gon be good homey. Just be patient, and play ya position." "If you say so." Kinky D agreed outwardly, but deep in his heart he wasn't hearing that shit. It's fucked up cause when the heat did turn up, Roylee would be the main one banging it out with the Skull Gang; while Kinky D just hung off his coat tail. Don't get it twisted, Kinky would sling that iron; just not without Roylee by his side.

# CHAPTER 18

# I NEED A VACATION

"Say honey bun, you got the passports and shit huh?" Tamia loved when Teelee called her that. It was a little nickname he had given her since they had been together. Her face lit up, as she flipped through all their important documents they were going to need while away. "Yeah bae, I'm going through them now." Tamia suggested they use traveler's checks to keep from exchanging their American money. St. Bart's currency was the Euro, something Teelee and Tamia was unfamiliar with. "You ready for this?" Teelee asked, walking up behind Tamia and planting a kiss on her neck. "What, ready for this." Tamia grabbed Teelee's magic wand through his basketball shorts. "Not that maw, but we could fit that in before we leave" Teelee replied, as he rolled on Tamia's plumped ass. "Boy you betta stop, before you start sumthin. We gon be late getting on the boat." "You the one started." Teelee eased back, because he knew if they got started they would have definitely been late. "For real, you ready for this love trip we bout to embark on." "Baby I'm ready to go anywhere you going." Tamia meant every word. The love she held in her heart for Teelee was like a disease that spread every minute that passed. She never felt a love like this before. Even with his flaws Tamia could find no wrong in Teelee. She had yet to tell him she had found out his real age. This past weekend she got the chance to spend some quality time with Celeste. Rambling on about her precious son, Celeste revealed Teelee's real age. She couldn't find herself being mad, or the least bit moved by the discovery, she actually chuckled. Her feelings were still strong and climbing. "Bae come here. I wanna talk to you for a minute." Tamia led Teelee to the bed. By the look in her beautiful hazel eyes; Teelee knew whatever she was about to say was serious. Baby you know I love you right? The love I hold for you is unexplainable. I want what we have together to be solid; not all that shaky shit we both probably been involved with in the past. I know without a doubt that my man is mine, and I'm aware of everything about him." "What you gettin at maw?" Teelee asked trying to cut through the chase. "Baby you know I know your real age?" Teelee had almost forgot about lying about his age. He knew she had to find out through his mother. His intentions were to tell her the real deal, but like always the streets deprived him of doing so. "Maw I was gon tell you bout that." "Baby I'm not trippin. I just want to know why you couldn't tell me your real age in the beginning." "I'mma be real wit you. When I saw those beautiful eyes from across the room at that party, I got a lil intimidated. I've never felt like that when approaching a woman.

Then, when I came ova to y'all table, and felt your beautiful vibe. I knew I couldn't say or do anything to fuck it up. I thought fasho you was gon say I was a lil boy, who was way too young for you. So yeah I did lie, but for good reasons." "Let me tell you something. I don't want you to ever feel like you can't keep it real wit me in any situation. We gotta trust each other and be friends before anything. Our friendship and honesty is what gon make this here last. You feel me baby." "Yeah I feel where you comin from. Now come here and gimme a kiss." Of course they did what they said they wasn't going to do. Fortunately, the intensity of their conversation made their climax strong and quick. There common ground had been laid. Their souls were brought together a little bit closer making their love for each other grow another notch.

Teelee rented a limo for the occasion. He felt if they was going to do it big, they might as well pull out all the stops. It also saved them from having to park their cars down at the port. Many people came back to broken car windows, stolen rims, and all other types of vandalism. This was definitely going to be a trip they would all remember. St. Bart's was the perfect place to consummate the new love bird's commitment to each other. The Caribbean getaway was a lover's paradise. Brandon spoke highly of the exotic island. He'd done numerous of trips for couples seeking to get away. Lil Man and Teelee had finally found those special women that gave them what they were longing for; genuine happiness. Thugga on the other hand was still stuck in a limbo. Caught up in the fame of the street life, he just couldn't find himself settling for one woman. All throughout their years of growing up, Thugga was always the one with two or three girlfriends at a time. He felt there was too much of him to be secluded by one woman. Brandon had hooked Teelee up with a great package deal. The deal included a cabin for each one of them, and breakfast, lunch, and dinner at a five-star restaurant on the cruise ship. Their itinerary was filled with lots of activities; from snorkeling to water skiing and three rental cars to transport them around the island. Not only did Brandon get a nice commission check, Teelee popped him off for getting them a great deal. The whole trip came out to be fifteen thousand. All expenses paid. "Yeah we'll be out in a minute. Tiger that's the limo outside. You sure you got everything you need." Celeste volunteered to watch Tia until they got back. She was undoubtedly in good hands, giving Tamia a great deal of assurance her baby girl would be okay. The stress free feeling Teelee was giving her was irreplaceable. "Yeah Jellybean Brown. I'm set, I got everything." "Jellybean Brown. Who the hell is that?" Teelee asked, obviously not liking the nickname Tamia had given him. "That's you bae. Why, you don't like it?" "No maw, I'm not feelin that one." "Don't worry baby, that's my personal name for you. Can't nobody call you that but me." "Why you don't pick another one. That sounds like some funny shit." "No it don't baby" Tamia replied, putting on her puppy face. It was no way Teelee could deny Tamia when she did that. "Aight, but don't call me that shit in public." That would really weigh heavy on his reputation in the streets. From Teelee the young, cold blooded killer, to Jellybean Brown. Definitely not a good look. The limo driver secured their luggage in the trunk of the limo, and they were off to pick up everyone else.

As they pulled up to Marc Morial Convention Center, located in downtown New Orleans. They could see the huge Carnival cruise ship docked at the port. "This what I'm talkin bout right chere" Lil Man stated, feeling the excitement of the trip. They all sat in the limo feeling like the Dons of the N.O. It was really an overwhelming feeling for them all. A year ago they were all sitting on Big Head Unc porch, plotting on a money making scheme. Now they sat in a top of the line limo with the best clothes money could buy. They had money that couldn't fold anymore, only stack. They were going on a trip most people would die to go on. To top it off, they were still the same hungry cats they started off as. The money didn't go to their heads by the least. They would still rock a nigga block, and hang around all the normal spots. It was just in their nature to be hood niggas. "I like to propose a toast" Teelee said lifting his glass of champagne. Everyone followed suit. "To success, because that's what we had in the past year. We've struggled, hustled, and achieved what we set out to do. All I want to say is, I love y'all and this is just the beginning." They all clanked glasses, and downed their champagne. They got their luggage squared away before boarding the ship. The limo driver confirmed their pick up time on the day they would be returning. Before heading to their cabins to get settled in, they all chilled on the deck of the ship. The ship was really beautiful. It was three decks high with swimming pools and Jacuzzis. Indoor basketball courts, a fitness center, and a night club. The personality of the staff was similar to the crew on the "Love Boat." "Baby I'm so excited" Tamia said as she put her arms around Teelee's waist. The horn of the ship went off as they were about to set sail. Many people waved goodbye to their loved ones as the boat eased onto the waters. The scene was similar to something you would see on a movie. "Say maw won't y'all go get things settled in the rooms" Teelee suggested to the women. "All you had to say is you wanted us to leave" K-Real said playfully rolling her eyes. Of course she knew Teelee wasn't referring to her, but she just played the part so she could get Twin and Tamia away for a minute. She was Teelee's protégé. Soon as the women walked off, Teelee's cell phone rang. It was Lanzo. Perfect timing for the departure of the women. Teelee didn't talk any of his street business around women; well Tamia to a certain extent, just not so much in depth. He didn't want her to have too much knowledge of anything, because if the heat of the Feds ever came it would put her in jeopardy. "Wzup my Latin amicus." "Hey Mijo, what's the deal? Have y'all left yet?" "Yeah we just pulled off from the port a few minutes ago." "Well look I'mma let you go enjoy yourself. I was just checking on you. I wanted to let you know Conco is going to be making that delivery to Raceland." "Fasho, I got you. I'mma see you when I get back." "Alright kid, go enjoy yourself. Tell that pretty lady of yours, I said hi." "Aight Lanzo, will do." "That was Escobar huh?" Thugga asked, looking at the raging water the ship's tracks left behind. "Yeah he said the shipment to Raceland go be delivered on schedule." "Son can you believe how far we've come?" Lil Man asked, running his hands through his dreads. “Sometimes it’s unbelievable.” “I already know homey. It seemed like yesterday when we were sittin on Unc porch, plottin to get out feet wet in the game.” Teelee knew getting at Tossy was a nice come up, but he didn’t know it was going to bring them far as it had. One thing he did know their ambition was going to eventually get them somewhere, and to his surprise this is where it got them. “Say son why you ain’t bring one of ya lil broads?” Lil Man asked. “Man I just feel like none of them groupies deserved to come on such a personal trip, ya feel me.” “What about Tyler?” “Son that broad too much of a headache. I’m tryna enjoy the trip, not go crazy on this bitch. I think I probably would have threw her disgusting ass off the third deck.” All of them broke out laughing as they pictured Tyler flying off the top deck of the ship. “I’m still worried about leaving Rafee behind” Teelee admitted, as he thought of how chaotic Rafee could get. “Son, I already told you. If sumthin gon happen, its gon happen regardless. Homey gon be aight. I told Pistol to keep an eye on him for us.” “I hope you right. We got too much to lose ova some bullshit, ya heard me.” “Trust me son, shit good. Don’t stress ya self. This supposed to be our time to chill.” From there they all separated to go get settled in, and prepared for their first night headed to Caribbean heaven.

“Maw you packed my electric shaver?” Teelee asked, rumbling through their luggage. Tamia and Teelee were preparing to hook up with the crew. They planned on having dinner and enjoying the luxuries the ship had to offer. “Yea bae, in the little carry-on bag.” That’s one thing he could count on as far as Tamia was concerned.

She was very reliable. She made sure all their things were in line, and on point. "You found it baby?" Tamia asked coming out of the bathroom. "Damn you lookin good" Teelee said damn near drooling over Tamia's sexiness. Tamia was working her Alexander McQueen, spaghetti strapped dress. The pecan colored dress blended perfect with her eyes. She topped it off with the Jimmy Choo stilettos to match. The dress hugged every curve in her body like a 96 Impala hitting a curve at 100mph. "Yeah bae, you wearin that shit." "All for you handsome" Tamia replied doing a spin so Teelee could see the slit down the back of her dress. Teelee just stood there dumbfounded. "Baby go get dressed. Everybody probably waitin on us." Teelee shook the lustful thoughts out of his head, and headed to the bathroom to get ready. Teelee stepped out looking pretty sharp his self. His tan linen pants suit, courtesy of Giorgio Armani, gave him a debonair kind of look. The Ferragamo loafers that adorned his feet, sealed the deal on his suave appearance. When Teelee exited the bathroom, Tamia had the same reaction he had. "Damn bae, you lookin some good." "How good?" Teelee asked, pulling Tamia into his arms. "Good enough to eat." Tamia licked her lips and attempted to grab Teelee's love stick. "Hold up baby, we gon be late. Lil Man just hit me up. They at the restaurant waitin on us." "Aight, but it's on tonight" Tamia responded, winking her eye at Teelee. When they made it downstairs everyone was chilling at the bar area of the restaurant. When the elevator doors opened, Teelee could have sworn he saw Thugga kiss Real on the neck. He shook it off as if he was tripping. He knew the big boss playa wasn't sneaking around with the gangsta girl. If he was it would eventually come out in the future. "What's good family" Teelee said as he and Tamia approached the bar. "We coolin, waitin on y'all. For a minute we thought we was gon have to send up a rescue team." Lil Man loved to fuck with Teelee about how he lost track of time when he was around Tamia. "Gurl I'm lovin that dress." Twin recognized Tamia' great taste in clothing. The vibe she got from Tamia was of a humble, loving, classy type of broad. Twin's characteristics fit in the same category, giving the two some things in common. At first Twin thought Tamia was some boogie bitch, considering how beautiful she was, not saying Twin was an ugly duckling. She was definitely saying a lot in the beauty department. She had creamy mocha tone skin, and high cheek bones. She could pass for Keisha that played on Belly, body and all. "Gurl you like" Tamia asked appreciating the compliment. The saying that "great minds think alike" was confirmed, because Tamia had the same thoughts lingering in her mind about Twin. They both felt they would become really good friends as time passed. "Y'all ready to eat?" Thugga asked signaling for the hostess so they could be seated. "Man I'm starving" Thugga stated. They managed to get a great seat by the window giving them a terrific view of the Atlantic Ocean. The restaurant was really upholding its five-star status. It was located at the top deck of the ship. The table areas were secluded off for privacy and a pianist had the musical atmosphere on point. The scene really set the tone for the night. "How are y'all this lovely evening? My name is Isaiah. I'll be your waiter for the night." "Say bruh, anybody ever told you, you look like the dude that use to play on the Love Boat." Back in the day that used to be one of Teelee's favorite shows. "Yes, I get that all the time. Many people compare the staff here to the staff on that show. Okay let's get you guys started with a beverage." Give us a bottle of Cristal" Lil Man requested as he skimmed through the menu. "So wzup Twin, I see you been havin my lil round love drunk these past couple of weeks. I ain't never saw him strung out like this. What's your secret?" Teelee was giving Lil Man a taste of his own medicine. In all actuality they both were in the same predicament love wise. They just love fucking with each other. They had been doing it so long it just came natural. "I just show my baby a lot of affection. That's a key ingredient to fulfill all your man's desires." "I see why my nigga like that." "So you're not?" Tamia asked, giving Teelee that look that got him every time. "You know you got me baby. I'm just fuckin wit my lil homey, ya heard me." "Check that shit baby girl" Lil Man said counter punching Teelee's attack. "It's all good. I can admit it. I got it, I got it bad." Teelee's imitation of Usher hit song, *"You got it bad"* made everyone break out into laughter. "Boy you so stupid" K-Real said wiping the tears of laughter from her eyes. "Oh yeah my auntie told me to tell y'all to come through. She wants y'all to get a feel of how things are ran at the clinic. She's having a grand opening at one of her new spots next month." There was a rumor that Candy made 500 thousand in one month from her clinic in the New Orleans East. "Teelee I'm tellin you, y'all made a damn good decision investing in my auntie business. She really done well for herself; as well as us. The company is growing fast." "Trust me I know. One day I saw Candy in a new Aston Martin. That car alone let me know she was on top her shit." The evening was going great. The women got better acquainted while Lil Man, Thugga and Teelee reminisced on the good ole days. After dinner they all separated to go enjoy their significant others. K-Real and Thugga claimed they were going to the casino. Teelee had a feeling that was a lie. The vibes the two were giving off was a little too obvious. Tamia even noticed while they were having dinner. She nudged Teelee's leg. "You see that bae" Tamia whispered as she witnessed K-Real feed Thugga a shrimp. All Teelee could do was smile, because his instincts were leading him right. Thugga had fell in the web of the black widow.

"This view is beautiful baby" Tamia said snuggling up against Teelee. They were on the top deck of the ship enjoying each other's company. They stood watching the moon at its brightest. The cool breeze coming off the Atlantic Ocean was delightful. The waves in the ocean tossed and flipped like two lovers entangled in hot passionate sex. The top deck of the ship was clear, giving Teelee and Tamia the privacy to enjoy one another however they pleased. The whole vibe and scene was intensifying their sexual appetite they both had for each other. "Damn maw you smell so good" Teelee whispered, as he rained small kisses all over Tamia's neck. Without saying a word, Tamia led Teelee to one of the plush leather lawn chairs circling the deck of the ship. Tamia instructed Teelee to lie down. The lustful stares that they both shared explained all they wanted to say and do. Looking deep into Teelee's eyes, Tamia never broke her gaze as she let her dress slide down pass her breast. "Tiger what you doin?" Teelee asked shocked by Tamia's actions. Tamia gently put one finger over Teelee's lips letting him know that she was in control. All Teelee could do was go with the flow, and hoped no one walked up on their little freak show. The cool breeze that swept across the deck caused Tamia's nipples to harden. They were so luscious, they made Teelee's mouth water. Tamia straddled Teelee putting her juicy cantaloupes in his face. Teelee immediately took one into his mouth. "Umm baby" was all Tamia could say as Teelee made love to her breast with his mouth. Tamia quickly unbuckled Teelee's belt, freeing his pulsating rod from its prison. With a nice quick move Tamia slid her panties to the side and inserted Teelee's hardness into her awaiting wetness. It felt like Teelee had fallen off the boat and into the ocean, warm and wet as Tamia was. Placing her hands on the head part of the lawn chair, Tamia began to ride Teelee slow and hard. Which caused Teelee to throw his head back in enjoyment. She was giving him the ride of his life. The sexual energy between the two made them cling to each other like a magnet. In between their tongues doing the tango, all they could do was let out moans of pure pleasure. Awe baby, damn you feel good" Teelee stated. "Baby I love you so much. It feels soooo damn good. Don't move keep it right there" Tamia commented. Teelee had hit that forbidden spot causing Tamia to rotate on him even more. A few more rotations led to them both exploding together, creating a world unknown to man. After gaining their composure they went for round two, this time with Teelee taking the lead. The funny thing about the whole situation was, Lil Man and Twin were on the opposite side of the ship experiencing the same amount of pleasure. Who knows what Thugga and K-Real were up to. The way they were acting, it definitely couldn't be held under wraps to much longer.

The next morning Teelee was up early feeling good from the exclusive night him and Tamia shared. The way she put it on him, it's a surprise he wasn't singing expressions of love. While Tamia slept, he wanted to surprise her and arrange for breakfast to be sent to the room. Instead of calling and ordering room service he chose to go order it in person. He didn't want to risk waking Tamia from her beauty sleep. On the way down to the restaurant he opted to stop by Thugga's room to see if he was up. Approaching his door, Teelee could have sworn he heard moans and banging against the wall. In his mind he blew if off as if Thugga had caught him a freak on the ship. Joking around, posing as a room attendant, Teelee proceeded to see who Thugga had in the confines of his cabin. "Room service" Teelee called out as he knocked on the door. Suddenly the noise stopped, and Thugga swung the door open wrapped in nothing but a sheet. "I ain't order no fuckin room service." What Teelee saw had him lost for words. K-Real was laying in the bed butt ass naked. "Nigga you playin early in the mornin huh?" Thugga asked as if the scene Teelee was seeing was something ordinary. K-Real didn't bother covering up. She felt like he was no one to cover up for, she had already had sex with him in the past. "So this why y'all two rolled solo" Teelee said closing the door. "We was gon tell y'all the deal, but I guess you done caught us in action." K-Real's nonchalant attitude really threw Teelee for a loop. She was really a street nigga, in a woman's body. She had slept with him, Lil Man, and now Thugga and she was sitting there acting like what she was doing was normal. "Y'all grown, I can't tell y'all what to do. I can't understand why y'all didn't just say what was up." All Thugga could do was smirk. He sparked the Keep Moving him and Real blazed before they got busy. "Wait till Lil Man hear this shit hear, he gon die laughing." Teelee threw the comforter over Real's naked body. "Girl cover that shit up. That's my boy shit now. You can't be exposing it like that." "Nigga get the fuck. You know I ain't trippin on that shit, besides Real like one of the niggas anyway." "So what's up? You feel like comin wit me to the restaurant. I'm bout to go get my Tiger some breakfast." The look on Thugga's face was saying, no I'm bout to finish what I was doing. Teelee disregarded it and threw Thugga his clothes, hanging on the chair by the bed. They walked out the room leaving Real in the bed. When Lil Man found out he laughed his ass off. He couldn't believe it. The rest of the cruise to the island was quite awkward. They weren't used to the sudden love connection between the two. It was kind of weird in the beginning, but they brushed it off quick. Shit didn't change, they were still all, Skull Gang 4 Lyfe. Nothing would ever change that. No matter what happened.

You could see Port Gustavia from a distance, as the cruise ship rode the raging waters of the Caribbean Sea. Everyone stood on the top deck of the ship, watching the beautiful scenery. The big horse shoe shaped port, was flooded with yachts and boats of all sizes. The ship had to dock at the port, because the water that surrounded the island was too shallow for the big ship. St. Bart's was small in size, but humungous in beauty. The eight square mile of arid volcanic rock was absolute paradise. The island held its own weight in beauty amongst the others. "Man this shit off the chain" Thugga said scanning the port through his Prada sunglasses. "That boy Brandon said it was nice, but I ain't know it was gon be like this" Teelee said with Tiger in his arms. "My auntie came out here for her last anniversary. She said the food is delicious, and the people are really nice." "Twin I think it ain't a place on earth Candy haven't been yet" Teelee stated. "Yeah she's been damn near around the whole world." "I'mma take you around the world. You gon come?" Lil Man asked, with Twin cuddled in his arms. "Where ever you go, you know I'm there" Twin replied looking into Lil Man eyes. "That's wzup" Lil Man commented. "Wzup my Thug. You ready for this here?" Real asked, rubbing her ass up against Thugga. "What you talkin bout the island, or this here?" Thugga slapped Real on the ass, making it jiggle in her sundress. "Yeah that, and the island daddy" Real replied, pushing her ass further into Thugga's pelvic area. "Say y'all need to go to y'all room wit all that" Lil Man joked. "Go to the room. Nigga how y'all was gettin down on the top deck the other night. Y'all could have got arrested for indecent exposure." Twin held her hand over her mouth, as an expression of embarrassment spread across her face. "Nigga what you was spyin on a nigga?" Lil Man was on the constant look out for any spectators so it was hard to believe that Thugga witnessed what happened. "No nigga! Me and Real came out to get some air after we hit up the casino. When we was about to walk out on the deck, we saw Twin handling yo ass." Twin was even more embarrassed hearing Thugga said those words. "Don't trip Twin, we ain't see much. I dragged his ass from up there soon as we peeped what was going on." "I'm glad they ain't see us" Tamia whispered in Teelee's ear. They both smiled, because they were both doing the same thing just on different sides of the ship. "Look bae, they got old colonial styled houses" Tamia said pointing at the homes spread all across the town. Gustavia was filled with old fashioned homes. Some of the buildings still had cupolas on top of the roofs. A cupola was a small gazebo like structure, used for lighting back in the old days. Some of the houses were painted in bright Caribbean colors. The cool blue waters were so clear; you could see the multi colored tropical fish swimming throughout the ocean. "Awe baby, this is so beautiful" Tamia said loving the island already. When the cruise ship pulled up to the port, the people of Gustavia was in place to greet the tourist. Their dark skinned tone showed their African descent, but their speech clearly showed the mix of French culture. The people of St. Bart's spoke French with a Creole twist. As all the people aboard the ship made their way down the gang plank, they were handed brochures of the island. "Bonjour Beaux Yeux. Welcome to St. Bart's" one of the island men said to Tamia as they made their way off the ship. "Merci Beaucoup" Tamia replied as she walked by. Teelee was lost for words. This woman amazed him every day. "Bae when you was gon tell me you knew how to speak French." "I don't speak it fluently, but when need be I show my

Creole heritage." "I know a lil bit to girl, but not too much" Twin admitted. "My great auntie speaks it fluently though." "I guess we all learning sumthin new" Lil Man said, while smiling at Twin. "We learn something new every day" Twin replied winking at Lil Man. "What ole boy just told you?" Teelee asked. "He told me I have really beautiful eyes." "So when you learned to speak like that?" "When I was little, my momma used to bring me by my great grandmother in Franklinton, Louisiana. She used to teach me words every time I was out there." "You sound pretty good. I wanna see how it sounds when we." Teelee leaned in and whispered in Tamia's ear. "When we havin sex." "I'mma see if I can make that happen for you baby" Tamia winked, as they made their way to catch the local ferry. When they made it to the island, they were taxied to their beach front villas. Brandon had arranged for them to stay in some beautiful beach front estates. The villas were often rented out by many celebrities, and athletes. When Tamia and Teelee walked through the door of their villa, Tamia instantly fell in love with the décor. "This is beautiful!" The interior layout of the villa was lavish. The hardwood floors were so shiny; you could see your reflection. There were three steps at the end of the foyer, leading to the living room area. The burgundy leather sofa set blended perfect with the hardwood floors. There was an electric fire place, to liven up the mood on a romantic night. The wall on the east end of the villa was all glass, giving a perfect view of the Caribbean Sea. The whole estate was electronically ran from the fire place, to the stove in the kitchen. Everything was operated by the push of a button. On the walls of the living room and master bedroom hung 52 inch flat screens. There was even a Jacuzzi on the back patio, facing the beach. The master bedroom was amazing. The canopy bed, draped with sheer curtains made the villa even more exotic. Teelee left the bags by the door, as he went to take a look out the long glass window. "Damn maw, this shit wzup right chere." Tamia walked up beside Teelee, and wrapped herself into his arms. "This is so beautiful. Thank you baby." "Anything for you beautiful." Teelee gently kissed the nape of Tamia's neck. The beach that their villa sat on was very peaceful. Lorient beach was the total opposite of St. Jean beach. Whereas St. Jean was party central. Lorient was lover's cove. "How bout you let me hear you speak some of that French shit, while I do this." Teelee leaned Tamia up against the glass window and began to dine in. "Bon appétit" Tamia said seductively while her eyes rolled back in her head. "Now I know what that means" Teelee replied before he commenced to clean his plate.

Everyone already planned to chill amongst themselves the first night. Tamia and Teelee loved the peaceful alone time they had. They joked, walked along the beach, and watched a movie or two. As Teelee drifted off to a nap, Tamia had plans to do something special for him. She wanted to show Teelee how much she appreciated all he had done for her. She called around the island and arranged a candlelight dinner in their villa. Tamia had the dining and living room area flooded with different size candles, she even had white rose petals scattered all over the floors of the villa. Tamia had the chef arrange one of Teelee's favorite meals. Steak and potatoes with freshly tossed salad, including a spread of fresh fruit. Tamia topped if off with champagne and chocolate covered strawberries. She went all out for her man. Teelee was awakened by the smell of food floating throughout the villa. As he stretched, he realized Tiger wasn't next to him. He quickly jumped out of bed to see where his beauty wandered off too. Teelee's eyes and mouth opened wide as he watched Tiger stand in front of him looking radiant as ever. She had her 6 inch Christian Louboutin heels on, with a cream see through surprise from Victoria Secret. Her honey colored braids sat in the middle of her back. Tamia cascaded them all to one side to give herself a sexy look for the night. The look was topped off with the diamond earrings and bracelet Teelee bought her as a surprise gift for the trip. Tamia looked like a goddess standing there. Since Teelee was lost for words again, Tamia broke the silence. "Are you hungry handsome" Tamia stated, while gliding over to Teelee taking his hand. "I wanted to show you how happy you've made me baby. All this here is for you. Thank you Teelee for making me so happy." As she walked Teelee to the table, he noticed the rose petals he stepped on. "Damn she did the damn thang. Look how amazing this woman is" Teelee thought as he followed Tamia's lead. He loved that she appreciated all he done for her. What she didn't realize, it was effortlessly. She deserved it all, Teelee truly loved Tamia. "Got damn maw! How you did all this, and you looking like all that. Baby you look good than a muthafucka" Teelee commented while the bulge in his boxers became alive. Tamia smiled and kissed Teelee on the lips, while sitting him at the head of the table. As they sat and enjoyed their food and conversation, Teelee was hungry for what wasn't on the table. He couldn't help but stare at Tiger, the entire time they ate. Her voluptuous breast had his mouth watering. Her thighs and ass had him on fire in his seat. Tamia got up from her chair, seeing the lustful look on Teelee's face. She straddled Teelee and fed him fruits, while drinking champagne. "Teelee, I love you" Tamia said seductively with her eyes glowing. The perfect light from the candles and the sweet smell coming from Tamia had Teelee hypnotized. "I love you too. You know I'mma make you my wifey huh?" "O really" Tamia smiled at the thought of becoming his wife. He swiftly got up from the table with Tamia legs still wrapped around him, and walked to the bedroom. The little Victoria Secret number was not a keeper. Teelee destroyed it trying to get to her treasure. Tamia kissed him slow and soft while stroking his hair. They made love to each other throughout the night like it was their first time.

The next morning, they all got up bright and early to check out what all the island had to offer. There was a shuttle bus scheduled to give a tour of the island. Everyone agreed and they were all listed to be picked up. Tamia and Teelee's villa was the last stop before the tour began. Their estates weren't too far from each other, which meant they all shared in an equal amount of paradise their first night on the island. "What it do fam" Teelee said, greeting everyone as him and Tamia boarded the shuttle bus. "What's good wit y'all?" Lil Man asked, noticing the glow on Teelee and Tamia's face. "Look like y'all had a damn good night." "Shid nigga y'all lookin the same way" Teelee replied taking a seat right behind Thugga and K-Real. "We did" K-Real admitted, turning around looking at Teelee and Tamia. "My thug showed his ass last night." "Too much info for ya boy" Teelee replied. "This is a nice shuttle bus" Tamia said, looking around the interior. There were 15 inch flat screens mounted on the ceiling on each side of the bus. While the shuttle navigated around the island, a brief history was shown on the small televisions throughout the bus. The plush leather seats were so soft and comfortable; you'd probably fall sound asleep if you sat still too long. Each seat was also equipped with ear buds so you could listen to the information being shared over the screens. Suddenly the driver of the shuttle came over the speakers. "Welcome to St. Bart's. My name is François. I'll be your tour guide for today. During the tour you all will be able to see some of the most exquisite attractions the island has to offer. As the tour progresses, you will have the option to listen to my verbal narration or you can listen to the DVD play a brief rundown of the history. Our first destination is to get a view of the many beaches that flood the island." As the shuttle made its way to one of the first beaches, everyone was amazed at how beautiful the island was. It was a tropical paradise. There was so many coral reefs that circled the island, enclosing the magnificent crisp blue water. "The beach to the left is St. Jean's beach" the tour guide announced. "This beach is suitable for water sports and all the surrounding facilities have been created for that purpose. Live reggae bands and calypso bands perform nightly at the two clubs located on the beach as well." "We gotta go see how they rockin on the club level" Thugga suggested, as the bus proceeded to the next part of the island.

"We could definitely do that" Teelee said as he continued to take in the beauty of it all. "Awe look bae, they have parrots in those trees" Tamia said, directing Teelee's attention to the beautiful birds. "This salt pond area to your left is very marshy, and is a habitat for tropical birds. "Damn that one right there is colorful than a muthafucka" Lil Man said, pointing at the big bright parrot. "This beach to your right is called Gouverneur beach. It is known for its crystal white sand. "Baby that is beautiful huh" Twin said marveling at the beautiful scenery. The sand was so white from the sun shining on it, that it temporally blinded your eyes. Lil Man leaned in and whispered something in Twin's ear. "I wouldn't mind havin you naked on that sand." "Boy you stupid" Twin replied. "This final beach to the right is called Saline beach, it's utilized by tourist who have no problem showing off their valuables. "Oh baby look, they naked for real" Tamia said covering her eyes. "That's the beach I wanna hit right there my thug" Real said nudging Thugga's leg. "Girl you nasty" Thugga replied. "Don't trip though, I'm lovin that." "Y'all was made for each other" Teelee replied, shaking his head. "You know what round, your right. This my Bonnie right chere, ya heard me." The tour concluded after a couple more stops. Everyone was brought back to their villas. They all planned to hit Caribbean Lynx. They were informed that the hottest reggae bands performed there. Tamia loved reggae music. It was one of her favorite forms of music, besides R&B and Rap. Sean Paul was scheduled to perform so that sealed the deal even more on their party destination for the evening.

It was a beautiful night to hit the beach and party. The

temperature was very pleasant. The light breeze that circulated around the island carried a wonderful Caribbean aroma. Everyone had their rental cars delivered to them so they could have transportation to the club. Teelee had just hung up with Lil Man and Thugga. Teelee and Tamia were late getting ready like always. The quickie had them lost for time. "Come on maw, everybody on their way." Teelee sat on the bed putting on his low top white Prada tennis shoes. Teelee planned on being comfortable and clean at the same time. He went with his black and white Sean John linen short set. He even went easy on the ice. He chose to wear his diamond link chain, his 3 carat pinky ring, and his Frank Muller. Tamia chose to wear her white strapless Chanel dress, with her white Chanel wedges. She accessorized lightly, because she wanted to really enjoy herself tonight. Only a few bangles and some earrings. Tamia had her hair braided by her Haitian coworker for the trip. She needed something very low maintenance. Her honey color braids hung in the small of her back. The color really intensified her hazel eyes. For tonight's occasion she decided to put them in an up-do while a few hung loose around her face. "You ready baby?" Teelee asked as he walked into the bathroom. "Yeah baby, just let me put on my lip gloss." "Damn maw, you lookin hot tonight" Teelee said admiring the way Tamia looked. The Chanel dress fit every curve on her body. "Thank you baby. I see you got your swag on deck tonight too" Tamia said while landing a big kiss on Teelee's lips. "Damn that taste good. Gimme another one." "No baby, we gon be late" Tamia said pushing Teelee back. Teelee's phone rang. *"I'mma muthafuckin hustla-*

*A muthafuckin hustla -H-U-S-T-L-E-R- I'm hustling."* Teelee answered his cell phone leaving Tamia to finish up in the bathroom. "Yeah what it do?" "We outside homey." "Thugga and Real out there to?" Teelee asked grabbing his money and keys off the night stand. "Yeah nigga come on. We ain't bout to be waitin on you and Tiger ass all night." "Say Lil Man." "Nigga what?" Click. Teelee hung up in Lil Man's face. Soon as Teelee clamped his blackberry in its case, Tamia came out of the bathroom. "Come on bae, I'm ready." They hit the lights to the villa, and they were out the door.

Caribbean Lynx was lit up like New York City. The club sat right on the beach, giving it a nice feel. It didn't have any walls, enabling the breeze that blew off the ocean to circulate around the club. There was a huge crowd present to see the dance hall king; Sean Paul. "Feel like we back at home" Thugga said noticing all the dread headed people walking around. There were two dance floors. One in the middle of the club and one on the sand of the beach. The cover charge was 100 dollars per person. The line to get onto the beach was very long. The concert would be over by the time the people at the end of the line got to the front. Teelee flashed that mullah and got all of them to the front of the line. Teelee pulled the big bouncer to the side. "Say homey, I need a V.I.P. table for me and my people." "That's gonna cost a couple of francs my friend." Without saying anything, Teelee placed ten hundred dollar bills in the massive hand of the big bald headed bouncer. "Right this way sir" the bouncer said lifting the rope to let them in. The bouncer personally led them to an exclusive spot sectioned off for celebs, and

V.I.P. customers. Not even 5 minutes after they sat down, Sean Paul was hitting the stage. *"Just gimme the light, and pass the drooo."* The club went wild as everyone held their lit lighter in the air. "Yeah this what I'm talkin bout" Thugga said with his lighter high in the air. "Feel like we back at home for real. They buckin in this bitch." "Light the purpa my thug" K-Real said passing Thugga a cigar filled with some granddaddy. "Would you all like anything to drink" the waitress asked, as she approached the table. "Yeah give us a bottle of Dom Perignon" Lil Man requested. As the waitress went to fill their order, everyone stood up and joined in with the excitement. *"Could I be yuh protector, yuh buff in every sector, every man around dem, waan tun yuh inspector?"* "Bae I gotta use the restroom" Tamia said grabbing her Chanel handbag. "Come on gurl, I'mma go wit you" Twin said following suit. "Real you coming?" Tamia asked. "Yeah come on. I can't let y'all go by y'all self." "I'll be right back baby" Tamia said giving Teelee a small kiss on the lips. "Aight hurry up back. These niggas buckin a lil to hard in this bitch. I don't wanna have to shut this bitch down" Teelee said meaning every single word. The atmosphere was pretty wild. You wouldn't think with the island being small as it was, but there were hood niggas and hood bitches everywhere. The club erupted when Sean Paul began to perform *"Here comes the boom."* It was extreme mayhem in the middle of the dance floor. "Damn them niggas wildin" Thugga said pointing to the middle of the club. People were pushing and shoving, not caring who they knocked down. "Come on homey, let's go get Tiger and nem" Teelee said leading the way across the club. It was good Teelee suggested they go get the girls. As they made their way through the crowded dance floor, they walked up on a group of young wild cats harassing Tamia and Twin. Real was standing her ground like a true gangster. "Nigga you betta get the fuck" Real barked. The short dread headed cat wasn't trying to hear it. He challenged the rejection. "Say baby, stop that. You know you wanna come have a drink wit me and my comrades." "Nigga please, I piss on niggas like you" Real said, standing face to face with the young goon. Tamia and Twin had to fight off the others. "Bitch come ova here and stop playin wit me" as Tamia arm was being grabbed by one of the young cats. Soon as dread said that, it was like the Matrix. Teelee grabbed the young cat by the throat, preventing him from saying another word. Thugga and Lil Man grabbed Twin and Tamia and moved them behind them. "Nigga who you callin a bitch" Teelee growled as spit flew out of his mouth into dread's face. By now they were all faced off. It was three to four. They had one up on Teelee and the gang, but that didn't matter. The young maniacs could handle ten of them boys if need be. As the other three proceeded to start the rumble, Lil Man and Thugga beat them to the punch. Lil Man threw a quick two piece at the first one that ran up, while Thugga broke the Heineken bottle over the other cat's head. By then Teelee had knocked young dread clean out. The crowd backed up, giving them more than enough room to scuffle. "Baby watch out" Tamia screamed, trying to get around the crowd. As Teelee was about to turn around, the fourth guy was coming across his head with a Heineken long neck. You would think the bottle would have knocked Teelee out. It was the total opposite. The hit made Teelee even angrier. As blood ran down Teelee's face, he threw a flurry of punches at the guy. The final hook to the jaw took the young cat off his feet. Teelee blacked out as he stomped the dude head into the ground. "Baby them people" Twin screamed, as the police tried to make their way through the crowd. "Lil Man and Thugga grabbed Teelee. "Come on son, them people comin." "Fuck them people" Teelee growled, continuing to stomp the dude to a bloody pulp. Lil Man and Thugga had to literally drag Teelee away. Luckily by the time the police made their way to the middle of the dance floor, Teelee and the gang were making their escape. They exited through the other side of the club, while the police walked up on four bloody busters. Everybody jumped in their cars and headed back to their villas.

Tamia ran to the bathroom as soon as they made their way through the door of the villa. She came back with a towel, band aids, and peroxide. "Come on maw, let's go sit on the beach" Teelee said holding his Sean Jean shirt on his wound. It was just a cut that bled like a gash. The bleeding had actually slowed up. "Boy are you crazy! Let me take care of your head first." Teelee walked out the door, making Tamia have to follow him. "Come on bae, I gotta clean your head up" Tamia pleaded, trying to catch up with Teelee. By the time she caught up with him, they were already on the beach, which was his plan. "Come on maw, sit down." Teelee grabbed Tamia's arm pulling her down on the sand. "Don't move, I'm bout to tend to your head" Tamia demanded while taking control. All Teelee could do was lie back. "It's not as bad as I thought" Tamia said. "I told you. The blood made it look worse than it was" Teelee replied. After Tamia cleaned Teelee up, they laid back on the cool sand. They were enjoying the breeze coming off the Caribbean Sea. The sound of the water tussling around was soothing, as the waves continually rolled in. "Baby you went crazy in the club" Tamia said, cuddled up in Teelee arms. "I get crazy over you. No nigga ain't ever disrespecting you as long as I'm livin" Teelee said running his fingers through Tamia braids. "I love you baby" Tamia expressed, as she puckered her lips toward Teelee. "I love you to honey bun" Teelee replied getting a taste of Tamia's lip gloss. As they released from their kiss, Tamia suddenly screamed. "What's wrong maw?" Teelee asked. "Look bae" Tamia said while pointing at a funny looking crab not even five feet away from where they were. The crab's long antenna like eyes sat on top of his body. It creep Tamia all the way out, because it stopped and looked directly at her. Teelee slung some sand and ran it off. It was known as the ghost crab. They lived on the beach in burrow like sand dunes. Seeing it for the first time would scare anybody. "Come on maw, let's go inside before you have a heart attack." Teelee whisked Tamia off her feet so they could head back to the villa and take a hot shower. After they showered, they sexed each other to sleep.

The next morning their plans were halted. Teelee had to arrange for everyone to fly out on a charter plane. There was a huge category 4 hurricane headed for the island. Everyone was disappointed, but soon got over it. They'd rather be safe than sorry. A hurricane that size would kill a lot of people, especially on an island small as St.

Bart's. Being killed while on vacation wasn't an option. They immediately packed up, and headed to the small airport known as Gustaf. Their getaway was short, sweet, and crazy. The main reason for going to the exclusive island was to get away from chaos. To their surprise, they were faced with the same shit they had to deal with back home. "You could take the nigga out the hood, but you definitely can't take the hood out the nigga.

## CHAPTER 19

## IT'S WAR TIME

"Bet a hunid I hit this ten nigga" Rafee said, shaking the dice in one hand and holding a Keep Moving in the other. Rafee and Kinky D was locked in an intense game of craps in Big Head Unc backyard. What made the game so intense was, Rafee was down by three g's and chasing. Instead of calling it quits and coming back another day, Rafee chose to keep on shooting. He just couldn't let a cat like Kinky beat him in nothing. Rafee felt Kinky D was a weak ass nigga. He was a loud mouth hanging off another niggas coat tail. Rafee really despised dudes like Kinky, because he felt they just took up space and wasn't built for the streets. Rafee felt if a nigga couldn't hold his own weight in the game, he shouldn't even be allowed to play in it. "Nigga bet, you ain't sayin shit." Kinky D peeped Rafee's stash. He estimated him to only have three hundred left. "If this nigga fall off on this point, I'm bout to get the fuck" Kinky thought as Rafee blew on the dice. Rafee turned his New Orleans Hornets fitted cap to the back, schooling the dice at the same time. "You ready chump, ten out the door." Rafee did a quick shake and tossed the dice in the air. The dice bounced and danced repeatedly until they landed on five. "Add five more" Rafee schooled the dice, then let them roll once again. After a couple of more shots, Rafee finally fell off, "4-3." "Ah nigga, I knew you wasn't go hit that point." Kinky scraped his money off the ground, and slid it in his pocket. "Nigga shoot! It's yo dice." "Nah round, I'm good." "Here." Kinky went in his pocket and threw Rafee two crumpled up one hundred dollar bills. "Nigga what the fuck is this?" Rafee asked. "I'm done homey, that's what this is." "Nigga what you mean you done." "I said I'm done. I broke you round. Come back tomorrow. I'mma give you ya get back." Normally Kinky would have never tried to play Rafee, but considering the fact he felt he was entitled to quit when he was ready and Roylee was around the corner on St. Anthony. Kinky felt he was safe. "Nigga you betta pick them dice up and shoot." The seriousness in Rafee's voice sent chills up Kinky's spine. In spite of the fear he stood his ground, refusing to continue on with the dice game. "Say round, I said I was through. How you go make me shoot the dice?" Without speaking another word, Rafee rose up off the ground. As soon as he pulled his Hornets sweat pants up around his waist, he simultaneously came off his hip with his Forty with the dick. "Nigga you know what, fuck shootin the dice. Empty out yo pockets, bitch nigga." "Say Rafee, man what you doing?" "Nigga what it look like I'm doing. I'm robbing a bitch nigga." The way Rafee held his grip on the Forty made Kinky know he wouldn't hesitate to send hollow tips through his frame. Kinky D was well aware of Rafee and his menacing acts, which made him want to kick his self in the ass for agreeing to shoot dice with him in the first place. He told his self if he made it out the situation, Rafee and all his Skull Gang potnas was going to get their issue. "Say round, it ain't gotta be all this. Everybody lose sometimes." Rafee could smell the fear leaking from Kinky's pores, as he rambled on. "Nigga I ain't tryna hear all that sucka ass shit. Your bitch ass shoulda been kicked out the game, but no you wanna continue to swim in the bayou full of alligators. Just take this as payin dues nigga." Kinky came out his pockets with the three g's he won off Rafee, and the two g's he came to the game with. "Nigga that's all you got?" The barrel of the Forty was in the middle of Kinky's forehead. Rafee did a quick pat down making sure the nigga didn't have his burner on him. As Rafee made it to the small of his back, Kinky hoped to God this trigger happy manic didn't shoot him upon finding his nickel plated .45. "What do we have here." Rafee pulled the gun from Kinky's waistband. This is a pretty muthafucka right here. I should shoot yo ass wit yo own gun nigga." The statement made Kinky tense up, because as quick as Rafee removed his Forty, he replaced it with Kinky's .45. Rafee pressed the barrel of the four nickel to Kinky's forehead with so much pressure that it was forming a perfect circle in his skin. "Nigga you know me. You niggas act like shit was sweet when I was locked off in prison. Nigga I want you to hear me, and hear me clear. All that sucka ass shit is out the window. I'm puttin this shit in beast mode outchere. You niggas betta be on ya P's and Q's." Kinky D was spooked the fuck out. He could have sworn Rafee was about to bust his melon right there in Unc backyard. To his fortune, Rafee let him make it. What Rafee didn't know was, he should have killed Kinky because extreme havoc was about to be brought upon their hood.

"Yeah I'm outchere on the block. What you bout to come through and fuck wit me." Roylee sat in his Hummer rapping with his girl Tanya. He hadn't been on the block for months due to his spot in Raceland. No matter how much money the spot in Raceland pulled in, it couldn't compare to the love he got from his old stomping grounds. As he looked at the little kids running around St. Anthony, he remembered his days as a youngster. Running around without a care in the world. Now those times were gone. He had his own responsibilities. That's the reason he put it in over drive everyday he placed his feet to the concrete. His girl Tanya had recently informed him that they were pregnant. His motivation to hustle increased, putting him in a no holds barred mode. Every dollar that came across his path, he was going to get for the sake of his seed growing in his girl's stomach. He had finally got Kinky D to stop trying to wedge a war between Teelee and the gang. That was a plus considering he needed all the money he could get. Many nights he contemplated taking on the challenge of taking over his allies' throne, but he quickly withdrew those thoughts. With all the tension within his crew about taking over, it was hard not to wonder on the position he would be in if Teelee and the gang was out of the way. He was definitely certified to go to war. Roylee was one of the most ruthless cats coming out of the 7th Ward. Many people feared the young killer; old heads and all. The physical part of the war was no problem, it was the disadvantages that it would bring. Money was just too good, and he wasn't going to let his selfish greed destroy what he had going. "Hit the locks nigga." Kinky D frantically knocked on the passenger side window of Roylee's Hummer, breaking him out of his deep thoughts. From the looks of it, Roylee knew whatever it was, it wasn't good. "What's good playboy?" Roylee asked hitting the unlock button on the driver side door. "Say round shit done got real" Kinky said with a serious scowl on his face. "These niggas got me fucked up! It's about to go down!" "Wo, wo, wo, slow down son. What the fuck you talkin bout?" "That bitch ass nigga Rafee just robbed me!" "Hold up, what the fuck!" "Man we was shootin dice on Touro and the Blade in Unc backyard and I hit him out about 3 g's. The nigga felt played when I told him I was about to quit, then he pulled his burner on me." Roylee had been having a gut feeling that something like this was going to happen. All the negative tension running through the veins of his crew, something was bound to pop off. He tried all the tactics he could think of to prevent this inevitable situation from happening, but like a pressure cooker with too much pressure inside, it's bound to explode. His goals of stacking much as he could from his spot in Raceland was about to be a thing of the past. No matter how much he wanted to squash the shit that just happened, he couldn't. This kind of disrespect could not be tolerated. If it was you were labeled as a pushover. Pushovers didn't last long running on the murderous streets of New Orleans. It was either get it in, or call it quits. Calling it quits was definitely not a part of Roylee's forte. He'd rather kill his self, than to go out like a sucker. "Look here Kinky, stay here and wait for Tanya. When she get here tell her I said to meet me at the spot in about an hour. Tell her I had to go take care of sumthin."

"What you mean stay here and tell Tanya, nigga I'm rollin wit you."

"Look here Kinky this shit bout to get real ugly my nigga. I need to make sure all our steps are calculated right. One slip up and we all dead. I'm not bout to run the risk of a nigga seeing you, and peepin the play. You got plenty of time to buck wit these niggas. Let me send the first message." Roylee knew he had to attack the situation correctly. Kinky D was on some emotional type shit, and could cause all of them to get killed. That's the one thing Roylee learned growing up beefing in the cold streets of the "Murda Cappy." Never let your emotions or anger dictate your next move in the act of murder. It could cause you to get picked up on a murder charge, and you're thinking pattern thrown off track; disabling you from making a wise decision. Roylee knew this was about to be a long drawn out war between the two sides. Just like he was ruthless, he knew his enemy was no pushover either. In fact, he knew the Skull Gang held more heavy hitters than his clique did; especially Teelee. He would have to work extra hard because he knew Teelee was the mastermind of their whole organization. The nigga was a cold hearted, stone cold killer; just like his self. It was about to be World War III, within their hood and it was nothing either one of them could do to stop it.

"Say Nardy, where you be at?" Nardy was a young goon Roylee had put under his wing years ago. Roylee peeped the potential in him a while back when a situation took place around the neighborhood strip club, "The Show." Roylee had been acquainted with the young cat, but never knew his certification in the street. This particular incident showed Roylee that the young killer had a head on his shoulder, and he wouldn't hesitate to rock a nigga to sleep. "Wzup cutie, you tryna get a lap dance?" Nardy scanned the big booty yellow bone for a second, before he allowed her to touch him. Nardy was only eighteen, but his awareness stayed on point. He knew niggas got caught slipping all kinds of ways. The life he was living wasn't no room to be off his game. "So wzup baby, you gon let me do my thang or what." As soon as Nardy was about to agree to the lap dance, he noticed his self being grilled by a group of dudes from the other side of the strip club. Immediately a red flag went up. In his mind he thought; either they sent the bitch over to throw him off his game, or they were waiting for him to leave the club. "Look phat, hold this spot down. I'mma be back. I gotta go take a piss. Here, hold this till I get back." Nardy put his blue LA Dodgers fitted cap on her head, as he headed towards the restroom. "Aight baby, but don't be long. Time is money, ya heard me." Nardy felt the cold hard stares penetrating him as he made his way to the bathroom. He had no real intentions of going to the restroom. It was just a diversion plan to get him out of danger. Soon as Nardy entered the bathroom, he went straight for the window. Whoever these cats was, they really didn't know they were about to get a brutal wakeup call. Fucking with the heartless young killer was a big mistake. "Yeah I'm waitin on you." Roylee leaned against his Cutlass Supreme talking to one of his cronies. He was parked on the neutral ground, right across the street from the strip club. It had been a great night on the block, so he felt like treating his self to a couple of drinks, and maybe a little head on the side. Soon as Roylee was about to make his way to the other side of the street, he noticed something funny. His instincts told him to chill for a minute and peep out the scene. Standing in a dark alley, that sat right off the corner of the club was a cat he was familiar with. The way he was dressed, and the AK47 that he held in his grip was something else he was familiar with. Those signs made him get back in his car. He wanted to peep out what the young goon was about to pull off. Minutes later a group of men emerged from the doors of the strip club. Upon seeing the three men coming out the club, young Nardy up the choppa. He riddled all their bodies with baby missiles. "BOOM, BOOM, BOOM, BOOM, BOOM, BOOM, BOOM." The three men didn't stand a chance. Young Nardy slaughtered every last one of them. Roylee stuck around until Nardy emptied the last bullet out of the clip. The boldness of this young killer sparked interest in Roylee. A week later Roylee summoned the young goon to meet up with him, giving him a proposition to roll with his team. Young Nardy agreed, and they had been close ever since. "I'm ova here at the gamblin shack, why what it do playboy? You sound fucked up." "Say lil homey, some shit just kicked off. I need you to meet me on St. Anthony. I'mma be waitin on you, ya heard me." "Say no more my nigga, I'm there." Nardy pulled up moments later in his black Ram Air Trans Am. Without speakin a word, Roylee jumped out his Hummer and into Nardy's whip. They had been on many murder capers together. All the preliminary shit need not be said. "Pull around the corner, so we could jump in the rock rental" Roylee said, cocking his blue steel 9. "So who mama we bout to send to the grave yard in a black dress?" "That bitch as nigga Rafee, that run wit them Skull Gang niggas. The nigga call his self tryna play my lil round. I got sumthin for his ass though." "Nuff said Whoa. I'm on the plane, ready to take off." Over the years of running with Roylee, Nardy had really grown into a well-rounded, street certified, gangster. The nigga stayed ready to put that work in; wearing mostly army fatigues, and Prada tennis shoes. The nigga was known as the young soulja, with much swag. His Native American heritage gave him a handsome look, with a grimy edge. His bronze skin complexion, and the two long braids he wore in his hair; made all the groupies want him in their bed. Roylee and Nardy jumped in the Ford Taurus and were off to start a war that would go on for quite some time.

"Here Gutta, roll this up" Thugga said jumping back in Rafee's Lexus 430. Thugga had stopped by his spot on Frenchman to pick up some fire Kush. Thugga and Rafee switched cars for the day. Rafee had grown tired of the luxury of the Lexus, and wanted to push some shit with speed so Thugga let him hold down the Corvette. "That's that good my nigga. Egghead said he ain't got a batch like that in a minute." "Say son, I need you to shoot me to my whip after we smoke. I gotta drop a package off to my youngin." Gutta had the 8th Ward on lock, ever since Thugga plugged him in with that snow white. Thugga knew linking up with the young grinder was going to pay off. Gutta was flipping five cakes a week, which increased Thugga's network even higher. "I got you. I gotta swing round that way anyway. My lil bitch just moved around there. I gotta go christen the house, ya heard me." "Thugga you a wild boy son. You don't worry if one of them hoe's gon ever set you up?" "Nigga I'm Thugga, Cal Cutta! None of them bitches or them bitch ass niggas bet not ever get the nuts to fuck wit me, ya heard me! Spark that shit up, fuck all the dumb shit."

Roylee and Nardy rode up and down every street backatown, in search for any signs of Rafee. "Turn right chere, lemme see if the nigga on Frenchmen St." As soon as Nardy spent the corner on Frenchman and Tonti St., Roylee spotted Rafee's Lexus. "There the nigga go right there." Thugga didn't even peep the black Taurus creeping up on the side of them. Before he could get the chance to do anything, Nardy pulled the Taurus in front of the Lex, blocking them in. All Thugga could do was duck, as Roylee hopped out and dumped 19 hollow points in the driver side of the Lexus. "BOOM, BOOM, BOOM, BOOM." Roylee and Nardy jumped in the Taurus and sped off, knowing that was the start of a very bloody war.

"Thugga my nigga say sumthin!" Thugga was curled up on the floor, under the steering wheel. Gutta didn't know whether to get out and buck at the niggas or concentrate on Thugga. The hit Roylee and Nardy pulled off was so quick, him nor Thugga stood a chance. "Say round them bitches shot me." Thugga's voice almost went unheard. The many bullets that riddled his body was draining the life out of him. Gutta hopped out the Lex and ran to the driver side. In the past he heard it wasn't good to move a person that had been shot, but he disregarded that notion. He knew if he didn't get Thugga to a hospital quick, he wasn't going to make it. He had been hit one time in the shoulder, but the adrenaline pumping through his veins helped him ignore the pain. From the direction the bullets were penetrating the Lex, Gutta knew it was a hit. He only got hit because of how close he was. Blood was splattered everywhere. Gutta couldn't tell where Thugga was hit. "Come on homey, I'm bout to get you to the hospital." Gutta lifted Thugga off the floor of the Lex. "Them bitches shot me round." "Be cool son, stop talkin. I'm bout to get you to the hospital." Gutta opened the back door of the car, and lied Thugga on the back seat. Even though him and Thugga hadn't known each other for too long, he felt pain in his heart to see his lil homey in that position. Gutta jumped in the driver seat of the Lex, and punched the accelerator. He knew if he got Thugga to Charity Hospital in time, it was a good chance they could save him. "Them bitches shot me" was all Thugga could say. "Who shot you round! Who the niggas was?" "Ro, Ro, Roylee." That's all Gutta heard before Thugga passed out on the back seat. "Thugga!" Gutta screamed. Gutta grabbed Thugga's wrist checking to see if he could feel anything, as he navigated his way to the hospital. He felt something, but it wasn't strong. He knew if he didn't get to the hospital quick, Thugga was going to die on the back seat. With some skillful driving, he finally made it to the emergency room. Gutta pulled up on the ramp, and hopped out to get some help. "My people shot up bad! Come on! I need some help!" Gutta snatched a nurse that appeared to be taking a break. "O my God, Paul grab a stretcher! We got a gunshot victim!" As they wheeled Thugga in the hospital, Gutta tried to follow but was stopped. "Sir you're gonna have to wait out here. Your friend is going to be just fine." Gutta wanted to slap the shit out of the nurse for making that dumb ass statement. She said that shit like Thugga only had a brush burn. "Bitch go help my people. Your encouragement ain't helpin." From all the blood on Gutta's clothes, it appeared as if he was in bad shape. He paced back and forth in the lobby of the hospital, until it snapped. "I gotta call Teelee and them boyz." Gutta ran out to the car to see if he could find Thugga's cell phone. He searched the back seat, and couldn't find it. Suddenly Gutta heard Thugga's ring tone "My boss bitch" by Mac the Camouflage Assassin going off in the front seat. He desperately searched until he found it on the driver side floor. "Hello, hello." "Wzup Thugga baaby" Lil Man said. Lil Man had been waiting at the studio for Thugga. He was calling to see what was up. "Lil Man this ain't Thugga. This Gutta, say round Thugga just got banged up. Come to Charity AS.A.P." "I'm on my way" was all Lil Man said before the phone went dead.

Lil Man, Teelee, and Tamia pulled up to Charity Emergency room almost at the same time. When Lil Man called Teelee and told him Thugga had been shot, Teelee ran out the house in his boxers trying to get to Thugga. Tamia had to run behind him with some clothes, before he got pulled over for indecent exposure. Upon entering the emergency room, they saw Gutta pacing back and forth with a disdainful look on his face. "Man what the fuck happened?" Lil Man asked in an aggressive tone. In Lil Man's mind everyone was a suspect. "Say homey we was sittin on Frenchmen smokin a gar when these two niggas pulled up on the car, and just went to bustin." "What niggas?" Teelee asked, coming within inches of Gutta's nose. "Look round, I feel your pain. As a matter of fact, I have the same intents y'all got towards the shit." Gutta had to show Teelee and Lil Man that he had nothing to do with the shit that just happened. The aggression coming from both of them showed him they felt he did. "I know what level y'all on, I'm being a hunid percent real when I say this. I ain't have shit to do wit this." Teelee analyzed Gutta's whole demeanor trying to see if anything was flaky. The obvious patched up wound on his shoulder gave Teelee a sign that Gutta could have been telling the truth. Teelee eased up so he could let his anger subside a bit. He knew right now his only concern should be if his homey was going to make it. Lil Man still looked at Gutta with a murderous stare. All his rationale had gone out the window. One thing was for sure, if Thugga didn't make it. All hell was going to break loose, literally. "So what the doctor said?" Teelee asked. "They ain't said shit yet. I been waitin for the nurse to come tell me sumthin. I think they got him in surgery. Say Teelee whenever we see what's good with Thugga. I got sumthin you definitely want to know." Tamia tried her best to console Teelee. His pain, was her pain. "Come on baby, sit down for a minute." As Tamia led Teelee to sit down, K-Real burst through the hospital doors. Her hair was all over her head, her eyes were puffy, and she had a look in her eyes that showed her pain and murderous intentions. "What the fuck happened!" K-Real ran up to Gutta so fast it caught him off guard. Lil Man grabbed Real. "Say Real be cool. He said he ain't have shit to do wit it. Don't trip, we gon see what it do. We gotta see wzup wit homey first and foremost." The piercing look Real was giving Gutta, made him believe the gruesome rumors about the venomous soulja girl. K-Real backed up, giving Gutta some breathing room. "Come sit down Real. We gotta just pray he go be good." Teelee was the only one that could control the female pit bull. Her homey, lover friend, was lying in there between life and death. Her anger calmed and the pain in her heart increased. Just the thought made her wanna pass out. "Where's Pistol and Corey?" Teelee asked. "They on their way from Bogalusa" K-Real replied, as she stared off into space. Tamia had called her mom, while on the way to the hospital. Shorty worked in the Trauma unit at Charity Hospital. Soon as some news developed on Thugga they would find out immediately. Everyone had made it down to the hospital. Thugga's mom, Rafee, Corey, Pistol, Ms. Mary, Money, and even T-Mac were all there. They all were on pins and needles, awaiting the news on Thugga. Shorty C came out, and informed them he was still in surgery. They were trying to dislodge one of the bullets that went in his neck, inches away from his juggler vein. The only thing she could say was, "keep on praying." Thugga's mom was a nervous wreck. Every time the doors to the Trauma unit would open, she jumped. As much as she prayed for this not to happen, it was only a matter of time. She was very well aware of her son's life style. She grew to accept the fact that he was a product of his environment, but she could never bring herself to accept the fact that he may die one day in the streets. She silently prayed to herself that whatever the outcome was, she would be able to handle it. After numerous hours passed, Shorty C emerged from the doors of the Trauma unit. By the look on her face, everyone knew it wasn't good. Shorty walked up on Thugga's mom. All she could do was pull her into an embrace that only a mother could relate to. "Nooooo!" The loud shriek Thugga's mom let out, caused everyone to break down. All Shorty could do was hold her tighter, as the tears began to fall from her own eyes. Shorty felt extreme empathy for Thugga's mom. K-Real ran out the hospital screaming and hollering. Pistol had to run after her to make sure she was good. Gutta couldn't believe his ears, as he dropped his head in sorrow. Teelee and Lil Man were in a state of shock. The both of them refused to let the thought of their brother being dead enter their hearts. "He can't be maw" was all Teelee could say, while Tamia held his head to her breast. Her eyes were filled with tears as well. Thugga was just like a brother to her. He loved the genuine love Teelee and Tamia had for each other. Rafee sat with his head down as the burning tears fell from his eyes; he promised his self for every tear he dropped a nigga was going to die. Money and T-Mac was extremely hurt as well. Thugga was their big brother, and mentor. The hatred that brewed in their hearts for Thugga's death, would be poured upon the 7th Ward in future years to come. Ms. Mary consoled Corey, who was not taking the tragic event well at all. This tragedy left deep holes in each and every one of their hearts.

One thing was for certain; their pain was going to be felt for a long time throughout the streets of New Orleans.

It had been a week since Thugga's death, and the pain only increased within Teelee's soul. He just couldn't accept the fact that his partner, brother, and business associate had been taken from him. He refused to be around anyone, even Lil Man. Tamia was worried sick; he hadn't been home since the day Thugga died. She wanted desperately to let him know that his pain was her pain, and they would get through it together. Teelee felt he needed time to his self to dissect the situation. He also didn't want to put her in harm's way. After they all departed from the hospital, Gutta informed Teelee on the people responsible for Thugga's death. Upon hearing who killed Thugga, Teelee's heart took upon a veil of pure evil. Even the pupils of his eyes seemed to turn completely black. Every thought that entered his mind was filled with evil and destruction. He vowed to his self that he would destroy Roylee and everything that was close to him. Lil Man spent most of his time taking his pain out on his mix tape. No one had seen Rafee since the day at the hospital. When the reason behind Thugga's death surfaced; everyone in the clique despised Rafee for his actions. If only he could have walked away from that dice game; Thugga would still be alive today. Knowing he was the cause of his comrade's death, he couldn't face anyone; at least not until he touched one of Roylee's souljas or Roylee himself. The 7$^{th}$ Ward would definitely be the reason the murder rate rose for the year. Frank Maynard would really have his work cut out for him. Teelee had been spending the past few nights at the Best Western hotel, located in the East. He wasn't traveling in none of his personal whips. He wanted to be very inconspicuous to the streets when he made his first move. No one would be ready for his wrath. Teelee cruised up Morrison road in the Impala Tamia rented for him. He sat behind dark tinted windows. He didn't give a fuck about the fine he would have to pay upon returning the car. His main concern was staying off the radar until he dropped his first bomb on the bitch niggas that killed his brother. The beef that just kicked off was no ordinary beef. The beef that Teelee and the gang was locked into was a never ending process. It would never get squashed until all were dead, and even then the next generation would inherit the beef. Lil Wayne's *"Damn I miss my dawg"* pumped through the speakers of the rental. Teelee turned up the Hennessey bottle he had been nursing all day; and sang along with the lyrics of the song, as he pulled to the red light on Read Road. *"My nigga-my nerve-my muthafuckin man-* THUGGA." So engulfed in his thoughts, he never paid attention to the N.O.P.D. squad car that pulled out of the Shell gas station. "WHOOP, WHOOP." "Awe fuck, I don't need this shit right now!" He really didn't need the police harassing him. The Glock 19, with the extended 32 round clip under his left leg would definitely send him on a trip to the Feds. Thinking everything would be cool, he pulled over as he made a left turn on Read. "I got my license and registration. These bitches ain't got no probable cause to search my shit. Fuck it's the jump out boyz!" Teelee knew there was a chance they might try and search the car. As a matter of fact, he knew for sure they would search the vehicle upon seeing who was behind the wheel. The heat was still on from those other incidents, dealing with Thugga's trial. Teelee recognized the short stocky officer exited the squad car. He was familiar with him from patrolling the 7th Ward, years ago. His resume wasn't good. He was one of them pick your charge type assholes. Even though the situation didn't look good, Teelee still held his composure. A nervous individual was the first thing the police looked for when they were on the verge of harassing someone. Teelee was a well-seasoned vet to all that type of shit. If it was his destiny to go to jail, he knew it was nothing he could do to stop it. Teelee slightly cracked his window, giving him enough room to hand the officer his license and registration. He was well aware of his rights, so they couldn't play him for a sucker. "Oh look who we have here. The infamous Mr. Teelee." Without speaking a word, Teelee stuck his license and registration out of the window. It was no need to talk. The quicker they ran his name, the quicker he could go about his business. The officer grabbed Teelee's paperwork out of his hand, as his partner made his way around to the passenger side of the Impala. Could you tell me the reason y'all pulled me over?" "The tinted windows on this car are pretty dark. I'm pretty sure they are well over the regulation limit." Teelee knew that was a bullshit excuse, because the windows on his personal cars were even darker. He hardly got pulled over, while driving his other vehicles. Shinning his flash light throughout the car, the officer recognized the Hennessey bottle on the passenger seat. He immediately made his way back to the squad car, where his partner was running Teelee's information in the computer. "Mark I think I just found our probable cause to search his vehicle." "Oh yeah, and what might that be?" "I noticed a bottle of alcohol lying on the passenger seat. We could check his alcohol level." "That might work. As a matter of fact, I'll call backup, because I know he got some kind of unregistered weapon in that car." From the length of time it was taking the two cops to run his name, Teelee knew they had to be up to something. Teelee had a feeling the reason they were taking so long because of the bottle lying on the seat. It was no doubt in his mind that they would try and perform a search now. Not having any gum, or anything to kill the smell of alcohol on his breath; he went for the next best thing. He retrieved a penny from the middle console of the car. The copper from the penny would definitely mess up the Breathalyzer machine. Teelee looked in the rearview mirror and noticed another police car pull up. "These bitches done called the Calvary for a nigga." Teelee slid the Glock under his seat, and prepared for the inevitable. Just as Teelee was about to call Tamia and tell her to get ready to come and bond him out, the short stocky cop tapped on his window. "Would you step out of the vehicle please?" "For what, all my shit legit." "We're going to need you to perform a Breathalyzer test." "Y'all think a nigga been drinkin cause he got liquor in the car. I ain't doing no trippin. We could do that." Teelee knew for sure he was good on the test, but the burner under his seat, he wasn't so sure about. He knew there was a fifty, fifty chance they would try and search the Impala. As Teelee exited the car, he noticed the cop kept his hand close to his police issued Glock 9. "You ain't gotta be nervous. I ain't bout to try and pull nuthin off." "What makes you think I'm nervous?" the cop asked, never taking his hand from by his gun. "Cause you clutchin ya heat like I'm a wanted murderer or sumthin." "Step back to the trunk of the car." Teelee proceeded to comply with the officer's request, while his partner did just what he had already predicted. "Say hold up, what the fuck you think you doing? Y'all can't search my shit" Teelee said, headed towards the officer. "Hey get back. Where do you think you're going?" At that moment the short stocky cop drew his gun. While he contained Teelee, his partner continued the search. The other two cops were out of their squad car, giving aid to their co-workers. As one of the officers made his way around to the driver side of the Impala, Teelee tensed up because he knew it was his destiny to go to Orleans Parish Prison tonight. "Bingo" the officer yelled as he retrieved the Glock. All Teelee could do was smirk at the short stocky cop. Running was out of the question. He was cornered in from every angle. "I might as well go in easy." He didn't feel like taking a trip to Charity Emergency room, before going to jail. "This is a nineteen Mark. Looks like our boy here is going away for a nice while." "Fuck you pig! I'll be out in less than eight hours. When I get out, I'mma be sure to get my lil goons to run a train on your daughter." The thought of Thugga being dead, mixed with the intoxicating feeling he was experiencing made him not give a fuck. He knew above all "Money Talked and Bullshit Walked." There was no way Sheriff Foley was going to hold him. He practically ran the streets of New Orleans. The rental was towed away and Teelee was brought down to Orleans Parish Prison where he was booked with,

"Felon in possession of a firearm."

"Turn the volume up in my headphones" Lil Man said preparing to lay his dedication song to Thugga on his mix tape. He had been in the studio day and night for the past three months. He made sure every track and every verse was on point. Their crazy trip to St. Bart's was the only break he had in between. The grief he was experiencing was unbearable. This was his only way to release the pain of his brother's death. Of course the thirst for Roylee's blood still roamed throughout his soul. He knew before moves were made, they had to lay his homey to rest properly. Teelee left him with enough information to sustain his anger for the moment. Lil Man understood the reason why Teelee distanced his self from everybody, including him. He knew his boy better than anybody. He knew what Teelee was planning was precise and effective; except this time, nobody would be spared. Lil Man's first cousin Dee was in place to sing the hook. The emotion and intensity in the song could be felt though the mesmerizing track. The bass of the drums gave you a heartfelt feeling on the inside. "You ready?" Lil Man's engineer asked, while adjusting the volume in Lil Man's headphones. "Yeah let's do this." In that moment it was like Lil Man transformed into a lion in the booth. He took his fitted cap from his head, letting his long dreadlocks hang over his face and shoulders. His voice roared over the track, as his emotions took control.

*"This fo my nigga Thugga-raised up in the gutta-born up in da hood-he be a block lover-fo that doe and that cane-he be a*

*Glock bussa-words can't explain, I miss my nigga Cal Cutta-shit'll never be the same-there won't be another Thugga-I'mma get ya youngin through the struggle-you been wit me from the start-you my blood brotha-side by side-now you're gone feel like my life smothered-but fuck it-I'm in the middle of the storm for ya-son I ain't going nowhere-I'mma bust back-dare one of them bitch niggas to bust back-*

Dee's part fit right into the flow of the song. As he let his soulful voice serenade the track.

*We'll be miiissing yooou-can't stop thinking bout youuu-I can't explain the pain-Shit'll never be the saammee.*

Thugga's dedication song was successfully laid. Lil Man really put his all into the whole mix tape. The finish product was looking to do big things, according to his associates. The word was Weezy Wee was interested in Lil Man's work. Occasionally Lil Man would dip by the rap star's house and chill. With Lil Man living directly across the street from him, they became acquainted. Maybe this could be Lil Man's big break, maybe not. The course of this beef the Skull Gang was facing would determine all of their futures.

Tamia leaned against the Porsche Cayenne awaiting Teelee's release from Orleans Parish Prison. When Teelee called from the pay phone in Central Lockup, Tamia dropped everything to go get her man. She dropped Tia off in the project by Denise, while on her way to the bail bonds man. She really didn't want Tia around while she handled business like that. She felt exposing Tia to that kind of situation wasn't cool. She tried her best to conceal the negative side of Teelee's life. When the phone rang she knew what time it was. All she said to Teelee was, "I'm on my way." She thanked God it wasn't anyone calling telling her he was killed. She was well aware of what to do when situations like this happened. Teelee had laced her up with all the things she would need, in the event he would ever go to jail. She knew exactly who to go to, and exactly what to say. No matter how bad she didn't want to admit it, she had become a "Gangster's Girl." Her future still envisioned Teelee becoming that great man. She loved the fact that Teelee was a bad boy. That was one of the main things that turned her on about him, but she knew the consequences of that lifestyle. She couldn't fathom him continuing down that path. Teelee constantly dropped several hints that he wanted to marry her. If their relationship was going to work, a definite change had to be made. As Tamia looked down at her diamond encrusted Cartier watch, Teelee bought for her birthday. A crowd of people emerged through the doors of Central Lockup. In the midst of all the people, Tamia spotted the love of her life instantly. Even with the five o'clock shadow Teelee had grown, he still was amazingly handsome in Tamia's eyes. "Wzup my baaby" Teelee said walking up swooping Tamia in his arms. "Hey baby!" Tamia lit up like a Christmas tree, from the feel of Teelee's embrace. "You miss me maw?" Teelee asked, looking deep into Tamia's hypnotizing eyes. He had to admit it, he really missed Tiger the past couple of days. "Do I, boy you bet not never leave me worried like that again." Teelee was lost for words concerning Tamia's statement. He really couldn't promise that, especially with the charge he had hanging over his head. The beef that had been placed on the grill ran through his mind as well. All Teelee could do was kiss Tamia to get pass the statement. "Come on baby, let me get you home so I can bathe and feed you. I'll bring you to Ralph office tomorrow." Teelee really needed Tamia tonight. She left Tia in the project by Denise until the next morning. She had plans to show Teelee just how much he was missed.

As Tamia parked the Porsche in the garage of the condo, she noticed the dazed look on Teelee's face. She wished it was something she could say to make him feel better. She knew his heart was heavy. Teelee walked into the condo and breathed a sigh of relief. He was happy to be back home and smell the scent of a hot meal. Tamia knew he would be starving after sitting in jail all night. She cooked chicken with gravy and rice, mix vegetables, yams, and vanilla cake. "Baby I'll start the water in the tub" Tamia stated. Teelee didn't have to say a word, she knew what he needed. Teelee knew Tamia would make the perfect wife. They understood each other so well. It was nothing he wouldn't do for her and Tia. Before Thugga's untimely death, he was secretly planning how he wanted to propose to her. He had her ring custom designed by Jack Sutton Jewelers. Teelee decided to officially ask her tonight. With Thugga passing and the beef cooking, he didn't want to waste any more time. While Tamia was preparing their bath, Teelee walked in the bedroom to retrieve the ring. He opened the pink ring box and smirked. Pink was Tamia's favorite color. Here it was cold blooded, block hugging Teelee, holding a pink ring box, ready to seal the deal on his love for Tamia. He knew Tamia would lose her mind once she laid eyes on the ring. It was a seven carat, emerald cut diamond with baguettes, set in platinum. He knew how much she loved emerald cut rings. Tamia called out to Teelee from the bathroom. "Baby come on, your bath is ready." Teelee closed the box and prepared to change Tamia's life forever. "Come on take that dirty shirt off, you smell like the jail house." Teelee stopped her as she prepared to take his shirt off. "Maw come here, sit down." Teelee took Tamia by the hand and led her to her vanity set. As she sat on the bench, Tamia suddenly became nervous. "What's wrong, what happened now?" "Ain't nothing wrong maw, calm down. I just need to talk to you for a minute." Teelee got down on one knee and began his expressions of love to Tamia. Her legs began to shake when she realized what was about to happen. With tears starting to form in her hazel eyes, Teelee took her little hand into his. "Maw I told you this more than once, but I say it cause I mean it. I never felt love like this before in my life. You bring me so much peace in this rough life I'm outchere living. It's nothing I won't do for you. You see past all the rough spots in me. Tiger marry me, and be my wife." Tamia was a ball of tears. She couldn't stop her hands and legs from shaking. When Teelee opened the box, Tamia could have passed out. The ring was on full bling. "Awe baby, yes I will." Teelee put the ring on Tamia's finger and smiled. Tamia put her arms around his neck and kissed him. "Teelee I love you. I just can't stop crying." Teelee wiped her tears away and kissed her on the forehead. "Stop crying baby. You like the ring?" "Boy are you serious, I love it! It's beautiful, it's just what I wanted. Oh shit, I got a wedding to plan now. I gotta call my momma" Tamia commented. "Well damn baby, can you bathe your man first." "Oh I'm sorry baby" Tamia replied, with her sad puppy face. "Let me get my baby cleaned up." Tamia began to undress Teelee. "Maw throw them clothes away, I don't want that shit." While they sat in the Jacuzzi style tub and soaked, Tamia just stared at her ring. Teelee had his head rested on her breast. Suddenly his mind fell back on his brother. He wished it was something he could have done to save Thugga's life. Tamia began to stroke his hair. "Baby I can't say I understand your pain, but I'm here. We'll get through this together, okay. They soaked a little while longer until his stomach starting growling uncontrollably.

Tamia tried to find a movie they could watch to take Teelee's mind off the pain for a minute. She popped in *"Coming to America."* "Maybe some laughter would ease his mind" Tamia thought. As they ate Teelee's mood lightened up a little. Tamia lay cuddled in Teelee's arm. She felt so safe whenever she was with him. She didn't know what she would do if something ever happened to him. Tamia turned to kiss him and before you knew it, Teelee was taking his T-Shirt off of her. Tamia was naked on his lap kissing him even more intensely. She removed his boxers and tank top. She slid him into her nice and slow. As Tamia rocked back and forth on him, Teelee could feel her wetness dripping out of its warm place. The way Tamia moaned and seductively whispered in his ear turned him on.

"Oh Teeleeee, Oh Teeleee, I love you." He gripped her ass and thrust his self into her even more. Teelee picked her up and had her against the wall in midair. She looked Teelee in his eyes and let out constant moans of ecstasy. He was giving her exactly what she needed, all of him. While Tamia tightened her muscles on Teelee, he nibbled and sucked her breast like they were candy. The way her eyes kept staring into his, made Teelee lose it. Tamia joined in his explosion and climaxed to no end. When Teelee released his grip and let her down she almost collapsed. Her legs were like jelly. They didn't bother making it to the bedroom. They slept cuddled up, right there on the plush carpet.

Looking in the face of his dead brother was real challenging for Teelee. Rhodes funeral home was packed to capacity. Teelee didn't permit Tamia to attend the service. He didn't want to take any chances with her safety. Seeing that it was an extremely large crowd trying to attend the service, the funeral home manager had to limit the amount of people that entered. The fire marshal would have shut the place down due to the huge number of people trying to attend the service. The massive crowd was almost as big as when 2Pac was laid to rest. There was a variety of people present to lay the 7th Ward thug to rest; from gangsters, pimps, dime pieces, and hoes. Everyone showed up to show respect to Thugga, the number one 7th Ward stunna. Baby, Slim, and Lil Wayne did a brief drop in. They were in Miami working on their latest C.D. when they heard the news. Juvey, and B.G. was there as well to show their respect. Turk was locked up at the time so he couldn't attend. Thugga was decked out in his usual thug wear, but in a formal way. His black Marc Jacob's button up shirt and pants blended well with his marble casket. The morticians at Rhodes really did a good job with Thugga's appearance. It seemed as if he was sleeping. "So I guess this is it huh homey? This where we part ways." Teelee's emotion were so out of control that his words were caught in his throat. "Look here son. I promise on Lil Jamal; I won't stop until every nigga on that block dead. I love you my nigga. See you on the other side." In that instance Teelee removed his diamond flooded chain, and Skull Gang piece and put it around Thugga's neck. Teelee took his seat and joined the rest of the fam. New Orleans born, Atlanta raised, R&B sensation Lloyd took the podium. He definitely brought new life to the old classic, *"Gangsta Lean."* The crowd was flooded with a sea of sorrowful emotions, after the beautiful performance. Thugga's mother was handling the whole situation better than everyone expected. God really blessed her with the strength to lay her son to rest. Of course she had her moments, but for the most part she saved face for the sake of her beloved son. She knew he would have wanted her to stay strong and hold it down for him. K-Real wasn't speaking at all. All of her responses consisted of nods of her head and hand signals. Her big Dolce & Gabanna sunglasses hid the pain in her puffy eyes. She had yet to tell everybody about her and Thugga's little secret. Lil Man was the only person that knew K-Real was pregnant with Thugga's baby. It slipped out one day while the three was headed to Harrah's Casino. Lil Man thought it was so hilarious. It killed him not to tell anyone. Thugga made him promise that he wouldn't let their little secret leak until the right time. In her mind, even though it wasn't good to do this to your child. She vowed that the streets of New Orleans hadn't seen the last of Thugga. She would shape and mold lil Ronnie to be as ruthless as his father; if not worse. Lil Man stayed on point keeping everything safe, just in case Roylee and his gang tried to pull something while the funeral proceeded. There were goons posted up all around the funeral home. You would have to be one bad motherfucker to penetrate the steel curtain Lil Man had secured around the family. Pistol and Corey was in their positions wishing one of them niggas made a move. Grief and beef was all that circulated through their minds. The grief was the fuel they were going to use to devour the beef. It was so much tension within the confines of the funeral home. As Reverend Frank stepped up to the podium to give his eulogy, everyone looked to him for a word of comfort. Reverend Frank had known Thugga, Teelee, and Lil Man ever since they were knee high to a grass hopper. It saddened him to see Thugga in that casket, because he knew all three of them had potential to be great men. Weather people wanted to accept it or not, God was the source and this was his call. Frank stood dressed sharp in his Armani suit. His powerful voice drew everyone in ear shot, to pay close attention. "Ladies and gentleman; family and friends. We are here today to lay this beautiful young brother to rest. Before we proceed let us bow our heads. Dear Lord I ask you to rain down a sense of comfort in this place today. I ask dear Father that you accept this young soul into your heavenly kingdom. Dear Father I ask that you put the right words in my mouth to comfort and encourage the family during the loss of their precious loved one. All power lies within your hands. I know with faith in you, every obstacle and dilemma that we may face we'll get through. In Jesus name I pray, Amen. Ronnie Bennett was a delight to anyone who had the pleasure to know him. We all are gathered here today to celebrate his tragic death. Ronnie Bennett better known as Thugga touched the lives of many people. While this young man's exterior lifestyle seemed too dramatic, the wisdom of our Lord teaches us to be full of joy in the assurance that man shall reach his full potential. Each man must face trials and adversity. Thugga's life and now his passing had undoubtedly initiated new courses in the lives of relatives, friends, and foes alike." The statement Reverend Frank made was so true. This tragic event would outline a pattern of destruction through the lives of many that will be involved in this bloody war. Frank wiped his brow that formed perspiration from the powerful message he was giving. God was truly in the midst. "No we don't mourn Thugga's passing in ignorance. For we know he shall be with us through what will change as a direct result of present circumstance. It is with great and deep sincerity, we thank the Lord of life and love for his grace and tender mercy. In closing I just ask that God bless and keep our beloved brother Ronnie Bennett, Amen." God really rained down a veil of peace and comfort, because as Reverend Frank stepped down from the podium the cries subsided and was replaced with humble smiles. Thugga's soul was at rest, and would be permanently engraved in the hearts of those who were close to him. Everyone was ushered up to the casket to view Thugga for the last time. Teelee, Lil Man, Corey, Pistol as well as all the rest of the pallbearers, took their position to carry the casket to the hearse. As soon as they gripped their hands around the rails of the casket, the doors to the funeral home opened. To everyone's surprise; it was Rafee. He was dressed in an all-black Dickey jump suit, with Thugga's picture plastered all over it. The look on his face was filled with pure grief. As he made his way down the aisle, everyone beamed in on him. Even though he was the reason Thugga was dead, Teelee and all the rest of the gang was happy he came. With tears streaming down his face, Teelee and Rafee locked eyes. Teelee saw the pain in his eyes. With a nod of approval Rafee took his place and carried Thugga's body to its final resting spot. After Thugga's body was secured in its plot off of Gentilly and St. Anthony, the celebration began. The second line started from the gravesite and led all the way backatown. Teelee rented a stretch Hummer and got a picture of Thugga, as well as pictures of all of them plastered all over the limo. The brass band led the way, with Thugga's mother and the rest of the Skull Gang following behind in the limo. Lil Man had thirty armed goons surrounding the limo, so the massive crowd that followed the second line couldn't get too close. Everything went smooth with no gun play involved. They all knew once the bullets went to piercing the air, it would be a long time before they stopped.

# CHAPTER 20

# BUCK BACK

"Pass the gar nigga" Rell demanded, as he turned his alpine touch screen radio up. Rell was one of Roylee's main men. Before the beef kicked off, Rell handled all the money drop offs. Rell had been a part of Roylee's entourage ever since Roylee was grinding dime for dime. He was a very loyal soulja. The only thing Roylee disagreed with, was Rell's want to be so flashy. Roylee always made a point to stress the importance of staying low key. Rell always blew it off as if Roylee was just hating, and didn't want to see him shine. Right after the hit on Thugga, Roylee arranged a meeting with all of his top people. He instructed that everyone be on top of their game, because they were at the start of a very dangerous war. Rell being the hard headed, never want to listen to nobody type; he disregarded what Roylee said. He brushed it off like this war was something to play with. Cruising down St. Bernard Ave., Rell was headed to bring his cousin Teedy to get slugged up. Mr. Smiles on First and Claiborne Ave., was the place to go. It was a sunny afternoon. Rell decided to put the top down on his drop top SS Camaro. His ground shaking kicker fifteens, raddled everything they passed. He definitely was on beam. "Say Rell, when we leave the dentist I want you to shoot me to the mall. I gotta go cop them new *"Jays"* that just came out." Teedy was young and very naïve to the streets. He thought his cousin Rell was the toughest nigga walking the face of the earth. He looked up to Rell, and wanted to be just like him. Teedy's mother knew her nephew was no good. She always stressed to Teedy not to ride around with Rell, but it was only so much she could do. They were first cousins and grew up together like brothers. The old saying, "A hard head, makes a soft ass" was so true. In Teedy's situation it won't make his ass soft. It would get his head bust. As Rell and Teedy pulled up to the red light on St. Bernard and Roman St., a homeless looking dude with dreadlocks approached the Camaro. He was attempting to clean Rell's windshield. Rell never thought to look the windshield washer in the face. He was so caught up into showing off for some hood rats walking along the side walk. Rell and Teedy didn't notice the bum draw to twin desert eagles. "Girl he got a gun" one of the hood rats yelled while running. All Rell and Teedy saw was the flash of fire jumping from the desert eagles. Rafee dumped every last bullet out of the massive guns. "BOOM, BOOM, BOOM." The bullets were coming so fast and close that they exited Rell's body and entered Teedy's. The impact from the high caliber desert eagles tore Rell's face completely off. The afternoon air was filled with the smell of blood and flesh. As Rafee fled the scene, he dumped his dreadlock wig a block away. By the time the police made it to the scene, all witnesses could tell them was a bum with dreadlocks fled the scene. That was the downside of having dreads in the N.O. You were always considered a suspect to a crime.

Lil Man sat behind his desk listening to beats for *"Gangsta Gumbo Vol. 2."* The first mix tape was doing really well. It was really buzzing over the net, getting a good deal of positive feedback. Lil Man's business associates were currently working on a deal for him to go on tour with Weezy. For now, it was just lingering in the air. Lil Man wasn't sure if he was going to accept, with the way the beef was cooking. As he twirled his four carat pinky ring around his finger, he let the melody of a potential track take control. He had a natural gift with music. As the melody circulated through his mind, he envisioned what he would lay to the hot track. He immediately came up with the concept and vibe of lyrics he would bless the track with. His studio was his own personal design; which really set the tone when he was in beast mode. Lil Man spent top dollar on every piece of sound equipment he had in the studio. The walls were covered with hologram skull heads, representing his Skull Gang family. Money green and black was the colors that covered the walls as well as the furniture. Plush leather sofas and chairs were in place for the all night flights in the booth. When you stepped in the booth it was like you stepped in a whole new world, "Gangsta Lil Man's World." Lil Man had everything he needed. He could design, lay, and even manufacturer his own CD's within the confines of his studio. He even had a T-shirt printing shop setup in the back. In New Orleans an establishment like that brought in a lot of revenue. For the simple fact, there was always someone buried every week. The most popular ritual in the N.O. was to get pictures of the deceased printed on a shirt. Lil Man saw the opportunity and took it. Seeing he didn't have the time to run it, he let his girl and her sister deal with the venture. Suddenly there was a buzz at the front door, breaking Lil Man's creative flow. He muted the track on his computer, and proceeded to see who it was. As he looked at the surveillance camera he hit the button to the front door letting Teelee in. "What it do son" Lil Man said greeting his brother from another. They shared a one arm hug and sat down. "What's good my nigga? You in here grinding huh" Teelee asked while leaning back in one of the leather office chairs that sat in front of Lil Man's desk. "Yeah you know me son, gotta make sumthin shake for the fam ya know." "I feel you round" Teelee replied. "I been waitin on you nigga. Where you been?" Lil Man asked, pulling a Keep Moving cigar stuffed with some purp out of his desk drawer. "You know how Tamia get man. She never want me to leave her side. I swear I got that girl spoiled." "Nigga get the fuck! Yo ass spoiled too. I swear y'all was made for each other." They shared a laugh, but as quick as it came it was gone. Staring at the full size picture of all of them that hung on the wall behind Lil Man's desk, made Teelee's pain resurface. No matter what anybody said, or the amount of time that passed, it still didn't ease the pain of their beloved brother. "I miss my nigga" Teelee said damn near tearing up. "Man me to homey. I never thought we would lose one in the dangerous three, even wit all the wild shit we pulled off. I always thought we would make it through and enjoy the fruits of our labor." Lil Man ran his hand through his long dreadlocks, as he leaned back contemplating on the old days when they didn't have a pot to piss in or a window to throw it out. "Fuck all this grief shit. Let's get ready to eat this beef we got cookin" Teelee said standing to his feet. He began to pace the floor. "What you got in mind round?" "I got some info on where the nigga Roylee ducked off at. Him and his bitch stayin out there in Baton Rouge. I don't know where he lay his head at, but I know a spot the nigga gon be heading too." "Oh yeah, I almost forgot" Lil Man said pulling up the rebroadcast of Channel 4 news on his computer. "Rafee called me last night and said he checkmated two of Roylee's people on St. Bernard yesterday." "That shit was all over the news. Tamia was telling me about it, but I didn't catch it." Lil Man clicked play as the rebroadcast began.

> *Good evening, I'm Keith Black reporting live on the scene. It has been a bloody afternoon out here in the Seventh Ward of New Orleans. Minutes ago two men were brutally gunned down at the red light of St. Bernard and Roman St. Witnesses say the new modeled Camaro, was ambushed by a man with dreadlocks posed as a window cleaner. The two men were reported dead on the scene. Their identity has not yet been released. The suspect fled the scene on foot. He's being described as a black male, stocky in build, with extremely long dreadlocks. If you have any information in this case, please call Crime Stoppers at 1-877-555-000. Back to you Mary Ann…*

Lil Man clicked the rebroadcast off. "That's what the fuck I'm talkin bout" Teelee exclaimed as he rubbed his hands together. "Where son at anyway? He ain't got at me since last week." "Rafee on a manhunt Teelee. He feel he got to start his own graveyard in honor of Thugga. He still down wit the team, its just sumthin he dealin wit within his self. He ain't gon be fully back until Roylee and that bitch nigga Nardy in the dirt." "It's all good. Son can do him, but he betta catch Roylee before we catch him." "So what you got planned?" Lil Man asked sparking the blunt. "Peep this." Teelee ran his scheme down to the tee as they smoked numerous of blunts. They reminisced over their beloved brother and all the crazy shit they had pulled off. The plan Teelee had cooking was damn near full proof. Roylee would have to have an angel on his side to duck the wrath of Teelee and Gangsta Lil Man.

"Counselor call your next case." "Yes your honor. Case number 8011156, Jamal Tsion Lee vs. The State of Louisiana. Your honor we're set for arraignment." "Who is the attorney of the defendant?" "Your honor Wayne Williams is the defendants counsel." It was the first time Teelee had to appear in court for the gun charge. The case stayed in the districts attorney's office for almost ninety days. Well over the time limit mandated for the review of a pending case. The court section Teelee had been assigned to wasn't bad. The honorable Judge John Haney was stern yet understandable. Wayne Williams had won many cases in his section, not just jury trials either. A few times he came out on top with trials by judge. Wayne Williams assured Teelee that everything would pan out fine. Teelee arrived in court looking as if he was a respectable law abiding citizen. Teelee was decked out in his cream colored Hugo Boss blazer and slacks, with a white polyester V neck shirt. He finalized the outfit with his cream colored Cole Haans, with the white sole. Tamia definitely played her part. She looked like a loving wife in her cream Chanel pants suit, with some cream Prada heels. Tamia wasn't fronting, the look she had was genuine. It was Teelee who was perpetrating. They looked great and the impression they were trying to make was accomplished. Wayne Williams made specific instructions that they dressed really nice. He explained how the Judge was big on family. The more they swayed him into believing that Teelee was a family man caught in a bad situation, the better the chances of Teelee walking away without any jail time. The courtroom was filled with family members awaiting the outcome of their loved ones' case. As Judge Haney flipped through a file, Wayne Williams came through the doors of the courtroom. "Wayne Williams you're late as usual" Judge Haney said, while looking underneath his wired framed glasses. Judge Haney very well knew the symptoms of a coke head. He dealt with them for years in his probation program. He knew Wayne Williams had a cocaine addiction. Many times he wanted to call him on it, but he had no evidence to prove it. He told his self if Wayne Williams didn't clean his self-up, he would surprise him with a urine analysis test. Teelee noticed the sloppiness in his lawyer as well. He made a mental note to check him on it immediately. Right now he had to let him work his magic. The case was only in the beginning stages, but with Wayne

Williams's mouth piece; it was possible that everything could be over in arraignment. "Your honor, I'm here for Jamal Tsion Lee" Wayne Williams said, unloading his briefcase on the defense table. "I'm well aware of that Williams. Counselor are you ready to accept the defendant's plea?" "Yes your honor, but before we proceed I need to approach the bench." Karen Steel was a very successful district attorney. She sent many harden criminals away for the rest of their natural lives. She was very aware of who Teelee was, therefore when she received the case she shouted for joy. She just knew she would be the one to take down the infamous Teelee. David Silva couldn't handle the weight when it was on his shoulders. To her disappointment a force more powerful had stepped in. All she could do was hope they left the case alone and let the state deal with it. Wayne Williams approached the bench as well. As they conversed in hush tones, Tamia squeezed Teelee's hand assuring him that everything was going to be okay. Tamia's support kept Teelee's confidence intact. Allowing him to believe everything was going to work itself out. Without Tamia by his side, he doubted that he would be sane at the moment. Teelee was on edge from losing his beloved brother, to catching this bogus ass charge. He knew without Tamia's loving comfort it was no way he wouldn't be half crazy at this point. As Teelee was checking the time on his Frank Muller, Wayne Williams was making his way towards them. He signaled for Teelee and Tamia to follow him in the hallway. "Look this the deal. The prosecutor said the Feds are looking into the case." "I already knew it. So what's up?" Teelee asked, preparing for the worst. Tamia had already begun to tear up. It didn't matter if Teelee had to spend a week in jail, Tamia was going to take it real hard. He was her rock and she couldn't fathom him being away from her side for any amount of time. "Well they are just investigating the case for now. Nothings official yet, so we have time to play with." "So I'm done for the day?" Teelee asked pulling Tamia beside him. Yeah you just gotta get your reset and were done." As Wayne Williams was about to walk back into the courtroom, Teelee grabbed him by his arm. Teelee whispered in his ear, "You lookin real sloppy, you betta fix that shit. If your sloppiness is the cause of me going to the Feds, you know what time it is." The look Teelee gave Wayne Williams said more than enough. He knew he had to be sober while working on Teelee's case, because his habit could very well cost him his life. Wayne Williams headed back into the courtroom while Teelee and Tamia stood in the hallway. "Baby tell me you're not about to leave me" Tamia said with teary eyes. "Look Tiger I can't promise you that, but what I can promise you is I'mma try my hardest not to. If I do I'mma need you to hold it down for me and be strong okay." "That ain't even a question. You know I'm down by law." "Well look we gotta get married soon. We can do at the court house for now." "What about the wedding though?" Tamia asked. "Of course we still having the wedding baby, I gotta give you that. I just gotta put my last name on you before somebody try and snatch you up." Teelee tried to make Tamia smile to ease her hurt. "Boy stop being stupid. You know I'm yours." "Well come here and show me you mine." Teelee pulled Tamia into his arms, as he gently planted a kiss on her forehead. They headed back into the courtroom to get Teelee's reset paper. There was a fifty, fifty chance that Teelee could go to the Feds or walk away free. The future would undoubtedly unfold itself. Whatever it was he would have to deal with it when it came. The beef he had going was too serious for him not to stay focus.

"Baby come on we gon be late" Tamia shouted while heading to the door. This time she was ready and Teelee wasn't. Teelee and Lil Man went out last night to celebrate Teelee getting married. He was really feeling the effects from last night. He usually didn't get a headache when he got drunk, but with all the Hennessy and Heinekens he drank at Ray's, it was understandable why he felt that way. After they left the courthouse to arrange to be married the other day, Tamia and Teelee got all the proper paperwork they were going to need. Luckily for them, there was a slot available for the following day at the civil courthouse. Teelee looked in the mirror still trying to shake the monstrous hangover he had. Outwardly he didn't look bad, but internally he felt like shit. He grabbed two Aleve's out of the medicine cabinet, and washed them down swiftly. As he sprayed on his Issy Miyake cologne, the thought of Tamia being his permanently made his hangover subside a bit. Teelee knew he had been blessed with a beautiful woman. Sometimes it was hard to express it the way he really wanted to. His mind was still caught up in the streets. The only love he knew how to share was that "ghetto love." That's all he was exposed to his whole life. Tamia gave him something he never felt before. "Baby what's taking you so long?

You okay?" Tamia asked walking into the bathroom. "I'm ready maw" Teelee replied while turning the light off. "Tia lets go" Tamia said, picking up her purse from the coffee table. Tia came running from her room looking cute as a button. She was so adorable, looking like a smaller version of Tamia. The only thing that Tia didn't inherit was Tamia beautiful hazel eyes. "Hold me poppa" Tia whined as she held her arms out for Teelee to pick her up. "Come on my lil meow cat." That was a cute little nick name Teelee had adorned her with. Teelee swept Tia up in his arms, and they were out the door. They decided to ride in Tamia's brand new white Range Rover. Teelee had just surprised her with it last night when he came from partying with Lil Man. She was so excited when she opened the door and saw Teelee pull up in the beautiful truck. It was definitely something to talk about. Teelee had it custom made for Tamia. It had twenty-four inch Lexanis on it and "Tiger Eyez" stitched in the head rest. Everything in the car was customized just for her. He made sure to have a camera in the license plate, to make sure no one ever followed her home. "Put our John Legend CD in" Tamia stated. "What song you wanna hear maw?" "You know what song. *"So High"* the one we chose for the wedding." As John Legend crooned his soulful lyrics, Teelee stole glances at his beautiful wife to be. He knew he was making the best decision of his life.

"I'mma go and park the truck. You and Tia go head up. Momma and everybody should already be up there." Teelee let Tamia and Tia out in front of the courthouse, then headed to park in the lot across the street. When Teelee made it to the courthouse, everyone was there. "Damn bae, that took you a minute. You couldn't find a spot?" Tamia asked while making last minute adjustments on her makeup. "I forgot the camera at home, so I ran to Walgreens to get one." "You ready son?" Mr. Daniel asked with a big smile across his face. He was really proud of Teelee. It showed him that Teelee was taking on responsibilities, and committing his self to a covenant with God. Mr. Daniel loved Tamia like a daughter, and couldn't think of anyone better to marry his son. "Yeah Pops, ready as I'mma ever be" Teelee replied. "Mama baby getting married. I'm so proud of you son. I can't wait for the real wedding." Celeste was ecstatic. "Look at my son-in-law looking all good. Come give your mother-in-law a hug" Cheryl said with her arms wide open. "Wzup Ma, you ready for me to be your son-in-law?" "I couldn't think of anybody better baby." "Come on y'all the Judge said she's ready" Tamia said. Judge Sandra Sears was the person performing the ceremony. Let me guess, this is the bride and groom. You two look lovely." Even though it wasn't there actual wedding, Teelee and Tamia was flawless. Teelee was rocking one of his favorite brands, Ralph Lauren of course. Cream Ralph Lauren pants, cream button down Polo shirt, with a cream and khaki colored Ralph Lauren vest and finalized the fit with some khaki and cream loafers. Tamia was killing the scene with her cream and beige Chanel blazer with the skirt to match. She complimented the set with her Jimmy Choo heels. The only thing a hater could say about the couple was they stayed on their style game. "Would you all please step over here" Judge Sears requested. "Are y'all ready?" They both replied yes, and the ceremony began. "We are gathered here today in the sight of God and man to join together in marriage Jamal and Tamia. What we do today is done in conformity to the laws of the State of Louisiana and in the tradition of men and women. Jamal and Tamia you stand before me requesting that I marry you. Do you both do this of your own free will?" They both responded with a simple, yes. "There will be trials and tribulations, joy and sorrow, but when you experience them with one another how much better they'll seem. Whenever you two look back on this moment, you'll see it as one of the happiest of your lives together." Celeste, Shorty, and Tamia were beginning to tear up. As Jamal and Tamia exchanged vows and promises to each other, they felt complete love in the room. Judge Sears finished up the ceremony. "Now by the power vested in me, and the State of Louisiana. I now pronounce you husband and wife. You may seal your promise with a kiss. From the moment they put their lips together, they both knew in their hearts they had a life full of drama, pain, and joy. Hopefully the joy would surpass the pain and they could have a marriage enter locking their souls eternally. Teelee picked Tia up and kissed her on the cheek. He placed a tiny diamond encrusted key around Tia's neck. She held the key to his heart just as much as Tamia did. They all shared hugs and kisses and headed off to Pampy's to celebrate with the bride and groom. Teelee and Tamia only wanted a small gathering of immediate family and friends. Teelee wanted to take Tamia on a getaway after they were married but his pending case prevented him from doing so. He promised Tamia when the big celebration came, they would go all out sparing no expense. As the celebration came to a close, Shorty took Tia along with her to let the newlyweds spend time alone. "Come on Mrs. Lee, I got plans for you tonight" Teelee said as he took Tamia by the hand. Teelee spared no expense on the getaway spot in Mandeville, La. that Lanzo recommended for the newlyweds. Tamia smiled at the naughty look in her husband's eyes. The realization of officially being Mrs. Teelee had her on a natural high.

"Real where you at?" Teelee asked as he cruised down I-10. "I'm at home. Why?" "I'mma be over there in five minutes. Don't go nowhere." Teelee had made up his mind to ship K-Real off for the safety of Thugga's seed. Upon finding out about it he was shocked and saddened at the same time. Teelee felt bad that his homey wouldn't get the chance to raise his seed. He knew he had to be ten steps ahead of the game, because the beef was getting thicker by the day. He had been contemplating the decision for a minute now. He already had it in his mind that the task of convincing K-Real to leave wasn't going to be easy. Real was thirsty for blood just like the rest of them. Her motivation to put Roylee to rest was just as high as everyone else. The chemistry between K-Real and Thugga was a match made in heaven. The two shared most of the same views, motivations, and desires; they couldn't think of nobody better to chill with. Real was definitely Thugga's ride or die chick. It was never a moment that Thugga had to lace Real up on what to do. She always stayed on top of her game. The funny thing about their connection was the fact that they never planned it. It just happened. It all started back when Thugga was locked up on his murder charge.

K-Real was always there showing her support. She handled all of his street affairs; making sure all of his clientele was taken care of. Through all of that she still took care of her own customers, and responsibilities within the organization. One Saturday during visitation it was like cupid had hit both of them with an arsenal of arrows. The attraction between the two became stronger as the weeks progressed. K-Real made sure Thugga had a visit every week. If Teelee, Lil Man, or Tyler couldn't make it, Real would show up making her even more attractive. The traits Real had was exactly what Thugga was looking for in a woman. Most women couldn't satisfy the 7th Ward thug's needs. K-Real's gangster edge turned Thugga on and it was nothing he could have done to turn it off. Real found what she had been looking for; a thug to the fullest. Real was taking Thugga's death real hard. It seemed like every one she had genuine love for was taken away from her. Starting when she was young with her mother and father, and now this. She didn't even get the chance to enjoy what they had. It was like a blink of an eye of happiness for her. Her goal was to make a life full of pain for Roylee and everyone that was close to him. Teelee pulled up in front of Real's condo in Kenner. He was thinking of angles to use to persuade K-Real into leaving for the safety of the baby. True enough he was the only one that could control the female pit-bull, but in this situation he wasn't too sure. "Say Real I'm outside. Come open the door. Upon entering Real's condo, Teelee knew she was taking Thugga's death extremely hard. The squeaky clean condo Teelee he was used to seeing was in a disarray. There were clothes thrown all over the place. The thick carpet that covered the floors looked like it hadn't been vacuumed in weeks. Dishes over flowed the sink and Real looked a mess. Her hair was all over her head. Her eyes were puffy with bags underneath them; making Teelee aware that she wasn't getting any sleep. Teelee took a seat on the sofa next to Real not saying a word. All he could do was pull her into his arms. As soon as her head hit his shoulders the tears started flowing like the Mississippi River. This was the first time Teelee had ever witnessed the venomous soulja girl cry. "Why Teelee? Why is he dead?" As K-Real asked that question Teelee was asking his self the same thing. Why his brother was buried six feet deep. "We both know why Real baaby. It's just too hard to accept it. Look at me Real." Teelee lifted K-Real's head from his shoulders. With a long deep stare Teelee gave it to Real raw and real as it gets. "Look Real, Thugga dead. Ain't nuthin me, you, Lil Man, or anybody else could do about it. Teelee understood under K-Real's grimy exterior that it was still an emotional feminine side she tried so hard to cover up. In this situation he couldn't cater to her emotions. Her life, his life, and every life involved in the Skull Gang depended on how strategic they handled this beef. It was no time to be soft. It was time to be ruthless and smart. That meant disregarding all feelings. "Real I'mma have to send you away." At that moment all the tears stopped, and the rage emerged. "What the fuck you mean leave?" K-Real stood to her feet. "Look Real I know you tryna get it on wit these niggas, but what you fail to realize is you got my nigga seed in your stomach. You think I'm bout to jeopardize you and the baby.

In K-Real's heart she knew Teelee was right, but she refused to give in that easy. "I ain't going nowhere" Real said defiantly. "I'm not askin you Real, I'm tellin you. You gettin the fuck out of the N.O." Now Teelee was standing. With a hard stern glare, he was able to quickly demobilize K-Real's front she was putting on. "Well how long you tryna send me away for?" Real asked while taking a seat in defeat. "Just until you have the lil one. After you have the baby I'mma see bout you comin back. For now, it's too dangerous for you to be down here." "Well where am I going?" "I got you a lil spot up in Atlanta. Tiger gon send you money every month. You ain't gotta worry bout shit." After many minutes passed, K-Real finally agreed. As much as she didn't want to admit that Teelee was right; she couldn't dispute his decision. The baby was her only way to keep Thugga's legacy alive.

"Say round guess who I just saw ridin up Music and Villere St.?" Gutta had the whole 8th Ward on watch for Roylee and Nardy. One of his lil souljas had just spotted Nardy riding up the block. Being that the young gunner felt he was untouchable he felt no need to lay low, and be inconspicuous. He believed if it was his time to go, it was nothing he could do to stop it. Gutta made a vow to his self that he would ride for the cause. Even though he and Thugga didn't know each other very long, he still felt obligated to enter the deadly war. Thugga helped him elevate his hustle when no one would give him a chance. Everything Gutta got he earned. No handouts involved. Even with the business he and Thugga had going. He made sure his money was right every time he clocked in. Thugga recognized the loyalty in Gutta and what started out as business became a genuine friendship. Gutta felt in his heart that he didn't have to know Thugga for a long period of time. Just the fact of him being a real solid nigga made him pick up his tool and enter a never ending beef. "Who nigga? I ain't got time for the guessing game" Gutta commented. "Nardy, he comin yo way right now. He in a two door black on black Monte Carlo." Hearing Nardy's name and the fact that he was in his territory made Gutta temperature rise. "Aight, I'm out." Gutta grabbed his Mac 11, and headed out the back door. From where his house sat he would have a good shot at Nardy. Gutta spotted the black Monte Carlo two blocks down. He positioned his self behind an old broke down Ford Mustang. From the position Gutta was in, it was no way Nardy would escape the rain of bullets about to pour down. As the Monte Carlo inched closer, Gutta wrapped an army green soulja rag around his hand and cocked the Mac 11. Click, clack. "This here for my nigga." A woman coming out of her house noticed Gutta across the street with the Mac in his grip. She quickly pushed her daughter back in the house and closed her door. Whatever was about to happen she immediately disregarded it, and made sure her and her daughter was away from all windows and walls. Most people in New Orleans that cherished their lives and the lives of their loved ones; had the same attitude towards situations like that. If it wasn't your business, the best thing to do was to act like you didn't see shit. The chance of somebody kicking down your door and killing you and your whole family was very high. As the Monte Carlo approached the stop sign in front of the

Mustang, Gutta made his way to the front of the car. "Yeah I'm on my way now. I'm in the 8th Ward." Nardy was on his way to take his sister to her doctor's appointment. He didn't want to do it, for the simple fact he had too much beef going on. He was committed to the new found beef with Roylee and the Skull Gang and all the other unfinished shit he had brewing on the streets. It wasn't like he was sitting on the beef. He just hadn't got the chance to eliminate the situations. Now the war with the Skull Gang was another story. He knew he would have to buck with these niggas for quite some time. The only reason he agreed to take his sister was because she had no other way to get there, and he wasn't about to let her catch the bus. "Yeah, I'mma be there in a minute. You betta be ready too." Nardy hung up the phone with his sister and turned his Hot Boyz, "Let Em Burn" CD back up. Approaching an old broke down Mustang, Nardy noticed someone stooping down in front of it. Before he could back up or do anything, Gutta jumped in the middle of the street riddling the car with bullets. Nardy quickly threw the Monte in reverse, trying to flee deaths embrace. Gutta continued spraying the Mac 11, as he walked the Monte down. Nardy ducked under the steering wheel, navigating it all at the same time. To Nardy's advantage, the clip in the Mac ran out. Nardy had a chance to escape the hands of death. "Fuck!" Gutta yelled out as the Monte scurried around the corner. "You got away from me bitch, but you won't get away from me next time" Gutta said as sweat poured down his face. Adrenaline pumped through his veins like a shot of heroin at its purest. Gutta had officially committed his self to the beef. It was no turning back now. He was all in until the end. Moments later Nardy pulled up to his sister's house. His near death experience was no shock to him. The only thing that threw him off was not recognizing who it was shooting at him. The face was familiar, but he couldn't put his hand on who it was exactly. The front of the Monte Carlo looked like Swiss cheese. Whenever Nardy figured out who it was, he promised to send his momma his head with a dozen of roses. Before Nardy got the chance to get out the car his sister was making her way out of the door. The thought of his baby sister being in the car while that incident took place made him furious. From this day forward he wouldn't allow none of his loved ones to be with him throughout the course of this beef. "Boy what happened to you?" Nardy sister was only sixteen years old and due to have her baby in a matter of weeks. Gina was a beautiful young girl. She had a light brown skin complexion, with some long wavy black hair. She was thick as Betty Crocker cake mix. Nardy wanted to kill the baby's daddy upon finding out his baby sister was pregnant. The only reason dude was still breathing was for the sake of his unborn nephew. Gina was Nardy's heart. All while growing up Nardy took care of Gina like she was his very own daughter. This incident made him realize he had more people to think about then his self. If anything happened to him, Gina would have to fend for herself. If anything happened to her, hell had no fury on the drama that young Nardy would bring. "I'm aight Ne, go back inside. I'mma be ready in a minute." Gina knew something was wrong, but she never went against what Nardy said. She complied and went back into the house. Nardy pulled his Monte in the yard. He was planning on taking it right to the shop, but he had to talk to Roylee about the shit that just popped off. He didn't know if it was Roylee's beef or some untaken care of shit he had hanging over his head. It's fucked up when you beefing with that many people that you don't know where it's coming from. Entering the house Nardy walked up on Gina sitting on the sofa with her head down. "What's wrong Ne Ne?" Gina raised her head from her hands, eyes filled with tears. What happened?" "Ain't nuthin baby girl. I just had a lil fender bender, that's all." Gina gave Nardy a look that said "Stop lying to me" but she opted not to say it. Gina had a very humble spirit. Before she sparked an argument with her brother, she gave him the benefit to come out and say what really happened. "Why you looked at me like I'm lying or sumthin?" "Because you are" Gina replied humbly. "Look here lil sis, I'mma call you a cab so you can go to your doctor's appointment. Right now I can't have you ridin wit me. If sumthin happens to you while you wit me, I don't think I could live on wit that on my brain." "Nardy what's going on?" "You know me Ne Ne. I'm a street nigga, this street business." "Just promise me you gon be alright." Gina took Nardy's hand and held on to it for dear life. By her grip Nardy knew she was scared something might happen to him. "Don't trip Ne Ne. I ain't going nowhere, I promise. Ya big brother here for you." Nardy hugged his lil sister then got up to call Roylee. His whole not giving a fuck attitude had just changed. Young Nardy was now on some think first type shit. Not thinking about the most important people in his life could cause him to lose someone he cared for. That would never happen as long as he had breath in his body.

"Girl I'm so scared right now" Tamia said, while taking a sip of her lemonade. Tamia and her best friend Noki sat having lunch at Copeland's, one of Tamia's favorite places to eat. She needed the listening ear of her best friend right now. Tamia had been a nervous wreck ever since Teelee's court date. Just thc thought of the Feds being involved with Teelee's case gave her butterflies in her stomach. Even though Teelee stressed everything would be okay she still couldn't relax. Tamia was extremely emotional. It could have been something very small, she would worry her little head off about it. "Girl he gon be okay, you gotta keep your faith." Tamia and Noki had been friends for a very long time. They were thick as thieves. If they were out together, you wouldn't catch one without the other. Back in high school is where their friendship began. One day Noki walked up on some girls trying to start something with Tamia. Being that Tamia was very beautiful and rather short, the girls at school hated on her. Tamia drew a lot of attention from the guys at school. With knowing that Tamia was still a respectable young lady; refusing most of the guys that approached her. The girls at school peeped her fan base and hated her, not giving young Tamia a chance. Don't get it twisted, Tamia stood her ground. Her height was the only disadvantage to her. True in all she was small, but she was rather vicious. This time she was outnumbered. It was two against one. "This bitch think she all that" one of the girls snarled as they closed in on young Tamia. She was retrieving something from her locker when the two ran up on her. The security at Tamia's high school was worthless. "Bitch who the fuck you calling a bitch" Tamia shot back. She pressed her back against her locker preparing for the inevitable. She wasn't about to back down from these hood rats. Just as they were about to jump on Tamia, Noki interceded. "Say hold the fuck up, what the fuck y'all think y'all bout to do!" Just by her looks you would never think she was ruthless as she was. With a butter pecan skin complexion, almond shaped eyes, and an hour glass figure you would have thought she was harmless. A lot of people was fooled by Noki's looks also; which made her smash harder. When the group saw her step up, they immediately started to back up. "Say Noki, this ain't got nuthin to do wit you" the ring leader said. They knew at any given moment Noki would start swinging her lethal blade and she never missed a beat. "This shit do have a lot to do wit me. This my lil sister y'all trying to crowd. You hoe's ain't fightin fair!" "We ain't know this was yo people." "Well now you know, and y'all bet not fuck wit her! You hoes must be ready to go to the emergency room" Noki barked with her blade in her hand. The way the light hit the end of the blade sparked fear in all their hearts. "It's all good!" "Well get the fuck! Why y'all hoe's still standing here!" They departed Tamia and Noki immediately. "You alright lil mama?" Noki asked putting her blade back in her purse. "Yeah chic I'm cool. You ain't have to do that. I wasn't scared of them hoe's" Tamia replied. "It wasn't about you being scared, it's about them hoe's tryna jump you for nothing. I wasn't feeling that shit." "I'm Tamia chic. I always see you around but I never knew your name." "I'm Noki."

"Thank you anyway but I wasn't about to back down from them hoes." From that day forth they were click tight. No one dared to fuck with Tamia or Noki when they were together. "I don't know Noki, I hope your right. I don't want my baby leaving me. This case sound serious chic." "Of course I'm right. Now stop stressing and eat your food. We not about to let nothing ruin our day. Teelee gon be straight." Tamia and Noki spent the day together relieving Tamia's stress. They shopped till they dropped. No matter what Tamia was going through, she could always depend on Noki to lift her spirits. Teelee's court day to see what the Feds was going to do was vastly approaching, so she definitely needed the girl time and encouragement. Only God knew the outcome. She just wished it was in their favor.

# CHAPTER 21

# GONE, BUT NOT FOR GOOD

"All rise court is now in session" the deputy announced. The honorable Judge Haney is presiding. There were very few people present in the courtroom. Today was the day Teelee was going to find out the Feds decision on his case. The creeks of the doors to the courtroom as well as the solemn atmosphere made Teelee have a bad feeling about the outcome of the situation. "I don't know maw. Shit don't feel right" Teelee said to Tamia as he scanned every part of the courtroom. "Baby chill out, everything gon be alright. You just a lil nervous that's all." Tamia put her arm around Teelee's waist to give him a sense of calmness, even though she was nervous wreck herself. It wasn't the fact of Teelee being scared to go to jail. He was worried about being off the scene at the beginning of this dangerous war. He felt he was supposed to be on the front line at all times, for his deceased partner in crime. If it was the other way around he knew it wouldn't be no questions asked. Thugga would have been rocking until the sun came up. Tamia was a whole other issue. He knew she could hold everything down, it's just at times she got real emotional when it came to her husband. It was a time to follow your heart and a time to use your head. With the Skull Gang being in the position they were in, it was no time for any slip ups. They had to make sure they were game tight as well as the people close to them. Ain't no rules in beef. If one of your people got caught up, there was no mercy spared for them. They were all prey in the mean streets of New Orleans. Wayne Williams was on time and ready for whatever the state had to dish out. The only thing that could put a black cloud over the situation was if the Feds wanted the case. Teelee still had a chance to fight the case in Federal court. The only thing was his chances of winning was slim to none. The Feds conviction rate was 99.8%. It was so high due to the fact that there were informants, and the fact that the Feds never entertained a case unless they had a solid conviction. Nine times out of ten if you ended up in the hands of the Federal Government, the deck was already stacked against you. Your best bet was to cop a plea. If you made them put on their boxing gloves in trial and you were still found guilty, they were going to hit you with basketball numbers. "Counselor call your first case" the Judge said while wiping smudges off his glasses. "Yes your honor. Jamal Tsion Lee vs. the State of Louisiana. We were currently awaiting a decision from the Feds on this case. I'm requesting that I and the defendant's defense counsel approach the bench." "You may" the Judge replied. Wayne Williams and Karen Steel made their way to the judge's bench. The facial expression

Williams was given off gave Teelee the impression that shit wasn't looking good. Tamia gripped Teelee's hand tighter because she sensed the uneasiness in him. "Baby you okay?" Tamia asked looking into her husband's eyes. "Yeah baby I'm good. I just know shit ain't lookin right" Teelee replied never taking his eyes off the little meeting going on at the bench. As Wayne Williams walked away from the bench, he signaled for Teelee and Tamia to go in the hallway. When they made it in the lobby Wayne Williams took a deep breath before breaking the news to Teelee. "Well looks like the Feds want the case" Williams said in defeat. "That ain't a surprise" Teelee said pulling Tamia into his arms. Tamia had already begun to break down. Her little hands shook as her eyes released a river of tears. "No baby, you can't leave me" Tamia pleaded in between sniffles. "Its gon be alright baby. Be cool" Teelee said trying to ease Tamia's nerves. "Well how much time I got on the street?" Teelee asked with his wife tight in his embrace. "The D.A. is saying that they will notify you as well as me when they are ready to set an arraignment date." "So you ain't got no idea of what I might be lookin at?" Teelee asked. "No not as of yet, but I will immediately file for a motion of discovery" Williams said pulling out his digital date planner. "Call me tomorrow for 10:00, and I'll let you know what were up against." "Aight" Teelee replied as he began to brainstorm on his next move. Now that his time was limited. He had to make sure every area in his organization as well as his home was tight. Williams walked back into the courtroom while Teelee and Tamia remained in the lobby. Teelee looked down at his wife who was curled up in his arms. He knew he had to make sure she was safe and sound while he was away. Tiger held his heart in her hands. She was his life and it was no way he was letting anything happen to her. "Come on maw. Let's go" Teelee said leading Tamia out the doors of the courtroom. The first thing on his agenda was his wife, then Lanzo. He needed to make Lanzo aware of the news. He wanted to end his business with Lanzo on good terms. He didn't trust the Feds and he definitely didn't want to drag Lanzo down with him. He never knew when he might need Lanzo again. He wanted to make sure that door of opportunity remained open.

"Lanzo I need to see you A.S.A.P." Teelee called Lanzo immediately after pulling away from the condo. He didn't like to see his wife cry. It took him almost an hour to settle Tamia's nerves. Finally, she drifted off to sleep, giving Teelee a chance to go handle his business. He knew he had to get his shit straight immediately. His freedom clock was ticking fast, so he had to make sure he tied up all his loose ends. Putting Roylee's head on a platter was at the top of his list. It was no way Teelee was leaving the street without putting Roylee in the dirt first. "Wzup Mijo, something wrong?" Lanzo asked. "Yeah, shit done got serious" Teelee replied while lighting up a cigarette. "Look meet me at the restaurant." "I'm on my way" Teelee said. Teelee pulled Tamia's Range Rover into Bulls Eye Point seconds later. Teelee decided to take Tamia's truck just in case the Feds were already on his trail. Seeing the black GT Bentley parked in its usual spot made Teelee know Lanzo was there waiting on him. Soon as Teelee walked in the doors of the restaurant the hostess led him to the back where Lanzo was waiting. When he approached Lanzo got up to greet him as usual. "Wzup Mijo, you okay?" Lanzo asked, returning to his seat. "Everything go alright in court?" "That's what I need to holla at you bout." Teelee took a seat across from Lanzo. "The Feds decided to take the case." "Damn Mijo I'm sorry to hear that. So what kind of numbers are they talking?" Lanzo asked while lighting one of his expensive cigars. "I'm getting wit my lawyer first thing tomorrow." "So what's up?" "Say Lanzo I don't trust these bitch ass Feds. I feel we should end our business just to be safe, ya heard me." "I understand. You been straight up the whole time, so you'll always have an open door with me. I'll stay in touch through Tamia. I don't want nothing to do with them fuckin cock roaches. Go do your bid and come home. I'll be waitin for you, but this time I'mma pull you in on some other things." Lanzo took a sip of his cognac while winking at Teelee at the same time. Teelee didn't have the slightest idea of what Lanzo was talking about, but he knew whatever it was it would be lovely. "So what's the latest on that situation?" Lanzo asked as he stood to his feet. "Don't worry bout that. I got sumthin in motion for that as we speak." Teelee stood to his feet as Lanzo made his way around the table. "Handle your business Mijo. I'll be in touch." From there Lanzo walked off to the back of the restaurant where he disappeared behind a set of double doors.

As K-Real watched the many people trying to get to their designated flight terminals in New Orleans International airport, she contemplated on saying to hell with what Teelee was talking about.

She had a burning fire in her soul to eliminate everything Roylee and Nardy ever had love for. She wanted them to feel the pain and agony of losing someone very close to them. She felt killing them to quick would take away from the pain she wanted to bring into their lives. She was happy and honored to be having Thugga's baby, but she was furious that her condition was causing her to be exiled from the war they had under way. She glanced at Teelee who appeared to be so focused and unmoved by the tragic death of their partner in crime. She knew behind his Marc Jacob shades was a soul filled with pain and uncontrollable rage. She also knew that he had to handle the situation as is. If he showed his emotions and pain, the hurt and devastation would hinder him from making the right moves to checkmate everybody involved in Thugga's death. She knew this because he always stressed the fact of never letting anything hinder her from making the best decision in a life threatening situation; especially not somebody she loved. "Can you believe how much has happened from the time I put you on that clown ass nigga Tossy?" "Yeah Real we done came a long way" Teelee replied as he gazed at the planes taking off down the runway. Deep down in his heart he wished him and Tiger could be boarding one of those planes, and never looking back. That wasn't an option for him though, but it didn't hurt to ponder on the thought. "Baby boy I know right now you're hiding your true feelings. I'm not asking you to show them, but doesn't it hurt to hide the pain." Teelee turned and faced K-Real. Before speaking he removed his sunglasses, and looked Real dead in the eyes. "Of course this shit hurt, but you know what. I'mma take all my hurt and pain and put it into destroying every fucking thing breathing on that block. Women, kids, grandmothers; it don't even matter no more!" The fire Real saw in Teelee's eyes showed the same pain she was feeling. At that moment she understood the reason Teelee was sending her off. He didn't want to risk losing another one of his loved ones. "What did the lawyer say this morning?" Real asked. "He said it should take about a week for the D.A. to get all the evidence and statements they have against me." "So what kinda time he said you'll be facing if things don't go right?" "Not much, but I can't think about that shit right now. I gotta make sure we smash that bitch ass nigga first." Just then the stewardess for Southwest began allowing people to board the plane. "Here." Teelee gave K-Real a thick envelope. "What's this baby boy?" K-Real asked while looking into the envelope. It contained 25,000. "That should be enough to get you situated when you get down there." "You already gave me 10,000 last week." "Just take the money Real. I gotta make sure y'all all the way good. Me and wifey gon come down there sometime soon. Just go lay back and bring my nephew in the world safe." Teelee rubbed K-Real's baby bump protruding through her shirt. She was only five months pregnant, but lil Thugga was starting to make his presence known already. "You be careful baby boy, and you and Tiger betta bring y'all ass down there A.S.A.P. to check on us." I got you Real baby don't trip, and I'mma cut one of them bitch ass niggas fingers off for you." "Please do! I could get it bronzed and put it on my key ring." They both shared an evil grin showing how much they thought alike.

"Gimme a hug" Real demanded with her arms open. Real hugged Teelee like she wasn't going to ever see him again. In actuality she wasn't promised too. The war could go either way. One thing she knew without a doubt, Teelee and the gang was gon rock hard and destroy any and everything that got in their way. "Hit me up when the plane land in the A" Teelee said walking K-Real to the gate of the terminal. "Aight baby boy tell Lil Man and them boyz I love em, ya heard me." "I got you." As K-Real gave her ticket to the stewardess and went to board the plane Teelee waved her off; put his glasses back on and headed to his car. Now that Real was off to safety, it was time to turn the heat up on Roylee and his crew. He drove away from the airport bumping Mac the Camouflage Assassin's *"Murda, Murda, Kill, Kill"* with much "Murda" on his mind.

Pistol and Corey sat in their trap spot in Bogalusa listening to Juvenile's *"400 Degrees." -You see me- I eat, sleep, shit, and talk rap-You see that Mercedes on T.V.- I bought that- I had some felony charges- I fought that- Been sent to no return but still was brought back-*

They sat trying to figure out how and the hell they were going to find a "connect" in such short notice. Teelee had informed everybody that he cut ties with Lanzo because of his current situation. He wanted to pass the torch to one of them, but he remembered him and Lanzo' s first meeting together. "Teelee I meet with you and you only." Respecting the bosses wishes Teelee kept the thought to himself, and discontinued their business relationship. It seemed like the gang had been dismantled in a matter of months. First Thugga gets killed, then Teelee catches the bogus ass Feds case, K-Real gets shipped off and now Rafee was still M.I.A. On the outside looking in one would have thought the Skull Gang would soon be a thang of the past. One thing about the group of young killers, their hearts were big as the New Orleans Superdome. Giving up or quitting wasn't even words in either one of their vocabularies. They all came out the mud of the slums of the N.O. The adversity and struggle was nothing to them. In their minds change helped them sharpen their ability to adapt in harsh and desperate situations. "So what you think son?" Corey asked while taking a hard pull off the Kush filled cigar. "I talked to one of my people last night" Pistol replied. "He got some people down in H-Town that got coke by the boat load. He suppose to hit me back tonight if the shit official, ya heard me. Turn that shit down" Pistol suddenly said. He jumped up from the sofa quickly. "Wzup?" Corey asked following his brother's lead. Corey knew by Pistol's sudden change in demeanor that something wasn't right. "Boom, Boom, Boom." The hard blows assaulting the front door was definitely not somebody coming to visit. Corey and Pistol both knew who stood behind the door and it wasn't the sweep stakes man coming to bring a million dollars. Pistol looked out of the peep hole and witnessed the whole apartment complex being surrounded with Federal agents. "What the fuck" Pistol said in shock of what he was witnessing. "Wzup nigga" Corey asked while looking out the peep hole. When he got a glimpse of what stood on the other side of the door, he had the same reaction as Pistol. "Open the door, D.E.A." the officer yelled with an arrest warrant up to the peephole.

"Come on son we gotta get the fuck outta here" Corey said. The spot didn't contain any drugs, but the guns they had was a whole different story. Most of the guns in the house was definitely going to send them away for a nice bit of time. All the serial numbers had been scraped off and most of all the firing pins were filed down; making the weapons fully automatic. As they made it to the back room Corey pulled the string to lift the blinds so they could open the window and jump out. As they attempted to climb out, they noticed about ten Federal agents with ski mask over their face hit the back fence to the apartment. "Fuck them bitches got us surrounded!" They closed the window and headed back to the front of the apartment. Instead of trying anything else, they sat back on the sofa and sparked the Kush back up. It was no sense in trying to flee they had nowhere to go. They were cornered in from all angles. The only thing that weighed heavy on their minds, was why the fuck the Feds was about to kick down the door and bring them to jail. Somebody had to be talking because their whole operation was full proof. They never dealt hands on with any of their clientele out there. They just were around to make sure everything went alright. The few people they had moving the work were the only ones that knew who really was in control. That was something they would have to deal with later. Right now the Feds were sending threats to kick the door down and the only solution to their problem at that moment was to get high as they could. "I guess we're bout to take a trip to the Feds huh" Corey stated. "I guess so" Pistol replied leaning his head back on the sofa. In that instance the door came tumbling down and twenty Federal agents emerged through. The thick purple haze smoke circulating the apartment created a veil that was diminished, as Pistol and Corey were thrown to the ground and handcuffed. They were brought back to New Orleans Parish prison where they were booked in the Federal holdover. They were charged as felons in possession of firearms, as well as conspiracy to sell over one thousand grams of cocaine. When it rained it poured, and in the Skull Gang's case it was Hurricane Betsy.

Soulja Slim famous *"Slow Motion"* track played in the background. *-Uh I like it like that- she workin that back- I don't know how to act- Slow Motion for me- Slow Motion for me- Slow Motion for me-Move in slow motion for me.* Roylee and one of his goons sat watching a big fine caramel stripper move in slow motion down the pole in Shakers, a well know strip club in Baton Rouge. Roylee had relocated out that way for the safety of his girl and unborn seed. He knew without a doubt Teelee and the gang wouldn't hesitate to kill his fam if they got the chance to. Only a few people knew where he laid his head at. His momma didn't even know where he stayed. He felt too many people knowing where he was would be dangerous, and could be leaked easily. Everywhere he moved he was accompanied with two of his most deadly gun slingers. T-Man and Kane, two blood brothers that spilled a lot of blood on the pavement of the streets of the N.O. They almost looked like twins, they both had long dreadlocks that hung down their backs. One standing 5'9 and the other 5'10. They had charcoal black skin and some really small, chink looking eyes with their soulja signs stamped in between them. The crosses symbolized your certification in all aspects of the game, whether it be hustling, jacking, murder, and anything in between. The two were responsible for at least thirty murders in the city of New Orleans, and that's not including the hits they took out of town. T-Man was the silent assassin, and Kane was the kill a nigga in broad daylight type of killer. Each having qualities that were very well needed in the raw beef Roylee had going on. After the death of Rell and his cousin Teedy, Roylee really tighten up his game by bringing the two chaotic brothers aboard. There was around the clock security placed around his girl. He made sure every time he ventured off to the city he had T-Man and Kane on deck, if young Nardy wasn't with him. The assassination attempt on Nardy and the hit on Rell and Teedy showed Roylee and his crew that the Skull Gang had many arms around the city. While Roylee and Kane chilled off in the club, T-Man maintained his position outside the club. He sat in Roylee's Hummer clutching a fully automatic Tommy gun with a hundred round drum; alert and aware of everyone pulling in and out of the club. "Wzup baaby, you tryna have a gangsta party wit us or what?" Kane asked. He slapped the stripper's bare ass as she gave them a full view of what she had to offer. Her big round ass was mesmerizing, as she made her ass cheeks move in sequence. "Sure daddy, but you gotta bring my girl too" the stripper replied. She turned over on her back, busting her legs wide open so they could get a better view of her clean shaven kitty cat. "Shid nigga ain't doing no tripping. Where she be at?" Kane asked while throwing loose dollar bills all over the stage. "She coming pick me up. She ain't working tonight" the stripper replied as she bent over touching her toes. "Wzup round, you bout that?" Kane asked Roylee. With a nod of approval from Roylee, Kane confirmed the after party by dropping ten one hundred dollar bills on the stage. "We gon be waitin outside when the club ova" Kane said. "What y'all ridin in daddy?" the stripper asked while picking her money up from the stage. "We in a royal blue H2" Kane replied. "Aight then fellas, I'mma see y'all in a minute." "What's ya name baby girl?" Kane asked. "Brown Sugar" the stripper replied before exiting the stage. The bounce in Brown Sugar's ass made Kane anticipate being behind that thing while she was throwing it back. Roylee on the other hand was enticed but not to the point he was off his game. He knew too many people didn't know where he was at, but he couldn't get to comfortable. Getting relaxed would definitely get his head knocked off. That's why Roylee relied more on T-Man than Kane. He knew T-Man didn't let nothing cloud his focus or judgment. Females and the notion that he was untouchable made Kane weak in a way. In serious beef, nothing or no one should cause you to be off your base. When you allowed that kind of shit to happen, you became prey to the same wolves you were in battle with. That was one of the main reasons Roylee kept Kinky D off the scene most of the time. He knew Kinky moved off emotion. That could get all of them knocked off real quick. He only allowed Kinky D to buck when he felt it was okay. In order for them to survive this beef they were going to have to submit to Roylee's authority. He was the only one that knew the most important ingredient in war, and that was how well you strategize. Roylee and

Kane had a couple more drinks, made it rain a few more times, and then headed out to the truck. When they made it outside T-Man was posted on side of the club in a dark alley. He had to call out to them to let them know where he was at. "Hey yo" T-Man yelled while sticking his hand in the air. "What the fuck you ova here in the cut for?" Kane asked as him and Roylee walked in the alley. "You get a better view of the area from ova here playboy" T-Man replied. He had his Tommy gun in one hand and a blunt in the other. "Son we got these strippers on deck. One of them hoe's caramel wit a big ass. Your favorite type, ya heard me" Kane said while taking the blunt from T-Man. "Let's go get in the truck" Roylee advised. When they left out of the strip club it was almost closing time, so their jump offs shouldn't have been too far behind. Just as they were about to spark up another blunt people started coming out the doors of Shakers. T-Man remained alert to everything moving, while Kane's only interest remained on where Brown Sugar was located. Roylee leaned back in the driver seat attempting to call his girl when a black Tahoe with dark tinted windows pulled up in front of the club. Kane immediately spotted Brown Sugar as she emerged from the doors of the club. "Hold up son, I'm bout to go see wzup wit these hoe's" Kane said as he jumped out of the Hummer. T-Man and Roylee maintained their positions as they watched Kane jog up to the black Tahoe. T-Man kept his eyes glued on the truck while Roylee talked on his cell phone. Something wasn't right about this picture. He could just feel it. When Kane made it to the truck Brown Sugar was just getting in the passenger seat. The driver of the truck who was obviously looking for something she had lost on the back seat, had long black silky hair. The passenger seat was preventing Kane from seeing her face. "So wzup daddy, y'all following us?" Brown Sugar asked as she ran her fingers through her short cropped hair. She actually looked cuter with her natural hair than the long blonde wig she wore while at work. "Hold up baby girl" Kane said. As he attempted to answer his phone the driver came from the back seat with a small AK47. T-Man was already out the Hummer headed in the direction of the Tahoe, but it was too late. By the time Kane looked up the AK47 bullet was ripping through his skull. In a rage T-Man let the fully automatic Tommy gun loose. "Tat Tat Tat Tat Tat." As T-Man progressed Teelee hopped out of the Tahoe spraying the Choppa in the direction of the Hummer. By then Roylee was out of the truck bucking back. The Rugger nines bucked fiercely, making them sound like they were fully automatic. Everyone that was leaving the club broke for cover. The bullets were coming from everywhere. T-Man and Roylee continued to close in on Teelee who was shielded by the Tahoe. As they attempted to corner Teelee in, Lil Man came from the side of the club spraying the AR15. Sirens were heard in the distance making them all snap out of their tunnel vision. Lil Man had managed to make it on the side of the Tahoe where Teelee was. "You aight son?" Lil Man asked. "Yeah I'm good, but we gotta get the fuck. Them people gon be swarming this bitch any minute." There were two dead bodies on the scene, Kane and Brown Sugar. All the ducking and hiding she tried to do didn't help. Ten of the many bullets that were flying at the Tahoe, managed to find her body as a domain. It was better she die that way, because Teelee and Lil Man was going to off her anyway. She was just a pawn in their deadly chess move they had planned. If she knew it was going to cost her life, she would have never accepted the measly two thousand dollars. Roylee and T-Man had already hopped back in the H2 and was pulling out of the parking lot. The tragic death of his brother made the evil inside him increase to the point he only shed two tears. The rest of his pain was going to be felt severely. In the back of his mind he knew this day was destined to come. He knew Kane's looseness was bound to get him knocked off, but he wasn't ready for his brother to leave him like that. The fact of the matter was Teelee and the gang would have to be on top of their game. Never slipping in any type of way, because the young heartless killer was pumping the same chaotic blood through his veins. He wasn't going to stop until he was dead or all the members and the family members of the Skull Gang was eliminated. Lil Man pushed Brown Sugar's dead body out of the truck and he and Teelee smash the gas fleeing the scene. Roylee had escaped death; leaving Teelee in a deeper rage. Teelee's plan was very strategic; the set up with the stripper, him disguising his self with the wig; all the way down to Kane walking up to the truck. Roylee was way smarter than Teelee expected. He knew at that moment that this beef would last a very long time, because Roylee was on the same shit he was on. *"Think first, Plan correctly, and Smash precisely."*

Lil Man was waiting on his business associates at his studio. Fletcher and Corey had recently informed him that they had received an answer back from Weezy Wee's manager. The immediate call for the meeting gave him the feeling that the news was good, but his reaction wasn't nearly what they expected. He just replied with a simple, for sure. He sat contemplating on how close he and Teelee were to putting an end to Roylee. When they heard the police sirens headed in the direction of Shakers, it took everything out of him to peel his self away from gunning at Roylee and his goon. They did kill Kane, but the main one they wanted got away. The other peons was expendable on both sides. Teelee and the gang definitely wouldn't hesitate to sacrifice one of the foot souljas that chose to enter in the bloody war. In Roylee's case it was the same. He didn't give a fuck if they lived or died. As long as they played their positions to the fullest, he was cool. That's what made the nigga even more dangerous. The fact that he could easily brainwash and recruit people that was about that gun play and not give a fuck about their lives. All the members in the Skull Gang were close and if one of them were lost it would cause pain. Lil Man took all those facts in consideration. That was the main reason he was having second thoughts on going on Weezy Wee's "I Am Music Tour." Suddenly the buzzer to the front door went off, breaking Lil Man out of his thoughts. Lil Man looked at the overhead monitor and realized it was his associates. He buzzed them in, while he downed his double shot of Hennessy. "Lil Man baby, you ready for this?" "What might that be Corey?" Lil Man asked, unmoved by his associate's excitement. Fletcher noticed Lil Man's demeanor and interceded. "You alright Lil Man?" Fletcher asked. He took a seat in front of Lil

Man's desk. Corey followed suit, as they awaited Lil Man's response. Lil Man let a minute pass before speaking. "Ain't nothing. What's the good news that got you niggas so excited?" Corey and Fletcher were two very successful music industry managers. With both of their wonderful talent in the industry they felt it would be a good idea if they teamed up and collaborated. Thus far, they were successful in all their endeavors in the Hip Hop business. They both were graduates from Loyola University in Uptown New Orleans. Obtaining bachelor degrees in their craft, they had done the work and mastered the business. Their portfolios of artist was unrevealed, but let's just say they were huge benefactors in the climb to make these artists successful. Fletcher knew Lil Man was holding back what he was really feeling, but he continued on in spite of. "Well as of yesterday you could be an official artist on the roster of the "I Am Music Tour" with Weezy" Fletcher informed Lil Man with a big smile on his face. A brief smile appeared on Lil Man's face, but as quick as it appeared it disappeared. "Look I'mma have to get back at y'all on that, ya heard me" Lil Man said while pulling a blunt from his desk drawer. As he lit the purple haze, Corey and Fletcher sat there looking dumbfounded. They couldn't believe Lil Man's response. "Man you serious" Corey said as he stood to his feet. "Say homey, I said what I said. It ain't gon change till I say so. As a matter of fact, get the fuck out my office! Both of y'all" Lil Man barked now standing on his feet. By the look in Lil Man's eyes and the two guns that lay on the desk, they opted to just let him be. They didn't want to be the breaking news for the day. They left out of the studio leaving Lil Man with his issues. Deep down Lil Man was elated to hear his hard work was finally starting to see some progress. On the other hand, this beef was at its beginning and his Skull Gang fam was going to need him as much as ever. Going away was something he just couldn't see at the moment. His loyalty to his team was over anything. Pistol and Corey were in the Fed holdover awaiting what their destiny was going to be. It was a good possibility Teelee was going to be taking a similar trip as well. Leaving Thugga's death unresolved wasn't even an option. The thoughts rambled through his mind so much, he had nearly smoked the whole blunt of Kush in five tokes. "Man I gotta call Teelee" Lil Man said aloud as he picked his cell phone up.

"What you thinkin bout baby?" Tamia asked. Teelee was lying in bed, staring at the ceiling fan as it spun around in circles. Tamia and Teelee were enjoying the comfort of their new spot out in Mandeville, La. Teelee didn't want to leave his wife in danger in the event he had to go serve time in the Feds. He gave up the lease on his condo and paid out Tamia's lease also. Teelee had been planning on closing out their leases a while ago, because they were paying for two spots, but living at one. The only way someone would be able to locate them, is if they followed them. That wasn't possible, courtesy of the cameras mounted in their back license plates. Lil Man's smart thinking had rubbed off quite well. Their new spot was a beautiful two story, five-bedroom brick home. It was surrounded by nothing but woods. At first Tamia wasn't feeling it, but the police station and 24 hour police patrol eased her nerves a bit. Teelee's thoughts ran a mile a minute. Being that close to Roylee and not being able to kill him, irritated the fuck out of him. He knew his freedom clock was getting shorter by the day. The thought of not putting Roylee in the dirt was driving him to the point where that was the only thing on his mind. He hadn't seen his son in months. Every time Nunew tried to contact him he would send her straight to voicemail. It hurt him to deprive his son of his attention he deserved, but he knew until his business was handled he would never be able to show his son the love he needed to show him. His mind was clouded with too much evil shit. It wouldn't be wise to expose his son to that side of him. "Just wondering what the future holds for us." "What you mean baby" Tamia asked sort of confused. Teelee noticed the confused look on her face and proceeded to explain his self a little clearer. Teelee set up in the bed and wrapped his arms around Tamia. "I'm not meaning in that way maw" Teelee said while taking Tamia's little hand in his and kissing her on her cheek. "I'm talkin bout the things you say you see in me. I wonder will I ever be able to up hold that position." Teelee sighed and ran his hands through his soft grain of hair, which began to grow out of its normal taper fade. "Of course you will be able to up hold your position" Tamia said. She put her hand under Teelee's chin, turning his face towards hers. "You know why?" Tamia asked. "Why baby?" Because you are destined for it. I can see it now. Under all that evil that's covering your heart, I can still see that light shining in your soul. You're a good man baby." Teelee didn't know what the hell he would do if he didn't have Tamia in his life. She was his support system, best friend, soul mate, lover, and wife all wrapped in one. Tamia knew that Teelee was in some serious beef, but she didn't know the details of what transpired in the street. Teelee kept her away from that for her safety. Don't get it twisted though, she was laced up like a pair of Polo boots. Teelee had bought her a baby 9. He would often bring her to the gun range to teach her how to shoot. She was a beast now with that iron. Soulja Slims "If Its Beef" came on as Teelee cell phone rang; it was Lil Man. "Wzup son" Teelee said while getting up off the bed. "I need to holla at cha homey. Where you at?" Lil Man asked. "I'm out here at the spot with Tiger. Where you at?" "I'm at the studio, ya heard me." "Aight I'm on my way. Gimme bout an hour." "Aight round, I'mma see you when you get here." Teelee hung up the phone and started getting dressed. "Baby where you going?" Tamia asked pouting as usual. She never liked Teelee to leave her side at night. She was always scared he wouldn't come back. "I gotta go holla at Lil Man at the studio." "Why he can't come out here? I have a bad feeling right now. Something's telling me you shouldn't go baby." "Maw sumthin always tellin you I shouldn't go" Teelee joked as he slipped on his Deion Sander Nike tennis shoes. "I'mma be right back baby" Teelee said while walking up to the side of the bed. He kissed Tamia on her forehead. From the moment his lips touched her skin, she knew he wasn't coming back. Tamia was usually always right in her assumptions. As Teelee walked out of the door all Tamia could do was lie back down and snuggle next to his pillow. As she slid her hand under her pillow to get comfortable, she felt a small piece of paper. She pulled if from underneath the pillow.

It appeared to be a poem written by Teelee in red ink.

### *"MY MOST PRIZED POSSESSION"*

*When I first laid eyes on you, you took my breath away. At that moment I knew we were destined to be. I had found the one thing I had been longing for. A true companion; somebody I could share my heart, even the things I had hidden in the dark. In the midst of my world filled with evil, you have shown me things I never knew was there; like me being a leader, good father, and somebody that cares. No woman in my past ever compared to you. That's why I swear to you, whatever happens in the future. You will forever be my most prized possession…I truly love you…*

*Love Always, Your Jelly Bean Brown LOL….*

By now the whole paper was wet with tears flowing from Tamia's eyes. She never knew Teelee was poetically inclined. Actually Teelee didn't know it either. He just let his heart pour over the paper. Tamia grabbed her cell phone from the nightstand and called Teelee. She wanted to tell him how much she loved his poem and to come back home. The phone just rang until his voice mail picked up. "Fuck" Tamia cursed as she tried calling him again. After six hours passed and a hundred attempts to reach Teelee; Tamia began to panic. As she began to throw on her clothes, her phone rang. Her intuition gave her a feeling of who it was. Her hands trembled as she pressed send on her phone. "Hello, you have a collect call from." "Maw it's me baby, press 1" ……

# EPILOGUE

Teelee never made it to the studio to meet up with Lil Man. Exiting the Causeway Bridge entering into Metairie, he was stopped by a State trooper that sat onside the bridge. The officer's reason for pulling him over was a "routine stop." Yeah right. Teelee had a U.S. Marshall warrant out for his arrest. Teelee instantly knew something was wrong. The officer was taking a long time running his paperwork through the computer. When the officer came back and informed Teelee he had a U.S. Marshall warrant out for his arrest, he didn't know who the U.S. Marshalls were. He thought the trooper was referring to the Coast guard. When the trooper made it known that the U.S. Marshalls were the Feds, everything became clear. The Feds had pulled off some slick shit. They hadn't even sent him a notice informing him that they were ready to set an arraignment date. They just ordered that he be picked up immediately. That was the main reason he made the moves he made, because the Federal Government was never fare. Tamia all but passed out when she found out her husband was in Federal custody. She knew her intuitions were leading her right. If Teelee could have just listened, he would still be with her in the comfort of their home. Tamia called Shorty C for a word of advice and Shorty gave her the rawest, realest advice there was. "You knew what type of dude he was when you started fuckin with him. Now stop that crying and handle your business like you're supposed too." Tamia was thrown for a loop by

Shorty abruptness, but it soon sunk in that she had to do just that. Tamia had to keep it gangsta for her man. She accepted the roll to be involved with a street nigga. Now it was time for her to be tested by her loyalty to him. When Lil Man informed Teelee of his news about the tour, Teelee encouraged him to proceed. He made him understand that it would be too risky for him to be out there by his self. Pistol and Corey were still awaiting their faith, and Teelee was in the same position. K-Real was in a secluded spot in Atlanta. Rafee was on his own mission, only popping up at unpredictable moments. Lil Man staying on the battlefield by himself would have been suicide. He eventually saw it Teelee's way, and informed Fletcher and Corey that he would be joining the tour. What everyone in the Skull Gang failed to realize was, there was two blood thirsty pit bulls right up under their noses. They had the same intentions towards this beef as they did. The evil brewing in their hearts would definitely cause havoc on the opposite side. The violence and bloodshed was at its very beginning, and it was nothing none of them could do to stop it. All they could do was strap up their Soulja Reeboks and buck to the sound of the beef, "Close, Attend, and Hut" ….

# ABOUT THE AUTHOR

Originally brewed and served up in a steamy pot of New Orleans. Mixed and sautéed with the most challenging obstacles and adversities; this young soldier has seen, lived, and endured everything the grimy street life the Crescent city has to offer. In the midst of his struggles, a clear vision of these harsh realities have been embed within his mind. Through his incarceration he's been blessed to bring these realities to life through ink, and give the world a better understanding of what leads a lost soul down a destructive path; that he's all too familiar with. It is his life's mission to take the cover off this new myth that living the *"thug life"* is a trend. It's a misconception that he vows to break.

www.ingramcontent.com/pod-product-compliance
Lightning Source LLC
Chambersburg PA
CBHW030748030726
47497CB00001B/191

* 9 7 8 0 6 9 2 6 7 2 4 5 7 *